Letter From a Stranger

Barbara Taylor Bradford was born and raised in England. She started her writing career on the *Yorkshire Evening Post* and later worked as a journalist in London. Her first novel, *A Woman of Substance*, published in 1979, became an enduring bestseller and was followed by twenty-six others, including the bestselling Harte series. Barbara's books have sold more than eighty-two million copies worldwide in more than ninety countries and forty languages, and ten mini-series and television movies have been made of her books. In October of 2007, Barbara was awarded an OBE by the Queen for her services to literature. She lives in New York City with her husband, television producer Robert Bradford. *Letter From a Stranger* is her twenty-seventh novel.

To find out more about Barbara, her books and sign up to her newsletter visit www.barbarataylorbradford.co.uk

Books by Barbara Taylor Bradford

Series
THE EMMA HARTE SAGA
A Woman of Substance
Hold the Dream
To Be the Best
Emma's Secret
Unexpected Blessings
Just Rewards
Breaking the Rules

Others
Voice of the Heart
Act of Will
The Women in His Life
Remember
Angel
Everything to Gain
Dangerous to Know
Love in Another Town
Her Own Rules
A Secret Affair
Power of a Woman
A Sudden Change of Heart
Where You Belong
The Triumph of Katie Byrne
Three Weeks in Paris
Playing the Game

Series
THE RAVENSCAR TRILOGY
The Ravenscar Dynasty
Heirs of Ravenscar
Being Elizabeth

BARBARA TAYLOR BRADFORD

Letter From a Stranger

HarperCollins*Publishers*

HarperCollins*Publishers*
77–85 Fulham Palace Road,
Hammersmith, London W6 8JB

www.harpercollins.co.uk

Published by HarperCollins*Publishers* 2011

I

A catalogue record for this book
is available from the British Library

ISBN: 978 0 00 730414 1

Set in Sabon by Palimpsest Book Production Limited,
Falkirk, Stirlingshire

Printed and bound in Great Britain by
Clays Ltd, St Ives plc

MIX
Paper from
responsible sources
FSC **FSC® C007454**
www.fsc.org

Again for my husband Bob, and as always
with my love

Contents

PROLOGUE

Istanbul
April 2004

PROLOGUE

The letter, contemplated and worried about for such a long time, was finally written. But it was not mailed. Instead it was put in a drawer of the desk so that it could be thought about, the words carefully reconsidered before that last irretrievable step was taken.

The following morning the letter was read once more, corrected and locked away for the second time. On the third day it was perused again and the words deftly edited. Satisfied that everything had been said clearly and concisely, the writer copied the final draft onto a fresh piece of writing paper. This was folded, sealed in an envelope, addressed and affixed with the correct stamps. The words AIR MAIL were written in the top left-hand corner of the envelope, which was then propped against the antique French clock on the desk.

A short while later, the young son of the cook was summoned to the upstairs sitting room. The envelope was handed to him, instructions given, and he was told to take it to the post office at once.

The boy left the villa immediately, waving to the gardener as he trotted through the iron gates of the old-style Turkish *yali*.

3

This was situated on the Asiatic side of Istanbul, on the shores of the Bosphorus, in Üsküdar, the largest and most historical district of the city.

As he walked in the direction of the post office, the boy held the letter tightly in his hand, proud that he had been given such an important task by his father's employer. He was only ten, but everyone said he was capable, and this pleased him.

A light, balmy breeze wafted inland from the sea, carrying with it the hint of salt and the sounds of continuous hooting from one of the big cruise ships now ploughing its way down the Bosphorus, heading towards the Black Sea and new ports of call.

The boy hurried on, intent in his purpose, remembering his instructions . . . the letter must be put in the box marked 'International'. It was going to America. He must not make the mistake of using the one that was for domestic mail. He was soon leaving the shoreline behind, walking up the long road called Halk Caddesi. The post office was at the top, and within minutes he found the letter box marked 'International' and dropped the letter in the slot. He then retraced his steps.

When the Bosphorus was in his line of vision once more, the boy began to run; he was soon pushing open the gates of the *yali*, heading for the kitchens. He found his father preparing lunch, and dutifully reported that he had posted the letter. His father picked up the phone, spoke to his employer, then ruffled his son's hair, smiling down at him. He rewarded him with pieces of Turkish delight on a saucer.

The boy went outside, sat on the step in the sunshine, munching the delicious sweetmeat. He sat there daydreaming, had no way of knowing that the letter he had just mailed would change many lives forever. And so drastically they would never be the same again.

The writer of the letter knew this. But the consequences were of no consideration. Long ago, a terrible wrong had been done.

4

The truth was long overdue. Finally it had been revealed, and if there was retribution then so be it. What mattered most was that a wrong had been righted.

PART ONE

The Letter

Read it a hundred times; it will forever keep its freshness
as a petal keeps its fragrance. It can never lose its sense of
meaning that once unfolded by surprise it went.

Robert Frost: The Figure a Poem Makes

ONE

The view from the second-floor terrace was panoramic, and breathtaking. Justine Nolan, who knew it well, was nevertheless always startled when she saw it, even after a short absence, and today was no exception.

She leaned against the white-painted wooden railings, gazing out at the sweeping line of the Litchfield Hills flowing towards the distant horizon. Their thickly wooded slopes rolled down to verdant meadows; beyond them Lake Waramaug, set deeply in the valley, shimmered in the sunlight like a great swathe of fabric cut from cloth of silver. As usual, Justine caught her breath, filled with intense pleasure that she was back at Indian Ridge, the house where she had grown up and spent much of her life.

It was a clear bright day, with a blue sky and bountiful clouds, but there was a snap in the wind, a hint of winter still, and it was cold for April.

Shivering, Justine wrapped her heavy-knit red jacket around her body as she continued to devour the view . . . the white clapboard houses, so typical of Connecticut, dotted here and there on some of the meadows, and to her right, set against a stand of dark-green trees, three silos and two red barns grouped together in a distant field. They had been there for as long as she could remember, and were a much-loved and familiar sight.

Unexpectedly, a flock of birds swept past her, unusually close to the railings, and she blinked, startled by them. They soared upward in a V, a perfect formation and quite beautiful. She stared after them as they flew higher and higher into the haze of blue, and then turned around and went back into the house.

Picking up her overnight bag, which she had dropped on the landing a few minutes earlier, Justine carried it into her bedroom and immediately unpacked, putting away sweaters, trousers, shoes, and her toiletries bag. Ever since childhood she had been neat, very tidy in her habits, and it was her nature to be well organized. She hated clutter, which had to be avoided at all cost.

Glancing around the bedroom, smiling to herself, she experienced a sudden rush of happiness. She loved this room, and the entire house . . . some of her happiest times had been spent here at Indian Ridge, especially when her father was still alive. She and her twin had adored him.

She was glad her mother had kept the house, and that she and her brother Richard could continue to use it at weekends, as well as for long stretches in the summer. It was their mutual escape hatch, a safe haven and a place where they could relax from their busy schedules in New York.

For the past month Justine had stayed in Manhattan, working on the last stage of her newest documentary about Jean-Marc Breton, the world's greatest living artist, supervising the cutting with the director and the film's editor. It had been arduous – long days and nights of work; hours and hours and hours filled with tension, stress, anxiety, good and bad surprises, friction at times, and some disappointments. But when they had viewed the final cut, and not without some trepidation, they had been jubilant. The film, which they had considered to be problematical right from the first day of shooting because of the temperament and dictatorial attitude of their subject, had turned out to be good. Very, very good, in fact, much to their collective relief.

Now Justine prayed that the network would feel the same when she screened it for them next week. Miranda Evans, the head of documentaries for Cable News International, would view it with total detachment, which always pleased Justine and her team. Miranda brought no prejudices or preconceived ideas into the screening room, which was why Justine trusted her judgement. That impartiality was a rare quality. Miranda had believed in her right from the start, and had funded most of the *Blood Diamonds* documentary, another tough subject.

Suddenly, worry edged into her mind. She took a deep breath and pushed it away. *The film was excellent,* and it *was* the final cut. *And that was that.*

She shook her head, grimaced to herself, wished she could let go of a project the moment it was at an end. But she couldn't; it always took her time to move on. And then she automatically went into a different mode, was filled with deflation, anxiety and a sense of loss.

She had mentioned this to Richard last night, and he had started to laugh, understanding exactly what she meant. Her twin and she were very much alike. He had pointed out that she was going up to the house to mentally and physically replenish herself, and fresh and exciting ideas would soon pop into her head when she was completely rested. And with that he had ended their phone call on a somewhat teasing note.

He's right, of course, she decided, as she went out of her bedroom and down the stairs. Nobody knows me like he does, just as I know him inside out. She felt a small trickle of sadness running through her when she thought of Richard's wife, Pamela, who had died two years ago of cancer.

To the outside world Richard was calm, strong and stoical,

in control, but *she* knew how heartbroken he was inside. He kept up a good front, and ploughed on doggedly, because of his five-year-old daughter Daisy. She planned to look after them both this weekend: mothering one, and being a loving companion to the other.

At the bottom of the staircase Justine turned right, walked towards the small sitting room overlooking the lawn, which she also used as an office, mostly to do the household accounts and bookkeeping.

She had settled Daisy in there when they had arrived from New York half an hour ago, and her niece was still sitting at the desk with her box of crayons and colouring book spread out before her.

Kim, the nanny, had the weekend off, and Tita, one of the housekeepers, was hovering over her, encouraging her to use as many crayons as she wanted. 'All the colours of the rainbow,' Tita was saying, her voice loving.

Afternoon sunshine was streaming into the room and Daisy's pale blonde curls shimmered in the light. What a lovely child she is, Justine thought, adorable in a variety of different ways, and it's so hard not to spoil her.

Justine couldn't help smiling to herself as she watched Tita being so attentive to Daisy, helping her. Tita and her sister Pearl loved Daisy as if she were their own, and, in a sense, she was. The two women had lived and worked at Indian Ridge for years and were part of the family by now.

She and Richard had grown up with them, and they appreciated everything the two of them did to keep the house, the gallery and their work studios in tiptop shape. They considered themselves blessed to have Tita and Pearl; Richard deemed them to be the salt of the earth.

Stepping into the room, Justine said, 'What are you colouring, Daisy?'

Daisy and Tita both turned around on hearing Justine's voice, and Daisy explained, 'It's a vase of flowers, Auntie Juju.'

'She takes after her father,' Tita grinned. 'She's got that talent he's had since he was a boy.'

A small smile struck Justine's face, and then she laughed. 'Unlike the two of us! We weren't very good painters, were we? Mine were a series of giant blotches.'

Tita joined in her laughter. 'And mine, too, and there was more paint on me than the canvas.'

Daisy, staring intently at her aunt, said, 'How much does it cost to go there?'

'To go where, darling?'

'*To Heaven*. I want to take my painting to Mommy. I'm doing it for her. I've got a lot of quarters in my piggy bank. Maybe ten dollars. It's a big pig.'

Justine was unable to speak for a moment. Her throat was suddenly constricted. Swallowing several times, she finally managed to say, 'It's a bit more than that, I think.'

'Oh.' Daisy nodded, pursed her lips. 'I'll have to get some more quarters then. I'll keep the painting for Mommy, and take it to her later. When I've saved up.'

'That's right.' Justine's low voice sounded hoarse. To her relief Daisy turned back to her colouring book, her blonde head bent over it once more in concentration.

The two women exchanged glances.

Tita was on the verge of tears, her dark eyes stricken. She was biting her bottom lip, struggling for control.

Clearing her throat, Justine said, 'Come on, Tita, let's go and plan the picnic for tomorrow.'

'A picnic!' The five-year-old swung her head, her bright blue eyes suddenly sparkling. 'In the gazeboat?'

'*Gazebo*, darling,' Justine corrected gently. 'And yes, it will be there, weather permitting. And guess what, Auntie Jo is coming with Simon.'

'Oh goody! Simon's my bestest friend.'

'We'll be in the kitchen if you need us for anything, Daisy.' Justine beckoned to Tita, who almost ran out of the room ahead of her; she followed in concern.

Tita was clutching the sink, hunched over into herself, still fighting the tears.

Crossing the kitchen quickly, understanding exactly how she felt, Justine put her arms around Tita and held her close. 'I know, I know, it's hard. Some of the things she comes out with take my breath away, tear me apart, and Richard too. But suddenly she brightens up – you know that, Tita. Especially if she's distracted. And she does forget.'

'Yes . . . but I suffer for her. I can't help it.'

'We've got to keep her busy, Tita. Look how she reacted when I mentioned the picnic and Simon. And I've learned a lot from Kim, who packs her days with activities, keeps her very busy when she's not at school. We've got to do that this weekend, as we've been doing for the last two years, actually.'

'I know, I know . . .' Tita cut herself off, blew out air, pulled herself together, and said, 'I'll put the kettle on. Let's have a cup of tea.'

'Good idea.' Justine smiled at Tita, squeezed her arm. 'She'll be all right.'

Tita nodded and went to fill the kettle.

Justine walked over to the fire and stood in front of it, glancing around. The kitchen was a comforting room, warm, inviting, and one of her favourites in the house. Copper pots and pans hanging down from the saucepan rack affixed to the ceiling gleamed brightly. In between the pots were strings of onions and garlic, bunches of lavender and thyme, whole sausages and salamis, all of which added a French Provençal feeling.

It had always been the hub of the house, where everyone congregated, because part of it was furnished as a living room. A sofa and wing chairs, a television set and a Welsh dresser were all grouped near the fireplace, while a large wooden table, which seated ten, was used to divide the room; beyond the table were countertops and the usual appliances. With its terracotta tiled floor, pale-peach walls and floral fabrics, the kitchen had a certain charm and a welcoming air about it.

The phone started ringing, and Justine stepped over to the small desk in a corner near the fireplace, and picked up the receiver. 'Indian Ridge,' she said, and immediately sat down in the chair when she heard her assistant's voice. 'Hello, Ellen.'

'Hi, Justine. I guess you made it up there in record time.'

'I did. What's happening?'

'All's well. I just had a call from Miranda's PA, and she wants to see the film on Tuesday afternoon at four o'clock, instead of Thursday morning. I told her I thought it would be fine, but that I'd better check with you. There's nothing in your book.'

'I've a pretty empty week, I know that. So yes, we'll screen the film whenever Miranda wants.'

'I'll confirm it with Angie. Everything's okay there, I suppose.'

'It is. I'm here with Tita, and Daisy's busy with her colouring book. I haven't seen Pearl yet – she went to the market; and apparently Carlos and Ricardo are up on the ridge, working on Richard's current project.'

'The guest house.'

'Which we don't really need. On the other hand, he needs it, Ellen, because it gives him work to do up here. It takes his mind off things.'

'There's still a lot of grief on him,' Ellen murmured. 'I wish I knew somebody nice to introduce him to.'

'He wouldn't be interested, I'm afraid,' Justine shot back.

'Anyway, I'll now come back on Tuesday morning instead of Wednesday. Have a nice weekend, Ellen.'

'And you too.'

As she hung up the phone, Justine had no way of knowing that her world, and Richard's, was about to change forever.

Two

Later that afternoon, when Daisy was taking a nap, Justine went into the small sitting room and sat down at the desk. It did not take her long to open the mail that had accumulated during the month she and Richard had stayed in New York.

The bulk of it was junk, which she promptly threw away; she then checked the bills, clipped them together, and looked at half a dozen invitations for local events, put these to one side as well.

At the bottom of the pile there was a square white envelope made of paper that looked foreign to her. Definitely European, she thought, as she picked it up.

Justine saw at once that it was addressed to her mother, Deborah Nolan, and that it bore an Istanbul postmark. Who did her mother know in Istanbul, of all places? On the other hand, how would *she* know? Her mother had friends all over the world. Looking at the back of the envelope, she saw there was no name of sender nor a return address. She stared at it for a moment longer, thinking that it may well be an invitation, such was its shape and size. She frowned, wondered whether to open it or not. Eight years ago, when her mother had moved to California, she had given them the use of this house. Her instructions to them had been very few: keep the house in good shape, pay the monthly bills and forward any letters if they pertained to legal matters.

This arrangement had worked well since its inception. Their mother paid the annual state tax, they took care of the overall upkeep and the salaries of the Chilean family who continued to run Indian Ridge with them – Tita, her sister Pearl, Carlos, Pearl's husband, and his father Ricardo.

Now, for the first time in eight years, here was a personal letter. Justine shrugged, picked up the paper knife, slit the envelope, and took out the letter.

She noted the name engraved at the top of the writing paper, someone she had never heard of, and began to read.

ANITA LOWE

Dear Deborah:

I have wanted to write to you for some time, unfortunately my courage constantly deserted me. Now this letter cannot be put off any longer. You do not know me. I did come to see you in London when you were a baby but you won't remember that. I am your mother's closest and most long-standing friend and I write to you because I am extremely worried about her. For years she has been troubled and unhappy because of the estrangement between the two of you. Lately she has become even more morose and filled with a heartache I cannot bear to witness.

She longs to see you and Justine and Richard. She loves them dearly, just as she loves you. You are her only family.

I must ask you this, Deborah. Why are you keeping her away? I do not understand your behaviour towards your mother. Surely nothing is so bad that it cannot be repaired. Whatever the reason for this estrangement you must end it immediately, before it is too late, before she dies. After all, she is almost eighty, as you well know. And so I beg you to reach out to your mother, get in touch with her, bring her back into your life and the lives of her grandchildren. It is in your power, and yours alone, to end her suffering and heartbreak.

With great sincerity,
Anita Lowe

Justine was speechless. She sat staring at the words she had just read, feeling as if the earth's tectonic plates had just shifted under her feet. Her shock was enormous. She noticed that her hand shook as she continued to hold the letter, then realized she was shaking all over. She could hardly believe what she had just read. Her grandmother was still alive? How could that be? What was this all about?

Taking a deep breath, she put the letter down on the desk, and endeavoured to control her swimming senses. After a few minutes she managed to calm herself, and leaned forward to reread the letter, wanting to absorb the words . . . they revealed something so momentous it took her breath away.

Her grandmother was still alive.

Therefore their mother had told them a horrendous and wicked lie ten years ago. She had told them their grandmother, Deborah's mother Gabriele Hardwicke, had died suddenly in a private plane crash.

Her mind began to race. Was the letter genuine? Or was it a hoax? How could it be? Unless someone wanted to cause trouble. If so, why? For what reason? The letter had been written to their mother and it had the ring of truth to it. It was genuine, all right; there was no doubt in her mind about that.

Then unexpectedly it hit her. A wave of joy. *Gran was alive.* Blinking back the tears in her eyes, Justine noted the postmark. The letter was mailed at the beginning of April. Now it was almost the end of the month. The letter had been sitting here in this lacquered tray for three weeks. No one had responded to Anita Lowe. But then how could a response be made? There was no return address. And where was her grandmother actually? In London? Or was she in Istanbul? With Anita Lowe? She had frequently moved between both places in the past. And why had this woman not given more details of her grandmother's whereabouts? Because she believed that Deborah knew exactly where her mother was. Obviously, that was the answer. Which brought her back to the lie her mother had told them.

Ten years ago, the day after they had graduated college, Deborah had explained their grandmother's absence from the ceremony. Whilst they were in the midst of their final exams, Gabriele had been on a private plane that had crashed in Greece. No one had survived, no bodies had been retrieved.

Closing her eyes, thinking back in time, Justine remembered her mother's words quite clearly. 'I didn't tell you about Gran's death because I didn't want to distract either of you when you were both under pressure.'

But none of that was true . . . this letter now revealed that. And their beloved grandmother was alive somewhere out there. The adoring grandmother who had come to stay with them so often and been such a big part of their lives.

According to Anita Lowe there was an estrangement between her mother and grandmother. About what? Something truly terrible? It must be, since it had lasted ten long years. All of those hours, days, weeks, months and years *lost*. Gone forever. For God's sake, *why?* She had no answers for herself.

Fury with her mother swept through Justine, and she automatically reached for the phone, wanting to confront her; then her hand fell away. Her mother wasn't in Los Angeles. Three days ago she had flown to China on a buying trip for her interior design business. From China she was going to Hong Kong, would not be returning for six weeks. She could not call her now. The time was all wrong.

She looked at her watch. It was almost three thirty. Richard would not arrive from New York for another hour. She needed to talk to him; they had to make a plan . . . the first thing they must do was find their grandmother. Before it was too late.

In the small back hall, Justine took Gran's old loden green wool cape off a peg, threw it around her shoulders, then went outside. She needed to think coherently, to settle herself before her brother arrived.

A few moments ago she had been about to call Richard on his cell phone, then had instantly changed her mind. She knew she must curb her desire to immediately share this shattering news with him. That was their usual way of doing things, their modus operandi, and always had been.

As twins they were joined at the hip, and there was an extra special bond between them, an emotional attachment and a link that she realized was not exclusive to *them*. All twins were like that. But this afternoon she understood she *must* wait until he arrived, so that she could show him the letter and discuss every-thing with him face to face. Together they would come up with a plan of action, she was certain of that. They had been the best team all of their lives.

Crossing the back yard, she mounted the white wood staircase built into the hillside. Carlos, Pearl's husband, had obviously repainted it recently, and it gleamed in the sunshine. Ten steps took her straight up to a wide landing, where on the left side of the hill there was a large gazebo, also freshly painted in readiness for the spring weather.

Her grandmother's gazebo.

Justine paused and then stepped into it. She squeezed her eyes shut, remembering the happy times they had spent here in her childhood. Opening her eyes, she glanced around, aware that anxiety about Gran was paramount. She couldn't help worrying, wondering how she was, now that she knew she was not dead.

She left the gazebo and went on climbing the staircase until she came to the end. It stopped in front of a stretch of green lawn; just beyond was the gallery, originally built by her grandmother, then revamped by her father, and remodelled in certain areas by her brother four years ago.

The gallery was beautiful, made of limestone, and was two storeys high; long, simple, yet elegant in its architecture, the central building was flanked on each end by a studio. Each one had limestone half-walls topped with huge plate-glass windows. The studios were actually part of the gallery and the whole structure was finished with a sloping, green-tiled roof. This was new, and had been designed by her twin, considered to be one of the best architects in the business today. She thought it was an inspired touch. The green-tiled roof appeared to float above the gallery and the glass 'boxes', and there was a lovely unity and fluidity to the entire building which was somewhat European in its design inspiration.

Justine went into the gallery and turned on the lights, then took off her loden cape, put it on a small wooden bench just inside the door. Because of the many paintings hanging in the gallery, some of which were rather valuable, the air was permanently controlled and remained the same temperature year round. It was cool and peaceful, and she appreciated the airiness, the spaciousness, the vaulted ceiling, the stillness and calm that existed here.

Slowly, she walked through the gallery, not focusing on any of the paintings as she sometimes did, simply moving determinedly through the flowing vast white space. Richard had designed a large, freestanding partition on rollers, which he called 'a floating wall', because it could be easily rolled around at will, and repositioned anywhere. He had used several of them in the centre of the gallery, on which were hung some of his own paintings, as well as many by other artists. Justine moved between them with ease, pushing them gently aside as required.

Within seconds she was approaching the far end of the gallery, heading toward the corner where paintings by her grandmother were displayed. Coming to a standstill, she zeroed in on one of them in particular which she had admired for years. It was a painting of two girls, most likely in their teenage years, and they were standing in a flower-filled meadow with dark green hills in the distance under an azure sky. The girls were enchanting in their gauzy summer dresses, their skirts billowing around them, their hair blowing in the wind. She had known for as long as she could remember that the taller of the two girls, the blue-eyed blonde, was her grandmother, Gabriele. The other had always been anonymous. Her identity a mystery.

Could she be Anita Lowe?

Leaning forward, Justine read the little wood strip on the wall next to the painting. It was called *Friends in the Meadows*. Underneath the title was the name *Gabriele Hardwicke*, and the year it was painted, *1969*.

Unexpectedly, she remembered something – her grandmother's penchant for detail, how she had kept careful records of almost everything.

Reaching for the small painting, Justine lifted it off the wall, carried it into Richard's design studio adjoining this end of the gallery. Carefully, she placed the painting face down on an empty table and stared at the back of the canvas. And there it was, a small label, close to the frame and yellowed with age. On it was written *A & G: 1938*. And the label was secured under a piece of Sellotape.

Gabriele had painted this from memory, hadn't she? And did the *A* stand for Anita? Perhaps. Certainly she couldn't help wondering about that, because in the letter Anita Lowe had said she was Gabriele's most longstanding and closest friend. So it must be her, surely? But in a way it didn't really matter whether this girl portrayed was Anita Lowe or not. Because the real Anita had spoken out most eloquently and effectively, three weeks or so ago, when she had finally put pen to paper after obviously hesitating about doing so for a number of years. She had helped her friend at last. Thank God she had. Vaguely, at the back of her mind, she now remembered her grandmother speaking about her best friend . . . Anita.

Carrying the painting back to the gallery, Justine hung it in its place, then stepped back and studied it for a few seconds. The other girl had brown hair and sparkling dark eyes, and there was something exotic-looking about her. She wondered why she had never noticed this before . . . perhaps because she had been looking only at the dazzling blonde girl who was her grandmother, the bewitching Gabriele. She knew, all of a sudden, that this was Anita.

Returning to the centre of the gallery, where the high-flung cathedral ceiling came to its peak, she sat down in the only chair, a white canvas director's chair. The cool white space, the silence and the overwhelming sense of tranquillity usually had a soothing effect on her, and today especially so: a perfect peacefulness was enveloping her. She closed her eyes, thinking of her gran and the last time she had seen her.

She was drifting with her thoughts when the shrilling telephone brought her up with a start. She fumbled in her jacket pocket for her cell phone, and pulled it out. 'Hello?'

'I'm almost there,' Richard said.

'I'm glad. Where are you?'

'What is it? You sound odd.'

'I'm fine. Where are you?'

'Just leaving New Preston. Why?'

'I want you to do me a favour.'

'Of course, what is it?'

'I want you to drive right up here to the gallery, where I'm waiting for you.'

'I'll come up after I've said hello to Daisy.'

'Please don't do that, Rich! You *must* come here immediately! Something's happened, and—'

'What? Tell me what's wrong!'

'I can't on the phone. Please, Rich, just come here first. *Please.*'

'All right. See you shortly.'

Impatient, anxious for her brother to arrive, Justine stood up and headed in the direction of his glass-windowed studio. She would wait for him there. As she approached the glass cube, another painting caught her eye, and she went over to look at it, stared for a long moment. It was of her and her brother and had been painted by a famous portraitist in New York when they were about four.

The woman had captured them very well. How alike they looked with their fair hair and dimples and the same light blue eyes. Yes, definitely twins, she muttered under her breath. And emotionally co-dependent.

Their father had commissioned the painting, and he had always loved it. But not their mother. In fact, she was very much against it right from the beginning, before it had even been painted.

Now it struck her quite forcibly that her mother's reaction had been odd, and she couldn't help wondering why. What on earth had she had against it? No answer to that conundrum, she thought. But Deborah Nolan had been an odd bird then, just as she was an odd bird now . . . scatter-brained, a flake – and sometimes downright irresponsible. And a liar, she added to herself.

Sighing under her breath, turning away from the portrait, she went into Richard's studio and glanced around. As usual it was sparkling clean, thanks to Tita and Pearl and their dedication to Indian Ridge.

Suddenly she heard the crunch of tyres on the gravel. Not

wanting to wait for him, she hurried out of the studio, almost running through the gallery to the front door.

A second later Richard was alighting from the car, striding towards her, a worried expression in his eyes, his face tight with anxiety.

'I know something's wrong,' he said, mounting the steps. 'So come on, tell me. And how bad is it?'

She ran into his arms, hugged him tight, and then, as they moved away from the door and went inside, she answered, 'Really, really bad. But part of the problem is good. *Wonderful*.'

She closed the door behind them, took hold of his arm and led him down the gallery. 'Let's go to your studio, I want you to read a letter I found today. But I must warn you, Rich. It's going to shock you.'

THREE

The moment they entered Richard's glass-enclosed studio, Justine sat down in one of the small modern chairs and indicated that her twin should take the other one.

He shook his head, went over to the empty drawing table and leaned against it, his tall, lean frame looking lankier than ever. It struck her that he had lost weight.

'I don't want to sit,' he explained, his eyes not leaving her face. 'I think best standing up.'

'I knew you were going to say that.'

'You always know what I'm going to say, just as I know what's going to come out of your mouth . . . but not today, I don't think.' A brow lifted quizzically, and he continued to stare at her.

Justine nodded, put her hand in her jacket pocket and took out the envelope, handed the letter to him. 'I'd better give you this.'

Richard looked down at it, his brow lifting again. 'It's addressed to Mom—'

She cut him off. 'And be glad she isn't here, didn't get to open

27

it, and that *I* did! Otherwise we might never have known the truth.'

His blue eyes narrowed. 'What do you mean, Juju? What is this all about?'

'*Gran*. I have to tell you something . . .' She cut herself off and took a deep breath. 'The letter says Gran is still alive, Richard.'

'*What?*' He was flabbergasted by her words and he shook his head vehemently. 'That can't *be* . . .' His voice trailed off; he was so shocked he was unable to finish his sentence.

'It's true,' she answered, trying to keep her voice steady.

Richard pulled the letter out of the envelope and began to read it avidly. When he came to the end, he went over to the empty chair and sat down, looking as if he'd just been punched hard in the stomach.

Justine saw how truly stunned he was, as she herself had been earlier. All of the colour had drained from his face, and he was immobile in the chair. It was obvious to her that he was shaken to the very core of himself. And why wouldn't he be? The news was incredible.

'It's hard to come to grips with it, Rich, I know that, and I—'

'Do you believe it?' he interrupted sharply, then looked down at the letter he was still clutching, bafflement on his face.

'I do, yes. It has the absolute ring of truth to it, and why would this woman write such a letter if Gran wasn't alive? That doesn't make any sense,' Justine pointed out.

'I wonder why she didn't write to Mom before?' He gazed at Justine, puzzlement still flickering in his eyes.

'I've no idea. But I do think something important has happened recently, which made Anita Lowe put pen to paper. Finally. She does say that Gran seems more unhappy – "morose" was her word – and look, Gran might even have been taken ill. Or maybe, in her desperation, Gran asked Anita to write.' Leaning forward, Justine stared into her twin's face. Her own was very serious and her eyes were troubled.

'You could be right,' Richard muttered. 'In fact, I'm sure you are.'

'We have to find Gran as quickly as possible,' Justine announced.

'Yes, I agree.' He rose, walked over to his desk, a huge slab of thick glass balanced on top of two steel sawhorses. Sitting down behind it, he was thoughtful for a few seconds, staring out of one of the windows at the trees.

He finally brought his gaze back to his sister. 'She *lied*. Our mother lied to us ten years ago. What a rotten thing to do. Telling us Gran had died. It was wicked, cruel. I remember very well how upset we both were, how we grieved for her.' He snapped his eyes shut for a moment, and when he opened them he finished in an angry voice, 'It's the most unconscionable thing I've ever heard of, and it is *unforgivable*.'

Justine was silent. He had voiced everything she had thought earlier; but then they were like two halves of one person and had been since the day of their birth. There was only fifteen minutes' difference between them; Richard had always teased her that he was the eldest, having been born first.

She said, 'God knows what happened between Gran and our mother to cause this . . . *estrangement*. But to carry it on for ten years seems outrageous. Really ridiculous to me. It's all our mother's doing, obviously.'

'Certainly Anita Lowe indicates that, Justine. Anyway, let's not forget our mother was always a bit ditzy.'

Justine was taken aback. 'That's putting it mildly, don't you think?'

'I'm being kind, I guess. She was actually a weirdo when we were growing up. Unreliable, irresponsible, a flake, and you know *what else*.'

Justine frowned. 'I do know, but let's not go there today,

okay?' The thought that their mother might have been a little wild and unfaithful to their father always troubled her.

'*Okay*. I know exactly how you feel about *that*.'

Justine simply nodded, thinking about their mother, and their strange childhood, and how much they had depended on their father. He had brought them up, if the truth be known. After a moment, she said, 'For her to tell a lie of such magnitude, and to *us*, her children, about her *own mother* . . .' She paused again, sighed, and finished in a voice so low it was almost inaudible, 'It was evil, Rich; such an evil thing to do.'

'Yes,' was all he said, knowing how right his sister was. After a moment, he asked, 'Isn't she in China?'

'Yes, and I know what you're thinking. You want to confront her right now. On the phone. But the time is off, and anyway I think we should wait, confront her in person. I want to see her expression when she understands that we know *exactly* what she is – a bitch – and that we know what she did to Gran.'

'And to us. We've been hurt. We'll deal with our mother when the time is right though. How are we going to find our grandmother? Shouldn't we call our mother, demand to know?'

'No. She won't tell us. She'll say Gran is dead. We'll do it through Anita Lowe. I have a feeling they live close to each other,' Justine replied.

'So you're saying Gran is in Istanbul, not London, is that it?'

'I think she probably is, because Anta lives there obviously, and she must know Gran's not well. We have to go to Istanbul.'

'I agree. But when?'

'Immediately. She'll be eighty in June. I don't think we should waste any time.'

Richard stood up, and Justine turned around and also stood as Daisy came running down the gallery, calling, 'Daddy! Daddy! Here I am . . . I'm coming to get you, Daddy!' Tita was following hard on the child's heels.

Justine said, 'Let's talk later. Your daughter is looking for you.'

'All right, later this evening,' he murmured.

'Listen, Rich, just one thing. Do you mind if I tell Joanne about this situation?'

'Why would you want anyone to know about this horrendous thing our mother has done?' he asked, sounding horrified.

'I don't, and Joanne isn't *anyone*, Rich, she's our best friend, we grew up together. But the point is this . . . *She* knows Istanbul well, and has a lot of contacts there, many friends. We're going to need help, and I think she can give us names and some good introductions.'

'Then tell her. Confidentially, though,' he answered.

Walking around the desk he swung his child into his arms as she came rushing into his office, her face full of smiles.

A few seconds later Richard was carrying Daisy out into the gallery, as she begged, 'Swing me, Daddy, please swing me.' And he did so.

Putting her down on the floor, he wrapped his arms around her from behind and, turning slowly, he swung her around and around, her legs flying out in front of her, her happy laughter echoing in the quiet gallery.

Richard started to laugh too, and watching him Justine was pleased he was enjoying this carefree moment with his daughter. She knew how upset he was about their mother's incredible lie, as angry as she was herself about the whole terrible matter. Still, he was sheathing it well at this moment, and for obvious reasons. He did not want Daisy to know there was anything amiss.

The thought of their mother enjoying herself in China, having a great time there, as she undoubtedly was, filled Justine with sudden fury, made her see red. Then she blinked, and turned to Tita, who was standing by her side, speaking to her.

'I'm sorry. I missed that,' Justine said. 'What did you say?'

'That Richard's a great father.'

'That he is, Tita. By the way, I'm thinking of asking Joanne to dinner. I'm assuming there's enough food.'

'Oh yes. I made three cottage pies, and Pearl has a ham baking, and there'll be lots of vegetables. Plenty for everyone.' She grinned. 'An army.'

Justine smiled. 'As usual! I'll call Joanne now, and I'll let you know if she's coming later.'

'No problema,' Tita answered, and went down the gallery, calling to Daisy, 'See you soon, Honeybunny.'

Justine continued to watch her brother, wondering if he would be able to come with her to Istanbul. He wanted to desperately, she knew that; on the other hand, he was still working on a huge architectural project. His new boutique hotel in Battery Park was almost finished, and she was aware that the final and rather complicated installations would be taking place in the next couple of weeks. She just wasn't sure he could break free – and anyway, she was not afraid to go alone. Justine was accustomed to travelling the world for her documentary filming, but Richard was overly protective of her, and he wouldn't want her to go by herself; also, he was as anxious to find the truth as she was.

Richard finally stopped turning and put Daisy down. He held her close to his legs, stroking her hair, asking, 'You're not dizzy are you, Bunnykins?'

'No, I'm not, Dad, I'm good.'

He looked across at his sister, standing in the door of his studio, and said, 'About our friend . . . I think I would prefer it if you just said you might be planning to shoot a documentary in Turkey, and leave it at that.'

'Agreed. It's better to stay . . . cool on this matter, don't you think?'

He nodded and, releasing Daisy, he walked over to Justine and said, sotto voce, 'That letter is lethal, and our lives will never be the same again.'

'I know,' she responded, staring into those blue eyes remarkably like her own. 'A lot of lives are going to be changed.'

FOUR

Once Richard had left with Daisy, Justine walked slowly down the gallery, dialling her closest friend, Joanne Brandon. There was no answer; she left a message and headed into her own glass studio.

Years ago, this had been her father's office, although its design was totally different today. The huge plate-glass windows Richard had installed gave it spaciousness, wonderful clear daylight and spectacular views of the property.

Her desk was a replica of Richard's, also of his design, a slab of heavy glass on steel sawhorses. Hers was a bit more cluttered than his, with several photographs in silver frames, mementos of some of her trips abroad, a Tiffany carriage clock Joanne had given her for her twenty-first, and a silver hunting cup filled with matching pens, another sign of Justine's tidiness and perfectionism. Behind her, a glass console table held her computer and keypad. She turned it on, and a few minutes later, when she glanced behind her, she saw there were no messages.

Sitting back in her chair, she let her thoughts wander, waiting for Joanne to call back. They had been friends since childhood; Joanne's mother had owned a house lower down on Indian Ridge

Hill, and they had grown up together. Joanne had inherited the house, and their friendship had continued into adulthood. Joanne's mother had been a widow, and Justine's father had gone out of his way to give Joanne a great deal of affection and later good advice after her mother had died.

Tony Nolan. He had been struck down in his prime by a fatal heart attack, and he hadn't even known he had a heart problem . . . twelve years ago. Justine was well aware that it was because of him that she and her twin had turned out so well. He was the one who had brought them up, given them a regime, a routine in their lives, instilling in them duty, responsibility and a genuine work ethic.

He had shown them a great deal of love, devoted himself to them, and, as a consequence, she and Richard had turned out to be wholesome, loving and relatively normal adults. Certainly they were well grounded.

Tony Nolan had taught them about ethics and integrity, given them a sense of honour. *Being truthful* was a phrase never far from his lips. Yes, he had been a truly good man and a wonderful father, and his values had been of sterling quality.

Quite unexpectedly, more than two decades fell away, and Justine saw him in her mind's eye on the day Pearl, Tita and their mother Estrelita had arrived at the house. He had hired Estrelita, a Chilean, to be the housekeeper at Indian Ridge, because their mother was always away on decorating business.

To her father's surprise and dismay, Estrelita had brought along her daughters, who had just arrived from Chile. She remembered how her father hadn't had the heart to send the two girls back to Estrelita's family in Chile, and so he had allowed them to stay. But he had hired an immigration lawyer at once, had undertaken to sponsor them. It helped that Estrelita had worked in New York for some years and had a green card, and matters had proceeded smoothly.

My God, twenty-two years ago, she muttered under her breath. She and Richard had been ten years old, Pearl eighteen, Tita sixteen.

Because their father had allowed the girls to stay, they fully understood they must help their mother in the house, and they had done so. But Pearl and Tita had longed to cook because they loved food, and it was her father who had taught them.

Justine closed her eyes, lost in sudden memories of her childhood, and saw them as they were all those years ago. She heard her father's booming laughter, the girls giggling and Richard joining in the banter and the fun.

She had been troubled at that time because of her mother's continuing absences – taken away from them by her work. Suddenly Justine now understood how much she had resented that in those days.

Rousing herself from her thoughts, sitting up straighter in the desk chair, Justine opened her eyes. And yet Pearl and Tita were still there, dancing around in her head. How devoted and loyal the two of them had been and still were.

They had stayed on after Estrelita had been taken seriously ill and had died here at Indian Ridge. The old house had become their beloved home over the years, just as it was her brother's and hers.

Pearl had been married at the local church fourteen years ago and her father had given Pearl away; she and Tita had been bridesmaids. Pearl had married her third cousin, Carlos Gonzales, who had come to visit Pearl and Tita from Miami and had never left. Tony Nolan had given him a job as a gardener and carpenter; and after Carlos had married Pearl, *his* father had come from Miami to live with them, and help out at Indian Ridge. Like his son, Ricardo was a hard worker and a talented carpenter.

As she looked back, Justine realized that her mother had never really been part of their childhood at Indian Ridge, although her grandmother had. Deborah Nolan had always been aloof, remote, and had somehow managed to stand outside their joyousness over the years. In a certain sense, she had been like a stranger looking in.

What had made her mother tell that horrendous lie ten years ago? She had ruined Gabriele's life, certainly caused her heartache. And she had caused them unnecessary grief. Only a monster would do something like that, something so cruel. *Evil.* What her mother had done was evil.

Her cell phone rang. She picked it up, put it to her ear.

'It's me. Jo.'

'Hi. Where are you?'

'I just arrived from New York. When did you get here, Juju?'

'Early this afternoon. Any chance you can come to dinner with me and Rich? We need to pick your brains, quite aside of wanting to see you.'

'I can. Delia will give Simon his supper. What do you want to pick my brains about?'

'*Istanbul.* I have to go there for work. I need some introductions, your best contacts.'

'God, I wish I could come with you, but I can't. My contacts you can have. And what time do you want me for dinner?'

'How's seven?'

'It's a deal.'

The kitchen was filled with the most delicious smells . . . apples redolent of cinnamon, bubbling on the stove, sweet potatoes baking, and the most dominant of all was the spicy fragrance of the cloves studding the ham in the oven. Justine felt ravenous all of a sudden, her mouth watering, and she realized she hadn't eaten lunch.

The moment Pearl saw her hovering in the doorway she put down the wooden spoon she was holding and rushed over to her, put her arms around her and held her close to her ample body. Just as Tita was petite and slender, her older sister was well padded and motherly. And yet they looked very much alike with their dark curls, dark eyes and permanent smiles. They both had warm and loving dispositions.

Finally releasing her, Pearl looked her over appraisingly. 'Seems to me like you've lost weight!'

'I have, that's true. I've missed your cooking, Pearl, and you, too.'

Pearl beamed at her. 'Joanne coming to supper?'

'Naturally. Who'd pass up a chance to eat a meal cooked by you? You're the best in the business.'

'Flattery, flattery.' Pearl laughed dismissively but looked pleased as she went back to the stove, stirred the apples in the pan and turned them off. She opened the oven door, glanced at the ham and nodded to herself, satisfied it was cooking nicely.

Justine walked across the floor and sat down at the big table. 'Where's Daisy?'

'Tita took her up to her room to clean her teeth, wash up. She'll be down soon to have her supper at six.' As she spoke, Pearl stared at the kitchen clock, saw that it was five forty-five and hurried to the countertop under the window. She picked up a cottage pie in a glass casserole and carried the dish to the oven. 'Got to get this brown,' she muttered, more to herself than Justine.

'Where's Richard, do you know?'

'He went up to his room. How about Parisian eggs to start?'

'Gosh, Parisian eggs. I love them! We haven't had them for ages. That's a great idea.'

'Good. Better check I've got anchovies and mayonnaise.' Gliding over to the pantry, she went on talking. 'Your grandmother taught me how to make Parisian eggs. She warned me . . . the eggs had to be boiled at the last minute. She used to say, "They must be really, really warm, Pearly Queen."'

Pearl swung around, suddenly laughing. 'Remember how she used to call me that, Justine? She said it was after the pearly kings and queens from that place in London.'

'The East End, and the pearly kings and queens are always Cockneys.' Memories flashed before her eyes unexpectedly: Gran in the kitchen here, teaching Pearl how to make cottage pie, steak-and-kidney pie, and fish and chips, as well as those hard-boiled eggs with mayonnaise and anchovies on top which they all enjoyed.

'They wore clothes with pearls stitched on them,' Pearl announced, closing the pantry door.

Justine slipped off the stool. 'I'm going to get ready, but I'll set the table first.'

'No need, Tita did it,' Pearl grinned. 'It's set for three.'

Justine laughed at the knowing expression on Pearl's rosy-cheeked face, went out to the hall and up the stairs.

Richard's door was ajar. She pushed it open and looked in. 'Hi! I spoke to Jo. She's coming over for dinner.'

He was at his desk. He turned around, nodded. 'Good, it'll be nice to see her.'

Justine came into his bedroom. 'I did some research on Istanbul on the Internet,' she said. 'I remembered something all of a sudden, Rich. When Dad and Gran worked together at Dad's showroom in the D & D Building on Third Avenue, they imported stuff from Turkey.'

Richard threw her a knowing look. 'I thought of that myself. They had two companies, Exotic Places and Faraway Lands, and they bought furniture and accessories from China, Japan, Thailand and India. And Turkey, of course. Didn't Gran used to go there from London? To Istanbul, I mean?'

'I think she did with Uncle Trent,' Justine said.

'They were close friends,' Richard murmured. 'When he died thirteen years ago, Gran was very upset.'

'Not long after Trent died, Gran went back to London . . . she said something about buying carpets to me,' Justine said.

Instantly something occurred to Richard. '*Hereke!* That's where the carpets are made. Dad showed me one when I was at the showroom with him on a Saturday; they're made of silk, I think. Very beautiful, and expensive. The more I think about it, she knows Istanbul quite well – and you're right, Juju, Gran's more than likely there. It's suddenly dawned on me that she had some special friends in Turkey.'

'I want to leave next week, and as soon as I can,' Justine announced. 'Do you think you'll be able to come?'

Looking across at her, he shook his head, his expression one of regret and concern. 'No, I don't. I've that big installation starting next week, and although I know Allen Fox is capable of overseeing it, Vincent Coulson will throw a fit if I'm not there. He'll want me on the spot twenty-four/seven, and you know it.'

'Yes, I do, and I will be all right, honestly. I can go it alone. I've done it before when I've been on foreign locations for my films. Don't worry about me so much.'

'How can I change after thirty-two years? I'll always worry about you, Juju. But it's not only that, I'm as concerned about Gran as you are, and I just feel I ought to be with you, helping to find her.'

'Listen, Joanne's been to Istanbul three times, twice on vacation and once on location for a movie she was handling. She'll be helpful with contacts, and you know I'll call you every day. And as soon as you can get away, you will.'

'And I'll bring Daisy.' He jumped up. 'Talking of Daisy, I said I'd sit with her while she has her supper. When's Jo coming over?'

'Seven o'clock. You'd better go down and be with your adorable daughter. I'm going to tidy up.'

FIVE

'You look great,' Joanne Brandon exclaimed, walking across the worn Persian carpet covering the drawing-room floor. 'Hard work and no play agrees with you!'

Feeling more relaxed for the first time that day, Justine smiled and rushed to meet her closest friend. 'You don't look half bad yourself . . .' She left her sentence unfinished as she grabbed hold of Joanne's hands.

'Come on, give me a hug,' Jo said.

The two women embraced, then stepped away, gazed at each other for a long moment.

Justine said, 'You've done something to yourself . . . it's a new hairdo! *Shorter*, and I love it. Very chic.'

'And you're leaner, fitter, and your hair's different, too. *Longer*, glossier. You glamour puss, you.'

The two of them broke into peals of laughter, both recalling how they always used to greet each other with comments like this . . . about their appearance. They had once again fallen into the old trap, on purpose, of course, since it had become something of a joke these days. When they were teenagers they had accused each other of being overly vain.

Joanna went and stood in front of the blazing fire as she usually did, enjoying the warmth, especially on this cool April evening. Justine walked over to the round table in the corner, where bottles of liquor and glasses stood, along with a white wine in a silver bucket. 'Is this all right?' Justine asked, her hand on the bottle. 'It's Sancerre.'

'Couldn't be better.'

After pouring the wine, Justine carried the crystal goblets over to the fireplace, handed one to Joanne. They clinked glasses.

'So the picture went well, did it?' Justine asked, sitting down opposite her friend.

'The best I've worked on yet,' Jo answered. 'The stars were great, had no problem with my PR demands, knew their lines, no temperament or tantrums. And we came in on time and on budget. *Thank God*. I was glad to get back to New York, and Simon. Poor kid, he really missed me. But there was no way he could've been in Los Angeles when I was working. I didn't want him to miss school either, and anyway his father wouldn't have liked him to be out of New York.'

'No, he wouldn't. How's *he* doing?'

'Oh, the same as usual. Bad tempered, bossy, impatient. Nothing's ever right. He's a negative man, Malcolm Brandon is, and a trifle petty.'

'But he can turn on the charm when he wants to.'

'Don't tell me. He does it now, even though we're divorced. But how about you? How did your editing go in the end? You sounded worried sometimes.'

'A heavy month, as I explained on the phone when you called. But the documentary came out great in the end. Jean-Marc Breton was a devil to work with, but ultimately he was brilliant and his art is just superb. Breathtaking really. His paintings are so vivid, so colourful, and Provence and Spain are wonderful places to film! I'm showing it to Miranda Evans on Tuesday afternoon. She saw some of the rushes when she came over to France, and she's also seen the rough-cut. Even though I say it myself, the finished product is . . . perfect.'

'Knowing you, it wouldn't be anything else. What did she say about the new title?'

Justine made a moue. 'At first she wasn't sure about it . . . after all, "Proof of Life" means different things to people. *Show me that the hostage is not dead*, is one example. That's what the police say to a kidnapper, or a fugitive holding someone against their will. To me it meant that if I could film the world's greatest living artist, an extraordinary painter, who was a recluse, non-communicative, and an eccentric, then I had *proof of life* that he wasn't dead, like so many people thought he was. He's hardly ever seen in public these days, and there has been a lot of gossip and speculation about his well-being. And I've just proved he's alive and kicking and as right as rain, to submerge myself in a bunch of clichés.'

'Clichés are *true, the truth*, used frequently, which is why they are called clichés.' Jo took a sip of wine and eyed Justine speculatively over the top of the glass. 'Is he really the lady-killer he's said to be, or is that all part of the myth and the legend, and all that jazz?'

Justine's face changed slightly and she remained silent, her blue eyes suddenly thoughtful, her face solemn.

Knowing her as well as she did, Joanne had the feeling she had accidentally stepped on dangerous ground. Taking a deep breath, she murmured, 'I guess he's a man with what is called *fatal charm*. Isn't that so? Did you succumb to it?'

'No, of course not, don't be so silly,' Justine answered swiftly, her voice rising slightly.

Joanne nodded; she thought: *I don't believe her*. She's blushing. What is she hiding from me? Clearing her throat, Joanne murmured, 'The whole world says he's irresistible to women.'

'I resisted, take my word for it.'

Richard asked, 'Resisted what, Juju?' He came strolling into the drawing room, went to hug and kiss Joanne, and then poured himself a glass of wine, joined her on the other sofa.

His sister said, 'Jo was teasing me about Jean-Marc Breton, or rather about his reputation as a womanizer. I was just telling her that I resisted his so-called charms.'

Richard knew that his twin was embarrassed for some reason, and wanting to alleviate this, he said, 'I thought he was truly a decent kind of guy when I met him, Jo. Fascinating to talk to, well informed about a lot of things, and it goes without saying that it was a great privilege to meet him in his home. And to be shown around his gallery by the maestro himself was an honour.' Richard took a swallow of wine. 'He didn't strike me as a man who went around pouncing on women.'

'I didn't say he did!' Joanne cried, and then laughed. Focusing on Justine, she changed the subject. 'When are you planning to go to Istanbul?'

'Next week, once I've shown the final cut to Miranda on Tuesday. I feel certain she'll like the film, and when I get all the business with CNI out of the way, I'll be on my way.'

'So are you going to do a documentary on Istanbul?' Joanne's auburn brow lifted questioningly.

'I'm not sure. I have an idea I want to pursue, and if I think it'll work, then yes, I might well be filming there later this year.'

'So what's the idea then?'

'You know I'm superstitious, Jo,' she murmured, sidetracking her friend. 'I never talk about an idea until I've developed it and finally got it nailed.'

'I understand. I have a great friend there, and she'll be extremely useful. First of all, she speaks perfect English. She's actually a professor of archaeology. However, being smart, she knew she'd never make a proper living doing that, so she started a boutique travel business. She knows a lot of people, and everything there is to know about all of the ancient sites, ruins, palaces, and the history of the country from the Byzantine period through the Ottoman Empire up to today. Ask her anything. She'll have the answer. I've already sent her an e-mail explaining that I will call her tomorrow.'

'What's her name?' Richard asked.

'Iffet Özgönül, and her company is called Peten – Peten Travels, actually.' Opening her handbag, Joanne took out a sheaf of papers. 'Here's some information I pulled up on my computer about her and her background. And also some pages about Istanbul.'

Justine took the papers eagerly.

Richard and Joanne started to talk about a barn on her property which she wanted to convert into a studio, and Justine buried her head in the sheaf of papers, the computer printout. It was a relief to have them.

She had suddenly grown apprehensive when Joanne had launched into a discussion about Jean-Marc Breton and his reputation as a lady-killer. So called. Making a documentary film about a great artist, his work and his life had been problematic enough; things had grown much more complicated and complex when he had fallen for her. She had made a decision months ago not to discuss the making of the film with anyone, and she certainly had no intention of speaking about her relationship with him.

Brushing thoughts of the Frenchman aside, she went on reading about Iffet Özgönül, liking the sound of her. This was a person who could no doubt help her in a variety of different ways, and it was very likely that Iffet would be able to find Anita Lowe, who was the key to Gabriele's whereabouts.

The sudden appearance of Tita in the doorway made Justine look up, and she raised a brow. 'Do you want us to come to the table?'

'Please, *now* Pearl says, for the eggs.'

'I'm famished,' Richard announced, standing up. 'Come on, Jo, and bring your drink.'

Tita disappeared down the corridor and Richard led Joanne and his sister into the small cosy dining room next door, which had once been the breakfast room, full of sunny yellows and greens and glass furniture. Richard had redesigned it. Removing all of the glass pieces, except for two étagères on either side of the fireplace, he had used a colour scheme of scarlet and black . . . scarlet on the walls, a black floor plus mellow antiques made an enormous difference.

'This has been a terrific transformation,' Joanne remarked, as Richard pulled out a chair for her, then went to help Justine.

He whispered against his sister's cheek, 'Where's the letter? I left it on my desk.'

'I have it in my pocket,' she murmured, and then, looking across at Joanne, said, 'I agree with you about this room, and although I was only half listening when you were discussing the barn, I think Rich has some great ideas for remodelling it.'

'He does. But then he's the best,' Jo responded.

'I like Iffet before meeting her,' Justine murmured.

'Here're the Parisian eggs,' Pearl announced, striding into the room with a tray of plates, followed by Tita, who handed one to each of them.

'Oh my, Parisian eggs like your grandmother used to make . . . I just love them.' Joanne picked up her fork, and began to eat at once.

How weird it is that no one has mentioned Gran for ages, Justine thought. And now, today, her name's on everyone's lips. Anxiety about her grandmother edged into her mind, as it had done on and off all day. Where was she? Was she well? Did she need money? What did she think of them? Her and Rich? Did she think they were in on this crazy estrangement, something promulgated by their insane mother? She hoped, no prayed, this was not the case.

Her mother. Deborah Nolan really was off her rocker, wasn't she? Two husbands since their father had died; both had divorced her – or she them, Justine wasn't sure which. What man would put up with *her* antics? She was skittish, silly, shallow, a spendthrift. Talented, tortured, tricky, troubled. Justine sighed under her breath. She could easily go through the alphabet, defining her mother, who had always been the absent mother, hadn't she?

'Penny for your thoughts,' Richard said, sitting back in the chair, gazing at his sister, worrying about her and their grandmother.

'Nothing much to tell you,' Justine replied. 'The eggs are good.' She grinned at him.

'And how. I've demolished them already. Great idea on your part.'

'It was Pearl's actually. By the way, I saw Carlos and Ricardo carrying some big planks of wood over to your building project this afternoon. How's it coming along?'

'They're doing a great job, and it'll be finished by the summer. But it's really just a simple bungalow, Juju, not a stately home.'

She began to chuckle. '*Simple?* Don't be silly, it's beginning to look like something rather splendid, in my opinion.'

Joanne said, 'I can't wait to see it. When am I going to get the tour?'

'Nothing to tour, as you call it, Jo – not yet. But I'll show you around tomorrow before tea in the gazebo.' He smiled lovingly at Joanne. 'I heard all about tea from Daisy. She's so excited that you and Simon are coming.'

'So am I, so's he,' Jo murmured. She wanted to add that Justine and Richard were the only family they had, and that they loved them very much; that she and Simon were dependent on them in so many ways. But she refrained.

She stole a look at Richard, surreptitiously, as she had been doing for as long as she could remember. She had loved him all of her life, had hero-worshipped him, but he had never shown much interest in her, at least not romantically. And then one day she had been swept off her feet by the sweet-talking, fast-talking, aggressive Malcolm Brandon, who had turned out to be a glib dud. And Richard had married Pamela. Who had died. And Jo had divorced the glib monster of Wall Street fame.

As she sat eating cottage pie and savouring this favourite, it suddenly struck Jo that Richard did not seem so full of grief tonight. Distracted, yes. Preoccupied, yes. *And worried*. He was worrying about something.

She was suddenly absolutely certain he was not pining for Pamela at this moment. There was a difference in his demeanour; he appeared jumpy, on edge, and worry clouded those wonderfully blue eyes. He was thinking hard; she knew when he was doing that, had been aware of this even when they were kids.

Jo let her gaze rest on Justine, thinking that she was also different tonight, had retreated into herself after her comments about Jean-Marc. And yet . . . well, there *was* something else bothering her best friend. Was it a problem with their mother?

Deborah, the darling of every man who met her, that's how Jo thought of her, and had since she was old enough to think about sex. The Sexpot. That's what some people called Deborah Nolan. The sexiest sexpot on two legs. How old was *she* now? In her fifties? Yes. Fifty-three or thereabouts. But no doubt as beautiful as ever, with her sculpted face, flowing dark hair and liquid grey eyes. Come-to-bed eyes, that was the way Malcolm had described them, looking as if he fancied her. He fancied a lot of women and had a lot of women and that's why they were divorced. And she was glad they were.

Clearing her throat, Joanne said, 'There's something wrong, Rich. I know there is, Juju.' She fixed her eyes on them.

They stared back at her and said nothing.

'Look, I've known the two of you since we were little kids, and we have a shared past. You can't pretend with me. You're both preoccupied and worried.'

48

Justine turned to her twin, her expression quizzical as she looked at him.

Richard pursed his lips, frowned. He said, 'There *is* a problem, Jo, you're correct. But I don't want to talk about it now. Not here. Let's finish dinner; Tita and Pearl have been working so hard in the kitchen. We can talk about it over coffee. Fair enough?'

'Yes, of course,' Jo answered, wondering what could be wrong.

Six

Tita brought coffee to the drawing room, and then disappeared.

Once they were alone, Justine took the letter out of her jacket pocket; leaning forward, she handed it to Joanne sitting on the sofa opposite them. 'The reason Richard and I are upset, worried, is because of this and what it reveals.'

Taking the letter from her, Joanne began to read, and as she did so she visibly stiffened. Finally, when she lifted her head and looked at them, her eyes were full of shock. '*Why?*' she asked, her voice shaking. 'Why did your mother tell you Gabriele was dead? Why did she *lie* to you?'

'We don't know,' Richard answered quietly. 'And we've no idea what this estrangement is about either. We're as mystified as you are.'

'But this is just horrible . . . that's not even a strong enough word to use . . . it's *horrendous*. And just think of your poor grandmother. Oh, God, I can't bear it. How upset she must have been all of these years. What an appalling thing . . . to be dismissed in that way, to be kept away from you.' Tears welled in Joanne's light-green eyes, and she blinked several times before continuing, 'She must have missed you both. Longed to see you. Gabriele must have suffered in the worst way.'

'We think so, and we totally believe Anita's letter, don't we, Richard?' Justine looked at her brother, and he nodded.

She sighed. 'Obviously Gran's not doing too well, and we need to find her as fast as we can.'

'That's the real reason you're going to Istanbul, isn't it? You genuinely believe she's there,' Joanne now asserted, staring at Justine pointedly.

'Yes, I do.'

'We both do,' Richard interjected.

'Couldn't she be in London, though? After all, she *is* English, and she had a house there. I know she said she was selling it years ago, but surely she took an apartment . . .' Joanne's voice trailed off when she saw the negative expression settling on Justine's face.

Richard said slowly, thoughtfully, 'I've read the letter several times now, and I honestly think that she is with Anita. There's every indication of that, reading between the lines.'

'I'm going to call Eddie Grange first thing tomorrow,' Justine announced. 'He was my line producer on this last documentary, and I need him to check a few things out for me.'

'Such as what?' Richard asked, glancing at her curiously.

'He can look in the London phonebook, see if Gran's listed, for one thing—'

'Why not try calling the international operator?' Richard interrupted, raising a brow. 'Or the Internet, check it out that way.'

'Don't be daft!' Justine exclaimed. 'Talking to the international operator takes an hour, maybe even longer, and you always get routed through New Delhi or somewhere else in India, so forget *that*. Eddie's my best bet.' Justine grimaced, then finished, 'However, I know she's not living in London. And on second thoughts, I'll go on the Internet later.'

'How can you be so sure she's not in London?' Joanne asked.

'Gut instinct, to be honest. But listen to me, Jo. Anita is her most longstanding, closest friend. Anita says this in the letter, very pointedly in fact. So under these awful circumstances, when you're missing your grandchildren, have been banished from your family, wouldn't you want to be with your closest friend? Especially if you were getting on, and Gran will be eighty this coming June.'

'You're right, under such circumstances I would want to be with my closest friend, which is you . . . Iffet will find Anita Lowe if anyone can.'

'I hope so. And by the way, don't go into that when you speak to her tomorrow. Just say I'm thinking of making a documentary there. I'd like to keep this situation confidential, and so would Rich.'

'I wouldn't have said anything to Iffet, I really wouldn't,' Joanne answered. 'And anyway, you can trust me to keep your confidence. I always have.'

'I know it wasn't necessary to say that to you, Jo, because you're family to me, and to Rich. But I just wanted you to be clear how I am going to handle the matter when I get there. I'll talk about business first before bringing up Anita.'

Joanne nodded, gave her a reassuring smile.

Richard said, 'Can't you go with Justine? It would make me feel better, Joanne, if you could. I'm afraid I'm stuck here for the next two weeks with my big installation at the hotel in Battery Park.'

'I'm stuck too, Richard. I just signed a contract to do the public relations on a movie being shot in Manhattan.' Frowning, she added, 'I don't think I can get out of it.'

'Nor should you even attempt to,' Justine murmured. She put her hand on Richard's arm lovingly. 'I'll be all right, Rich. I'm thirty-two like you. A grown-up. And perfectly capable of travelling alone.'

Richard smiled, hugged her to him. She was his best friend as well as his twin and the most important person in his life except for his little daughter. The thought of ever being without Justine terrified him.

Joanne said, 'When I was working on that crazy movie over there a few years ago, Iffet was indispensable, Richard. She'll make things easy for Justine.'

'That puts my mind at rest,' he murmured.

'So when do you plan to leave?' Joanne asked Justine.

'Next Wednesday, the day after I've screened the film for Miranda, and she's signed off. Which I know she will. By the way, I checked the airlines this afternoon. There are quite a few flights from Kennedy to Istanbul. Night flights.'

'That's correct, and it's about ten hours to Istanbul. Make sure you book a direct non-stop flight, which is the best. You don't want to have to change planes in a foreign city.'

'I'll take an afternoon flight, either on Delta or Turkish Airlines. Both have direct flights.'

They went on talking about Justine's trip for a short while longer, and then eventually Joanne stood up. 'I'd better go. Thanks for dinner, the two of you. And I'm sorry.' She stared at them. 'What I mean is, I'm sorry your mother did this awful thing to Gabriele, and to you. But let's face it, this is also *wonderful* news – your grandmother's alive and not dead after all, and I for one can't wait to see her again.'

'We know you love her,' Richard said, walking out of the drawing room with his sister and Joanne.

They saw her to the door, but stood talking to her on the step for several minutes longer.

Justine suddenly said, 'I used to think you were wary of our mother, Joanne. Perhaps even a bit frightened of her when we were growing up. Were you?'

'Wary perhaps, but not frightened,' Joanne answered, frowning to herself. 'You know, I think I was actually in awe of her, and also rather intimidated.'

'That's a funny word to use,' Richard said, scrutinizing her for a moment. 'She wasn't particularly intimidating. Know what, I always thought our mother was ditzy. A real flake.'

Joanne nodded in agreement. 'She *was* those things, yes. I suppose I was intimidated by her beauty, that's the best way of describing it. And the way she affected grown men was incredible. They were struck dumb when they set eyes on her. To be honest, I never thought she was a bad person. Nor did I think she could ever do something so . . . so cruel, so very mean.'

'Neither did we,' Richard said in a hollow voice.

Justine was silent.

Justine awakened with a start, lay there feeling disoriented. There was light in her bedroom and for a split second she thought it was morning. Then she realized that it was the moonlight filling the space with its soft, silvery glow.

Throwing back the bedclothes, she slid her legs to the floor, went over to one of the windows overlooking the garden and stared out. Riding high in a cloudless black sky was a huge full moon. It was extraordinarily bright; the light it gave off was unusually powerful, and she stood admiring it for a moment, then turned away, got back into bed.

Thoughts she had had before falling asleep came back, gave her a jolt, as they had earlier. *Did her mother know where her grandmother was living?* Obviously Justine couldn't be sure that she did, but there was a line in Anita's letter which suggested differently: *Get in touch with her before it's too late*, Anita had written. Of course, Anita might have just been making an assumption. Unless she had the true facts, was aware that Deborah *could* reach out, because she knew where to contact Gabriele directly. These were some of the thoughts that had hovered at the back of her mind over dinner. She had shoved them away. Now they were back again.

There was a sudden tapping on her door; it was opened gently. 'Justine. Are you asleep?'

'No, Rich,' she answered, sitting up as her brother came into the bedroom and closed the door.

'It's okay, I'm wide awake,' she murmured. He sat down at the end of the bed; there was a puzzled expression on his face.

'What is it?' she asked, noting a flicker of concern in his eyes.

'I woke up about half an hour ago, because something was troubling me, I guess. I was remembering what Anita said in the letter to Mom. She told her to get in touch with Gran. But look, she didn't say where, didn't give Mom an address.'

'I was thinking exactly the same thing only a few minutes ago! It woke me up . . . well, we do have the same thoughts fairly often, don't we?'

'Yep. So, do you think Mom has Gran's address?'

'It's hard to say. *Maybe*. On the other hand, Anita might merely be making an assumption that she does. Why?'

'I was wondering if we should call Mom after all? In China. Do you know the time difference?'

'Thirteen hours. They're ahead of us. I don't think we should call her, Rich, honestly I don't.'

'Why not?'

'It's dangerous.'

'In what way?'

'In every way. First of all, she'll go nuts if we say that we know Gran's still alive, and that she lied to us. She'll deny it, shout and scream. If we challenge her, explain how we found out, she'll say the old lady who wrote the letter has dementia, doesn't know what she's doing or saying. You know what she's like, and she'll keep on denying everything, she'll lie in her teeth. She'll never admit Gran's alive. And anyway—'

'But we can cope with the hysteria and the histrionics. We have in the past.'

'This situation is different, because I sense there's something

55

rather big, important behind the estrangement, and I think Mom's the *guilty* one. Gran's innocent of wrongdoing, of that I am really, *really* certain. Our grandmother always had her feet on the ground; she was extremely well mannered, even tempered, level headed, practical, and a very nice woman. I often wondered where Mom got her temperamental nature from – or rather, from whom. Listen to me, Rich, the thing is this . . . I believe it would be dangerous to let our mother know we *know* what she did, how she's kept Gran away from us all these years. If she knows where Gran is, and also Anita, then who knows what could happen? She might go and see them, scare the wits out of them by harassing them.'

'I don't think she'd do them any physical harm,' Richard protested, then frowned, 'Is that what you're getting at?'

'No, I'm not. I agree, I don't think she'd attack them physically. *Verbally*, yes. And that kind of abuse can be very disturbing to anyone, most especially two old ladies. And what if one of them had a heart attack or a stroke because our mother scared them?'

'Yes, I see what you mean: she can be very voluble. And vicious. She's got a nasty tongue.'

'Only too true. She's a loose cannon, in my opinion. Capable of anything. So no, I don't want to phone her and ask her where Gran lives. I'll find Anita, and she'll take me to her. Don't forget, I was a journalist before I became a filmmaker, and I know how to track someone down.'

'And there's Iffet. Jo thinks she's going to be of great help to you.'

'She probably is.' Justine glanced at the clock. 'My God, it's almost two o'clock! Hey, Rich, I can call Eddie in London, get him to flip through the phonebook.' She reached for the phone on the bedside table, and Richard grimaced. 'Don't call him at this hour, for heaven's sake. It's only seven o'clock in London.'

'Knowing Ed, he'll be up.'

'But won't he think it strange that you're calling him in the middle of the night here?'

'I guess so.' Putting the receiver back in the cradle, she said, 'I'll give him a shout later. In the meantime, I wouldn't mind a cup of tea . . . or hot milk. Something. And guess what, I'm hungry.'

'So am I. So it's settled then, we're going to leave it alone. By that I mean we're not going to call our mother in China? Or wherever the hell she might be?'

'Correct. I'm going to find Gran, and it's not going to take me as long as you think. I've a good feeling about this friend of Joanne's, and I trust my own instincts. Gran's in Istanbul. And a good-looking English woman, with a hint of regality, is more than likely part of local society, moving in the right circles.'

'You're right. Let's go down to the kitchen. I'd love a mug of hot tea and some cake or cookies.'

Justine leapt out of bed, threw on her robe, and she and her twin went down the stairs to the kitchen. As she put the kettle on, Richard opened the refrigerator door but, finding nothing he wanted to eat, he went into the pantry. 'Oh, my God, there's a coconut cake in here,' he exclaimed, carrying out the cake stand with a glass dome.

Justine stared at him. 'If you touch that cake you're in *real* trouble! Pearl will have your guts for garters!'

'That's one of Dad's expressions!'

'Borrowed from our grandmother. And I believe Pearl made the cake for the tea party in the gazebo tomorrow.'

'*Whoops*. I'll go and put it back.' A moment later he emerged from the walk-in pantry with a glass biscuit jar. 'What do you think? Will Pearl get mad if I have a couple of these cookies?'

'I think you're on safe ground.'

* * *

The fire had burned low, but there were a few glowing embers left, and so there was a warm and cosy feeling in the kitchen. Richard and Justine sat at the big square table, sipping their mugs of tea and munching on the cookies.

Neither of them spoke for a while, but their frequent and sometimes long silences were never awkward. Rather, they were comforting. It had always been like this since they were born. They were totally at ease with each other, and on the same wavelength. Very often they had the same thought simultaneously, and said what the other was thinking. *Twinship*. That was the way Richard described it, much to Justine's glee.

As children they had done everything together, had gone to the same kindergarten and high school. Later, they went to Connecticut College in New London, a choice that had been perfect for them, as it turned out.

Joanne had asked if she could join them there, and they had been delighted when she got in. And so the childhood triumvirate had continued from their young adulthood into their college years, and afterwards.

Justine and Richard understood each other completely and on every level, and now Richard suddenly said, 'We've both clamped down on our anger, and that's best for the moment, don't you agree?'

She nodded, and said in a low tone, 'But the day of reckoning will come, you know.'

'A confrontation with our mother would be an indulgence at this moment, Justine. The most important thing is to get you on your way to Turkey.'

'Agreed.' Reaching out, she put her hand on his, resting on the table. 'I know you're going to worry, but I'll call you every day, I promise.'

'Day or night, any time, my phone will be on.' He shook his head, squeezed her hand. 'I hope Gran's all right. I can't bear to think what the last ten years have been like for her . . . she must have been so hurt.'

'And lonely,' Justine remarked softly. 'That's the worst thing of all for anyone. Loneliness.'

PART TWO

The Search

To reach the port of heaven, we must sail sometimes with
the wind and sometimes against it – but we must sail, and
not drift, nor lie at anchor.

Oliver Wendell Holmes

Seven

Justine recognized Iffet Özgönül at once. It helped, of course, that the woman she zeroed in on was standing next to a tall man holding a sign with the name NOLAN printed on it in large letters.

But Justine knew it was her. She fitted Joanne's description: slender, petite, a brunette with short curly hair and a big smile on her face. And now she was waving. Iffet had been told what to expect by Jo, no doubt about that: a lanky blonde American with long hair and blue eyes.

Waving back, then turning around, Justine beckoned to the young man carrying her two bags, and strode forward, increasing her pace. He hurried after her.

A moment later the two women were shaking hands, and Iffet was saying in perfect English, 'Hello, hello. So pleased to meet you. And welcome to Istanbul.'

'I'm glad I'm here, and pleased to meet you too, Ms Özgönül.'

'Oh, please, call me Iffet, everyone does.'

'Iffet it is, and I'm Justine, okay?'

'Of course. And it's a name we Turks know well. Centuries ago we had an emperor called Justinian, who built the now famous Haghia Sophia Church . . . But you don't need a history lesson now. Let's go to the car. And by the way, this is Selim, our driver.'

The tall man bowed courteously, and smiled; Justine smiled back and thrust out her hand, which he shook.

Iffet led her through Atatürk Airport and outside to the car, which turned out to be a small minibus. As the young baggage man was stowing her bags in the back, Justine glanced at Iffet and asked, 'Are we picking up other people?'

'Oh, no, not at all. But I always use these little buses.' Lowering her voice, she added, 'They're cheaper than regular cars, and more comfortable.' With a smile she hurried over to the baggage handler, and handed him money, thanking him.

Justine also thanked him. 'I could have done that, Iffet,' she murmured. 'Look, I have the tip money right here in my pocket.'

'Oh no, it's fine, really. Come, let us go . . . isn't it a beautiful day?'

'It surely is,' Justine answered, lifting her head, looking up. The sky was a perfect cerulean blue, with a few white clouds floating above in the vast sky; it was sunny and warm – perfect spring weather. She took several deep breaths, glad to be outside after the long night flight, and then bounded up the steps into the minibus.

Once they were on their way, Iffet asked her what she wanted to do that day, if anything at all, and also told her that she had booked her into the Çiragan Palace Hotel Kempinski, following Joanne's instructions.

'Yes, she told me she wanted me to stay there, that I would love it. As for doing something, I believe I'd like to take it easy today. I did sleep a bit on the plane, but not much. I was sort of restless, frankly. I'd prefer to do nothing.'

'I don't blame you, Justine. The hotel has a pool. More importantly, also a spa. A good spa. Perhaps you should indulge yourself.' Iffet gave her a big smile, her whole face lighting up.

'You can even have a Turkish bath, if you want. However, that might knock you out.'

Justine began to laugh. 'Joanne's a big fan of them, and insisted I had *one* at least. But not today.'

Changing the subject, Iffet now said, 'I'm thrilled that you're thinking of making a documentary here in Istanbul. May I ask what it's about?'

'I don't really know yet,' Justine admitted, giving her a wry smile. 'I need to see the city, poke around, learn about the people, the life, and about Istanbul's history, politics and religions. I do know that the latter fascinate me. I've done a bit of research, Iffet, and I think it's amazing that Muslims, Jews and Christians have lived peacefully side by side in Istanbul for many centuries. What a feat that is. Unbelievable.'

'It is, and I will be pleased to help you with your research, Justine. I am at your disposal, as is my entire office.'

'Thank you.'

The lobby of the Çiragan Palace Hotel Kempinski was spacious and airy, with a high ceiling, handsome furnishings and enormous elegance in the grand manner.

Everyone from the doormen and bellboys to the assistant manager and the young public relations woman greeted them with courtesy and friendliness, and Justine realized that they knew Iffet well. That was the reason *she* was getting the royal treatment.

Within seconds of their arrival in the lobby, she and Iffet were whisked up in the lift by the public relations woman and the assistant manager. Alighting on the fifth floor, they were guided down the corridor to her room. When they were ushered inside, Justine saw at once that it faced the Bosphorus and had a magnificent view. It was large and comfortable, with a seating area in front of French doors, which opened onto a terrace furnished with chairs and a table.

'This is great, thank you so much,' she exclaimed to the hotel staff who had accompanied them, as she glanced around, taking everything in. Once they had explained everything, they departed, reminding her they were at her service if she needed anything.

When they were alone, Iffet said, 'I'm happy you like the room, Justine. When I came over to inspect it this morning I was also pleased. I had requested one overlooking the Bosphorus, but they're not always available.'

'Thank you. And it suits my needs perfectly. I'd love to take you to lunch here, Iffet, to discuss a few things. Do you have time?'

'I kept today open for you, and thank you. We should perhaps have lunch on the terrace, it's a beautiful spot. Unless you prefer to be in air conditioning.'

'No, outside. I'd just like to tidy up, if you'll excuse me for a few minutes. But before I do that I need to do one other thing . . . find a telephone book.' As she spoke, Justine glanced around the room, opened the wardrobe, then a cupboard and a chest of drawers, shaking her head, looking disappointed. 'Not one in sight.'

'I can get a number for you immediately.' Iffet pulled out her mobile phone and asked, 'What is the name of the person?'

'Anita Lowe. And listen, I haven't found her on any Google search, or anywhere else on the Web. But why not give the local book a shot?'

Iffet explained, 'I shall call my office, that is the fastest way.'

Justine nodded, picked up her handbag and went into the bathroom. After washing her hands and face, she took out a hairbrush and attacked her mane of long blonde hair. Once it was sleek, no longer a tangled mess, she put on lipstick and sprayed herself with perfume.

Her mind was racing as she stared at her reflection in the

bathroom mirror, her thoughts focused on her grandmother and Anita. She knew she wouldn't rest until she had found them. Her appearance didn't matter; they took precedence in her head.

Straightening her black blazer, pulling out the collar of her white shirt, she decided she at least looked tidy, if nothing else. Grabbing her bag she went back to the bedroom, ready for action, prepared for what the rest of the day held.

Iffet glanced at her when she came in, and said in a regretful voice, 'Anita Lowe is not listed in the Istanbul phonebook.'

'*Oh*.' Justine pursed her lips, then she said, 'Could you try another name, please? *Gabriele Hardwicke*. That's Hardwicke with an *e* at the end. Again, I tried to find her number without success.'

Once again Iffet dialled her office, passed on the name and waiting patiently. After a few seconds she shook her head. 'No luck.'

'I wonder how I'm going to find these two?' Justine muttered, almost to herself, then forced a smile onto her face. 'Thanks for trying, Iffet. Shall we go to lunch?'

'I am ready.'

Going down in the lift, Iffet suddenly turned to Justine and asked, 'Do you have an address for either of the two ladies? If so, you could write a note. I can have it delivered in an hour. There is a special service I use.'

'I don't have an address for either,' Justine replied as they stepped out into the lobby. She thought: If I had an address I'd be hightailing it over there already. Swiftly she continued, 'I really do need to find Anita. I'm fairly certain she lives in Istanbul, and—' Justine cut herself off abruptly, and stood stock-still in the middle of the lobby, staring at Iffet.

Staring back, Iffet asked, 'What is it? What is wrong?'

'I've just thought of something. If a person owns a house in Istanbul, or an apartment, would the property have to be registered with a government agency? You know, for local taxes?'

'It would, yes!' Iffet exclaimed. 'Ownership of property has to be registered at the deed and land office at the local municipality. Tapu ve Kadastro Dairesi, that's the name of the land office. I must put one of my staff on this immediately. If you'll excuse me, Justine, I must speak in Turkish to that person. It will be quicker.'

'No problem.'

Taking a few steps away from Justine, Iffet again used her phone, and within a split second was talking rapidly to someone in her office.

'It is being taken care of,' she announced a moment later, a huge smile on her face, her brown eyes sparkling. She glanced at her watch. 'It's twelve thirty now. Lunchtime. So I might not receive the information until tomorrow.'

'That's all right, and thank you. Come on, let's go and have lunch.' Together Justine and Iffet walked across the lobby, through the lounge, the indoor café and out onto the terrace.

They were shown to a table in a corner, one that had a spectacular view of the hotel, its gardens and the swimming pool. Beyond was the Bosphorus flowing down into the Black Sea. As usual it was busy with varied traffic. Today there were sailing boats, private yachts, tourist boats and the ferries, plus a couple of cargo ships. In the distance, a huge cruise ship sat stationary on the far horizon, silhouetted against the bright blue sky like a behemoth.

'What a fantastic sight this is!' Justine said.

'It is lovely. If you didn't want to move you could stay here and keep very busy. There's the spa, a hair salon, many shops, bars, restaurants, swimming and tennis.'

Justine smiled. 'But I do want to move, I want to see this city, get to know it.'

'I have made a list for you.' Iffet immediately pulled a sheet of paper out of her bag. 'A list of churches, such as the Haghia Sophia, the little Haghia Sophia, both built by your male namesake, Justinian. The Blue Mosque, the Topkapi Museum, and various palaces. I'll take you wherever you want to go tomorrow.'

'I'm in your hands, you're the expert, but I wouldn't want to miss the Grand Bazaar and the Spice Bazaar.'

'I have them on the list for Saturday,' Iffet answered, then glanced up at the waiter who had appeared at the table. She ordered sparkling water and so did Justine, and both women took the menus he handed to them.

'I'm not a foodie, not very adventurous when it comes to food,' Justine explained, 'and I see several things here that I like. A club sandwich, for one, and a number of good salads. Do you know what you want, Iffet?'

'Like you, I am a simple eater. I will select one of the salads.'

'And I'm going to go for the club sandwich.' Justine beckoned to the waiter who came over and took their order, and then Justine said to Iffet, 'Have you ever been to New York?'

Iffet shook her head. 'But I do know London quite well. I go there often. Do you want to travel here in Turkey? Is there anywhere special you'd like to visit?'

'I've always wanted to go to Ephesus, but I'm afraid I won't be able to do it this trip. Perhaps next time.'

'If you make your documentary.'

'That's right.'

The two women liked each other, had clicked immediately during the drive from Atatürk Airport, and their conversation was nonstop both before and during lunch. On the plane, Justine had re-read Joanne's computer printouts and the travel guide she had given her, and because she was a quick study and had a retentive memory, she was able to have an intelligent discussion with Iffet. But always at the back of Justine's mind was an image of her grandmother, and thoughts of Anita Lowe. But she knew that once she had located one or both of them she would be able to relax. For the moment she remained tense inside, anxiety ridden.

At exactly two o'clock, Justine interrupted their conversation about the Basilica Cistern, a vast underground water system, saying to Iffet, 'I'm sorry to cut this short for a moment, but I must call my brother. He's expecting to hear from me about now.'

'That is perfectly all right, Justine, I shall give you your privacy.' Iffet made to stand up and leave the table.

Justine put out a hand, touched her arm, exclaimed, 'No, no, that's not necessary. I'm just calling him to let him know I've arrived safely and am in your care.' She shook her head, sighed lightly. 'He worries about me a lot.' Taking out her mobile phone, she dialled Richard's apartment, and within a few seconds she heard his voice.

'It's me, Rich,' she said. 'Safe and sound in Istanbul, sitting by the Bosphorus having lunch with Iffet. It's exactly two o'clock here, and I guess you're having breakfast in New York.'

'I am. A piece of toast and a mug of coffee standing up in the kitchen. How was the flight? How's Istanbul? What's the hotel like?' he asked in a rush of questions.

'The flight was great, just under ten hours, and landed on time. Istanbul is fascinating, what little I've seen of it. The weather is fabulous, and so is the hotel. Oh, and Iffet is lovely . . . a friend already.'

'So you're in safe hands all round, and I can relax.'

'Of course you can. Anyway, you know very well I can take care of myself. Any news, anything special happening?'

'Nothing at all. Daisy is great, work's going good, and the first part of the installation is under way. So far without any hitches.'

'Great. I obviously don't have any *news* about anything. Too soon. I'll call you tomorrow at this time, but my phone's always on if you need me. Big hug, love you.'

'Love you too, Juju. My arms around you.'

After clicking off, Justine smiled at Iffet and confided, 'He fusses about me, but he just can't help himself. I guess I'm the same with him. We're twins, and we're almost literally joined at the hip.'

'Oh, twins! I understand about twins. I have a friend who is a twin, and she and her sister are the same way.'

'I can imagine. But it's fantastic in so many different ways. Now, getting back to our interrupted conversation, you were telling me that the Basilica Cistern goes back to Byzantine times and was laid out under Justinian.'

'It's a cavernous vault underneath Istanbul. We can visit it if you are interested, it *is* open to the public.'

'I'd love to see it.' Justine opened her black leather handbag, pulled out her black Moleskine notebook. She found the page she was looking for, said, 'I put the Basilica Cistern on my list, along with the two big bazaars.'

'Good. We shall cover everything in the next few days. Perhaps this little tour of ancient places in Istanbul will produce an idea for your documentary.'

'It just might,' Justine murmured. 'It just might.'

EIGHT

A voice filled the room. A man's voice. Melodic. Slightly high pitched. Singing in a foreign language.

Justine opened her eyes and blinked in the dim light. Struggling up into a sitting position on the bed, she listened more attentively as the voice finally trailed off, stopped. Now there was perfect stillness. No sound at all.

Sliding off the bed, where she had been dozing, Justine went over to the seating area. The French doors were open, and she stepped out onto the terrace, looking around. Leaning against the terrace railings, she peered down into the garden below, expecting to see an orchestra, the singer preparing to sing another song. But there was no band. No musicians. No singer.

Then, suddenly, she understood. What she had just heard was the voice of a muezzin standing at the top of a minaret, calling the faithful to prayer. Joanne had mentioned this last weekend, explained that it happened five times a day, that electronic amplification carried the muezzin's voice around entire districts, all of which were large and heavily populated.

The muezzin's singing had awakened her from her languorous

dozing, forced her off the bed, and she didn't care. In fact, she was glad. She had some serious thinking to do.

After lunch with Iffet, she had come up to her room, unpacked, put everything neatly away and called Eddie Grange in London. He had not been able to find out anything on the Internet about the two companies her grandmother had been associated with. Very simply, there was no evidence that there had been either showrooms or offices for Exotic Lands and Faraway Places. It was as if they had not existed.

She had thanked Eddie and hung up. This new information, and the fact that her grandmother was not listed in the London phonebook, more or less proved that she did not live in London any longer. Perhaps she had vacated the city long ago and settled permanently. Unless she had an unlisted phone number. But Justine doubted that. Her grandmother wasn't into the secrecy game. Unlike her mother, who was.

With her arms folded and resting on top of the railings, she stared out into the night, lost for a moment in the beauty. The sky was a lovely deep pavonine blue, the stars were coming out in a brightly scattered array, and there were twinkling lights everywhere, especially on the other side of the Bosphorus. The Asian side.

How odd it is, she thought, to be here in Istanbul and straddled between Europe and Asia Minor, on two continents at once. What an intriguing place this was. Straightening up, she realized she was more positive than ever that her grandmother was here, somewhere in this city. She felt it in her bones.

Now she couldn't help wondering if the search at the land registry office would produce an address for Anita? Gran? Of course it was possible that Gabriele had her own home here. She had been independent by nature, decisive and driven, had stood on her own two feet, battling the world, making everything work for herself and for them.

Justine smiled inwardly. She had inherited those traits from her granny, no doubt about that. In fact, her father had told her she was more like her grandmother than her mother. And it was true, thank God.

Why would her grandmother come to live here in Istanbul? Justine was able to answer that question instantly.

Her grandmother's lifelong friend Anita lived here, and there were several other good reasons as well. The weather was mild all year round, according to Iffet, and was certainly the perfect climate for an older woman; knowledge of Istanbul from years ago, when she was doing business; other old friends residing in the city; a lifestyle she enjoyed.

Justine went back into the room, turned on several lamps and sat down in a chair. She closed her eyes, focusing her mind on Gran, and intensely so.

To all intent and purpose, Gabriele Hardwicke had seemingly disappeared off the face of the earth. Just as if she *had* died. Justine knew she hadn't. She had Anita's letter to prove it.

Certainly there was nothing of her life remaining in London. Earlier today Eddie had told her so in no uncertain terms. *Zilch*, was the way he had put it. And certainly she had been surprised, even startled, when he had wondered aloud if her importing business in London had ever existed.

What if the same thing happened here? What if neither woman owned homes here? Then there would be no way to find them. She would be facing a brick wall . . .

A blue-and-white tiled wall. Unexpectedly she was seeing this in her mind's eye . . . a blue-and-white tiled wall in her grandmother's kitchen in New York. No, *several* walls. Tiles from Istanbul, Gran had told her. Like the blue-and-white vases, tubs, planters and urns her father and Gran used to sell to interior designers in Manhattan. And brass objects. And carpets. Those beautiful silk-woven carpets from Istanbul. No, from Hereke, a small town located outside the city.

As all this came rushing back to her, she thought: That's it.

She snapped open her eyes and sat bolt upright. Dealers in tiles, ceramic objects, antiques and carpets . . . those were the people she had to find, if it became necessary. Perhaps they would remember her grandmother, perhaps even still knew her, and therefore knew where she lived.

Justine went to the desk, began to make notes about the items that had been imported from Turkey by her father and grandmother. As she did this she felt an easing of the tension inside her, because she had thought of another way she might be able to trace Gabriele Hardwicke. She had to find her. She would not rest until she did. And she would start tomorrow.

At one moment, Justine roused herself from her unceasing thoughts of her grandmother and pushed herself up from the desk. She could not resist the pull of the terrace that opened off her room, and she went outside to sit under the night sky. She glanced up, marvelling at that midnight blue arc above her. The stars were amazing . . . so many of them here in Istanbul, littering a sky that was clear, peaceful and infinite.

Across the Bosphorus the lights of Turkey and Anatolia on the Asiatic side were pinpoints of brilliant colour glittering across the countryside, turning it into a fairyland. And downstairs people were already dining at the terrace café; she could hear the sound of muffled voices and laughter against the backdrop of a tinkling piano.

She immediately recognized the song, picking up the strains of 'Somewhere Over the Rainbow' from one of her favourite old movies, *The Wizard of Oz*. Her grandmother had loved that movie as much as she and Richard had when they were little. And she herself had always yearned for Dorothy's sparkling, scarlet shoes.

That's what I need, a Wizard, she thought, and a Good Fairy

and a Magic Wand. She let out a small sigh, and then it nudged its way in . . . that maddening thought of the estrangement. What *had* happened between her mother and Gran to cause this insane rift? She wondered then if it could possibly have anything to do with money? Her mother was a spendthrift – she knew that only too well from her childhood, her father's angry tones echoing in her head right now, as if he were standing next to her. Bankrupt was another word constantly on his lips. 'You'll bankrupt me, the way you spend,' he used to shout angrily, and there would be another row between her parents, doors banging and raised voices for hours.

But they always made up eventually, and things normalized again. But looking back she acknowledged that they were either in each other's arms or at each other's throats . . . it had been the most tumultuous of marriages. After one of these rows had occurred, her grandmother had not come to the country for a while. She had gone instead to Huntington to stay with her close friend and lawyer, Trent, at his house on the water overlooking Long Island Sound. Sometimes Gran took them with her, and she and Rich enjoyed those trips, and enjoyed being with Uncle Trent, who made them laugh and spoiled them and thought up fantastic treats. Her mother never wanted them to go out there to Long Island, mostly because she did not like Trent Saunders. Not at all.

She was jealous, Justine suddenly thought, jealous of Trent's presence in Gran's life. What was it that she had once muttered? 'Nobody can take the place of my father.' But her father had died when her mother was seven. She had idealized him. She had always been going on about Peter Hardwicke.

How odd that she had forgotten hearing her mother say that to Gran, and for so many years. Unexpectedly, it stood out in her mind now, perhaps because it informed her, told her some-thing important: Trent Saunders had been more than her grandmother's American lawyer, he had been a special friend, very special indeed. I hope he was, Justine thought, seeing her grandmother in her mind's eye, the lovely looking blonde with blue eyes and a mischievous laugh, always so elegant and charming, and ever the lady, the genuine thing. A class act.

Anger flared in her. Anger with her mother. For a split second, she was again tempted to call her in China, but resisted. Why alert her to anything? Far better to confront her when she had accomplished what she had come here to do. And yet again she was positive her grandmother's whereabouts would not be forthcoming. Her mother's modus operandi was always to deny everything.

Glancing at her watch, Justine saw that it was nine thirty, and she went into the bedroom. Picking up the phone, she called room service, ordered a green salad, a plate of assorted cheeses and a pot of English breakfast tea with lemon. This done, she found the zapper, turned on the television, found CNN, and sat down to watch the latest news, wanting to connect to the rest of the world again.

Even as a child she had loved news, was always thrilled to know what was happening around the world, which was why she had become a journalist. She had been, and still was, a news buff.

She watched CNN, found herself glancing at the rolling text at the bottom of the screen, and switched to Sky News out of London. Nothing but bad news tonight, she thought, as she gazed at the screen and the unfolding events. The voice of her first news editor at the local Connecticut paper now reverberated in her brain. 'Bad news sells newspapers,' he had constantly told his reporters. 'Don't bother to bring me good news.' Well, the world these days was one big bad news story on a global scale.

Wanting variety, she zapped again, found her own network,

Cable News International, and sat glued to the screen until room service came.

The waiter eventually arrived at her door, wheeled the table into the middle of the room, and placed it so that it faced the television set. She thanked him as she signed the room service bill, and then sat down, continuing to watch as she picked at the salad.

Suddenly Justine stiffened. *There was her own face*. On the screen. And an announcer's voice saying, 'Famed documentary filmmaker Justine Nolan takes you into the private realm of the world's greatest living artist, Jean-Marc Breton. Her filmed biography of the master, "Proof of Life", will air on this network in September as a CNI documentary special.'

Images of Jean-Marc Breton – his homes in Provence and Spain and some of his paintings – flashed across the screen and then were gone. And so was her face. The news continued to roll. Business as usual.

Justine was taken aback. She now realized what Miranda Evans had meant when she had said, immediately after the screening, 'We've got to maximize this, Justine. It's a brilliant film, and it's going to be a worldwide hit. I'm going to make sure of that. I'll prepare a campaign immediately, do some promos.'

Miranda had said this on Tuesday. Today was Thursday. So Miranda had done the work yesterday, splicing a few key frames together, writing a couple of lines to go with them, and having Eric Froman, of the golden voice, do a voice-over. Just a few good words had been enough to accompany those vivid visuals. And *voilà*! Here was a promo on air tonight. Miranda Evans was moving swiftly, working well ahead of time. She was obviously convinced she really did have a potential hit on her hands. But then Miranda has always promoted her, backed her with a network right from the beginning.

Wow, oh wow! Justine was pleased, and went to find her cell

phone, punched in Richard's number, needing to share this with her brother.

When he answered, she said, 'Rich, it's me. Is this a bad time? Or can you talk?'

'Hi. And it's okay, I'm in my office. What's happening?'

'Well, listen to this! Miranda's worked wonders already. I've just seen the first promo for "Proof of Life" on CNI. Imagine that. I saw it by accident, and obviously she had the promo made yesterday when I was flying here. I must admit, it took me by surprise.'

'Hey, that's great. I'll keep a look out for it tonight. And she is a fast worker. How was your day?'

'A bit disappointing, in one sense. Anita and Gran are *not* in the Istanbul phonebook. But I guess we knew that. Iffet is checking with the land registry office, to see if they're listed there. They would be if they own homes here. Eddie hasn't been able to find any trace of those companies Gran was involved with. You know, Exotic Lands and Faraway Places. As he put it, "there's zilch in London". He even suggested they might not have existed.'

'He's wrong. Gran talked about them to us, and she didn't invent such things. She probably closed them down many years ago, and he hasn't gone back far enough. Let's hope Iffet finds something positive.'

'I came up with a couple of other ideas. I thought Iffet could take me to see some dealers in carpets and ceramics. If I'm lucky we'll find somebody who knew Gran, and knows where she lives today.'

'Brilliant idea. I know you're on the right track, so just keep going. Call me tomorrow. I will have to run now, Juju, I've got a meeting starting in a few minutes.'

'It's ten o'clock at night here, so I'm going to bed soon. I'll call you tomorrow.'

They both clicked off, and Justine sat back, cut into a piece of cheese and placed it on a cracker. She had a brainwave. *Interviews*, she thought. I can do some interviews about "Proof of Life". Explain I'm here to do research, may make a documentary about Istanbul. Television, newspapers.

She jumped up, went to get her notebook, looked at the list of names Joanne had given her, contacts in the media here. A brainwave indeed. If she couldn't find Anita and Gran she would have them find her. The media was the key. I've got to put my face in front of Gran, she added to herself. It's the only way.

NINE

They were in the middle of the teeming city in the heat. It was unusually warm for May, according to Iffet, and Justine was relieved she had chosen to wear white-cotton trousers, a white-cotton shirt with a turquoise vest top underneath, and very comfortable shoes.

For the moment the two women were cooling off in the leafy gardens in Sultanahmet Square. Having started out early on this Friday morning, they had already been to Topkapi Palace, once the resident of the Ottoman sultans, in the adjoining district. When they had first arrived in this square, they had visited the Blue Mosque and then the Haghia Sophia Church, which faced each other across the gardens.

Justine had been impressed by both of these ancient monuments. The Blue Mosque, famous for its Ottoman architecture, had six minarets, a number of golden domes with spires and 250 windows. Once inside, she had been captivated by the blue-and-white ancient Iznik tiles lining the walls. Immediately they had reminded her of the blue-and-white reproductions which her father and grandmother had sold at their showroom in Manhattan.

Justine knew from Iffet that the Haghia Sophia Church was one of the world's greatest architectural achievements. It had been built by the Emperor Justinian in the Byzantine period. The enormous edifice seemed more like a cathedral to her.

Now turning to Iffet, Justine said, 'Thank you for showing me these extraordinary places. I've really enjoyed our morning of sightseeing, but I'd like to take a rest now, wouldn't you?'

'I would. I think touring these two religious places, plus the Topkapi Palace, is enough to take in on one morning.'

'I wouldn't mind going to the Spice Market later. But shall we go somewhere for lunch first?'

Iffet nodded, pulled out her mobile phone, and dialled. A moment later she was asking Selim, the driver, to come and pick them up. After listening to him for a few seconds, she clicked off, and said, 'We must walk down here, Justine, towards the Bazaar Quarter. It will be easier for him. It's all to do with parking.'

'This restaurant is an old favourite – of mine and everyone else's,' Iffet explained. 'But it is quite hard to find if you don't know where to look.' Her brown eyes danced. 'But here we are,' she added, walking past the main entrance to the Spice Market, and leading Justine towards a steep flight of stone stairs. 'It's called Pandeli's, and it's on the first floor.'

Iffet climbed quite swiftly; Justine followed on a little more slowly, telling herself she needed to get back to the gym. Immediately.

As they went inside the restaurant, Justine said in a low but excited voice, 'Well, this was certainly worth the climb, Iffet.'

'I know,' she answered with a laugh.

The two women were greeted warmly by a waiter and led to a table near a window. They both ordered sparkling water, and took the menus offered. Justine, glancing around, exclaimed,

'The aqua-coloured tiles are gorgeous and the domes architecturally stunning. What a lovely place.'

'It's popular with the discerning locals, and the food is delicious,' Iffet said. 'I hope you will try the *börek*, they are renowned here, Justine. Little pastry triangles with cheese and herb filling, and once they are fried they swell up and turn brown.'

'I'm going to try them. Actually, I'm quite hungry, I didn't eat much last night, and I never really have a proper breakfast.' She picked up the menu and scanned it, and realized she liked the sound of many of the items listed. Finally she decided to order sea bass cooked in paper. 'I'm going to have the fish,' she said.

'So am I.' Iffet beckoned the waiter, and ordered for them, took a sip of water before continuing. 'There are a lot of palaces to see, and other museums. We must go slowly. I do not want to tire you, Justine. It is a good idea to visit the Spice Market after lunch. Tomorrow perhaps you wish to go to the Grand Bazaar.'

'I'd love it. You see, what happens to me is that I get visually overburdened if I view too many buildings and objects. I lose my judgement. I'm better if I pace myself. And listen, thanks for this morning. You are very knowledgeable. I was genuinely fascinated by Topkapi Palace – and especially the women's quarters, the harem.'

Leaning forward, she then said, 'I had something of a brainwave when we were going around Topkapi. It suddenly struck me that I would like to do a biography of Istanbul . . . on film, of course. This place has such an extraordinary story to tell . . . I think I would call it "Biography of a City".'

Iffet was staring at her. 'What a clever idea. *Exciting*.'

Justine was speaking the truth. The idea *had* suddenly hit her in the face when they were viewing the harem. She understood at once how fascinating a story about Istanbul could be. It was something she decided she would research once she had found her grandmother.

Iffet was asking how she could help Justine with this idea for the documentary when her cell phone buzzed. She answered it, listened attentively, gave her thanks and clicked off. 'That was my office. I am so sorry, Anita Lowe is not listed at the land registry office.'

'Oh.' Justine felt a rush of dismay. She cleared her throat. 'And Gabriele Hardwicke? Is she listed?'

'No, she is not. If you knew which district they lived in, that could be a help. I could send someone to do an additional check.'

'I have no idea,' Justine murmured, and blinked, then glanced away.

Iffet realized immediately that Justine was tremendously disappointed. Her expression was crestfallen and her blue eyes looked moist, as if she might suddenly cry.

'It is *important* to you, isn't it, Justine? That you find these two ladies?'

'Extremely important.'

A silence fell between the two women. Iffet couldn't help wondering what this was all about and why her new friend was so upset.

Justine was asking herself if she should confide in Iffet, and immediately cancelled out that idea. She had met Iffet only yesterday, and could hardly tell her about the letter from Anita. She would hesitate to tell anyone. Her mother had done a horrifying thing and she didn't want a soul to know. Other than Joanne, who was like a sister to her. On the other hand, perhaps she owed this very nice woman a bit of an explanation. An edited version of the truth.

She was about to speak out when the waiter arrived with the *börek*, and so she sat back in the chair, wanting to wait until they were alone.

* * *

Justine realized that she and her brother might have made a terrible mistake. They had decided Anita Lowe lived in Istanbul because the letter she had written bore an Istanbul postmark. But she might have simply been passing through the city, or on vacation. The truth was they didn't have any idea where Anita lived, nor their grandmother either. And she was more anxiety ridden than ever.

For a moment her frustration soared. How foolish they had been, and she in particular. She pressed down on these feelings, and made up her mind to confide in Iffet, although only to a certain extent. She was far too ashamed of her mother's behaviour to reveal that awful part of the story. She would have to fudge the estrangement, and put the focus on finding the two women.

Taking steely control of herself, Justine drank some of the sparkling water, and settled back on the banquette, glancing around. Several rooms formed the restaurant, and they were all visible to each other through the wide doorways. The cool aqua-tiled rooms, the windows and the starched white-linen tablecloths created a fresh look, and the setting provided a pleasant respite from the noise of the nearby markets and ferry terminals; it was a relaxing haven away from the jostling crowds.

'I am glad I brought you here, Justine. I think you like it,' Iffet said before picking up a *börek* and biting into the small triangle of pastry.

'I love it, is it a new place?' Justine asked, also starting to eat her own *börek*.

'No, it's very old. It was opened in 1901 by a fellow called Pandeli, and it has been a success ever since.'

When she had finished eating the *börek*, Justine looked across at Iffet and said quietly, 'I think I owe you more of an explanation about my search for Anita Lowe, but let's have lunch first. We'll talk over coffee.'

This they did, after enjoying the sea bass cooked in paper

and the grilled vegetables. Both women smilingly declined the delicious-looking desserts, and ordered Turkish coffee. 'Rife with caffeine, but why not, for once?' Iffet murmured, smiling at Justine. 'What do you wish to explain about Anita Lowe?'

'I must start with Gabriele Hardwicke,' Justine murmured, holding Iffet with her eyes. 'She is our grandmother, and it is she I am looking for, and I believed I would find her through Anita.'

Iffet looked taken aback, startled, and was silent for a moment, then she said, 'And I haven't been able to find Anita for you. Perhaps there are some other ways I might be able to locate her, if you are certain she lives in Istanbul.'

'That's just the point, I'm not. But wherever she is, I do think my grandmother will be with her. They have been friends since they were young girls, and have remained close. Let me tell you how all this came about.'

Justine told her story swiftly, giving only the details, resisting any embellishments, and explained that she and Richard were out of touch with their grandmother because of a quarrel between Gabriele and her daughter, their mother Deborah. Finally she finished, 'And I'm worried about Gran because Anita indicated in her letter she is so despondent and misses Rich and me. Also, she might not be well – she is almost eighty.'

Iffet had listened attentively, and now she said slowly, thoughtfully, 'Everyone has been making assumptions . . . Anita, you and your brother. I shall make one. Let us assume Anita and Gabriele do live here. If that is so, there are several other things I could do. What nationality are they? American?'

'No, they're both English. As I told you, I think they grew up together. In London. Although my grandmother does have some sort of connection to Yorkshire, in the north of England. But why do you ask?'

'Because there are many foreign consulates here. Often foreign residents visit their consulates just to say hello, leave their names for future reference. Or for social events the consulate might give. There are also other organizations that foreign residents can join. I could make enquiries.'

'Thanks, Iffet, that's great, and I have a couple of ideas myself. My grandmother seems to have past connections to Turkey, buying ceramics, antiquities and carpets for a showroom in New York which she and my father ran. They sold to interior designers. I was wondering if you knew any dealers . . . one of them could have known Gran, might still know her.'

A dark brow lifted, and Iffet asked, 'What kind of carpets? Kilims?'

Justine shook her head. 'No, not kilims – they were woven silk carpets from Hereke.'

'This is a good thought of yours, Justine,' Iffet said, sounding enthusiastic. 'I know one excellent carpet dealer; we could go to the shop whenever you want. It's not far from here.'

'Let's do that. But here's my other idea, and I know you'll be able to help. Last night I was watching television, going to different news stations. When I clicked onto the network I work with, Cable News International, I was taken aback when I saw my own face. I couldn't believe it. There I was on Turkish television. The network had made a promo for my new documentary. That's what gave me the idea – to be interviewed on a local show. Anita or Gran might just happen to see me.'

The worried expression on Iffet's face had dissolved and she was smiling. 'Brilliant. I can arrange a television interview. What about a newspaper story? We have a Turkish daily newspaper called *Zaman Daily English*. I can phone them.'

'You've brightened my day, given me hope!' Justine exclaimed, a smile lighting up her face. 'Let's forget about the Spice Market today, head for the carpet shop instead.'

*　　*　　*

'We're going to Punto,' Iffet explained. 'It's close to the Grand Bazaar over there. It won't take long.' Five minutes later she was ushering Justine down a narrow street and through a heavy wooden door which stood open. 'The carpet dealer is located in this *han*. It is called the Vezir Han.'

'What's a *han*?' Justine asked, always curious about everything.

'A *han* is a big courtyard with several buildings around it, and originally, centuries ago, the *han* provided accommodation for travellers, their pack animals, plus their wares. At night the heavy door was locked for safety. Today these courtyards house workshops, and there are many of them all over Istanbul. Now, we must go around this corner and we will be there.'

A moment later, Iffet was leading her into a small, ancient shop called Punto. As they entered a young man came forward, smiling broadly. He bowed to Iffet, shook her hand, still smiling, and Iffet introduced him as Kemal, youngest son of the owner. After shaking Justine's hand he immediately led them down a flight of steps, and Iffet said in a low voice, 'He's taking us to the private room reserved for special customers.'

'I'm not a customer,' Justine whispered back.

'I know. And he knows we are mostly seeking information about Gabriele Hardwicke. I told him on the phone. He wants this to be done in private, and you will be shown rugs, as a matter of courtesy.'

'I understand,' Justine responded.

Kemal led them to a banquette, and said in English, 'Please be seated, ladies. Comfortable, yes?'

'Yes, thank you,' Iffet said, also speaking English. She then reverted to Turkish for a moment or two. Justine guessed she was explaining things to him. Kemal nodded, and disappeared, hurrying across the showroom, entering an office.

Turning to Iffet sitting next to her, Justine asked, 'What did you tell him?'

'I asked him if he could telephone his father, who is not here today, to enquire if he knows your grandmother. And then I spelled her name for him. He is sending out an assistant called Mustafa, who is going to show us some of the best Hereke silk carpets, and later a weaver will demonstrate how she works on a loom. I hope you don't mind, but we must show politeness.'

'I understand, and I don't mind at all.'

Mustafa arrived, introduced himself, shook their hands, bowed, and then brought out the first carpet. It was beautiful, as were the next two, but when he presented the fourth, throwing it down and pulling it across the floor, Justine caught her breath in surprise. It was a mixture of various blues, on a deeper blue background, and it was gorgeous, that was the only word to describe it.

'It's breathtaking!' she exclaimed to Iffet, and smiled up at Mustafa. 'I've never seen such a wonderful carpet,' she said, and it was obvious she meant this.

The young man beamed. 'Thank you. It is special. Rare. An Ozipek. The best name, a good name.'

Another young man appeared carrying a tray with glasses of tea on it, and both women took a glass. Leaning closer, Iffet murmured, 'It is the custom, serving tea. And we have to drink it, or they will be offended.'

When Kemal returned a short while later, Mustafa left the showroom and Kemal spoke swiftly in Turkish, after excusing himself to Justine.

Once he had finished, Iffet made a moue. 'Some good news. Kemal's father did know your grandmother. He told Kemal that an Englishwoman called Gabri did buy carpets from him. The bad news is that he hasn't seen her for some years. I am so sorry.'

'It's okay. And at least we know Gran did spend time in Istanbul. Gabri is her nickname, by the way.'

TEN

The man cut quite a swathe as he walked through the lobby of the Çiragan Palace Hotel Kempinski, was well aware of the glances cast his way. He was used to it, therefore paid no attention.

His name was Michael Dalton, and he was tall, lithe, and in excellent physical condition at the age of thirty-nine. Because of his arresting dark good looks and last name, the movie buffs who met him thought he might be the brother of the British actor Timothy Dalton. But he was not, nor was he in the business of treading the boards or making movies.

Michael Dalton was in a very different kind of game, and it was one that was close to his heart. It took him all over the world and threw him into a mix of very diverse people. He always held his own whatever company he kept, and his geniality, charm and ready smile were captivating, disarming and persuasive, camouflaging the true nature of the man. Only a scant few were ever allowed to see the real Michael Dalton, get a glimpse of his superior intelligence, inside knowledge of international politics and formidable understanding of world history.

There was a lot of speculation about what he really did for

a living. Some people said he was a secret agent with the CIA. Others maintained he was British-born, worked for British Intelligence, and went undercover for MI6. And there were those who insisted he was a negotiator, a fixer, a go-between for presidents and prime ministers. Others had decided he constructed huge financial deals for tycoons, tyrants and oligarchs. They insisted that was where all his money came from. But they were wrong.

Michael Dalton did exactly what he actually purported to do. He owned and ran an international security company with offices in London, Paris and New York. It was renowned, had a fine reputation and was highly successful with a raft of big clients, including major corporations, banks and multinationals.

Many of the other things bandied around about him happened to be true. He *was* an American, *had* been born in New York, *had* attended Princeton and Harvard, *did* have a law degree and *had* been engaged. Once. Now he *was* unencumbered and preferred it that way.

Michael Dalton had two mantras: *Those who retire die; he who travels fastest travels alone.* These thoughts were on his mind as he strode out onto the terrace of the hotel and glanced around. Only two tables were taken. In one corner there was a young blonde woman, in the other the man he had come to meet.

As he reached the table, put his hand on the man's shoulder, he received the response he fully expected, 'Take a gander at the other table, Michael. I've not seen such a beautiful blonde for *centuries.*'

Michael laughed and sat down. 'You never change, Charlie; you've always got one eye on a girl, even when you're doing business.'

Charles Anthony Gordon, who ran a private bank in London, laughed with Michael, and asked, 'What are you drinking? Not the usual Coca-Cola, I hope?'

'No. I'll have tea instead.'

'Guess what? I'll have the same. It's a bit too early for booze. So how do you feel now that you've broken off the engagement?'

'Relieved. I was just thinking that as I came out onto the terrace. I was also reminding myself that when a man retires he dies.'

'I expect that's a dig at me, old chap, but guess what? I think I'm going to change my mind.'

'You're not going to retire after all?' Michael sounded surprised. He stared at his old friend, who had not yet reached retirement age. 'I hope you mean it, Charlie!'

'I do. Scout's honour and all that stuff. You're looking pleased.'

'I'm thrilled. How come you changed your mind? You were so adamant when I was in London two weeks ago.'

'I know I was, and I did mean it. But I got talked out of it by our Scottish friend. He made good sense.'

Michael beckoned to a waiter, ordered English breakfast tea, one with milk, the other with lemon, and, once alone again with Charlie he added, 'I'm glad Alistair did a number on you. I can't tell you how essential you are to us. But then you know that.'

'I do, I suppose. Which is why I changed my mind. Got to do one's duty, protect the lands of the free and the brave.'

Michael leaned across the table. 'I'm glad I didn't bring a farewell gift for you.'

'Yes, it would have been a waste of money.' Charlie placed a cigarette lighter on the table and a packet of cigarettes. 'I know you like a smoke now and again – have one of mine, Michael. It's your favourite brand.'

'Thanks, I will.' Michael took out a cigarette, put it in his mouth and brought the lighter to it. 'It's in the packet, correct?'

'You've got it right.'

After taking several puffs of the cigarette, Michael stuck it in the ashtray to burn away, picked up the packet of cigarettes and put it in his jacket. He then pushed the lighter across to Charlie, who slipped it in his trouser pocket.

'I've got bad news, I'm afraid,' Michael now announced, focusing all of his attention on the Englishman. 'Those birds we spoke about when I was in London, I'm afraid they may be delivered to someone else.'

'*The pheasants?*' Charlie raised a brow. 'Damn and blast, and we were promised that wouldn't happen.'

'*C'est la vie,*' Michael murmured, as he grimaced and shook his head. 'Some people are untrustworthy.'

'Any chance of a diversion?' Charlie asked.

'I'm working on it. *That*, or perhaps extinction. I do believe those pheasants in particular have to be off the market . . . *permanently.*' When Charlie didn't respond, Michael exclaimed, 'If you can tear your eyes away from the blonde, I have a bit more news for you.'

'Oh, sorry. I couldn't help admiring her when she stood up. Quite the leggy colt, isn't she?'

Michael simply smiled, and said sotto voce, 'Stay close to our contact, make sure he understands we're now *all* behind him.'

'I will.'

The waiter arrived with the large pot of tea, and Charlie turned to Michael. 'Will you be coming to London in early June? If so, I'd like you to be my guest at Wimbledon.'

'No, I don't think I will be there then,' Michael answered, 'but thanks for the invitation.'

The two men walked through the gardens of the hotel, heading in the direction of the marble Çiragan Palace, a rococo building which had been in ruins for years until it became part of the new hotel. Now it had sumptuous suites, private rooms for special events, and a traditional Turkish restaurant, yet it had not lost any of its nineteenth-century charm.

Michael Dalton and Charles Gordon had been associates and friends for many years. Michael knew that underneath that English 'old school tie' exterior Charles presented to the world was a man of integrity, steely determination and dependability. He ran the bank his grandfather had started in 1903, and which his father had brought to prominence; Charles, a financial genius, had only made it more prosperous than ever over the last twenty-five years. He was now fifty-nine, but looked so much younger.

The bank was a client of Dalton Incorporated, and Michael's company handled all security matters for the bank and its top-level personnel. Charles and Michael had developed a special relationship over the last seven years, and exchanged a great deal of vital information about many other things, not always to do with the bank. Rather, these matters related to events that affected and often changed international politics. And so affected the financial world.

Now that they were entirely alone in the gardens, Michael turned to Charles, 'Have you just given me some names?'

'Yes, of three men. You'll find a little strip of paper underneath the cigarettes. They could become dangerous men. Although not everyone knows that. You must keep them in your sights at all times.'

'Enough said.' Michael immediately changed the subject, and asked, 'How long are you staying in Istanbul?'

'Five days, I'm here with my wife and two of our kids, Randolph and Agnes. I think you've met them. It's a nice weekend break for me, and gives me a chance to spend time with the family. I'm glad our trips coincided. How long are you staying?'

'I'm not sure. I'm here to see several top clients, so probably a week, then I have to go back to Paris for a few days. I just took on a new client there, who's become extremely security conscious of late.'

'A lot of people have since nine/eleven, and I can't say I blame them. It's a dangerous world.' Charlie grimaced, added, 'Why am I telling *you* that? If anyone knows what it's like out there, it's you.'

'A powder keg.' Michael shook his head. 'The world will never be the same again. And it's changing every day. And so fast it's hard for the average person to keep up. We just have to live life as normally as we possibly can.'

Charles Gordon made no comment, and the two men walked on in silence for a short while, as always at ease with each other. When they reached the old palace they turned around and walked back the way they had come, each lost in his own thoughts.

At one moment Charles said, 'I was pleased when I learned you were staying in the same hotel, Michael. It turned out to be convenient.'

'Yes, it did. And I'll be in and out, around, if you need me for anything.'

'I hope to God I won't,' Charles exclaimed.

'So do I,' Michael answered.

Once he was back in his suite, Michael took the cigarettes out of the packet, then shook it until a small slip of paper finally fell out. When he read the names Charles had written on it he was truly startled, and instantly understood why Charles Gordon had preferred to pass these names to him in this way, rather than say them out loud.

He tore the paper into small pieces, did the same with the packet and the cigarettes, and went and flushed everything down the toilet.

Returning to the sitting room, he opened the French doors and stepped out onto the terrace. How beautiful the Bosphorus looked at this hour. The sun was setting and the deep blue waters of the straits rippled with rafts of crimson, pink and gold, and the sky was aflame along the rim of the far horizon. He loved it here at this time of day. They had a name for it in the movie business. The Magic Hour they called it, and indeed it was exactly that. The world was a beautiful place. What a pity it was full of madness.

Taking off his blazer, he put it on the back of the chair and sat down, thinking about the clients he had to see here. But soon his thoughts drifted, and he focused on the words he had said to Charles a short while before. He had called the world a powder keg, and it was the truth. Anything could happen, anywhere, at any time.

As a historian he knew that the history of the world was actually a history of wars. Endless wars since the beginning of time. He was convinced that fighting was genetic, a compulsion man could not resist. There would always be wars because man had no choice. Making war was hardwired into the human mind. And whatever reason was given, it was to gain one thing, and one thing only. *Power*. He sighed under his breath. All *he* could do was what he was doing, and hope that sanity would prevail.

That expression immediately reminded him of Vanessa, his former fiancée, and the last conversation they had had four months ago. She had told him she hoped sanity would prevail and that he would sell his company, take the money he was being offered and run. With her by his side. He had known at this particular moment that she could not, would not change. She loathed what he did for a living, and wanted him to lead an entirely different life. In fact, she wanted to change him completely. Remake him into someone else.

And so he had run. Not with the money he got for his company, because he had turned down the deal, had declined to sell. He had run from her because the doubts he had had about her had suddenly become certainties. He understood she was not the woman he wanted to spend the rest of his life with. That woman was one he had not yet met but hoped he would. What he wanted was to be loved for who and what he was, for the man he had become. He did not want to be turned into an entirely different person, or be some woman's puppet.

The ringing phone brought him to his feet. He strode into the room and over to the desk. 'Hello?'

'It's me, darling. What time shall I expect you?'

'In about an hour, sweetheart. Is that all right?'

'Of course it is, and I can't wait to see you.'

'I feel the same way.'

She simply laughed and hung up, and he smiled as he walked back to the terrace to get his blazer. He loved that laugh of hers. It was full of joy. That was what he wanted in his life. *Joy.* It struck him suddenly that this was something he had not experienced for the longest time, not for the entire year he had been with Vanessa. She was not acquainted with joy. It was an emotion she didn't understand. Or perhaps didn't even have.

Nasty thought, Michael, he chastised himself as he returned to the sitting room, hung his blazer in the closet and picked out a silk tie to wear to dinner. He wanted to look his best tonight. He smiled again at the thought of the evening ahead.

ELEVEN

*I*stanbul. *City of contrasts. European. Oriental. Exotic,* Justine wrote in her Moleskine notebook, then added, *a cosmopolitan city: diverse in every way . . .* and put down the pen as her cell phone began to sing its little tune. Pushing back the chair on the terrace, she ran into the bedroom and picked it up off the bedside table. 'Hello?'

'It's me, Justine,' her brother said, sounding as if he was next door.

He had taken her by surprise, and she exclaimed, 'Is something *wrong*? Why are you calling me now? It's four o'clock in the morning in New York.'

'I couldn't sleep; I woke up about half an hour ago. And I felt a compulsion to call you. I suppose you're on the way out – it's noon there, isn't it?'

'That's right, and oddly enough I've been wanting to speak to you too, Rich, but obviously I couldn't, it was too early.' She cleared her throat, went on, 'How's Daisy? And how's the installation going?'

'Daisy's terrific, what with everyone fussing over her and all that jazz, and the installation has gone without a hitch, so far. It'll be finished on time. I guess you're down in the dumps?'

'I am, yes, a bit. I arrived here a week ago yesterday and still haven't found Gran, and it frustrates the hell out of me, Richard.'

'I know . . . just as I know you've done everything you can. Local television interviews, stories in the newspapers: everybody in Istanbul must be aware that you're there by now.'

'I guess so. I did think of one thing . . . maybe Anita and Gran do live here but are away somewhere, and haven't seen all the publicity about me and "Proof of Life". That's possible, don't you think?'

'Yes, it is . . .' He paused, then said somewhat hesitantly, 'Listen, Justine, I did have an idea—'

'What?' she asked, cutting across him, wondering what she could have missed. 'What idea?'

'We *could* call Mom. She must know where Anita Lowe lives, otherwise Anita would have written her address in the letter.'

'I'm not going to call her. You have to do it.'

'No, I can't, it would be better if you called.'

'No way. Tackling our mother on the phone won't work. She'll say that Anita Lowe has dementia or Alzheimer's. We've discussed this before. The only way we'll ever get the truth is to confront her in person and wrestle it out of her. You know what she's like – you grew up with her too.'

'Not really, if you think about it. We grew up with Dad, and Gran on the sidelines.'

'True. Honestly, I won't call her, Richard, and you shouldn't either. She won't tell us a single thing, and we'll only alert her that we're aware of the truth about her, what a despicable person she is.'

'You're correct in everything you say, but what are we going to do, Justine? We've reached a dead end.'

'That's the way it looks, and Iffet hasn't come up with anything either, though she's tried very hard. She had someone in her office check various organizations and clubs where foreign residents congregate for social evenings, and the British Consulate as well, but nobody seems to know them. As Eddie would say, we've come up with zilch.' Justine paused, fighting back rising anxiety mingled with frustration yet again.

'So, we're adrift at sea in a leaky boat,' Richard muttered. 'About to sink.'

Justine couldn't help laughing. 'That was one of Gran's favourite sayings.'

'Along with, "There'll be tears before midnight." That was another favourite . . . *warning*.'

'And "Stop crying, tears won't get you anywhere." Gran had a line for almost every situation, all from her auntie Beryl – at least that's what she told me. Anyway, I did come up with one possibility and it might just work. I was waiting until a bit later to call you, to pass it by you, see whether you agree that I should do it.'

'Tell me.'

'I'm going to take some newspaper ads and—'

'Ads!' he cried, his voice rising. 'That'll *embarrass* Gran, not to mention Anita Lowe, whom we don't even know. You can't do that.'

'I don't care about embarrassing anybody right now; I care about finding these two women, in particular our grandmother. Anyway, the ads aren't about them, but about my new documentary. It's called "Biography of a City", and it's all about the history and peoples of Istanbul.'

'When did you think this up?' he asked, sounding puzzled.

Justine could almost see him frowning as he spoke, and she answered, 'Since I've been here. And it's all started to come together in my head in the last few days – the documentary, I mean.'

'So what *are* the ads, actually?'

'I will ask foreign, English-speaking residents to come and see me, to talk about their feelings for the city, and their views. I will also invite Istanbulites who have unique stories to tell about their lives to come along also. *They* will speak to my researcher.'

'You have a researcher already?' Surprise now echoed in his tone.

'Yes. Iffet Özgönül.'

'She agreed?'

'I haven't actually asked Iffet yet. I'm going to talk about it with her today. We're having lunch later and doing a boat trip around the Bosphorus.'

Richard, far away in New York, remained silent.

'I intend to mention Gran and Anita in the advertisement. And you can be really helpful if you'll go to my apartment and take the photograph of Gran out of its frame and send it to me by Fedex today. It's on the chest in my bedroom.'

'Do you want the photograph to use in the ads?' Richard asked cautiously.

'Correct.'

'I don't think our grandmother will like seeing her picture in an advertisement in a newspaper, I really don't, Justine. It'll go against the grain.'

'I know that as well as you do, but I'm desperate to find her. And you are too, and so I have to use any means I can. I'm hoping she'll see her photograph and come to see me. Which is what Anita said she wanted in her letter. And if Gran doesn't see the ad, maybe Anita will, or another friend, and they'll tell her.' Taking a deep breath, Justine finished. 'Please back me up on this, Rich, it's so important.'

'I do back you, that goes without saying. I'll get the photograph this morning and send it out immediately. But listen, I hope you know what you're doing—'

'She won't be angry, I promise you,' Justine interrupted.

'I wasn't referring to Gran. I was referring to the fact that if you publish an advertisement in a newspaper, asking for people to come and talk to you about the city they live in, *thousands* will show up.'

Justine laughed. 'I doubt that: most people are very shy about such things.'

'You'll see,' he warned, and then laughed with her. 'My God, only *you* could think up something like this.'

'That's not true, you could. Very easily. You're my twin.'

'Do you always have to have the last word?'

'Yes, because you had the first when you were born fifteen minutes before me. Dad told me you yelled your lungs out.'

'I can't remember,' he answered, the laughter still echoing in his voice. 'Okay, so it's a deal. Talk to you later.'

'I'll send the ads for your approval, once they're done,' Justine said. 'I'll need your feedback.'

'Keep them simple. Remember, less is more.'

For the next half-hour Justine made additional notes about Istanbul in her Moleskine, and stopped, suddenly thinking about the advert. She now realized that Richard had been right on two points. Firstly, if she invited people to come and talk to her about Istanbul, hundreds might indeed show up. Secondly, her grandmother would most likely be unhappy to see her photograph in a newspaper. So she must rethink certain things, and carefully word the advert; she must make a decision also about using the photograph of Gabriele. Maybe it *was* a bad idea, after all.

As soon as she saw Iffet she would offer her the job as chief researcher on the project. She hoped Iffet would accept; she believed she would. Iffet was proud of her city and would want it to be shown in the best way, in the right light.

Now her next task, which had become a daily ritual, was to send her e-mails to Daisy, Joanne and Ellen at the office. All three were done swiftly, and Justine closed down her laptop and went to get ready.

Iffet had warned her it was going to be a very warm day again, and so after she had done her hair and make-up, she chose a light cotton dress and sandals for lunch and the boat trip around the Bosphorus.

The fact that they had not found the two women nagged at her unmercifully; on the other hand, Justine now found solace and renewed hope in the idea of the advertisement for the documentary about Istanbul. Also, she was looking forward to the trip on the boat, since it would show her different aspects of this city which she was coming to know and love.

'And if you would become the researcher on the project, I would be thrilled,' Justine said finally, looking intently at Iffet, having told her about the idea.

'I would be very happy,' Iffet replied in her lovely quiet way. 'I am flattered that you would ask me.'

'Thank you, Iffet, thank you so much. What a relief that is; my office will put you on the payroll of the new company I'm forming for the project. You just have to let me know what your fee will be.'

Iffet simply nodded. Taking a sip of the sparkling water, she then said, 'I believe Richard is correct. You cannot invite people to visit you here at the hotel. Hordes will come. Might I make a suggestion, Justine?'

'Yes, go ahead.'

'I think you should ask people to write or e-mail to my office, and we will sort them. We can select the right candidates for you to interview.'

'That's a fabulous idea! And who better than you to choose the people. After all, you're an Istanbulite.'

'I am, yes, although I was not born here. I come from the country. My family owns a farm – that's where I grew up.'

'And you left and came to the city, just like I did. I was born and bred in Connecticut, and Richard and I still use the house we grew up in. We go there for weekends. Does your family still have the farm?'

Iffet nodded. 'One of my brothers runs it.'

'Do you come from a big family then?'

'I have a sister Nimet and three brothers, Hasan, Ihsan and Ismet. My sister lives in Istanbul.'

'That's nice that she lives here . . . I guess the two of you emancipated yourselves, like I did.'

'That's true. Returning to the advertisement, what exactly are you going to say in it? About the documentary.'

The two women were sitting in the restaurant on the terrace of the hotel, and now Justine bent over from the waist, picked up her white handbag, rummaged around and found her notebook. After a moment of turning pages, Justine cleared her throat, began to read.

'Emmy Award-winning television producer Justine Nolan plans to make a documentary entitled "Biography of a City: The Life Story of Istanbul".' She paused, glanced at Iffet. 'That's the headline at the top and the text is quite simple, only a few lines which would run to one side of the ad. This is what I've written. *Justine Nolan's latest documentary "Proof of Life" will be shown on the Cable News International network this coming September. It is the life story of the man considered to be the world's greatest living artist, Jean-Marc Breton, and it will be viewed by millions around the world.*'

After another pause, she then went on, 'There will be a bit of blank space, and then I want to say something like this . . . *Now Justine Nolan plans to focus her camera on Istanbul, its history, religions, traditions, architecture and historical sites, food, as well as its diverse peoples. Do you have a story to tell about this city? If so please . . .'* Closing the notebook, Justine finished, 'That's as far as I've gone with the text, and now of course we can add your office address. What do you think?'

'It's perfect in length. Concise, to the point. When do you plan to have it in the paper?'

'Hopefully next week. I thought of using your photograph as the chief researcher, my own as the producer, and Gabriele's as the advisor on the project. She may see it, or a friend might, and she'll know I'm here. But that aside, I am truly serious about doing the film – the ad is not merely a ploy to find my grand-mother. I hope you understand that, Iffet.'

'You are a serious and sincere person, Justine, I know that. And your project is very exciting. I am delighted to be associated with it, and I will be happy to give you my photograph.'

'Thank you, and now perhaps we'd better order our salads. What time is the boat coming to pick us up?'

'It will be at the hotel jetty at two o'clock.'

TWELVE

Several hours later, Justine and Iffet boarded the sleek white motorboat anchored at the Çiragan Palace jetty, and went to sit in the glassed-in area behind the two men in charge of the boat. It was a sunny afternoon, extremely warm, and this part of the deck was cool and comfortable; there was a small table on which stood water, bottled drinks and a bucket of ice.

Once they were on their way, moving down the straits towards the Bosphorus Bridge, Justine went to stand in the open area of the boat. She was armed with her video camera and started shooting at once. As they sped under it she was amazed at the size of the suspension bridge. What a magnificent piece of engineering it was.

Iffet came to join her, explaining, 'We are going to the edge of the Black Sea. We'll turn and come back up on the Asian side. And we can do the trip again if you wish. For extra pictures.'

'That's a great idea, Iffet, and thanks for suggesting this. It's giving me a wholly different perspective.' Turning to look at her, Justine said, 'I've been thinking of bringing Eddie Grange in from London for a few days. He works as the line producer on the documentaries I make in Europe. I'd like him to get a feel of Istanbul, because I'm hoping he'll sign on for this new documentary.'

Iffet nodded, then asked, 'What is a line producer?'

'Exactly what it says: a producer who is on the line every day; in other words on the set, and actually overseeing the shooting of the movie by the director. I'm the executive producer, which means I'm in charge of everything and everyone. I'm on the set every day too, of course, but only for a few hours. I have to attend to the business end.'

'In other words, you're the boss.'

Justine grimaced, half laughed, murmured, 'You've got it.'

She started filming once more, and Iffet remained at her side, also enjoying being on the boat.

They were moving along up the other side now, passing many mosques, villas, museums, ancient buildings and parks, which were all visible because they were built on the shoreline. Iffet began to talk about the Asiatic side of Istanbul, pointing out monuments, famous landmarks and restaurants noted for their good food; she also gave her the history of this part of the city and Turkey in general. Justine was once again impressed with her knowledge, which was exceptional, and covered everything from archaeology to ancient and modern history, and many local traditions.

When they had come full circle around the Bosphorus, Justine said, 'Can you ask the driver to take us back to Central Istanbul, Iffet, please? I'd like to get some more shots of the skyline.'

'Yes, I will,' Iffet replied, then added, 'but he does speak English.'

'Sorry.' Justine followed her into the covered area of the boat, where she poured herself a glass of water, feeling rather foolish. Of course he spoke English. What an idiot she was. Tourism was big business here, and there were lots of American and English visitors, as well as people from all over the rest of the world.

Once they were stationary in the middle of the water, facing Central Istanbul, Justine started to film. She wanted to capture the city from various angles, and she moved around a lot.

After a while she stopped shooting and went over to the rail, looking across at the skyline. What she saw took her breath away again: domes of churches, synagogues and mosques huddled together; the spires of minarets standing tall and slender; gold glittering on the tops of spires and domes of these religious places. Grand old palaces, stately and elegant; modern hotels, apartment buildings, and museums. Beyond were crowded streets and narrow alleyways, the *hans*, chic shops, offices, restaurants and cafés; the Grand Bazaar and the Spice Market. Boutiques for fashionable clothes and jewellery were everywhere, along with stalls selling vegetables and fruits, fried fish and other local delicacies, Turkish Delight and Baklava. And mingled amongst them were the homes of Istanbulites. Over eight million people lived and worked here on the European side. There it was in all its glory – a great metropolis teeming with people of all kinds, from all walks of life.

A thought struck her and it made her stiffen, frightened her. *How would she ever find her grandmother in there?* Central Istanbul was overwhelming. I'm on a wild goose chase, she thought, and a sense of failure trickled through her. A sadness enveloped her as she walked back to the covered area, sat down, sighing under her breath. Damn, damn, damn. A needle in a haystack. That's what I'm looking for.

Waiting for her to say something, watching her intently, Iffet finally reached out and touched her arm. 'What is it, Justine? You look so *pensive* . . .' She let her voice fade away, conscious always of everyone's privacy; never wishing to pry, be invasive or intrude.

'I'll never find her,' Justine said at last, her voice full of anguish. 'Just looking out at that city over there makes me shrivel inside. It's not just a city, it's an overwhelming metropolis and of a kind

I've never seen before. Foreign to me in a hundred ways, yet oddly familiar in others . . . and, oh, how it *defeats* me. Gran is lost to me. I believe that now. She could be in a hospital or an old people's home. And then again she might not live here at all. It's been a waste of my time, this trip. Finding her is an impossibility.'

'Oh, Justine, do not say that! Do not give up hope.' Leaning forward Iffet said enthusiastically, 'I think the idea for the documentary is brilliant. And so is the idea of taking an advertisement.'

Justine lifted her head and looked at her new friend and suddenly felt ashamed of herself. She exclaimed tersely, 'Here I go again, moaning and whining, and feeling sorry for myself. I owe you an apology, Iffet. I've been extremely selfish since I arrived here a week ago. And you've been just wonderful, putting up with me the way you have, and doing all you could to help. I've been so self-absorbed about finding my grand-mother, I haven't given a thought to you, and that's not right when you've been so very, very gracious.'

'You haven't been self-absorbed. You've thought about Daisy and worried about Richard, and his state of mind, the loss of his wife, and you have had a *brilliant* idea. To do a biography of a city. Such a *splendid* idea, I believe. So please do not apolo-gize to me. It is not necessary. You are not leaving yet, Justine. You said you were going to get your line producer to fly over from London . . . Eddie. You said you wanted him to see the city. The other day you called it a city of a thousand and one dreams. I did think this was another good title, if I might say so. Please, do not lose hope – not yet. And remember the advert. That could bring results.'

Justine stared at her, thinking how extraordinary this young woman was, and she said swiftly, 'Iffet, you're such a blessing. You do cheer me up.'

'I am glad. Let us go around the Bosphorus one more time.

Another full circle. We will float down the Asian side, and you will take more photographs . . . such a different side of the city, very unique, so ancient.'

'All right, let's do it. I might as well get as much stuff as I possibly can.'

Iffet went over to Arzu and Nuri, the drivers, who were standing chatting to each other at the front of the motorboat. After giving them instructions, she returned to the canopied area where Justine was. Iffet sat down next to her. She asked, 'What is it? You are concerned. Are you all right?'

'I'm fine, thanks, Iffet. I was just thinking about an idea Richard and I discussed before I left New York. It's something I could do to find Gran, but I'm reluctant.'

'What could you do?' Iffet looked at her closely, intrigued.

'Hire a private detective. From an agency. Richard and I had thought of doing it, but changed our minds.' Justine turned to face Iffet. 'Now I'm not so sure we were right.'

'You said your grandmother is almost eighty. How old is Anita? The same age?'

'I should think so, since they apparently grew up together. They're probably both very frail now, perhaps not well even – in fact they could be ill.'

'I understand your reluctance to engage an investigator. However, I could find you the right person. Someone discreet. If you decide it is necessary.'

'It might be my last resort.' Justine's cell phone jangled, and she reached into her bag for it. 'Hello?'

'Hi, it's Joanne.'

'Jo, hello! I'm sitting here on a boat in the middle of the Bosphorus with Iffet. We've been cruising around the straits this afternoon.'

'I wish I'd been with you. And I could be if you need me.'

'What about the movie? Has something happened?' Justine asked, startled by Joanne's comment, immediately concerned for her dearest friend.

'Yep, you can say that again. I quit this morning. The director was fired a few days ago. The replacement is someone I don't like, so I just went to the producer and told him I didn't want to be on the film. There was a bit of a wrangle, mention of lawsuits, threats from him, and all that jazz, but he finally saw reason. I cannot work with Jude Hillyer, who's the new director. If you remember, I've locked horns with *him* before.'

'I do remember, Jo, and he's renowned as a difficult guy, a temperamental tyrant. I'm sorry you had to leave, you were crazy about that script, and the cast, I do know that.'

'So do you want me to come out for a week to help you look for your grandmother? I know from your e-mail this morning that you've had no luck.'

'That's great of you to volunteer, Jo, but to be honest, I really don't think there's anything else I can do. I am at a dead end. As I told you in the e-mail.'

'Oh, Justine that's *awful*, so heartbreaking for you. I know how frustrated you are. Listen, I'm happy to come for a few days.'

'I'm only going to spend another week here, doing some more research. Then I'm definitely coming back to New York. I want to make a deal for my new project with Miranda at CNI. So there's really no point you flying all this way. But thanks for offering.'

'Just give me a yell if you change your mind. Simon and I are going to spend Saturday at Indian Ridge with Daisy and Richard. A tea party in the *gazeboat*, as Daisy calls it, and we're staying on for supper.'

Justine was thrilled to hear this news, and exclaimed, 'Hey, that's just wonderful! And thank you for being there for them when I'm away. I appreciate it, Jo.'

Joanne laughed. 'It's my pleasure, Justine, my very great pleasure. I think Rich needs a bit of TLC at the moment, and I aim to give it to him. Why let any old stranger sneak in there ahead of me?'

'I endorse *that*. He does need some female companionship . . . ' Justine paused, and then added softly, 'And all sorts of other things, so do your best to give them to him.'

'Don't you worry, I will. Can I speak to Iffet?'

'Of course. I'll talk to you over the weekend. Here she is.'

She handed the cell phone to Iffet, and sat back, lost in sudden thoughts of Richard and Joanne. *Together*. As a couple. She had been aware of Jo's feelings for her brother for years. The timing had been all wrong then. Now, perhaps, the timing was right. As she thought this, she crossed her fingers and said a silent prayer.

PART THREE

The Reunion

Rich the treasure,
Sweet the pleasure;
Sweet is pleasure after pain.

John Dryden, *Alexander's Feast*

THIRTEEN

The driver had turned the boat around, and now it was moving up the Bosphorus towards the Sea of Marmara, leaving Central Istanbul behind. As they went past the Çiragan Palace Hotel, Justine turned to Iffet and said, 'I want to invite you to dinner tonight. But not at the hotel. You must choose the restaurant, since you're the expert.'

'No, no, that's not necessary,' Iffet protested. 'I invite you.'

Justine shook her head. 'We'll figure *that* out later, but please pick one of your favourites.'

Iffet had learned not to argue with Justine about something like this. She murmured, 'I shall make a reservation,' and went to sit under the canopy. Taking her cell phone out, she dialled her office.

It struck Justine that the Bosphorus suddenly seemed busier than it had been earlier, with two ferries moving across the water; there were also several motorboats like theirs obviously set on the same course. Nuri, who was driving, slowed their speed, obviously trying to avoid the wakes left behind by the other boats immediately ahead.

It was very noisy. Seagulls wheeled and turned against the

azure sky, their shrill squawking strident against the hooting of the ferries. What a cacophony of sound. It was like bedlam. Another phrase Gran used when we were being too noisy, she thought, and squeezed her eyes shut. Oh God, where was she, the elusive Gabri? Justine wondered then if her granny *was* dead, gone from this world.

Pushing that unacceptable thought away, she picked up her video camera and started to shoot the beautiful scenery, not wishing to dwell on anything depressing. Keeping busy had always been the best antidote for anything that troubled, worried or distressed her.

Eventually the boat was turning again, still guided by Nuri, who had set his sights on the Asiatic side, just below Karaköy, where the public ferries left for Üsküdar. He obviously wanted to stay away from *that* trajectory; did not wish to become involved in heavy traffic.

As they now progressed down the Asian side of Istanbul, Justine got a wonderful series of shots, including Leander's Tower, a white structure that stood mid-channel not far from the shoreline. All of this footage would help her to write the outline for the script, and could be part of the presentation to Miranda.

A moment later she began to zero in on several lovely villas, ancient *yalis* that had been restored. Two of them, surrounded by gardens that were lavish and beautiful, were balanced right on the edge of the Bosphorus. They reminded her of those grand houses on the canals of Venice, and they were equally as arresting and graceful in design.

Nuri had picked up speed, but unexpectedly he slowed down. She suddenly realized why. Another motorboat in front of them was drawing up to a jetty and had stopped. Three people were about to alight. It was apparent to Justine that Nuri did not want to make the sea choppier than it already was.

The people were now mounting the steps that led up to a long jetty which was attached to the gardens of the pink villa.

Nuri manoeuvred their boat past the jetty carefully, and she focused her video camera on the pink villa beyond, which was quite extraordinary.

The woodwork on the balconies was delicately carved and looked like fancy white lace set against the pink-painted wood walls. The garden was aflame with colour from the blue wisteria, the red Judas trees, bright pink peonies in abundance and the many multi-coloured tulips blooming everywhere. What a sight it was. Picture perfect, as the saying goes, she thought.

Justine zoomed in closer, and at that moment one of the women on the jetty turned around to catch hold of her blue chiffon scarf, which was blowing out behind her and about to fly away. As the woman grasped hold of it in the nick of time, she was looking in the direction of the camera. Her face was caught on film.

With a gasp, Justine stiffened, and almost dropped the camera. Captured on film was the face of her grandmother, framed by a halo of silvery-blonde hair.

She put the camera down swiftly, her hands shaking, and started to shout at the top of her voice, 'Gran! Gran! It's me! Justine! Gran, turn around again! Gran! Gran!'

The woman had not heard her, perhaps because of the wind and the other noises carried across the water. Already Nuri had left the pink villa behind and was increasing his speed. Justine began to scream at him. 'Nuri! Nuri! Stop this boat at once!'

Iffet, who was under the canopy and had been on her cell phone, jumped up, ran to Justine. 'What is the matter? What is wrong?'

'I saw my grandmother! Back there at that pink villa. I have her on film. Get Nuri to turn back. Please, Iffet. He's not paying attention to me!' Her voice broke. '*Please*. It's Gran. I'd recognize her anywhere.'

'I believe you,' Iffet exclaimed, and hurried to the glassed-in cabin where the drivers sat together. 'Please turn the boat around, Nuri,' she said in a low but firm voice. 'Didn't you hear Miss Nolan telling you to stop? To go back?'

The driver shook his head, and so did Arzu. 'It's very windy, very noisy on the water,' Nuri muttered, but he drove the boat around in a semi-circle, now pointing it in the opposite direction.

'Please return to the pink villa,' Iffet said in the same low but authoritative voice.

He did as he was told.

A few minutes later they arrived at the jetty leading up to the gardens and the pink *yali*. Only the man who had been on the boat was there, speaking to the driver.

Craning her neck, Justine could just see the two women who had mounted the steps with this man. They were standing in the gardens. One of them was wearing the blue chiffon scarf that had almost blown away, and her heart lifted.

Now Justine could not contain herself. She ran to the side of the boat, and shouted, 'Gran! Gran! It's me!'

The man came forward, stood staring down at Iffet and Justine, an expression of puzzlement on his face. 'Can I help you?' he asked in English.

Before Justine could say a word, Iffet explained swiftly, 'My friend thinks she knows the lady in the blue scarf. In the garden over there. She would like to speak to her.'

'I *must* speak to her!' Justine cried, and before Iffet could stop her she was jumping off the boat, climbing the steps, and rushing up onto the jetty at great speed.

The man was so startled as she pushed past him and ran towards the gardens, he remained rooted to the spot. But then he immediately recovered himself, and sprinted forward after her.

Because of the sudden commotion, people running, the woman in the blue scarf and her female companion dressed in red turned around, looking towards the jetty, obviously surprised, perhaps even alarmed.

Iffet clambered up the steps and ran forward as well, following behind the man and Justine.

Justine was screaming at the top of her voice, 'Gran! Gran! It's me.'

The woman in the blue scarf heard the words, and she stepped forward, stretching out her arms when she recognized her. Tears were streaming down her face as Justine plunged headlong towards her and came to a standstill just in time. She almost knocked her grandmother over.

'Gran, it's *you*! *Oh, Gran*. I've been looking all over for you.'

Gabriele Hardwicke was stunned, could hardly believe what was happening. Speechless, she stared up at Justine, gently touched her face. At last she spoke. 'Is it really you, my little love? Is it really you?' Her voice was shaking, her blue eyes welling with tears once more.

'Yes,' Justine whispered, and wrapped her arms around her grandmother, and Gabriele returned the embrace. They stood locked tightly together, weeping and clinging to each other.

Iffet's eyes were full of tears, so touched was she; and she was filled with relief. Justine had found her grandmother at last; this thought thrilled her and a sudden rush of joy swept through her. Brushing her eyes with one hand, she turned to the other woman and stretched out her hand. 'I am so sorry. I am being rude. I was moved because Justine has found her grandmother. I am Iffet Özgönül. I think that you must be Anita Lowe?'

The woman in red had been crying also, and she was wiping

her tears away with a lace handkerchief. She nodded finally. 'I am indeed Anita Lowe, and I am so very pleased to meet you, Miss Özgönül,' she replied and shook Iffet's hand.

'Oh, please, call me Iffet.'

'And you must call me Anita – everybody does, you know. And this is my grandson, Michael Dalton.'

The man stepped forward and took hold of Iffet's hand, his black eyebrows lifting quizzically, his dark eyes filled with warmth and sympathy. 'Pleased to meet you, Iffet. Call me Michael, and I must say that's the most dramatic entrance I've ever witnessed. It's also the first time I've been almost trampled underfoot by a blonde.'

Iffet was about to apologize on Justine's behalf, and then noticed the sudden amused look flickering on his face. He started to chuckle and so did she.

Anita said, 'It might have been unorthodox, as well as dramatic, but it was a very welcome entrance, I can assure you of that. Now Michael, Iffet, let's go over to them and guide them into the house. They can't just stand there weeping in the garden until midnight.'

The three of them walked over to Gabriele and Justine, who at last broke their embrace. Gabriele turned to Michael. 'This is my long-lost granddaughter, Justine. And Justine, this is Michael Dalton, Anita's grandson.'

The two of them shook hands, and then Anita hurried up to Justine and embraced her. Standing away from her, her dark eyes sweeping over her, she said, 'Perhaps it goes without saying, but you're a sight for sore eyes, my darling. Why did it take you so long to get here?'

Justine gaped at her, taken aback. 'Because I didn't have your address.'

Anita was equally startled. '*Oh*. Well, we'd better go inside and unravel all this, over a cup of tea.'

'Tea!' Michael exclaimed, laughter lingering in his eyes. 'Under the circumstances, I think champagne might be more appropriate. This *is* a celebration, after all.'

'Quite right,' Anita answered, taking command, ushering them all across the garden. They followed her. Gabriele and Justine were holding hands tightly, as if afraid to let go of each other. And neither of them could stop smiling.

'We always have tea in the gold room,' Gabriele said, leading Justine across the spacious hall with several tall windows, a glittering crystal chandelier and a highly polished parquet wood floor. 'So called because of the yellowish silk curtains which look gold at this hour.'

'Is this your villa, Gran?' Justine asked, still clinging to her grandmother's hand, constantly looking at her, hardly able to believe they were together at last, that she had actually found her.

'No, it belongs to Anita.' Gabriele smiled, her face lighting up. 'I live next door. I'll show you my little *yali* later, darling.'

'Can we sit over there near the windows?' Justine now asked, looking towards the many windows in a bay draped with yellow-gold taffeta curtains. 'I must call Richard. I can't delay telling him the news.'

'Of course we can. And you must call him immediately. Put his mind at rest.'

The two of them walked across a beautiful Turkish carpet, sat down together on a sofa, and Justine dialled Richard's cell phone. As she waited for it to ring through she realized she could hardly breathe, she was so excited. 'It's me, Rich,' she said as evenly as she possibly could when he answered.

'Hi, Justine, I'm afraid I'm in a meeting and I—'

'I don't care! You've got to listen for a minute. Someone wants to speak to you. Please get up, walk outside into the corridor. If you're in your own office.'

'I am. Okay, I'm going out into the hallway now. Who wants to talk to me? What's this all about?'

'I'll tell you the minute you're in the hall.'

'I'm there now. Who wants to talk to me?'

'Gran.'

'*What?*' he shouted, his amazement echoing down the line.

Justine handed the cell phone to her grandmother, and Gabriele said, 'Hello, Rich.' Her voice was trembling.

'Oh, my God! *Gran!* I can't believe it!' Richard's voice was shaking uncontrollably, and he began to cry, trying to push the tears back without much success. 'What happened? How did Justine find you? We thought we were at a dead end – that you'd disappeared forever. Tell me! Tell me!'

Gabriele was also in tears. She wiped her eyes with her fingertips, and said, 'It was a fluke. An accident actually. One of those strange things that sometimes happen in life, and when you least expect it.'

Pulling a handkerchief out of her jacket pocket, Gabriele blew her nose, and attempted to calm herself. She continued, 'It's wonderful to hear your voice, darling. I hope to see you soon, Richard.'

'I'll be there as quickly as possible. Oh, and Gran, I've got a little girl. Daisy. She's five. You're a great-grandmother now. Didn't Justine tell you?'

'She only just found me about ten minutes ago,' Gabriele said, suddenly laughing through her tears, and handed the phone back to Justine.

'Hey, Rich, it's me. Can you listen? Or do you have to go back to the meeting?'

'To hell with the meeting. They'll just have to wait. Go on, tell me how you found Gran.'

'I'll make it quick now. We can talk later. Iffet and I were cruising the Bosphorus this afternoon. I was using my video camera, getting shots of the Asian shoreline of Istanbul for the documentary. Our boat slowed down near a beautiful villa, because three people were getting off a motorboat in front of us. I was intrigued by the beauty of the villa and was zeroing in on it, when one of the women standing on the jetty turned around to catch hold of her scarf. And it was Gran. Her face was there, right before my eyes on my video camera. Then our boat suddenly sped ahead, and so we had to turn around, go back. I just barged up the steps onto the jetty and ignored a man trying to talk to me. I just ran, Rich, screaming Gran's name at the top of my voice. And she heard me, saw me. A minute later we were in each other's arms.'

'Oh, my God, it *was* a fluke! Like Gran just said!' Richard exclaimed, his voice still high pitched. 'If you hadn't had the video camera, you might not have seen her, and if you hadn't been passing the villa at that *precise* moment, you would have missed her altogether. *Que sera sera*, Justine.'

'*What will be will be*. Always our grandmother's motto when we were kids. And it *was* meant to be that I found her. I genuinely believed she was here. Until I became so discouraged this past few days.'

'Thank God you did believe it, and persisted, that's all I can say. I gotta get back to the meeting. I'll call later. You'll be with Gran, I guess.'

'Where else?' She clicked off, and saw that Gabriele was weeping and wiping her eyes, and Justine moved closer and put her arms around her.' We've so much to talk about, Grandma, and I've got all the time in the world.'

'No, you don't, actually,' Gabriele responded swiftly. 'I think tea has arrived and *pink* champagne. We mustn't keep Anita waiting.' Suddenly she began to laugh, her happiness at being with Justine reflected on her face. 'I'm afraid afternoon tea is a ritual with Anita. You'll think you're at the Ritz: she puts on quite a show.'

Justine couldn't help laughing, catching the hint of acerbity in her grandmother's voice. This was the root of her sense of humour and an English trait. How she had missed it, missed laughing with her grandmother about life, people and their many foibles.

Jumping up from the sofa, Justine offered Gabriele her hand.

Gabriele looked at her askance, exclaimed, 'What do you think? That I'm an old lady? Don't be so silly, Justine. I'm perfectly capable of getting up by myself.'

'Oh, sorry, Gran.' She eyed Gabriele and said with real sincerity, 'You do look wonderful, I must admit. Positively blooming. And so does Anita.'

'Oh, you must tell her that!'

FOURTEEN

Justine, who had been frustrated all week, felt frustrated once again. But only momentarily. She instantly pushed this feeling away.

What she wanted to do was get her grandmother alone, to talk to her, explain, question, and discuss the horrendous estrangement that had kept them apart. Decisive by nature, and with a penetrating mind, Justine needed to make decisions at once, get to the bottom of things immediately, and move on. *That won't happen today*, she thought as she settled back in her chair, glanced across at her grandmother and smiled.

Gabriele smiled back but remained silent.

Justine knew that Gran was also bursting with questions, needed to talk to her about intimate matters, private family things. Taking a deep breath, she told herself to keep calm. *They would talk later*. She would make sure of that.

Anita said, 'Ah, here come Zeynep and Mehmet.' As she spoke, a young woman came through the door pushing a double-tier tea-cart, and behind her walked the cook, dressed in his white chef's coat and wearing his white toque, that culinary mark of distinction. He was also pushing a tea-cart, a wide smile flashing on his expressive face.

'Madame,' he said to Anita, inclining his head, 'shall I serve the champagne first?'

'Oh yes, I think so, Mehmet.'

Mehmet popped the cork with something of a flourish, pouring the champagne into tall crystal flutes. Zeynep carried the tray of them around, smiling politely as she moved through the little group; they were seated in a circle around a large coffee table of Turkish design in front of the fireplace. 'Thank you, Zeynep, Mehmet. We can manage by ourselves now, I think,' Anita said with a warm smile.

'Please ring if you need anything else, madame,' Mehmet murmured, and he and the young woman left together, closing the door behind them.

Gabriele said, 'Mehmet's treats are very special, Iffet. And Justine, I know you'll like them. He does some of his own tasty bites as well as the usual English afternoon tea sandwiches and scones.'

Raising his glass, Michael announced, 'I think a toast is in order. Congratulations, Gabri, on being reunited with your granddaughter at last. And my compliments to you, Justine, for being such a clever sleuth. And cheers, everyone!'

Justine murmured, 'Not much of a sleuth, Michael. Finding Gran was a fluke.'

'Not really,' Anita murmured. 'Because I wrote the letter.'

'Yes, you did, but you didn't give an address. We didn't know where to find you.'

Michael and Gabriele both seemed startled, and exchanged knowing glances, then Michael took a swig of his champagne. Shaking his head, looking puzzled, he then turned to Justine. 'But you came to Istanbul anyway. That was very courageous of you.'

'Thanks, but it wasn't really . . .' She let her voice trail off under his penetrating stare, and she realized for the first time that he was very good looking. She had been far too preoccupied with her grandmother to notice how stunning Michael Dalton was. She turned her head, avoiding his eyes.

Anita said, 'I must have forgotten to write the return address on the envelope, which I always do. I can only think it was because I had written and edited that particular letter several times. I must have forgotten in my haste to get it posted. Anyway, your mother has my address, and Gabriele's as well. Why didn't she give them to you?'

Justine glanced at her grandmother, instantly noticed the flash of apprehension in Gabriele's eyes. She cleared her throat, then said swiftly, 'Let me explain what actually happened, Anita. My mother spends most of her time in California these days. She has a lot of clients in Beverly Hills, where she now lives. When your letter arrived at Indian Ridge, she was away. I was in New York and so was Richard. We were both busy with work projects and we didn't go up there for a whole month. So your letter went unread until I opened it. My mother had already gone to China for six weeks. She is on a trip around that country, buying objects for her interior design business. So I opened the letter, read it, showed it to Richard and left immediately. I'd tried to Google your number, or thought you just might be in the local phonebook. But Iffet checked, and neither of you are listed.'

'That's quite true, we're not,' Anita murmured with a small, rueful smile. 'I'm listed under the name Bentley, because after Maxwell died – that's my first husband Maxwell Lowe, a lovely man . . .' She sighed. '. . . I eventually remarried some years later. My second husband was Frank Bentley. But he too died, only two years after we married. Shame. And Gabri is listed under her professional name, aren't you, darling?'

'Yes,' Gabriele replied, and said to Justine, 'I use the name Gabriele Trent, and I'll explain about that later. I have a design studio at my *yali*, where I create fabrics, a line called Tulipmania. And that's why you couldn't find me in the telephone book either,' she finished, looking across at Iffet, smiling.

Iffet volunteered, 'I did check the land registry office as well.'

'You would find us only under Bentley and Trent there,' Anita explained, nodding her dark head. A bright smile unexpectedly washed over her face. 'But it worked out all right in the end, didn't it? Now, Iffet, Justine and Michael, go and help yourself to the tea sandwiches. There's smoked salmon, egg salad, cucumber, and various other things, and scones with strawberry jam and clotted cream. I always serve English breakfast tea.'

'I would like a cup of tea, Anita, thank you.' Iffet smiled at her hostess and rose, walked over to the tea-cart near the fireplace.

Michael also stood up. 'Can I pour you a cup of tea, Gabriele? And you too, Grandma?'

'That would be lovely,' Gabriele answered, and Anita simply nodded.

Justine jumped up, and went to join Iffet at the tea-cart; a moment later Michael was standing next to her. 'I'll pour their cups of tea if you'll hand the sandwiches around,' he said. 'I know how they like it.'

Justine turned to face him. 'You must have known my grand-mother a long time.'

'All my life – well, most of it. My mother married an American, Lawrence Dalton, and I was born and brought up in New York. But naturally my mother came to Istanbul to see her mother every year, and Dad and I came too. After my sister was born she came along as well. And Gabriele was often here at her *yali* next door. Our two grandmothers are joined at the hip.'

Michael began pouring the cups of tea, and Justine picked up two plates of tea sandwiches and carried them over to her grandmother and Anita, offering them.

Gabriele smiled up at her, her eyes overflowing with love.

'I need to know all about my great-granddaughter, Justine, did you bring photographs of her?'

'Yes, but they're at the hotel. The Çiragan Palace.'

'I'd like you to come and stay with me at my *yali*,' Gabriele said. 'Will you do that, darling?'

'Where else would I want to be, Gran?'

FIFTEEN

The afternoon tea party was a jolly event, and everyone was happy to be there together, thrilled about the reunion of Justine and her grandmother.

Gabriele herself was ecstatic, could hardly believe that Justine was sitting next to her on the sofa, at times squeezing her hand or hugging her tightly. It was also gratifying to Gabri that her granddaughter had remained very much the unspoiled, loving person she had been when growing up.

At thirty-two she was warm, charming and charismatic, her personality outgoing, her manner easy and unassuming. These traits aside, she had become a lovely woman with her long blonde hair, sculpted features and wide-set blue eyes. Tall and willowy like my mother, Gabriele thought, and my grandmother. Of our ilk, no doubt about that.

Her mind jumped to her daughter Deborah, most definitely a Hardwicke, with her late father's dark good looks. *Deborah*. Lost to her for so long. Not just for the past ten years but since her childhood, since Peter Hardwicke had made her his own, put his imprint on her, as his arrogant mother had. He had turned her into a bigot even as a child. She had become a silly snob with grand ideas about herself and who she was. They had influenced her far too much, and in a certain sense they had ruined her life, inculcating in her expectations that were dangerous – far fetched and beyond her reach, in fact. She was inclined to look down on everyone, full of class distinctions.

'Penny for your thoughts, Gran,' Justine said, looking at Gabriele, searching her face.

'Not really worth a penny. But you are invaluable. I'm so proud of you, Justine, the way you've turned out.'

'You might not be quite so proud if you knew what I'd been about to do,' Justine shot back with a grin.

Gabriele was sitting in front of a tall window. A shaft of sunlight turned her silver-gilt hair to gold, and in this light her eyes looked as blue as they had when she was a young woman.

Shaking her head, her face lighting up with spontaneous laughter, she answered, 'You could never disappoint me; you never did when you were a little girl. But tell me, what wicked thing was it?'

'I was going to use a photograph of you in an advertisement I was going to take, am going to take, in a Turkish newspaper. It was to announce my new documentary, but I hoped that if you saw your picture, or Anita did, you would contact me.'

'That doesn't upset me, or alarm me – you ought to know better than that, darling. Nor would it have embarrassed me. Which photo, by the way? I hope it's a good one.'

Justine chuckled. 'I asked Richard to send it to me today by FedEx. I will have it tomorrow . . . It's the one you gave me about fifteen years ago, and it was taken at Uncle Trent's house in Long Island.' Justine's eyes suddenly sparkled. 'And you know what, you're wearing a blue dress, the same colour as that scarf.'

'I remember that day very well . . . so you're making a new documentary?'

'It's called "Biography of a City", and it's about Istanbul, Gran. Originally, I used that story, a ploy really, to get Iffet to work with me. You see, I *did* come here to find you, actually. Then, in the course of this week, became inspired.'

'It's a very clever idea indeed. And you're still going to do it, even though you've now found me?'

'Yes, I am, Gran, because it *is* a great idea, and there is a real story to tell about this place. The documentary I just finished editing is going to be shown in September, and I did several interviews about it. With various papers here, and the English language paper as well. I did them hoping you would read about me, and come and find *me* at the Çiragan Palace.'

Gabriele frowned. 'When did they appear?'

'Earlier this week.'

'Anita and I just got back from Bodrum, down in the south, last night. We were away for several days, and obviously I never saw them.'

Justine nodded, hesitated, and then asked in a lower voice, 'Did you know Anita had written to my mother?'

Gabriele shook her head, and answered sotto voce, 'Not at first. She did that off her own bat, without mentioning a word. But then when she didn't hear from Deborah she got upset and eventually confessed to me. I was a bit startled at first. But it didn't surprise me she hadn't heard. I have written to your mother many times over the years, and she never responded—'

Iffet was walking across the floor, and Gabriele stopped and changed the subject. 'And how did you find Iffet?'

'She's a friend and colleague of Joanne's. Oh, my God, I was so excited to find *you* I forgot to tell *Jo*! I must call her immediately, if you'll excuse me.' Justine stood up as Iffet came to a standstill next to the sofa.

'I'm afraid I will have to leave now, Gabriele . . . Justine. Anita has kindly asked me to stay for supper, but I think it is better if you are all alone this evening. You have so much to catch up on.'

'But I did invite you to dinner,' Justine reminded her.

'I know you did. So kind, Justine. But that was before you found Gran.' Iffet laughed. 'I still can't get over it!'

'Neither can I,' Justine exclaimed.

Gabriele rose and, turning to Iffet, she murmured, 'Thank you so much for helping Justine. I can never thank you enough. I think God meant you to be on the Bosphorus this afternoon. I really do believe that. I've never believed in the randomness of things . . . I think there *is* a grand plan.' Stepping closer to Iffet, she kissed her on the cheek, and finished, 'I hope I'll see you in the next few days.'

'I'm sure you will.'

Justine said, 'Come on, I'll walk you to the jetty . . . and the boat.'

'Thanks, but you don't have to, Justine.'

Justine and Iffet walked together through the garden of Anita's *yali*, heading in the direction of the jetty. At one moment, Iffet said, 'Your grandmother is such a lovely person. And so good looking. Very English.'

'I know. And she's a wonder. So is Anita, just as attractive as Gran in her own special way. And very motherly.'

'I cannot tell you how excited I am you found your grandmother this afternoon. It is like . . . *a miracle.*'

'*A fluke.* But that's the way life often is, you know. Full of strange twists of fate, coincidences, accidental happenings that turn out to be blessings. All I know is that she's found, and I'm not going to lose her again.' Justine paused for a moment and took hold of Iffet's arm, and said, 'I can't thank you enough for being such a help, Iffet, and for your patience and kindness.'

'It was my pleasure. Will you make the documentary?'

'I fully intend to . . . Also, I'm still going to do the advert. I think the idea of picking out some Istanbul stories about people and their lives will work well. My plans haven't changed. And I still want you to work with me.'

'Of course. I would love to, Justine.'

'Oh look, there's Nuri waving to us from the jetty.'

On her way back to the *yali*, Justine paused for a moment and dialled Joanne's phone number. There was no answer. She tried her apartment in New York, and when the answer machine came on she told her friend the great good news about Gabriele, and clicked off.

The moment she walked back into the sitting room Justine was aware of a change in the atmosphere. As she glanced around she noticed that Gabriele and Anita seemed more relaxed. Michael was standing at the other end of the room, facing the window, speaking on his mobile.

Strolling over to the two women, she said to Gabriele, 'I just tried to reach Joanne but she wasn't at home. I left a message. She'll call back. I know she'd love to speak to you, Gran. Is that all right?'

'Of course it is, darling,' Gabriele answered. 'I watched her grow up; she's like part of the family. How is she doing? How is her life?'

'Jo's the same, always optimistic, like me. You know I can't stand negative people. She got married, to one of those Wall Street wonders who turned out to be a bad lad. They're divorced now. They have a little boy, Simon, who's Daisy's age. She does public relations for movies.'

'And Daisy? What's she like, my great-granddaughter?'

'Like you and me, Gran. Blonde, blue-eyed, tall; she's very precocious without being awful, bright as a button. And adorable, lovely.'

'And her mother?'

'Pamela died two years ago,' Justine said, her voice suddenly echoing with sadness. 'She had cancer of the uterus, went very swiftly. Richard took it extremely badly; he's been coping with a lot of grief and heartache.'

'Oh, Justine, I'm so very sorry,' Gabriele replied, a look of dismay in her eyes. 'Poor Richard, poor darling. How heartbreaking. A loss like that is so very hard to bear.'

Anita murmured a few words of condolence, and then giving Justine a pointed look, she asked in her rather direct manner, 'And what about you, Justine? Single, married, divorced?'

Justine began to laugh. 'Never married, so never divorced. I am single, free as a bird, and fancy free.'

'Is that a fact? Mmmmm, that gives me food for thought, my darling.' As she spoke, her sparkly dark eyes settled on her grandson near the window, the expression on her face thoughtful.

Gabriele, her eyes on Anita, began to chuckle, and she said in an amused tone, 'I can see what's going through *your* mind.'

Justine looked from Anita to her grandmother, then followed the direction of Anita's gaze, saw how focused she was on Michael. Turning to face the two of them, she spotted the conspiratorial expression on both their faces and, much to her mortification, she felt herself blushing bright pink. She opened her mouth to make some sort of pithy comment, but closed it at once because Michael was turning around, moving towards them.

Michael was speaking to them. 'I got out of the dinner. So I'm free as a bird,' he explained, walking across the room to join the three of them.

Anita began to laugh.

Gabriele's mouth twitched, but she managed to keep a straight face, suppressing her laughter.

Justine simply sat down on a sofa, still mortified, and said nothing. She was poker faced.

Anita murmured, 'Funny you should say that, Michael.'

'Say what, Grandma?'

'That you're free as a bird. Only a few seconds earlier, Justine said exactly the same thing. But she was referring to something else.'

Michael ignored this comment, took a chair opposite Justine, said to her, 'You have to decide if you want to move in with Gabriele tonight or tomorrow morning.'

'Tonight, of course.' She glanced at her grandmother and asked, 'Is that all right?'

'Don't be such a silly goose – naturally it's all right with me. Why wait until tomorrow? Haven't we waited long enough to be with each other again?'

'Absolutely,' Michael answered, before Justine could respond.

She stared at him, thinking that *he* certainly knew how to take command of a situation. He gazed back at her, smiled at her with such warmth she felt that odd tightening in her chest again, and quickly looked away, aware of the effect he had on her.

He said, 'Do you want me to *drive* you back to the hotel tonight so you can pack and check out? Or would you prefer to go across the Bosphorus on our boat?'

'Whichever you want, Michael,' she answered, managing to find her voice.

'The bridge might be very busy, full of traffic,' Anita pointed out.

'That's true. Then it's settled. We'll go by boat.' He stood up. 'Kuri, our driver, will wait for us and bring us back in time for supper.' Throwing a quick look at Gabriele, he asked in a loving voice, 'Does that meet with your approval, Aunt Gabri?'

'It does indeed,' she said.

Sixteen

Michael Dalton was sitting on the terrace of the Çiragan Palace Hotel, nursing a glass of white wine as he waited for Justine, who was upstairs in her room busy packing.

He was facing a dilemma, and wondering how to best solve it. Before he and Justine left his grandmother's *yali* to come here, Anita had drawn him to one side and told him to take care of Justine's bill at the hotel. 'Just charge it to my account there,' Anita had murmured. When he had demurred, explaining Justine wouldn't want that, she had become insistent.

His reluctance was based on his understanding of Justine Nolan. In the several hours she had been at the villa he had realized that she was independent, had a strong character, was very much her own woman.

It had taken a lot of guts on her part for her to come here without an address for Anita. It also told him how much she cared about Gabriele and that she had been determined to find her. Certainly she had thrown caution to the wind when she had embarked on this venture, not knowing what she would find. The conclusion he now drew was that Justine was not the kind of woman who would want Anita, or anyone else, paying her hotel bill.

He made a decision: he would play it by ear.

He laughed at himself inwardly, knowing full well that he liked her so much, was so attracted to her, felt such a strong pull towards her; he did not want to upset her in any way.

Michael had a weakness for brunettes, and yet here he was longing to grab hold of this tall leggy blonde, so sexually drawn to her he was actually startled at himself. Not his type, yet his heartbeat quickened when she had come close to him in the sitting room, and again on the boat when she had fallen against him as the motorboat had hit a series of wakes from other small vessels crossing the straits.

He was not a man who was a womanizer, nor had he ever rushed from woman to woman in his younger days, being selective and somewhat conservative in his choices. He had often been alone for long periods of time between romances . . . and yet here he was tonight, preoccupied with Justine, and he had only split up with Vanessa a few months ago. Vanessa. Justine. My God, they were as different as any two women could be . . .

He cut off this thought, and stood up swiftly, as Justine walked towards him, a smile on her face. He noticed at once she had changed, wore a blue silk shirt and navy blue trousers, carried a navy shawl. Her long blonde hair gleamed, and she had put on make-up.

He smiled as he pulled out the chair for her.

She sat down, and said, 'Sorry I took so long, but I decided to change clothes . . . it gets coolish here at night, I've noticed. Anyway, here I am. I left my bags with the concierge, and paid my bill, so everything's been done.'

'You paid the bill, did you? That means Anita's going to rap my knuckles.'

'Figuratively speaking, of course.'

'Figuratively speaking, yes. She wanted me to put your bill on her account here. But I must admit, I was hesitant, reluctant.'

'Oh, why?' Justine asked, staring at him. Now that she was with him again, she realized why she hadn't stopped thinking about him when she was upstairs packing. There was something about him that drew her to him, made her want to know him better.

'I decided you were the kind of woman who wouldn't want her tab picked up . . . that you might be offended or resent it.'

'Neither, but I wouldn't have allowed you to put it on Anita's account, because it's not necessary.'

'So I did the right thing?'

'Yes.'

'Would you like a glass of wine before we cross the straits?'

'One for the water, sure,' she said laughing.

He laughed with her, getting the analogy at once, and beckoned to a waiter, ordered the white wine. He said, 'When is Richard coming to see Gabriele?'

'As soon as he can. He has a good week's work yet on the installation. He just designed a new boutique hotel in Battery Park. He's very anxious to get here, though, as you can imagine.'

Michael nodded. Longing to know more about her now that he had her to himself for a while, he changed the subject when he said, 'You mentioned the name of one of your documentaries, something about babies with guns? Was that it?'

'That was it exactly. It was called "Babies with Guns: The Child Soldiers of Africa". I won an Emmy for it . . . I made it several years ago.'

'Congratulations, on the Emmy, I mean. And I'm sorry I missed it . . . that subject has always interested me.'

'I'll get you a copy if you want . . . and why does the subject matter interest you, Michael?' she asked, her eyes focused on him intently.

Before he could answer, the waiter brought the wine. The two of them clinked glasses, and Michael replied, 'I suppose because I'm often preoccupied with war. All kinds of different wars.'

'Oh, why is that? Are you in the military?'

Michael shook his head, took a swallow of wine.

'So what do you do for a living?' Justine probed, surprising herself at all the questions she was asking.

'I run a security company. The main office is in Manhattan. I've two others, one in London, the other in Paris. Actually, I studied law and then history, and graduated, but never became a lawyer, much to my parents' surprise.'

'I can imagine. So your mother is Anita's daughter?'

'That's right. Her name is Cornelia, and she's a lawyer, too.' He grinned. 'Well, she studied law at Harvard, where she met Larry Dalton, my father. And she did graduate, but never practised either. Because she fell in love and got married and very quickly had me, then my sister Alicia.'

'And did you go to Harvard too?' Justine asked, riddled with curiosity about him, suddenly aware that she had a need to know him inside out.

'I did, yes, and I enjoyed it. Fortunately, I realized I wasn't cut out to be a lawyer. One day I had an epiphany of sorts. I suddenly realized how patriotic I was and that I must join the Secret Service. I had this desire to serve my country. So that's what I did.'

'You became a Secret Service agent?' she asked, a brow lifting.

'Eventually, yes. I had to go through a lot of training at the Secret Service academy in Washington.'

'Did you protect the president?'

'Not until my last year with the Secret Service. Then I got hit by the barrel of a rifle. I was unlucky, I had an accident with my eye. It affected my vision to a certain extent, and obviously I was no good at protecting a president, or anybody else for that matter. So I did the next best thing. I left the Secret Service and I started my own security company, but I'm mostly behind a desk, running the business. Sometimes I travel to my different offices—' Michael broke off as his cell phone on the table buzzed. 'Hello?'

'Michael, it's your grandmother. Where are you? Did the two of you get lost?'

'No, Grandma,' he answered, laughing. 'We'll be there very shortly, just leaving the hotel.'

'Oh, that's good. Gabri and I . . . well, we miss you both.'

'See you soon.' Putting the phone in his pocket, Michael looked across at Justine, a smile still flickering. 'I think you got the gist of that?'

'I did. And they're quite amazing, those two, aren't they?'

Michael stared at her, nodding. 'I bet you thought you were going to find two old ladies with walkers, but what you got were two babes in Valentino dresses and heels. Full of piss and vinegar, as Gabriele would say.'

'I did, yes,' Justine agreed, laughing with him. 'And was *I* surprised.'

There was less traffic on the Bosphorus going over to the Asiatic side, and the water was calmer, so it was a much easier trip. Michael had been asking Justine lots of questions – about Iffet, how she had found her; and what the two of them had done to try and locate Gabriele.

She had answered him swiftly, with her usual directness, and he had marvelled at the clever ideas she had come up with, and her ingenuity and tenacity. 'My hat's off to you, Justine,' he said, when she had finished. 'And the idea of the advertisement was quite brilliant. Aside from drawing attention to you, to Gabriele, and alerting Anita you were here, I think asking Istanbulites to tell you their stories of the city was – and is – inspired. I'm sure my grandmother has lots of tales to tell you.'

'Then she'll be my first interview,' Justine said, smiling at him. 'In a way, the documentary is another fluke. I really did come here to find Anita and, through her, my grandmother. But I didn't want to go into a lot of private stuff with Iffet, so I told her I was investigating the idea of a documentary. However, I wasn't really serious about that until I started to tour the city, and began to understand its fascinating history. It seemed like a natural to me.'

Michael nodded and, glancing at her, his eyes slightly narrowed, he asked, 'Did you happen to be sitting on the terrace of Çiragan Palace last Friday afternoon? Late afternoon?'

'Yes, I was there. Why?'

'Did you notice a man ogling you?'

Justine gave him a long stare, and exclaimed, 'Yes, I did! He looked like an Englishman, and he kept stealing glances at me. Then another man, tall, dark, came and joined him. Oh, my God! Was that you? I didn't want to encourage that guy so I ignored him, didn't look around, do anything like that. I just sat making my notes and I never saw your face.'

'And I didn't look around either, because it would have been rude, and perhaps embarrassing to you. He's quite harmless, he just loves beautiful women, but all he does is ogle them, actually, Justine.' Michael chuckled. 'He's well and truly married, happily married.'

'He's a friend of yours then?'

'A client and a friend.' Michael sat back on the seat, a strange look suddenly crossing his face, and he began to shake his head.

Justine, who was totally conscious of him in every sense, asked, 'What's wrong? You've got the oddest look on your face.'

'Something just struck me, and quite forcibly. My friend was itching to come over to say hello, ask you to join us for a drink. And if he *had* done that, I would have had to come with him.

We would've all introduced ourselves, obviously. You wouldn't have known my name, but I would certainly have known yours. Justine Nolan has been part of my life for years.'

'And on hearing my name, you would have told me you were Anita's grandson, and that you knew my grandmother, and that would have been another *fluke*.'

'Exactly what I was just thinking,' Michael answered, and shook his head again. 'A missed chance.'

'True, but through another fluke it all worked out . . .' She cut herself off, and sat gazing into space for a moment.

Michael said, 'Now you've got an odd look on your face. What have *you* just thought of?'

'I was just wondering if life is . . . *a fluke*. I mean, is everything that happens in all of our lives . . . *a fluke*? Is life made up of random things happening – flukes, accidents, all those kinds of things?'

'I don't know, but I have had to deal with many coincidences in my life, both personal and professional . . . accidental encounters that have been meaningful in some way, and very *flukey* things as well.'

'My grandmother doesn't believe in the randomness of life. She thinks there's a master plan. When we were little she was constantly saying *Que sera sera*, what will be will be. She told Iffet that God had meant us to be on the Bosphorus this afternoon, and that God had meant her to be there too, and that's why we encountered each other.'

'And I guess God meant it to happen this Friday and not last week.' And He meant it to happen when I was here in Istanbul, not Paris, Michael thought, but did not say. Originally he had been planning a trip to see his French client in Paris, and then had unexpectedly changed his mind, decided to come here instead, and not for any special reason whatsoever. Another fluke?

Justine said, 'Has my grandmother told you a lot about me? I mean you did say I'd been part of your life for years.'

'Yes, she did talk about you from time to time, and over many years, even before this ridiculous estrangement, the problems with your mother. What's it all about, do you know?'

'I don't, Michael, but it is one of the things I plan to find out about. And I genuinely believe it's my mother who's at fault, not Gran.'

'It wouldn't surprise me,' Michael asserted. 'We're here. Kuri will help us with the bags.'

A moment later, the door opened and her grandmother was standing there on the step of her *yali*, smiling at the two of them. 'You don't have much luggage, darling,' Gabriele exclaimed.

'I travel light, Gran,' Justine explained, hurrying over to her, embracing her.

Michael, turning to Kuri, said, 'Give me those bags please, and thanks very much, Kuri, for your help. We won't need you again tonight, so you might as well get off for your supper. See you in the morning.'

The driver inclined his head, smiled, and disappeared through the curtain of trees.

Stepping back, Gabriele ushered Justine into her villa, telling her, 'This has been my home for years, darling, and I think you're going to like it.'

Michael said, 'Sure she will,' and went inside after them, carrying Justine's two suitcases which he put down on the floor. 'I'm going to leave you two alone for a while. I've got business calls to make to New York. I'll be having supper with you later.'

'See you,' Justine murmured. 'And thank you for helping me, Michael.'

'My pleasure,' he replied and, stepping outside, he closed the door behind him.

SEVENTEEN

The moment they were alone, Gabriele took hold of Justine's arm, and said, 'Come along, darling, let's go into the little sitting room. I have a great need to talk to you, and there's plenty of time to show you the villa, since you'll be staying for a while.'

'That's exactly what I want to do, Gran. Before *you* say anything, *I* must ask the first question. It's one which troubles me terribly, and Rich. What is this estrangement *about?*'

Leading her into the sitting room, Gabriele said, 'Let's go and sit near the fireplace. I always have a fire in the evenings at this time of year – it gets cool – and I'll tell you anything and everything you want to know.'

Justine took a seat in a comfortable armchair opposite her grandmother, and explained. 'Richard and I knew nothing about it, until the letter from Anita came and I opened it.'

'Thank God you did,' Gabriele exclaimed. 'If you'd simply sent it on to your mother, you'd be none the wiser, and she would not have replied, and we wouldn't be sitting here, the two of us.'

'So what did happen between you, Gran?'

When Gabriele remained silent, Justine said, 'Was it about money?'

Gabriele looked at her granddaughter alertly, thinking how bright and intuitive she was. 'You've hit the nail on the head, my dear. It *was* mostly about money . . . but then Deborah is somewhat avaricious, greedy, when it comes to material things. She never had enough of anything, and I'm certain she's still the same, isn't she?'

'I don't think a leopard changes its spots, Grandma, so I guess she is still as grabby. But to be honest, Richard and I haven't seen much of her since she went to live in Beverly Hills. That was eight years ago. Two husbands and two divorces later, I can't help thinking she might be on the prowl again for a rich man. That's why she won't come back to New York. Beverly Hills is now her preferred fish pond.'

'I would have thought that Palm Beach was better. More widowers, no?' Gabriele said, her tone slightly acerbic.

Justine burst out laughing. 'Oh, spot on, Gran! There's nobody like you. Anyway, please tell me about the estrangement.'

'It was like this,' Gabriele said, leaning forward slightly, her hands clasped together, her blue eyes fixed on her grand-daughter. 'When your father died twelve years ago, your mother immediately wanted to take over the showroom in the D & D Building. She told me she was going to run it as your father had. I said that she couldn't, because I was going to do that. Naturally she was up in arms, screaming and shouting, and being her histrionic self. Once she had calmed down, I explained that *I* owned the import company. The showroom lease was in my name, and I had financed most of the operation. Naturally she didn't believe me. She had assumed it belonged to your father, but in fact he only had a very small investment in it. In the end, I had to show her all of the legal papers to convince her.'

'So my father worked for you, and not vice versa, and yet

somehow everyone thought it was his company,' Justine murmured.

'I know, and it didn't matter to me. And with all due respect, your father wasn't the one who put that story around. It was your mother. Anyway, he and I made a good team; he enjoyed working with me, and so did I with him. He took a big burden off my shoulders. I paid him a handsome salary and he was genuinely content with the arrangement. Your mother had her own decorating company, and she was working. However, her business wasn't as successful as she would have everyone believe.'

Gabriele sat back in the chair, her expression sad. With a sigh, she said, 'Your mother was stubborn from the day she was born, and I'm afraid she thinks she's right about everything.'

'Oh, you don't have to tell me that, Gran. Rich and I realized long ago that she's a know-it-all. One thing surprises me, though: we thought her design company was big time, the way she talked. She was constantly away, as you well know. Travelling for business, she said. I often wondered about *that*, especially as I got older.' Justine threw her grandmother a keen and knowing glance. 'I don't want to interrupt, so please continue the story.'

'I decided the best thing was to pay her your father's salary every month, and keep her out of the showroom and out of my hair. I did it for peace and quiet, really, and to keep my business on an even keel. You remember Edgar Clarke, who worked with us when your father was alive, I'm sure. I promoted him to your father's position as manager, and he did a good job for me. Especially when I was in London or travelling. In the end, I decided to close the showroom in order to spend more time in London and here in Istanbul. After all, you were already in college.'

'I remember that, Gran, but we did miss you a lot when you were away. Dad was dead, and Mom was never around.' Justine fell silent for a moment, before saying quietly, 'What set her off *ten years ago?*'

147

'Several things, darling. About a year before that, I closed the showroom. I stopped paying your mother your father's salary. There was no longer an import company either. So what was the point? That was why she came to visit me in London in 1994. I still owned auntie Beryl's house just off Charles Street, and she stayed with me, trying to make nice, so I believe . . .' Gabriele's voice quavered slightly; she paused, cleared her throat before continuing a little unsteadily, 'One afternoon, when I was out at appointments, she broke into my writing case. Can you believe that? She actually broke the lock, and as bold as brass. She stole jewellery which auntie Beryl had left me in her will. Plus a large amount of cash. Deborah also read personal documents, and it was those that set her off on a horrible rampage.'

Gabriele took out her handkerchief and blew her nose, dabbed at her eyes. 'I was stunned that my own daughter would invade my privacy, *and* steal from me.'

Justine was aghast at this story; leaning forward, she touched her grandmother's hand, patted it. 'Don't cry, Gran. I'm here now, and Richard will come soon, and we'll make up for the pain she's caused you. I promise you we will.'

Gabriele forced a smile, nodded, but was quiet, falling down into herself, as she tried to recover her equilibrium.

After a few minutes, Justine asked, 'Did you get the jewellery back? And the cash?'

'I did, yes, because she made one mistake. The things went missing when the help was off. They were on holiday. She couldn't accuse them, and the house hadn't been broken into. And so it was obviously your mother who had taken my things. She didn't have a leg to stand on and I got everything back.'

Justine nodded. 'And what kind of documents did she find, Gran?'

There was a long silence, before Gabriele said at last, 'She found my marriage certificate. She discovered that I had married

148

Uncle Trent a year before he died – that's fourteen years ago now.'

'I'm so glad that happened, Grandma! He adored you, and he was such a lovely man, so kind and warm. But why didn't you tell anybody? Like Dad? Or me and Rich? Or our mother, your daughter?' So-called, Justine thought, remembering her mother's treachery over the years.

'I told your father. In fact, he was the one who urged me to marry Trent, and—'

'Why did Dad urge you to get married to him?' Justine interrupted, her curiosity aroused more than ever.

'Because he agreed with Trent that we *should* be married, in order to protect me should anything happen to Trent. You see, Trent was older than me, and he was diagnosed with leukaemia a year before he died, and although he and I had been together for many years, I'd always resisted marrying him.'

Gabriele paused, lifted her hands helplessly, shook her head, looking rueful, as if she could find no good reason for this attitude on her part. She stared out into the room, lost for a moment in her thoughts.

After a second or two, as Justine waited patiently for her to catch her breath, Gabriele finally continued. 'Trent was determined to make me his wife because he loved me, had loved me since the day we met, and because he had so little time left. He also wished to secure my future financially. He had never married, so had no offspring, but he did have a sister and a nephew. Being a lawyer he knew only too well how families could behave when money was involved. It occurred to him that his sister and her son might challenge his will. *If I wasn't his wife.*'

'I understand,' Justine murmured. 'You would be vulnerable, and that's what Dad and Uncle Trent were endeavouring to prevent.'

'That's right. So I finally, at long last, agreed to marry Trent, providing he left his sister and nephew the house in Long Island

and his New York apartment. I didn't want trouble. I'm not avaricious, and I basically agreed to get married to make Trent happy.'

'And did Uncle Trent agree to your suggestion?'

'He argued with me at first, but finally gave in, and left those two properties to his sister and nephew, who, by the way, were not only surprised at this bequest after Trent died, but also perfectly happy with what they got.'

'It was generous of Uncle Trent,' Justine murmured, and grimaced. 'So Mom found the marriage certificate and that set her off. One thing I don't quite understand . . . what was her anger about? Uncle Trent was dead by then.'

'I'll get to that in a minute, but let me explain something else. Many years ago, long before your mother was married to your father, I found a beautiful property in Connecticut. It was called Indian Ridge, the home we all loved except your mother, who didn't really care about it. Trent bought it, put it in my name and gave it to me outright. It has always been in my name and it still is—'

'Indian Ridge belongs to you! Not to Mom?' Justine's astonishment showed on her face and she gaped at Gabriele, staggered by this announcement, and thinking yet again what a pathological liar her mother was.

'That's correct, Justine,' Gabriele answered. 'When your mother came to London ten years ago she demanded Indian Ridge. She wanted me to give it to her outright. I explained I couldn't do that because it was in an unbreakable trust. The Somerset Trust had been created some years ago, and Indian Ridge is in the Somerset Trust for you and Richard, and your children, and then their children, and so on. You and he will inherit Indian Ridge one day, after I'm dead. It's a pretty straightforward trust. Your mother didn't like my news about the Somerset Trust. I pointed out to her that she had never really loved – or even liked – the house, but that she could live there for as long as I was alive. After that it would be yours, and you and Richard would be in charge and could do what you wanted about the house.'

'Grandma, I'm so stunned about inheriting Indian Ridge, and Richard will be . . . thank you so much. I don't know what else to say. It's so very generous of you, and somehow a "thank you" doesn't seem quite enough.'

'You are my family. My only family, now that my auntie Beryl is dead. She was the last of my mother's line except for me. Now you and Richard are the future line . . . You and yours will carry on after I'm dead. As for your mother, I don't know what to say about her.'

Justine was moved, so touched by Gabriele's words she couldn't speak. She was choked up and emotional for a moment or two, and she sat very still in the chair trying to steady herself.

At last, taking a deep breath, she said in a low voice, 'I bet Deborah went berserk, lost her cool.'

'She was furious. And that is when she vowed never to speak to me again, never see me again, and that you and Richard were barred from my life. That I could never be in contact with you.'

'So that's what the estrangement is all about. As you said, material things. Gran, I want—'

'Could I just finish this, darling, before you tell me what you need to say?'

'Yes, please do.'

'It's important you know that the Somerset Trust was created when you were children, because I knew how much you and Richard cared about Indian Ridge, and Tony too. Your father loved that place with all his heart, and had he lived he would have continued to reside there, since I also named him in the Somerset Trust.'

'But not my mother?'

'No, Justine, not as far as the house is concerned. It didn't matter to her, except for its intrinsic market value. She would sell it at the drop of a hat.'

Justine sat staring at her grandmother thoughtfully, and then asked at last, 'Why didn't you marry Uncle Trent when you were a younger woman? I mean, why did you wait until it was literally forced on you by Dad? Because Uncle Trent was ill and Dad knew he didn't have long to live?'

A deep sigh escaped Gabriele, and she leaned forward; her blue eyes, clear, full of intelligence, were fixed on her granddaughter. 'Actually I always longed to marry him, deep inside myself. But I couldn't. There was a terrible impediment, you see.'

Justine's eyes narrowed and she cried heatedly, 'My mother! She was the impediment. She didn't like Trenton Saunders. I was aware of that when we were little. She never wanted us to go with you to his house on Long Island. *She was the impediment, wasn't she?*'

'She was. But, darling, how did you know she didn't like Trent?' Gabriele sounded astonished, and looked it.

'Because I was a very observant child, if you recall. And she didn't exactly hide her dislike of him. I might go so far as to call it hatred. She harboured great hatred for Uncle Trent, and I can't imagine why. He was so lovely.'

'What you say is the truth. Your father loved Trent, and your father also loved me, and in the end he made me see sense. He said, "To hell with that bloody screwed-up daughter of yours. Just live your life and be happy, and make that devoted man happy while he's still on this earth." I've never forgotten your father's words.'

'Where did you get married, Grandma?'

'City Hall in New York. Your father came along with us, jokingly saying he wanted to make sure we did it. Then he took us to lunch at Le Cirque afterwards. We never told anyone. Except Anita, who knew Trent well, and Larry Dalton, Michael's father, who is my lawyer.'

'Oh, Gran darling, what a story, but if only you'd married

him years before . . .' She let her voice trail off. The past was the past, and nothing could change it now.

Gabriele said, 'We were married legally for one year. However, as far as I'm concerned, we'd been a married couple all of the years we were together. Thirty years, actually, and as I once said to Trent, "A bit of paper's not going to make much difference to us, or our lives." And he agreed.'

'It does when it comes to wills and the legal stuff, though, doesn't it, Gran?'

'It certainly does, darling. Now, I cut you off before. What was it you wanted to tell me?'

Justine took a deep breath, and as she thought of the words she had to say, she began to shake inside. 'Gran, you must have wondered why Rich and I never came looking for you ten years ago, and since that time—'

'I figured your mother had told you some awful story about my behaviour, or suggested that I had dementia, or Alzheimer's, and was in a home or an asylum, something like that.'

Justine's eyes filled with tears and they rolled down her face, as she said in a half-choked voice, 'She told us . . . she told us . . . you were dead, that you'd died in a plane crash.'

'Oh, my God!' Gabriele's eyes welled. 'Oh, my poor darling, you and Rich must have been so upset. And how could my daughter tell a horrendous lie like that?'

Justine jumped up and went to kneel next to her grandmother, took her hands in hers. Hands that had looked after her when she was ill, soothed her anguish when she was upset about something as a child. Those loving, caring hands, worn now and old, and she took them in hers and held them tightly, bent down and kissed them. 'Upset is not the right word, Gran. We were heartbroken, and we grieved for you for years. When we found out you were alive I was dumbstruck and couldn't wait to find you, and Rich felt the same way. And we were worried how you were doing, how you were . . . and we were afraid you'd think we didn't care, didn't love you, but you know we do.'

Bending forward, Gabriele put her arms around Justine and held her tightly. 'I've never thought badly of either of you. Ever. I know the stuff you're made of . . . let's face it. Your father and I shepherded you through your formative years.'

Gabriele wiped her eyes, and so did Justine, and suddenly they looked at each other and began to laugh.

Gabriele said, 'Thank you for finding me.'

Justine now gave her grandmother a very direct look, and said, 'I want to ask you something.'

'Go ahead.'

'Why didn't you come to New York immediately to see Richard and me? We wouldn't have been influenced by our mother. We knew she was a liar and a cheat. We would have believed *you*, Gran.'

'I thought you wouldn't see me, or have anything to do with me. Deborah had been in such a fury she had frightened me a bit. She can be verbally violent, as you know. Then, just as I was getting my courage back, thinking about flying to New York, she sent me a letter and enclosed an e-mail from you and Richard.'

Gabriele went over to the desk, took out some papers. She explained, 'Your mother wrote the following. "*Mother: Be warned. Richard and Justine feel the same way about you as I do. They don't want you in the family. They think you're a liar. Which you are. They are disowning you as I did. Stay away from us. Deborah.*"'

Justine was aghast. 'How horrible! It's not true. Honestly, it isn't.'

Gabriele said, 'This e-mail from you to her was enclosed. It says, "Dear Mom: Anyone who lies like your mother has no place in our lives. You did the right thing to disown her. We disown her too. We're on your side. Love Richard and Justine." I'm afraid I believed this.'

154

'Can I see the e-mail, please, Gran?'

'Here it is.' Gabriele handed both pieces of paper to her.

After reading the e-mail, Justine said, 'It *was* sent from my computer. But not by me. It's a forgery. She accessed my computer, sent it to herself. What a duplicitous woman.'

'I know what you mean,' Gabriele replied.

'And inventing that plane crash! How rotten she is.'

'Oddly enough, I did have a car crash just after I got back to Istanbul ten years ago, and I was incapacitated for a few months with a broken leg and a broken shoulder. I couldn't travel for a long time.'

'Thank God I found you, Gran. And thank God for flukes.' Justine paused, then looked over at the arched doorway. A sudden smile illuminated her face.

'Good evening, ladies,' Michael said, coming into the room. 'I've been sent to collect you by my boss, otherwise known as Anita. She'd like you to come and join us for supper. I'm here to escort you across the courtyard.'

Eighteen

It was a beautiful night, the midnight-blue sky sprinkled with the brightest of stars. A huge silver orb of a moon, which seemed much closer than it truly was, looked as if it had been strategically hung over the gardens, resembling a set design in a movie. In the distance, the Bosphorus appeared to have been painted with silver, and it shimmered in the moonlight.

The French doors were wide open, bringing the outdoors inside, the sweet scent of varied flowers mingling with the salty tang of the sea drifting in on the warm air.

The dining room in Anita's villa was unusual, circular in shape with a domed ceiling, the walls washed in pink, the floor covered in terracotta tiles. A round dining table took pride of place in the centre, covered in a floor-length Paisley-patterned cloth and partnered with antique French chairs.

Anita, dressed in a floating cyclamen and purple silk caftan, hurried forward to meet Gabriele, Justine and Michael, smiling broadly as she motioned them to come into the room. Taking hold of Justine's arm possessively, she led her inside swiftly, explaining, 'Mehmet has made a Sunday lunch for dinner, because Gabri told me how much you loved her Sunday lunches. Years ago, when you were growing up. We thought that's what you'd enjoy tonight.'

Justine broke into laughter, and looked over her shoulder at her grandmother. 'None of us have managed to get it right *ever*, Gran, not since you went back to London.'

'Mehmet will. He's an old hand at it,' Gabriele replied, her soft blue eyes dancing with happiness.

Anita indicated where they should sit: Justine between herself and Michael, with Gabriele facing her granddaughter across the table.

Taking her seat, Gabriele smiled at Justine, truly happy to gaze at her lovely face. Gabriele's joy at having Justine here in Istanbul knew no bounds; plus now, fully understanding *why* her grandchildren had not come searching for her before, she was also comforted. A sense of peace at long last.

Justine glanced at her grandmother surreptitiously, thinking what a beautiful woman she still was – one who looked younger than her years.

There were several reasons for this: a head of thick, luxuriant hair, the same silvery-blonde it had always been, a broad brow, high cheekbones and an extraordinary complexion that was relatively unlined. Also, her enormous vitality gave her an aura of youthfulness, and Justine had noticed how quickly she moved, and with grace.

Justine could not help but marvel at her, and at Anita. The latter was full of energy, just like Gran, and seemingly as fit; a good-looking woman, smart and well put together, with short curly brown hair and twinkling dark eyes. There was a deep bond between the two of them, Justine knew that, and earlier she had picked up on their knowing glances.

After sipping their wine, toasting each other, Anita touched Justine's arm lightly. 'I apologize again for forgetting to put my name and address on the back of the envelope. Stupid! Whatever was I thinking about?' She looked irritated with herself, and shook her head wonderingly. 'I must be getting forgetful in my old age.'

'No, you're *not*!' Gabriele exclaimed. 'Forget about age. It happened because you were obviously intent on getting that letter into the postbox. So *I* suspect, anyway.'

Justine turned to Anita, said gently, in a warm voice, 'But I did find you, and that's all that matters, isn't it?'

Michael suddenly interjected. 'Justine, can I ask you a question?'

'Of course,' she answered.

'Didn't you think of hiring a private investigator to find them?' He sounded puzzled, and threw her an odd look.

'Yes! Of course! Richard and I did discuss that before I even left New York. But we decided not to because we didn't want to upset—' She broke off immediately, looking slightly chagrined.

Laughing, Michael finished her sentence. '*Two old ladies.* That's what you were going to say. Correct?'

She nodded and laughed with Michael, and the two grandmothers did also, because they were aware they did not resemble old ladies at all. Not with their lovely hairdos and high heels, chic caftans and red lipstick.

A few moments later, Zeynep came into the dining room carrying a large platter, and Anita explained to Justine, 'This is *lakerda*, local tuna from the Black Sea.'

Zeynep offered her the platter, and Justine took two of the thin slices of fish and a piece of lemon. 'It looks delicious,' she murmured.

Michael started to talk to her about the places she had visited in Istanbul whilst 'on the hunt for Gabri', was the way he put it, and the two grandmothers also wanted to hear what other sights she had seen, where she had been. 'I've been to a *han*,' she told them.

'You have?' Anita sounded surprised to hear this and stared at Justine, frowning. 'Which *han*?'

'Vezir Han. Iffet took me to Punto, and—'

'Oh, my goodness, the carpet shop!' Gabriele interjected. 'I haven't been there for some years. I used to know the owner quite well.'

'I discovered that,' Justine responded, and recounted the story of *why* they had gone to Punto, and the fact that the owner actually did remember her, had even referred to her as Gabri. Gabriele and Anita looked at each other and smiled.

Michael said, 'Clever reasoning on your part.' He grinned at her. 'Quite the little detective, Justine.' He sounded amused.

'Not really, Michael,' she answered evenly, even though she was annoyed by his tone. 'I was a journalist before I started to make documentaries, and so I do know a bit about digging for information.'

Gabriele murmured, 'Tell us more about your latest documentary, Justine. We'd love to hear. Do you mind?'

'No, of course not, Gran. It's about a man who is considered to be one of the world's greatest artists, Jean-Marc Breton, the painter and sculptor. I did a filmed biography of him and his work, focused on his art, his studio in Provence and his homes. It's two hours long. In fact, there's a promo running currently on the network I'm associated with, CNI. You might catch it if you turn it on later. I did some interviews with local Istanbul newspapers about "Proof of Life", actually in the hopes that you might see them, read them, and know I was in Istanbul.'

'We were away. Oh dear, what a pity we missed them,' Anita said, shaking her head regretfully.

Gabriele nodded.

Michael stared at Justine. '"Proof of Life". That's a strange title for a documentary about a painter, isn't it?'

'It's a term used by the police and other agents; it's hostage terminology. I chose it because it *was* strange, and therefore people would be *intrigued*, would want to know what the story was about. And it is *apt*, because Jean-Marc has been a *recluse* for many years, staying *in the dark*, so to speak. Some people thought he *was* dead. But he wasn't dead, and that's why I thought "Proof of Life" was an appropriate title. The film *proves* he's alive.'

'When you explain it that way, then I agree with you,' Michael replied. 'And I for one can't wait to see it. I've always been an admirer of his art. What's he like?'

'Brilliant – a genius, in my opinion. A great artist,' she enthused.

'I meant what's he like as a person, as a man?'

'Oh, well, let me see . . .' Justine frowned, looked reflective. 'He's fascinating, charming and difficult – impossible, in fact, depending on the time of day, or the day of the week. He can be extremely irritating because of his temperament. But he's also one of the most attractive and beguiling men I've ever met . . .'

Justine stopped instantly, suddenly aware that Michael was staring at her intently, his eyes narrowed. She felt her neck growing warm, and then her face, realized she was blushing. She also knew that he had picked up on something in her words or her tone, or both, and she was angry with herself. She had given herself away.

After studying her for the longest moment, his eyes riveted on her, Michael murmured, 'It sounds as if he made a very strong impression on you, and a favourable one. You've no doubt made a wonderful documentary about him.'

She nodded, but did not respond, then noticed that Gabriele and Anita were looking at each other oddly. Picking up her glass, she sipped her wine, mortified. Michael Dalton was far too intuitive and clever. But then he'd been trained as a Secret Service agent, hadn't he?

There was a silence at the table. No one said a word.

Fortunately, Zeynep came in and removed the fish plates, and put down clean ones. The arrival of Mehmet pushing a meat trolley, with a large leg of lamb reclining on the carving board, seemed to lighten the atmosphere.

'This is going to be a treat, Justine,' Anita said, and forced a laugh, relieved that the chef had come into the dining room. 'And your grandmother says it's the best Yorkshire pudding outside Yorkshire.'

As she spoke she stole a glance at her grandson, wondering what was wrong with him. He had sounded so sarcastic a few seconds ago, and his eyes looked darker than ever. They became almost black when he was angry. Why was he angry now? *Aha!* Because of Justine's remarks about the painter. Oh, my goodness, Anita thought, he likes her. Maybe more than likes her? She hoped so. Vanessa had been wrong for him. Beautiful, yes, but hard, selfish, self-involved and manipulative, and not very bright. Street smart perhaps, but no intellect.

No one had been happier than she when her grandson had broken up with her. Anita wanted Michael to meet the right woman; wanted him to have the kind of woman he deserved.

Was Justine that woman? In her opinion she was. Justine was solid as a rock, had real character and strength, Anita had become aware of that this very day. She herself had fallen in love with Gabri's beautiful granddaughter, and in an instant. Had he?

Had her Michael been struck by lightning? She prayed to God he had. What she needed for him was a *coup de foudre*. She needed him to be swept off his feet, enraptured, captivated. And she needed Justine to experience the same feelings – otherwise it wouldn't work.

But now she must play hostess.

Mehmet was rattling on about the lamb and the Yorkshire pudding, smiling and gesticulating; finally he started to carve the joint with great skill. All slices were paper thin, in the way they liked them, the English way.

Gabriele and Anita were responding to the chef in their usual friendly manner, both of them hoping the atmosphere would change, ease up. They were so in tune, they knew each other's thoughts, just glanced at each other from time to time.

Michael was silent. Furious with himself. He never displayed weakness, never lost face, and yet he had done just that tonight. He had broken his own rule. Why had he overreacted to Justine's words about Jean-Marc Breton? Because he somehow instinctively knew she had been involved with the famous French artist, might still be involved. And he was . . . *jealous*.

How unbelievable that was. He had never been jealous before. And he had been confident about his ability to attract the opposite sex all his life.

Picking up his glass, he finished the white wine in a gulp, and pushed himself to his feet. Walking over to the sideboard, he picked up the decanter of red he had put there earlier, and noticed that his hand shook slightly. As he carried the wine over to the table, he wondered what the hell was wrong with him.

Somehow he managed to pour the wine into everyone's glass without spilling a drop, and when he placed the decanter in a silver wine coaster on the table he was glad to see his hand was steady again.

Mehmet served the lamb and Yorkshire pudding, adding gravy, and Zeynep carried the mint sauce to each person so they could help themselves. Roast potatoes and other vegetables were served, and indeed it was a typical English Sunday lunch, made in Justine's honour.

Michael had no appetite. His stomach was in knots, and that weird feeling in his chest had returned; it was like tight bands encasing him. How could she be affecting him in this way? He had just met her this afternoon, he hardly knew her. Oh, but you do, a small voice in his head told him. You've heard about her for years, and you felt something for her at once, the moment you saw her rushing across the garden to Gabriele as if her life depended on it. You raced after her, wanting to grab her, pull her into your arms. That was when she stole your heart.

*   *   *

Normality returned. The tension eased. And they all four settled down to enjoy the delicious lamb. As the dinner progressed, it was Justine who genuinely cleared the air by telling them about Daisy, and her antics, and so distracted them. The two grandmothers in particular were fascinated by her stories about the child.

After this, Richard became the subject matter for a short while, and Justine held them spellbound as she told them about her twin's life in the last ten years; his marriage, and his brilliant career as an architect.

At one moment, a little later, Justine suddenly turned her head and looked at Michael.

He became conscious of her gaze, also turned his face to look back at her.

She smiled at him.

He saw an odd expression in her blue eyes, one he could not quite fathom. Then he found himself smiling in return, unable to resist her. Within seconds he was more at ease with himself, and relaxed in the chair.

It took him a little while, but eventually Michael joined in the conversation once more, and so did Justine. There was a general air of goodwill between the two of them again. Naturally the grandmothers noticed this and were relieved. For these two not to get on, if only as friends, would be a disaster, since the families were so bound together.

After the summer pudding had been served and eaten, they went out onto the terrace and a few seconds later Zeynep brought them mint tea in glasses.

It was Gabriele who asked Justine to tell them more about the other documentaries she had made, and Anita and Michael listened alertly to her.

For her part, Justine was happy to discuss her work because it took her mind off Michael. From the moment she had arrived here she had been conscious of him, aware of every move he made, everything he said, the tone of his voice, the expression on his face. His presence overwhelmed her. He was larger than life. Clearly he knew it. On the other hand he had not thrown his weight around or done anything amiss. He had simply over-reacted to her. As she had to him. *Oh*, she thought. Oh, my God! That's what it is. *Struck by lightning.* Her heart trembled at the thought of him. He was tall, good looking and every inch a man. And she had fallen hard. *Had he?*

NINETEEN

'And that, Richard, is Gran's story of the estrangement, and what caused it,' Justine said, leaning back against the stack of pillows on the bed in her room at the *yali*.

Thousands of miles away, her twin was sitting at his desk in the glass cube that was his studio at Indian Ridge, his feet up on the desk, the cell phone pressed to his ear. 'So, to sum up, what you're saying is that it was all about money. Our mother cut Gran off from us because of *that*!'

'That's right, and we've always known she was grasping,' Justine answered. 'She was obviously furious when she heard that Indian Ridge was in a trust for *us*, and not her; that she couldn't have it, wasn't getting it.'

'Right on, Juju. And I must say, I for one am thrilled. It's great that Gran's done this for us, so generous of her. So, go on, tell me about Anita's letter, why didn't she put her address on the envelope? Forgetfulness, I suppose. Or perhaps old age.'

'*Neither!* I think it was overload. Writing the letter several times, which she tells me she did, editing it, copying it out for the last time, and getting it to the post office. And listen, they're not old. They're two stylish babes in Valentinos and heels. And bright red lipstick. Fit as a fiddle, and not a sign of dotage.'

'Oh, my God, are you trying to tell me we've got a handful on our hands?'

'Not at all, just a fabulous grandmother and her special friend, who's basically sweet, very motherly. They look marvellous, by the way, as no doubt you realize, and they're both pretty vital, really with-it.'

'Glad to hear it. So you've moved in?'

'Tonight.'

'What's Gran's house like?'

'Charming, Richard, and decorated in her usual style. Simplicity being the keynote, with some nice antiques, beautiful fabrics, mostly of her own design, from a collection called Tulipmania. She has a little design studio attached to the *yali*, and she's going to show it to me tomorrow. She was too tired tonight.'

'You must be, too. It's five here, so it must be midnight there.'

'It is, yes, but I sort of got a second wind. The excitement of finding her, our reunion, and meeting Anita. It's been busy, I can tell you,' Justine explained. 'The *yali* is smallish, but she did have rooms decorated for us, Richard. Can you believe that? Somehow she was always expecting us to suddenly appear.' Justine paused, finished, 'She had no idea our mother had told us she was dead.'

There was a moment of silence, then Richard exclaimed, 'God, that sounds awful, when you say it just like that. So blunt, cold, but that's what her daughter told us. Gran must have been hurt and upset to hear those words. She was, wasn't she?'

'Actually, she looked shattered, as if she'd been kicked in the stomach—'

'Well, she was, figuratively speaking,' Richard asserted.

'When she started to weep I went and put my arms around her, and comforted her as best as I could. She recovered – you know what she's like, a real fighter. After that we had a lovely evening . . .' Justine smothered sudden laughter, then said, 'She had Anita's chef make a Sunday lunch for dinner for me, for all of us. Because it was my favourite.'

'That's our granny. By the way, did you explain why I wasn't there with you?'

'Of course I did, and she understood and can't wait to see you. With Daisy. I told her all about your little sweetie-pie.'

'And she fell in love with her, right?' Richard said, chuckling.

'Naturally.'

'Justine, I just want to backtrack for a moment . . . I understood everything you've told me and realize that Mom still harbours her money-grabbing ways, but there's just one thing I'm not quite getting.'

'What's that?'

'You said Gran told you that our mother broke into her writing case in London ten years ago, and stole jewellery and cash, also *invaded her privacy* – those were your words – because our mother found documents and read them.'

'What are you getting at?'

'You said documents *plural*, but you only mentioned *one* document. Gran's marriage certificate . . . from her marriage to Uncle Trent. So what were the other documents?'

There was a long moment of silence, and then Justine finally said, 'Gran only mentioned the marriage certificate.'

'Are you sure she said documents *plural*?'

'Absolutely. She definitely did. But she only discussed *one*. So what were the other documents? That's what you're wondering. Also, why was our mother so upset? After all, Trent Saunders has been dead for years.'

'You're quite right, and I believe our mother saw something lethal; something that set her off on a full-blown rampage. But

Gran didn't tell you *what* that document was. I think Deborah read something that shocked her. Certainly something much more important than an old marriage certificate to do with a man long dead.'

'What could it have been?' Justine asked in a puzzled voice, sitting up straighter on the bed, a worried expression on her face.

'I have no idea. But I don't think our mother would go into a rage about Indian Ridge, which she never liked.'

Justine didn't say anything, frowning, her puzzlement intact. 'I find it very perplexing, Rich, now that you bring it up. And I can't even make a guess.'

'I'm surprised *you* didn't notice that she only told you about the marriage certificate—'

'So much was going on,' Justine interjected. 'I'd just found her. We had so much to discuss. I wanted to explain why we hadn't gone looking for her, and I also wanted to know what the estrangement was about. It was quite a lot to handle. And we got sidetracked in a way, because first there was tea at Anita's, and then the dinner, and so much happiness and chatter . . .' Her voice fell away.

Richard said, 'Why don't you ask Gran what she meant?'

'I don't think I can,' Justine protested. 'I don't want to put her through . . . *an inquisition*. My God, we haven't seen her for ten years, Richard! I'm not going to question her.'

'You're right, don't get excited. It was just a thought. And it doesn't matter,' he finished quietly, realizing his error.

'No, it doesn't,' Justine agreed. 'And anyway, if there's anything more to tell, she'll explain in the next few days. When we're more relaxed.'

'That's true.'

They talked a little longer about Daisy, and the weekend, and then Justine exclaimed, 'I forgot to ask you. Have you spoken to Joanne?'

'I have, yes, and she did get your message about Gran, and she was ecstatic that you found her finally. She didn't call you back because she didn't want to interrupt that first meeting with gran. She told me to give you her love, and she'll call you tomorrow. As I will. Now I have to go, Juju, to see my daughter. And you do, too. Hang up, you have to go to sleep.'

But she did not sleep.

It evaded her.

How could she sleep when she had so much on her mind?

Her brain was racing, working overtime. She tried to remember her grandmother's words *exactly*, replaying the conversation once again in her head. And she heard her grandmother's voice clearly, always so precise in its diction. *Documents*, in the plural. Her gran had said that. *Private documents*. She was certain of it.

What kind of documents had her mother read, and why had they set her off? Or was it only one that had done the trick?

Focusing on the kind of documents people usually kept safe, Justine made a mental list: a birth certificate, a marriage certificate, a child's birth certificate, divorce papers, a death certificate, a will. Or maybe two or three wills . . . Uncle Trent's? Gran's auntie Beryl's? She had left a will, and had favoured her niece Gabriele. She had heard stories about Beryl's affection for her grandmother years ago.

Had Deborah found evidence that her mother was much richer than she had previously thought? And she could be, no doubt of that. Gran had worked hard all of her life. And was still working.

Was her mother adopted? Could she have found this out for the first time that day, when she broke open her mother's writing case?

No, that was an impossibility. Gabriele Hardwicke was far too honest to have hidden such a thing from her daughter, and for decades.

On the other hand, her mother did not look like Gabri. Not at all. Nor like Richard and her, either. She wasn't as tall and lanky as Gran and them, nor was she a pale blonde. Deborah was shorter, curvaceous, and dark haired with grey eyes; their characters were different, as well. Deborah was bossy and slightly crazy.

She herself had often wondered from whom her mother had inherited certain unsavoury traits, her temperamental ways, her superiority, her snobbery. Certainly not from Gabriele Hardwicke, who was the exact opposite. And her granny had a much better character than her mother, who was mean-spirited.

She's not a nice person, Justine suddenly thought, nor is she loving. How could she have done what she did? Why did she act the way she did, on that day so long ago now? Ten long years ago. She had issued a terrible edict and she had kept it in place. Kept Gran and them apart. Punishment for something? Was that it?

It dawned on her then that Deborah Hardwicke Nolan clearly hated her own mother, and with such virulence she had cut her off from the rest of the family without a second thought, or any worry about the consequences.

What document had her mother read?

What secrets did her grandmother have?

Because there had to be secrets, hidden things, a *lethal* document, as Richard had said a short while ago. And how could *she* find out? Only two people could tell her the truth . . . her mother and her grandmother, and she did not relish the thought of asking either of them, Gran especially. It would be a rotten thing to do, a terrible intrusion on a woman who had been ripped away from her grandchildren years ago, and with such cruelty it was breathtaking. She had endured enough pain and sorrow already . . . Justine couldn't bear to contemplate what it had been like for her grandmother all these years.

She thrashed around for a long time, and then finally threw off the sheet and light eiderdown, got out of bed. Her grandmother had given her a beautiful room overlooking the Bosphorus and the gardens, which were immediately below her windows. Roomy and airy without being too big, it was beautifully decorated with a few choice antiques and fabrics patterned with tulips.

Opening the draperies, she looked down into the gardens and then across at the flowing Bosphorus, had the sudden and urgent compulsion to go outside. She needed to breathe in the night air, to feel the soothing power of nature all around her. Perhaps after that she would be able to sleep.

Sliding her feet into a pair of mules, she left her room on silent feet.

How beautiful the garden was at night. Bathed in moonlight, it was filled with the mixed fragrances of peonies, roses and night-blooming jasmine. Sweet and heady. There was a breeze ruffling the trees, and Justine felt immediately refreshed, her slight headache beginning to recede.

As she walked along a pebbled path towards the sea, she suddenly understood why her grandmother lived here, in Istanbul. The climate and the beauty of nature were intoxicating, and the way of life was relaxed, unhurried; a peacefulness reigned at the two *yalis*. And then there was Anita, her grandmother's friend since girlhood, her rock; they were each other's rocks, weren't they?

Unexpectedly, Justine came across a garden seat, and she immediately sat down under the blue-blossomed wisteria trees, relaxing against the wrought-iron back. Staring out at the straits, she realized there was a lot of traffic on it still: two cruise ships, a couple of deluxe yachts, and one of those great cumbersome barges that transported goods to foreign places. Of course. It was a major waterway, flowing from the Mediterranean through the Dardenelle Straits into the Bosphorus and on to the Black Sea. Other places, other worlds, far-flung destinations . . .

As she relaxed, she opened her mind and let Michael Dalton creep in at last. She had held him at bay since the moment she had gone to bed, and perhaps that was another reason why she had not been able to sleep. He kept intruding, slipping into her thoughts when she least expected it. He was unlike anyone she had ever met. She had been startled that he had picked up on her comments about Jean-Marc Breton, read something into them, connected her to Jean-Marc instantly. She snapped her eyes shut. That was a place she did not want to go to tonight. Or ever again. Jean-Marc was all the things she had said he was; she had portrayed him accurately. Sadly, she did not like him.

Justine opened her eyes, and sat up straighter on the bench, tensing slightly. All of a sudden she had heard noises, footsteps crunching on the pebbled path, and she swung her head, was immediately alert. On guard.

There was a flash of white in the moonlight. His shirt. And then Michael was a few feet away from the garden seat. His face was serious when he looked down at her and said, 'You couldn't sleep, could you?'

'No, I couldn't.'

'Neither could I. So I thought I'd come and join you. You and I have a lot to talk about.'

PART FOUR

Coup de Foudre

How do I love thee? Let me count the ways.
I love thee to the depth and breadth and height
My soul can reach, when feeling out of sight
For the ends of Being and ideal Grace.
I love thee to the level of everyday's
Most quiet need, by sun and candlelight.

Elizabeth Barrett Browning,
Sonnets from the Portuguese

Twice or thrice had I loved thee,
Before I knew thy face or name.

John Donne, *Air and Angels*

TWENTY

Michael sat down next to Justine on the garden seat, laid his left arm along the back of it and crossed his legs. He did not speak and neither did she.

Acutely aware of him, she pushed herself into the corner of the seat, hoping he would not hear her heart thudding in her chest. He flustered her; there was no other way of describing it.

Although Justine had no way of knowing it, Michael had a similar problem with her. He was thrown off balance when they were in close proximity. She affected him like no other woman ever had, and he was drawn to her on every level. He wondered what she thought about him. He had noticed that odd look in her eyes, the tantalizing smile when they were at the dinner table, but he hadn't quite figured it out. Not yet.

It was Justine who finally broke the silence, when she asked in a low voice, 'How did you know I was sitting out here?'

'I was in my bedroom, talking on the phone to my New York office. I walked over to the window and looked out. I saw you coming down the path from Gabri's *yali*.'

Justine simply nodded, made no comment.

He went on, 'Once I'd finished my call I decided to join you.'

'You said we had a lot to talk about before you sat down.'

'We do, but before we get to that, I want to apologize. I sounded kind of nasty when I made those gratuitous comments about "Proof of Life". But honestly, I didn't intend to sound mean, or sarcastic. The words just came out all wrong. I feel like a jerk. Will you accept my apology?'

'There's nothing to apologize for, Michael.'

'I think there is, but thanks for being so nice. Can we be friends again?'

She nodded. 'We weren't *not* friends.'

'Great.' There was a moment's pause before he went on in a more serious tone, 'I don't want to be intrusive, but I would like to ask you something.'

'Anything. And I'll try to answer.'

'Has Gabri told you what this rather long and baffling estrangement with your mother is all about?'

'She did explain it, yes. Like you, I needed to know, and so did my brother. Gran was immediately willing to talk about it earlier this evening. I think she *wanted* to get it off her chest, unburden herself. Talking about it was a relief for her.'

'Must it remain confidential, or can you share it?'

'I can share it with *you*. I'm afraid it was about money. And my mother's bad behaviour about money. My grandmother really is – well, an innocent bystander: that is the best way I can describe it. My mother has always been avaricious by nature, and I guess she still is. But the quarrel did happen ten years ago, and it's become ridiculous.'

Justine noticed at once that Michael looked astonished, and he sat staring at her for a few seconds. At last he exclaimed, 'She kept your grandmother cut off from her family because of a quarrel about *money*? How reprehensible.' He sighed, shaking his head. 'But then they do say money is the root of all evil.'

'In my mother's case, I believe it is.'

'What does your brother say? How's Richard taking it?'

'He feels the same way.' Justine looked at Michael carefully, asked, 'Do you think that Gran kept the reason for the quarrel, and the estrangement, to herself? Wouldn't she have confided in Anita?'

'I think she obviously would have done that, yes. But Anita has always told me she didn't know what the long estrangement was about. But, you know something, that doesn't mean a damn thing. Those two are extremely close.' Michael paused, staring into the distance, a reflective expression settling on his face. Finally, he murmured, 'Anita may very well have known for years, but kept it to herself. They're very protective of each other.'

'Oh yes, I've gathered that,' Justine said.

'Can I keep going? With the questions?'

'Yes, that's fine, Michael.'

'What did your mother tell you and Richard? How did she explain your grandmother's absence from your lives all these years. Ten years is a long time.'

Justine stiffened, dropped her head, staring down at her hands, wondering how to answer him. She actually didn't care what he thought of her mother. But she did suddenly wonder whether her grandmother would want *anyone* to know that her own daughter, her only child, had told her grandchildren that she was no longer of this world. It was somehow shaming, wasn't it? Her mother had done a truly shameful thing – wiping her mother off the face of the earth was unconscionable.

'Hey, it's okay, Justine,' Michael said, kindness echoing in his tone. 'Don't put yourself on a rack about this. It's not worth it. You don't have to tell me if you don't want to. I'm curious because I've spent time with Gabri over the years, a lot of time, and I know how she has suffered. Listen, Justine, you're here now, and that's all that really matters. She has you back with her, and that's the most important thing of all.'

She stared at him, still unable to speak.

He saw the tears trickling down her cheeks, and reached out for her, drew her closer to him very gently. Leaning forward, he wiped the tears off her cheeks with his fingertips. 'Don't cry. I can't bear to see you weep.'

Justine took a deep breath. As steadily as she could, she said, 'My mother told us Gran had died in a plane crash.'

Flabbergasted, Michael gaped at her. His dark brows grew together in a frown, and he asked in a tight voice, 'And when did she tell you this?'

'The day after our graduation. She had no alternative. She had to explain Gran's absence somehow, because Gran wasn't at the ceremony. Naturally we believed her. Who could ever imagine that our mother would tell such a rotten lie about our grandma?'

Michael nodded, but remained silent.

At last he responded, saying in a gentle voice, 'I'm so sorry this devastating thing happened to you and Richard. And most of all to Gabriele. It wasn't necessary, and ten years have been lost. Ten precious years, and at a time when Gabriele needed you both . . .' He didn't finish his sentence. He was choked with emotion, could not speak. He loved Gabriele, and she had been part of his life for as long as he could remember.

There was a long silence.

Almost without thinking, Justine reached for his hand, held onto it tightly. He squeezed her hand in return, sat side by side on the garden seat, thighs touching. Being together was comforting to them both.

Justine suddenly muttered, 'What my mother did is unforgivable . . .'

'It is, yes,' he answered in return. 'And that's the reason you never tried to find her until now, isn't it? You genuinely believed your grandmother was dead.'

'That's right . . . Listen, Michael, I have a question for you. Did something important happen recently? To Gran, I mean?

Was Gran suddenly taken ill? Did she have a heart attack? I can't help wondering, because I don't understand why Anita suddenly wrote that letter to my mother after all these years.'

Michael gazed at Justine for the longest moment, then answered, 'It's all my fault. I was worried about Gabriele. Over the last year she has become withdrawn, quiet, not her usual self, and I realized she was thinking about her approaching eightieth birthday. So, I just took the bull by the horns, so to speak, and told Anita to write a letter to your mother, asking her to end the estrangement.'

He paused thoughtfully. 'Of course, how was I to know that she would write it over and over again, become nervous about getting it in the mail, and so forget to put her address on the envelope in her haste?'

'You didn't know, and I'm happy you told Anita to put pen to paper. The letter brought me here and I'm glad I'm here.'

'So am I.'

He said no more, afraid he might spoil the beginning of something special. Because he knew it was a beginning. How strange life was. Yesterday they had never met, although he already knew a great deal about her. Nine hours ago she had rushed past him on the jetty, almost knocking him over. He had realized who it was at once, and had raced after her. And in that short span of a few minutes his life had changed. Irrevocably. There was no question in his mind that she was his destiny. And that he was hers.

Gabriele awakened with a start, and sat up in bed, feeling disoriented. She had just dreamed that she was back at Indian Ridge, tending to her rose garden, and now she blinked and looked around.

No, she was not in Connecticut. She was here in her *yali*, the much-loved home she had shared with Trent for many years. She *was* in Istanbul, after all.

But something *was* different.

She frowned, and then it instantly hit her. *Justine was here.* Her beloved granddaughter had found her. Something shifted inside her; perhaps it was her heart leaping, and leaping with joy. Justine was with her, and Richard would come soon, bringing with him her great-granddaughter Daisy. She could hardly wait.

Last night Justine had given her the photograph album, explaining that it had been assembled in a hurry over a few days, and that it was hers to keep.

It was full of pictures of Daisy, Richard and Justine. There were also some of Joanne, always a favourite of hers, with her little boy Simon. They're all back in the fold, she thought, or perhaps I'm the one who's back in their fold. Whichever it is, we're going to be together soon, all of us under one roof.

Gabriele knew herself well, accepted that she had been sinking down into herself, becoming uncommunicative in certain ways, solitary, sorrowful, and even occasionally depressed. Although she usually tried to combat that by keeping herself busy. Now, suddenly, she felt buoyant, excited, glad to be alive.

Her family. How important it was to have a family. They belonged to you, and you belonged to them, and when you were together everything was well with the world. You were all safe, protected, loved and cherished. That's the way it had been at Indian Ridge when Tony was alive. He had loved his children, and her and Trent. And his wife as well; but Deborah had made his life miserable, for the most part. Absent wife. Absent mother. Absent daughter.

Gabriele's thoughts settled on her. She had known for years that there was something radically wrong with her daughter, but had never really been able to pinpoint it exactly.

Then, ten years ago, when Deborah had thrown a hysterical fit after breaking into her writing case, she had finally understood.

Her only child was unbalanced, unhinged, and a sick woman, and had been for years. At the time she had wondered what it was that she had done wrong. Had she not brought her up in the right way? Was it her fault?

For a while she had experienced enormous guilt. But in the end she had let it go . . . because she had started to remember once more those years with Peter, the way her happy marriage had turned bad when their little daughter was five years old. It seemed he was more interested in his daughter than her. Then his overbearing mother had weighed in with her unwanted advice. Davina Hardwicke had actually called her an unfit mother, and had railed at her. And she had never understood why. Or what she had done that was wrong.

Nothing. I did nothing wrong. They wanted Deborah for themselves, and they took her away from me in a sense, even though we all lived in the same house. But we weren't a family, not really. My presence was tolerated, but seemingly not needed. I was pushed out.

Because I was different. I was not like them. I was tolerant and fair-minded, and had no prejudices. But the Hardwickes did, most especially Davina. Her late husband Oswald had been a major in the Indian army and, in the early days of their marriage, they had been stationed there. Oswald had been infected with the same snobbery endemic in some British officers in India and Arab countries. Racial superiority was a given. They referred to the Indians as the natives or wogs, looked down on them and anyone who was not an Englishman of the Protestant religion, including Roman Catholics; they deemed Arabs, Jews and the Asian races to be dirty, ignorant heathens; 'the great unwashed' was the way Davina had described them to her once, much to her horror.

Obviously, Oswald and Davina had influenced their only child, Peter. He was teeming with racial superiority and class distinction, and was equally snobbish and bigoted. He hadn't even had a good word for the Allies during the war, had hated the Americans, the French and the Poles. These disgusting traits had only grown with age and she was aware they had been absorbed by Deborah, who had idolized him. And idealized him after his death.

Gabriele thought the Jesuits said it best: Give me the child until the age of seven and I will give you the man. Or the woman, in this instance.

She sighed under her breath and let go of these thoughts.

Opening her eyes, she got out of bed; it felt warm in her bedroom, and she walked across to the window, opened it. As she looked down into the garden she saw them sitting on the garden seat. Justine and Michael. She smiled to herself, pleased that they were becoming friends, but also wondering what they were doing up at this hour. It was after two o'clock in the morning. Well, they could do what they wanted: they were both over twenty-one.

Later today, when she told Anita that their grandchildren had been keeping company in the middle of the night, her dearest friend would smile knowingly, a dark-brown eyebrow would lift, and she would start to plot and plan. But there was no way anyone could tell Michael Dalton what to do, and certainly Justine was her own person, an independent woman, used to making her own decisions at thirty-two.

Anita would hope and pray that they would get together. *And she?* What would she do? She would wait. She knew only too well that life had a way of taking care of itself. No one really had control of their own life. They thought they did but that wasn't true. Outside factors always intervened. And prevailed. God had a plan for everyone.

Once, long ago, she had lost faith in God. Had cursed Him, hated Him, blaming Him for every evil in the world. But evil was not God's creation. It was Man who had invented evil and set it in motion. And eventually she had managed to forgive God, absolve Him.

For a reason she did not understand, Gabriele suddenly remembered the baby, the little boy, instantly shocked that this thought had floated to the surface of her mind. Her chest tightened and her legs felt weak; she leaned against the window frame as a slew of devastating memories rushed back, swamping her. Then, with swiftness and ruthless determination, she pushed the unwanted memories away.

It had all happened long ago. Still, it was not true that time healed all wounds. Some of her own wounds had still not healed if the truth be known.

Justine was suddenly shivering, and Michael exclaimed, 'Know what, it's turned cold! There's a wind blowing up, we'd better go inside.' As he said this he jumped to his feet, gave Justine his hand and pulled her to her feet.

Placing his arm around her, holding her close, he hurried her toward the *yali*. When he saw the light shining through Gabriele's bedroom window, he said, 'Your grandma's up, I hope she's all right.'

'She probably went to check on me, saw I was missing and wonders where I am.'

'Probably,' Michael answered, knowing how possessive grandmothers could be. 'But she must realize you've not gone far. How could you?'

Within seconds they were going into the smaller *yali*, and as

Justine headed for the staircase, he called, 'How about a cup of hot tea? Or whatever?'

'Tea would be great,' she replied, running up the stairs, and headed for her grandmother's bedroom. Tapping on the door, she opened it quietly and looked in.

Her grandmother was sitting up in bed, reading a book. Justine slipped into the room, went over to the bed, smiling at Gabriele.

'I was outside talking to Michael, and we noticed your light on as we came back to the house. He's making me a cup of tea, would you like one, Gran?'

'I would, darling, thank you.' As she spoke, Gabriele threw back the bedclothes and slid her legs to the floor. Putting on her robe, she continued, 'I couldn't sleep either. We must all be suffering from the same thing. The excitement of your sudden arrival, I've no doubt. There you came, floating up out of the sea like a beautiful blonde mermaid. I was never so surprised, or excited, in my life.'

Justine laughed, took hold of her grandmother's arm and started to walk her out of the room.

'Thank you, Justine. But I can manage perfectly well,' Gabriele murmured, slipping out of her granddaughter's grasp. 'I'm not an old lady yet, and you must remember, age is just a number.'

Michael was standing at the bottom of the staircase with a grin on his face. 'I put the kettle on, Gabri, and I'm all gung ho for tea. But I'm thinking of having a brandy chaser as well. What about you?'

'Why not?' she answered, and glided past him into the living room.

He smiled at Justine. 'How about you?'

'I'll have a brandy chaser, if you are,' she said, and walked on, following her grandmother.

'I'll be in with the tea in a few minutes,' Michael said, and disappeared into the kitchen.

When Justine walked into the living room she found her

grandmother poking the fire, moving the embers around before placing a small log and chips of wood on them. 'That'll be a good blaze in a jiffy, Justine. Now come and sit here with me, my dear, and get warm.'

The two of them seated themselves on a small loveseat close to the fireplace and Justine remarked, 'Michael told me he's known you most of his life, so you must have been coming to Istanbul forever, Gran.'

'Over fifty years,' Gabriele answered, and started to laugh. 'But it doesn't seem like that long . . . whoever it was who first said "time flies" was correct.'

'And have you always lived in this *yali*?' Justine probed.

'Yes, but it was Anita's guesthouse years ago, and I used to come and stay with her and Maxwell, her first husband. Once Cornelia went off to boarding school in England, and then continued her education in America, things changed. Anita didn't really need this little *yali* any more, but she didn't want to sell it either. So for a long time, Uncle Trent rented it from her, and eventually she agreed he could buy it for me. And here I still am.'

'You've made this room look beautiful, Gran, my bedroom too, and your own. You're so talented.'

'I'll show you the rest of the villa tomorrow. I don't know what happened to the day. It's just slipped away.'

'I know what you mean.'

'Here I am with the tea,' Michael exclaimed, bringing in a laden tray and putting it down on the coffee table near them.

'There's a bottle of cognac over there, Justine,' her grandmother remarked, indicating a trolley in a corner.

In a few minutes the three of them were sitting near the fire, drinking the lemon tea and then sipping the brandy, enjoying the warmth from the fire and the drinks and their easy companionship.

Justine suddenly said, 'I have to go to the Çiragan Palace later today, to pick up the FedEx envelope from Richard.' She glanced at her grandmother. 'With your picture in it.'

'I'll take you,' Michael said.

'Oh, but Michael, no, I don't want to be a nuisance. And—'

'I have an appointment there in the afternoon,' he cut in. 'At three o'clock. If you don't mind waiting an hour for me, we can come back together. Or Kuri can take you back and return for me later.'

'I'm quite happy to wait and come back with you.'

He nodded. 'Then it's settled. Now, where shall I take you all for dinner tonight?'

'Oh, dear.' Gabriele gave him a knowing look. 'I'm afraid that might create a problem. Anita's planned a small dinner; she's invited a few friends to meet Justine.'

Michael offered her a reassuring smile. 'No problem, we'll have a party here, and I'll take you out to dinner before I leave.'

'Where are you going?' Justine asked, her voice rising slightly, and felt herself blushing. How stupid she was, revealing her feelings.

'To Paris to see a client,' Michael answered steadily, keeping his face neutral, not wanting her to know how pleased he was by the way she had spoken out. He knew he was right about her.

Gabriele asked, 'Are you coming back to Istanbul? Or going to New York?'

'No, Gabri, not New York. But I will have to go to London at some point. I have a number of clients there I have to see.'

Justine clamped her mouth shut, said nothing.

Gabriele simply nodded and also remained silent. But she was quite positive there was a spark between these two. Perhaps more than a spark.

TWENTY-ONE

'This is the most beautiful fabric,' Justine said, looking at a length of silk hanging on a coat rack in Gabriele's studio located at the far end of the *yali*. It was a soft pale blue, patterned with tulips randomly placed. These were a very bright snow white and had feathers and flames of the deepest burgundy. The mixture of the white and the burgundy on the petals – plus the green leaves – made the flowers stand out dramatically against the pale blue background of the silk.

'One of my favourites, too,' Gabriele said, joining her at the rack. 'I love the plain tulip because it is the most beautiful and elegant of flowers, but I just can't resist the multicoloured ones.'

'Neither can I. But when did you start designing these tulip fabrics, Gran?'

'About ten years ago.' She grimaced. 'I was very upset when I came back here after seeing your mother in London, and I didn't know what to do with myself. Anita and I had been running our ceramic and carpet export business for years, and it sort of runs on its own anyway. But actually, it was Anita who asked me to paint a picture for her bedroom wall. She asked me to do a still-life, a flower arrangement, and I ended up painting a vase of tulips. She loved it so much she suggested I use it as a pattern for a fabric. You see, years ago we had produced fabrics of my designs, and sold them here. I suspect she wanted me to be busy, to take my mind off your mother and the estrangement.'

'I'm sure she did, Gran, and I understand how upset you must've been,' Justine murmured.

'So I started designing again, using only tulips in my fabrics, and we ended up opening a new business together. To my shock it's been extremely successful, and the fabrics now sell all over the world,' Gabriele finished.

'I bet they do! You paint tulips beautifully, Gran; they look real, so life-like, I feel as if I can reach out and pick one. And I love the name you dreamed up. Tulipmania is so unusual. It was very clever of you.'

'Not so clever really, darling,' Gabriele answered. 'There was a period in the seventeenth century known as Tulipmania in Holland. The Dutch had gone crazy over the tulip for many, many years, and at one moment in time the price of bulbs skyrocketed beyond everyone's wildest imagination. A single bulb could cost as much as a grand house on a Dutch canal. Men spent fortunes, lost fortunes, made fortunes . . . all because of tulips.'

'My God, how extraordinary!' Justine exclaimed, sounding genuinely surprised. 'I've never heard anything about that period.'

'Actually, it all started here in Turkey.'

'What did?' Justine asked, turning around to look at her grandmother, who had walked over to her drawing board and was sitting in a chair.

'The popularity of the tulip,' Gabriele answered. 'It's beloved here. And all over Asia, as a matter of fact.'

'But I thought the tulip was a Dutch flower.'

'It was taken from Istanbul to Amsterdam by the Dutch in the fifteen and sixteen hundreds, and was soon a favourite. It then went to France and England, and became the most popular of all European flowers. But as I just said, it is native to Turkey and has been growing here for centuries, long before the Dutch heard of it. If you look carefully for it, you'll see it's used in many Turkish designs, such as the blue-and-white Iznik tiles, vases, urns and pots, and in local fabrics and carpets. You'll notice the tulip partnered with the carnation, which is another popular Turkish flower. However, the tulip reigns supreme.'

'Gran, how fascinating all this is, and I hope you'll talk about it on film when I do my interview with you for the documentary,' Justine said, sounding excited.

'Of course I will, I'll talk about anything you want.'

Justine smiled at her, and riffled through the other fabrics, each one even more beautiful. She thought: You won't talk about everything, though. You're holding out about something. What that is, I don't know, but I sense there's a secret. A mystery.

Gabriele interrupted these thoughts when she started to talk about the dinner Anita was giving that night. 'I don't know if you have anything to wear this evening, Justine, but if not I do have several caftans made out of various fabrics, if you'd like to choose one. And also some tunics to wear over trousers.'

'I would, Gran! Brilliant idea, because I didn't bring anything remotely appropriate for Anita's fancy dinner, and I'm sure it will be fancy, won't it?'

Gabriele chuckled. 'You've picked up on her style very quickly – she loves to make a splash, have fun. It will be fancy, yes, but elegant. I think it's going to be a buffet supper, and she's invited some interesting people. A caftan or tunic will be ideal. Come on, let's go upstairs and choose one. Whichever you prefer.'

'I'm so glad she's invited Iffet,' Justine remarked as they left the studio.

* * *

189

Michael Dalton stood at the end of Anita's garden on the edge of the Bosphorus, looking out towards the European side of Istanbul. He was expecting a call and had his mobile phone in his hand, waiting for it to come through.

It was the most beautiful morning. There wasn't a cloud in the blue sky nor a breath of wind. He caught a whiff of seaweed and salt on the air, and it brought back memories of his childhood. He glanced around. No two ways about it, the day was simply gorgeous. It boded well for his grandmother's dinner party tonight.

His mobile rang and he answered immediately, pressing the phone to his ear. 'Hello, Henry. How goes it this morning?'

'Not bad; in fact, all is well in the heather.'

'Tramping some moor somewhere, are you?'

'Yes, actually, I am.'

'Any birds?'

'Not to speak of. Grouse season's not until August, you know. And the rest have flown.'

'My birds? The ones I was promised?' Michael asked swiftly.

'That's right. And they'll never be seen again.'

'Oh dear. Extinction?'

'Exactly. But at least no one has to worry that they're floating around somewhere . . . doing damage to somebody's property.'

'Good to know. Thanks for calling, Henry. I'll be seeing you in a week, maybe ten days. Will you be back from the moors?'

'Naturally. Let me know when to expect you.'

'I will. And thanks, Henry. You did good.' Michael clicked off his phone, dialled Charlie's mobile. He was in Gloucestershire where he spent weekends at his country home near Cirencester.

Charlie answered his mobile phone after two rings. 'Morning, Michael. How's the news today?'

'Good morning, Charlie. It's good. I spoke to our friendly gamekeeper, and apparently those birds I mentioned are no longer available.'

'What happened to them?'

'They've flown,' Michael answered.

'Where?'

'Into extinction, I'm told. There's no longer a problem about the birds doing harm.'

'Thank God for that. Our mutual friend was worried about them getting into other hands. But we do have a situation of sorts.'

'Can you tell me?'

'The oligarch who sent you the cigarettes last week seems to have disappeared.'

'Are you sure?'

'Pretty much, Michael. Seemingly, he went off the radar on Wednesday. He was expected to attend a meeting at the Waldorf Towers in New York and never showed. Not surfaced yet.'

'There's nothing I can do, or you either.'

'Obviously not. We're not even involved. I just wanted you to be in the loop. He could be a problem for the world, and we must remember that, stay focused on him.'

'I appreciate the reminder. I'm coming in sometime later next week. I have to be in Paris on Wednesday to meet with a client. After that I'll hop on a plane, be around for a couple of days in your neck of the woods.'

'Great. I'll take you to dinner at Mark's.'

'Best place to go . . . it's quiet, and I like the food.'

'Talk to you later,' Charlie said and hung up.

Michael slipped his phone in his pocket, and walked over to the garden seat, sat down for a moment, wanting to think about the information Henry had passed to him.

The game birds were guns being touted by an international arms dealer. Miraculously, they were now off the market, and had apparently been destroyed. One of his security teams had been handling the matter for a client of his. The client was worried the guns were about to wind up in the wrong hands in his own back yard. Michael never asked too many questions on a phone, but whatever it was his team had done, the armaments were destroyed. Gone for good. He would learn about the details later when he saw Henry in London.

The Russian oligarch who so worried Charlie was none of his business – or Charlie's either. But Charlie had indicated last Friday that the man was dangerous and that he should be aware of that. Now the Russian had disappeared. Perhaps someone got to him before he could cause damage on a global scale. MI6 or the CIA? Or the FBI? Michael closed his eyes for a moment, focusing. It would be the FBI operating in New York. The CIA could only work on foreign soil, just like MI6. If it made the newspapers they would know soon enough.

He let out a long sigh, focused on Henry again. He was relieved those guns hadn't been used to create a revolution . . . in a moment or two he would call his client to let him know his country was safe. For the moment.

He heard footsteps on the pebbled path, and glanced over his shoulder. His grandmother was hurrying towards him and he jumped up, looking worried. 'Slow down,' he said, walking to meet her. 'I'm not going anywhere, at least not yet.'

'I know. But I couldn't complete my arrangements for tonight until I'd spoken to you.'

'I'm all yours,' he said, taking her arm, leading her back to the garden seat. Once they were sitting down, he said, 'So tell me your problem.'

'It's not really a problem. I just need your advice. Do you think I should hire a band?'

Michael was momentarily taken aback. 'How many people have you invited? Enough for a dance?'

Anita laughed, and exclaimed, 'Don't be so silly. I've got the four of us and Iffet, which makes five, and I've invited fifteen people, well, Gabri and I have between us. So we're twenty.'

'I do think a band is overdoing it,' Michael said, laughter in his eyes. How like his grandmother it was, wanting to make a splash. 'How about a trio?'

'I shall just call Abdullah, that's the man who plays the guitar so well – you've heard him before. He'll come and bring two or three of his musicians. That will be nice, don't you think?'

'I do.'

'You like her, don't you?'

'Who?'

'Don't say *who* like that, so innocently. Justine, of course.'

'I do like her, yes, a lot, if you must know. Remember, Gabri has spoken to me about her for years, so I feel as if she's an old friend.' Michael smiled at her.

'Do you think we're a bit brainwashed? Oh well, that doesn't matter, she *is* nice, and she's very beautiful, Michael, don't you think?'

'Yes, if you like long lanky pale girls with silvery-blonde hair.'

'You're making her sound awful, like . . . like a ghost.'

'I'm teasing you. Look how she just took off, came searching for Gabri . . . That took courage.'

'Yes.' Anita was silent for a moment, before saying, 'I'm very glad she found Iffet. I don't know what she would have done without her.' Anita felt a little rush of guilt again about the missing address.

Michael turned his head, glanced down the path and said, 'Here's Justine now, coming to join us.'

He rose quickly, and went to meet her, happy she had finally appeared. Grasping hold of her hands, he smiled, pulled her closer and gave her a peck on the cheek, restraining himself. 'It's nice to see you this morning, and looking so fresh and rested.'

'And you too, Michael.' Although she was five feet nine in her stockinged feet, Michael was six foot three and she had to look up at him. This pleased her; she liked men who were taller than she was. 'We were up late last night.'

'None the worse for it, though. Anita's planning a nice party for you; she's just been telling me about it.'

'It's so sweet of her to do this.'

'It'll be a fun evening.'

The two of them walked back to the garden seat, and Justine said, 'Good morning, Anita, and thank you for a lovely dinner last night.'

'My pleasure, Justine, and good morning. And where's Gabriele?'

'In her studio looking at some caftans and tunics, and that's why she sent me to find you. We need your opinion, Anita, and yours, too, Michael.'

Within minutes they were standing in the studio with Gabriele, who had hung four caftans on the clothes rack. She explained, 'Justine can't make up her mind which one she wants to wear tonight. So I suggested she bring you both to pass judgement and choose.' Gabriele smiled at Michael, and then glanced at Anita. 'You have a good eye – why don't you pick one out for her?'

Anita looked pleased, and said, 'Oh, I can tell you now. I think the pale blue would be perfect. It will match your eyes, Justine.'

'I like the red,' Michael said, although he didn't care what she wore. All he wanted at this moment was to grab hold of her hand and rush her away from the grandmothers and up to his room. Bad thought, Michael, he chastised himself. He then added, 'Although blue is Gabri's colour, and you do look so much like her, Justine.'

'A much younger version of me,' Gabriele said swiftly. 'Very much younger.'

'Why don't I just hold each one next to me,' Justine suggested, and went to get the blue caftan. Slipping it off the hanger, she stood in the middle of the studio and held the caftan against her body. They all murmured their approval. She then took the red one and did the same thing, followed with the green, and finally the white. Each caftan and tunic was patterned with the tulips, and they were obviously the most expensive fabrics from Gabriele's line.

'The pale blue,' Michael said at last. 'Either the caftan or the tunic.'

Anita nodded in agreement, and so did Gabriele.

Justine smiled at them all. 'Thank you . . . I always rely on family decisions,' she said, and felt herself suddenly blushing.

TWENTY-TWO

Michael was waiting for her at the jetty as they had arranged earlier. He was already on board, standing on the deck, and Kuri was at the wheel of the motorboat.

Michael waved and smiled when he saw her, and shouted, 'Come on down, I'll help you onto the boat. There's been a hell of a lot of traffic this afternoon, and the sea's very choppy.'

'Good thing I'm wearing flat shoes,' Justine said and started down the steps, endeavouring to keep herself calm. As usual, the minute she set eyes on him she began to shake inside. He had a disturbing effect on her, unlike anything she had known before.

When she was halfway down, she paused for a second. It was windy. His dark hair was ruffled, his loose, navy-blue shirt blowing around him; he looked devil-may-care and impossibly handsome. She knew that whatever happened she would always have that image of him in her head. She went on down the steps, her heart clattering against her ribcage.

'Give me your bag,' Michael said when she was standing in front of him. She did, noticing how much the boat was rocking.

'Now give me your hands.'

She did as he told her, then took a step forward over the side, holding on to him, and came on board with a bit of a wobble, falling against him. He staggered slightly, but steadied, held her tightly against him, and kept on holding her until she laughed, relaxed in his arms and stood firmly on the deck. Only then did he release her.

'I told you it was rough,' he said. 'It's the wake every other boat creates. Now come on, let's go sit over there.' As he led her to a long banquette, he called out to Kuri, speaking in Turkish.

Within moments they were speeding away from the jetty, heading towards the European side of Istanbul. Before they could start talking, Michael's cell phone began to ring, and he pulled it out of his shirt pocket, pressed it to his ear.

'Dalton here,' he said, then listened for a moment.

'Well, yes, that's all right, Aly. But I'm already on my way. So why don't we meet as planned and spend only half an hour on the papers. I'll study them again tonight. We can have breakfast tomorrow since that's what you prefer.'

Michael listened again for a few minutes, said goodbye and clicked off. Putting the phone in his shirt pocket, he looked at her, and said, 'The meeting won't take all that long after all, as you heard.'

'Business is business, and I don't mind waiting for you, however long you are. I told you that yesterday,' she responded. 'Are you working all the time, Michael? Even at weekends?'

'More or less, but I'm usually on the phone behind a desk, not out in the field. Today's meeting is about security management on a large estate – several estates, in fact, and I need to explain some of the installations we're about to do. Incidentally, just so you know, our grandmothers have an invisible electronic fence around their two *yalis*, so they're very well protected.'

'Yes, Gran mentioned that to me last night, and then again

this morning when she gave me a little tour of her villa. She added that you had them put in, as if I hadn't guessed.'

He glanced at her. 'They're quite a double act, those two, and I'm glad they've got each other. They keep each other's spirits up.' Still staring at her, he took hold of her hand, and moved closer to her on the banquette. 'And I can't tell you how happy I am to get you alone at last. Away from our darling grans and their eagle eyes.'

Justine began to laugh. 'They are rather doting, aren't they?'

'That's a strange word to use,' Michael said. 'Mind you, they are doting. But they're also watching us all the time, trying to guess how we feel about each other. To put it bluntly, I don't think they would be at all upset if we disappeared to my room or yours . . . for a bit of privacy.'

Noticing the odd look on her face, Michael frowned. He said, 'They're very modern and extremely romantic, you know. Especially when it comes to us. They're itching for us to get . . . well . . . get together, so to speak.'

Justine was silent for a moment, and then she smiled at him. 'I'm not surprised Anita is romantic; Gran probably is, too. But for the last twenty-four hours I've been so emotional with Gran I suppose I've missed certain things – undercurrents, whatever.'

'But not the way you affect me, I hope.' His dark eyes were riveted on hers.

'How could I?'

'Have I made it *that* obvious?'

'No. But you affect me the same way.'

'How? How do I make you feel, Justine?'

'Nervous, flustered,' she admitted, feeling relieved to tell him this. She held onto his hand even tighter. 'Anxious, shaky. Pick a word.'

Michael put an arm around her and drew her closer, then he leaned forward and kissed her on the mouth, very gently, quickly pulled back and looked at her. 'There, I've done it! Finally kissed you, although it was rather a chaste kiss, wasn't it? Not quite what I had in mind when I first saw you.'

'It was a lovely first kiss,' she replied, relaxing against his body.

He wrapped both arms around her and held her tightly until they arrived at the Çiragan Palace, where Kuri brought the boat alongside the hotel jetty.

They walked up through the gardens, heading towards the hotel, holding hands but not talking. Justine was relieved they had spoken so openly to each other on the boat. It had helped to ease the tension in her. Also, the way he had held her tightly in his arms on the bumpy ride across the choppy sea had been thoughtful and caring, and she had felt comfortable with it. At least I'm not in this on my own, she thought, and smiled to herself. And then she suddenly laughed out loud at the ridiculousness of this thought.

Michael glanced at her, asked, 'Why are you laughing? Care to share the joke with me?'

She hesitated, suddenly feeling foolish, and remained silent for a second, then quickly said, 'I was just thinking that at least I'm not in this on my own.'

'In what?' he asked, standing still, gazing at her. He wanted to laugh, too, knowing exactly what she meant, but managed to keep his face straight.

'You know what I mean, Michael.'

He nodded. 'You mean *I'm* in it, too, sharing the same disturbing situation.'

'That's right . . . it's not one-sided.'

'You bet it isn't.'

They went on walking, crossed the terrace and entered the hotel, making for the lobby. When they arrived at the concierge's desk, Justine asked if they had received a FedEx envelope for her, and it was promptly given to her by the smiling concierge.

Michael said, as they moved away, 'I've got about fifteen minutes before my meeting, so why don't I get you settled at a table on the terrace? I'll pop off to meet my client, and then join you after half an hour. That's all the time he can spend with me today. We can relax a bit, and have a drink before heading back to the *yalis*.'

'That's fine,' she answered, and walked out onto the terrace with him. It was obvious that he was well known here, and the maître d' made a big fuss over him, led them to a table in a corner of the terrace which looked out across the Bosphorus. After Michael had ordered tea and they were alone again, he said, 'How long are you staying in Istanbul?'

'I don't know . . . why?'

'Will you wait for me?'

'What do you mean?'

'I have to be in Paris next week. Then I must make a short trip to London to see the head of my company there. After that I'll head back. I was hoping you'd still be here, Justine.'

'Of course I'll wait for you to come back,' she said, and then felt the colour rushing into her face. Why did she always start blushing when she was with him? Clearing her throat, she said rapidly, in a rush of words, 'I was planning to stay with Gran until Richard arrived. We both want to spend some time with her.'

'That's good, she needs you both. These years have not been easy for her, and just seeing her yesterday, the way she . . . blossomed last night was great for me. I've worried about her a lot.'

'But she hasn't actually been ill, has she?'

'Not physically; she's a strong woman, like my grandmother. Good genes, I guess. They're both tough and very resilient. But emotionally Gabri *has* been upset at times, and particularly because family is so dear to her.'

'I realize she must have been unhappy, at a loss, and perhaps not even understanding our absence, why we hadn't tried to find her. I'm glad she has Anita and you.'

'And my mother when she is visiting. Everyone loves Gabriele; she's considered special in our family. In fact, she's a member of our family.'

'She's always been popular,' Justine murmured, and then, picking up the FedEx envelope, she opened it and took out the photograph and Richard's scribbled note. 'Just look at her, Michael, doesn't she look great in this picture?'

'She does. And you really do have a strong resemblance to her, don't you?'

'That's what everyone's always said, and of course we're both tall and blonde.'

The waiter arrived with the tea tray; after pouring a cup for each of them, he quickly departed.

Michael said, after a few minutes, 'I'd better go and see my client, get this over with.' He rose, squeezed her shoulder. 'See you shortly,' he murmured and left.

Justine sipped the tea and, leaning back in the chair, she relaxed for a while. Eventually she looked at her watch and saw that it was just after three o'clock. Eight in the morning in the States. Time to call Richard in Connecticut, and then she would make a call to Joanne after that.

Across the Bosphorus, the two grandmothers were also having tea. This afternoon the two of them were sitting in Gabriele's garden. Usually they were relaxing on Anita's terrace, mainly because Mehmet, her chef, wanted to present a traditional English tea every day, but today there was a great deal of activity in and around Anita's *yali*. Preparations were being made for the dinner party, which Anita had decreed must be festive; Mehmet was in the kitchen making delicious food for the buffet. At this moment two helpers were stringing lanterns around the trees on the terrace, another was placing votive candles in strategic spots, and two tables had already been erected on the terrace, each seating ten.

Gabriele said, 'It's so sweet of you to have a party for Justine – very dear of you, Anita.'

'Oh, don't be silly, it's my pleasure. I'm just thrilled she's here.' She turned to her oldest friend, and peered hard at her. 'I swear to God her sudden arrival yesterday has taken twenty years off you.'

'Do you know, I feel twenty years younger!' Gabriele exclaimed, smiling.

Anita took a sip of her lemon tea, and went on, 'Do you think they'll get together, Gabri?'

'I do, yes. I saw a spark between them yesterday, and—'

'Only a spark! I'd hoped for a flash of lightning.'

Gabriele chuckled. 'It might easily have been a *coup de foudre*, for all I know, and like you, I'm praying it was. They're ideally suited, as you well know, and I saw Justine looking at him very intently last night. I saw the yearning on her face, and I wanted to weep, it was so real and true.'

'Did you really? That's wonderful news. Do you think Michael saw it?'

'I don't know. But the good thing is they're both fancy free, as Justine called it yesterday. Aren't you glad Michael broke up with Vanessa? That he's free too?'

'You know very well I couldn't wait for him to realize what she was as a woman. Thankfully, he did.' Giving Gabriele a very pointed look, Anita continued, 'I've been on tenterhooks for the last few months, although I haven't said anything to you. I kept thinking she might pull a nasty surprise on him; tell him she was pregnant. But she hasn't, and I think she's already in another relationship. What a relief.'

'That wouldn't happen, Michael getting her pregnant. He's far too smart for that, darling,' Gabriele pointed out.

'He is smart, and he's been around the block a few times, but you know what men are like as well as I do. When they get an erection, that's what they're focused on, and nothing else.'

Laughing, Gabriele simply nodded, and poured herself another cup of tea. 'This is what I think we should do: give them plenty of space, let them be alone together as much as possible. Let things take their natural course.'

'Oh, yes, I agree with you about that.' Anita fell silent for a moment, staring out at the garden, and then she said softly, 'She reminds me so much of you, when you were her age, Gabriele. I remember once going to tea with you at the Ritz when I was in London, and people just gaped at you, struck by your loveliness. That's what my darling Max used to say about you: *everyone's struck by Gabri's loveliness.*' Anita sighed, and sat back in the chair. 'Well, we've had our good times, too, haven't we?'

'Thank God,' was all Gabriele said.

After a few moments, Anita leaned even closer and said, sotto voce, 'What did you tell Justine? About the quarrel, I mean?'

'I explained about her mother breaking open my writing case, and finding the marriage certificate, and I told her it was about Indian Ridge, my will, which was more or less the truth.'

'So you didn't tell her the real truth then? The truth from long ago?'

Gabriele looked at her askance, and her face paled. 'Oh, Anita, you know I couldn't do that! I can't speak about . . .' Her voice faltered.

Anita immediately reached out and touched her arm lovingly. 'I'm sorry, so sorry, Gabri, forgive me for bringing it up. The past is the past.'

'And so it must remain.'

'I promise it will. It is our secret, Gabri.'

'I trust you implicitly.'

There was silence for a while.

Gabriele was the first to speak, when she said in a quiet voice, 'I thought about . . . the baby, the boy, the other day, Anita. I was so startled he came into my head, and I don't know why.' She frowned. 'I'd had a dream, about . . . about . . . those days, and I didn't really remember the dream, it was so vague when I woke up, and then the baby came into my thoughts.'

She rested her head on the chair-back and closed her eyes. 'But I've had strange dreams, off and on, since auntie Beryl died,' she went on after a moment. 'Perhaps because she was my mother's sister, and the last link I had to my mother. I don't know the meaning of dreams, and you don't either . . . but let's face it, we *are* strange, us humans, and our emotions are so controlling of us, affect everything we do. So I believe.'

Anita simply nodded, remained silent.

Suddenly, Gabriele sat up straighter in the chair. 'We must not think of the past, not the good days nor the bad. We must lift our eyes to the future, and let's hope that those two can make sense out of what they are feeling . . .'

Michael was walking across the terrace towards her sooner than Justine expected. 'Here I am,' he said, sitting down, placing the large envelope he was carrying on the table.

'Did everything go all right?' she asked, aware that he appeared more serious than was usual, not his smiling self.

'It's fine. My client has some concerns about a few things on the overall security plans, and we'll make a few adjustments. But it's not a problem. He's just a bit impatient I'm afraid, wants it done overnight.'

'Which is impossible?'

'You've got it. I'll straighten it out with him tomorrow.' He looked at her, put his hand over hers. 'Shall we have a glass of champagne before heading back?'

'Why not?' she murmured, staring at him, her eyes searching his face.

'What's wrong? What is it?' He frowned, puzzled.

'You seem suddenly troubled; your face is very grave. Is it business?'

'Not the kind you think.'

'What kind is it then?'

'The business between us.'

She did not respond. Michael signalled to the waiter, who came over at once. After ordering two glasses of pink champagne, he turned back to her, picked up her hand and kissed the palm, closed her fingers over it, and placed it on the table.

After a moment, he went on, 'I want to tell you something, Justine, and it's this . . . I'm free, not involved with anyone. Didn't Gabriele tell you I broke off with my fiancée almost five months ago?'

'No, she didn't.'

'I'm surprised, under the circumstances. They're very chatty, those two grans of ours. And what about you? Is Jean-Marc Breton still around in your life?'

'No, he's not, and he never was in my life, actually, Michael. We had a brief, and I do mean *very brief*, involvement last year. But it ended quickly. I just had to stop seeing him for my own good.'

He nodded. 'Why? Or don't you want to discuss it with me?'

'That's not a problem. I discovered I didn't like him, and I didn't want to be with him on a permanent basis. Will you tell me why you broke off your engagement?'

'Pretty much for the same reasons as you. One day I suddenly saw Vanessa as she truly was, and I realized we weren't right for each other, that it wouldn't work. We are poles apart.'

The waiter arrived with the champagne and placed it in front of them. Michael lifted his glass; Justine did the same. They clinked glasses, and he said, 'To you, Justine.'

'And to you, Michael.'

They sipped the champagne in silence for a moment or two, both of them lost in their thoughts. Justine suddenly remarked, 'I believe you're right about the doting grandmothers. When you were at your meeting a while ago, I remembered Gran asking me *twice* if I liked you.'

'And what did you say?' Michael now asked, a dark brow lifting.

'Yes, I told her. *Yes.*'

He glanced away, looked into the distance reflectively, a smile touching his mouth fleetingly. When he brought his gaze back to hers his face was solemn. Taking hold of her hand, he asked, 'And are you saying *yes* to me?'

'I am.'

'I want you to know I'm not playing games, Justine.'

'I realize that; I can tell from your demeanour, the expression in your eyes, and your intensity. And I'm not, either.'

'I'm happy about that, and it's good to know we understand each other.'

'I know we do, Michael.'

'I realize that some people would look at us askance, say we're crazy; on the other hand our two doting grandmothers are obviously our gallant supporters, and that pleases me. They're wise, long-lived, know all about life, its many vagaries. And I, like them, do believe in love at first sight, and I guess you do too.'

'It's not a fallacy,' she murmured. 'Although it's never happened to me before.'

'Nor to me,' Michael said. 'But it *is* wonderful to feel this way. Don't you think?'

Justine simply nodded, not trusting herself to speak. She was shaking inside, unnerved by him once more.

He said swiftly, taking hold of her hand, 'Don't look so worried. I'm not a lightweight – also I'm almost thirty-nine years old, and I've seen a lot, been around the block, and I know what I'm doing. Okay?'

'Okay,' she repeated, at a loss for words. She had never known a man who was so honest, so outspoken about his feelings, and this pleased her. Suddenly, without reserve, she trusted him.

TWENTY-THREE

S itting back, Justine stared at herself in the mirror and was pleased with the way she looked. She did not usually make this kind of effort with cosmetics. Now she smiled, knowing *why* she had used eyeliner, pale blue eye shadow, mascara and blusher. *For Michael.* Being a pale blonde, she could so easily look faded, and tonight she wanted him to see her at her best.

Rising, Justine went to the clothes closet and took out a pair of black silk trousers, then put them on. She pulled the tunic over her head, and stepped into a pair of sandals that her grandmother had lent her. Then she left the room, walked down the corridor to see her.

As a child, she had always gone to her gran for an inspection, once she was dressed, and she was automatically doing it tonight. This made her feel suddenly happy, because Gabriele was in her life again, and an old ritual was unexpectedly back in place. It brought back memories.

Tapping on her bedroom door, she opened it and said, 'Can I come in, Gran?'

'Of course,' Gabriele answered, and swung around as Justine walked in and closed the door behind her.

'I've come for an inspection.'

For a moment, Gabriele couldn't speak; her throat was tight with emotion. How lovely her granddaughter looked tonight. She had swept her blonde hair into a chignon and paid attention to her make-up. Justine stood there smiling at her, so tall and elegant; she was proud of her, and what she had become as a woman.

'You're not saying anything to me,' Justine murmured, wondering if she had overdone the make-up.

'Because I'm rendered speechless, that's why. You are beautiful, Justine.' Walking over to a chest, Gabriele picked up a black velvet box and gave it to her. 'I was about to come to your room. I wanted you to have these. Trent gave them to me many years ago, and they were always meant to come to you one day. They match the colour of your eyes.'

Justine stared at her grandmother, opened the box and gasped. On the white satin were a pair of square-cut aquamarine earrings surrounded by tiny diamonds. 'Gran, they're just beautiful!' she exclaimed, stepping closer and kissing her. 'Thank you so much, I'll treasure them always.'

'Trent used to say aquamarines were specially created for blue-eyed women, you know.'

Justine put them on and turned to face her grandmother. 'They're perfect, don't you think?'

'I do, darling. When you go downstairs you'll knock 'em all dead. Although I'm sure it's only Michael you want to impress. I'm right, aren't I? You *have* fallen under his spell, haven't you?'

'Yes, I have,' Justine admitted. 'And the feeling's mutual. Obviously you and Anita have spotted our attraction to each other.'

'Attraction!' Gabriele gave her a strange look. 'What a mild word to use to describe what's been going on between the two of you. I prefer to call it struck by lightning.'

'Is it so apparent?' Justine's gaze was fixed on her grandmother.

'To *us*, yes. He can't take his eyes off you, and you're suffering from the same affliction. You appear to be mesmerized by one another. Dazed. Or perhaps I should say *dazzled*.'

'I've only known him two days, and yet I miss him when he's not with me. It's so strange, Gran, but I feel as if I've known Michael forever.'

'Not so weird, darling. You can be with a man for twenty years and never know who he truly is. Then again, you can meet a man and know everything about him in an instant. I have no worries about you with Michael. There's no one quite like him.'

'I realize that.'

Gabriele said, 'I trust him absolutely.'

'My coming to find you has changed my life.'

'And mine and Michael's and Anita's.' Gabriele studied Justine for a moment, loving her so much. Then she added, 'And it's all for the good.'

'I'm hoping Richard's life will change too.'

Gabriele looked at her alertly. 'What do you mean?' she asked, sounding baffled.

'Because I'm away, here with you in Istanbul, Joanne is taking over for me, keeping an eye on Daisy and Richard. Especially on Richard. She's been in love with him for years, and I'm hoping something special develops between them while I'm gone.'

'That would be quite wonderful, darling, and he does need a woman in his life. It can't be easy for him.' Walking across the room, Gabriele took off her robe and reached for the caftan. 'I'd better hurry now, finish getting dressed. Please go down and keep Anita company, Justine. Tell her I won't be long.'

It was a lovely evening.

The sky had already darkened, a galaxy of brilliant stars were littered across its arc, and there was a silver-disc of a moon floating over the Bosphorus, as usual.

Justine moved through the garden slowly, saw at once how magical it had become. Decorative Chinese lanterns were strung between the trees and flowering bushes were swaying gently in the faint breeze, and everywhere there were votive candles flickering in small glass holders, encircling tree trunks and lining pathways. A mixture of flowers plus scented candles mingled and filled the air with a heady fragrance.

She glanced about, looking for Anita, and discovered she was alone. There was no one in sight except for a trio of musicians, and the waiters hired for the evening. Then she heard his step as he strode across the terrace, looking around as she had done a moment before. He was dressed in a long-sleeved black silk shirt and matching black trousers, and there was a confident air about him, as there usually was.

She stepped forward, gliding from the garden onto the terrace, and he saw her immediately, stopped dead in his tracks. He stood staring at her, his expression a mixture of surprise and admiration.

Justine continued walking until she stood in front of him. 'You look great, Michael,' she said, smiling up into his face, and wondered if he could hear her clattering heart. She hoped not.

'And you take my breath away,' he answered. 'In fact you look so perfect I'm afraid to come anywhere near you, for fear of mussing you up.'

Nevertheless, as he said this Michael took a step closer, drew her towards him and kissed her lightly on the lips. 'Still far too chaste, that kiss. Well, we'll deal with that later, rectify it.'

'I hope so,' she answered in a low voice.

Michael took hold of her hand, led her to the bar at the end of the terrace, asked a waiter for two glasses of champagne. Suddenly there was the sound of music filling the air, as the trio began to play. A moment later they saw his grandmother heading in their direction, her red silk caftan swirling around her as she stepped out briskly.

Michael whispered, 'I made sure I'm sitting next to you at dinner,' and clinked his glass to hers. 'And Iffet's with us.'

'I'm glad,' she replied. Moving forward, she gave Anita a kiss and exclaimed, 'You look fabulous! You should always wear red.'

'I mostly do.' Anita gazed at Justine and continued, with a hint of awe in her voice, 'You look incredible. You're truly beautiful. Isn't she, Michael?'

'My glamorous, gorgeous girl,' he answered, putting his arm around Justine's waist, drawing her closer to him.

'*Yours?*' Anita said with quiet emphasis, peering hard at him. 'Is that actually true? Or just a figure of speech?'

'Ask her,' he responded, glancing at Justine, his dark eyes dancing mischievously.

'I am,' Justine replied in a steady voice, even though she was shaking inside. Or was it heart palpitations? He had such an enormous effect on her when they were standing as close as this that she was thrown off balance.

'That was fast.' Anita looked at them carefully. 'But fast is best. That's the way it was for Max and me. We took one look at each other, and that was it. Your grandfather was the love of my life, Michael, as I was of his. We were happy until the day he died.' A little sigh escaped her, and now, glancing around, she asked, 'Where's Gabri?'

'She'll be here in a few minutes, Anita. I went to see her before coming down and we started chatting. It delayed her.' Justine touched an earring. 'She gave me these. Aren't they beautiful?'

'Yes, I can remember the day she got them, a gift from Trent to match her eyes.'

'Yes, she told me.'

Michael exclaimed, 'Here's Aunt Gabri now, coming across the garden. I'll go and escort her over.'

Turning to Justine, Anita said in a confiding tone, 'If he says you're his girl in front of me then he really means it. And by the way, I've never seen him behave like this. I think he's serious. I assume you are too?'

'Yes, I am, Anita.'

'That makes me happy, and just know that he'll never betray you, that's the way he's made.' She took hold of Justine's hand and squeezed, held onto it. 'You're made for each other. I told your grandmother I saw it yesterday – love at first sight; it was written all over your faces.'

'It's never happened to me before.'

'It only occurs once in a lifetime. You can take my word for it. And I don't think it's happened to Michael before either.'

'I believe you,' Justine replied.

Michael brought Gabriele over to them, and hurried off, after explaining that he was going to get a glass of champagne for her.

'You look stunning, Grandma,' Justine said. 'What an unusual colour your caftan is.' Admiration echoed in her voice.

'It's supposed to be burgundy, but it's got a hint of aubergine,' Gabriele replied. 'I thought it was unique, though. I'm sure something went wrong in the dyeing process; however, *I* like it.'

Michael was back with the champagne and he gave the glass to Gabriele. Looking at each of them, smiling broadly, he declared, 'Surrounded as I am by three beautiful women I feel like a happy man with his own harem. Very spoiled.'

'You are,' his grandmother shot back, winking at him. 'And we all love you to death.'

'It's mutual,' he said, then added, 'Oh, I see Iffet on the jetty, and Daphne and Paul Leyland have just arrived too, along with the Drapers, Grandma.'

'Gabri and I must go and greet them,' Anita announced. Taking hold of Gabriele's hand, she continued, 'Obviously every-one's decided to come by boat tonight. Look how crowded our jetty's becoming.'

The moment they were alone, Michael kissed Justine on her

cheek. He murmured, 'After the meeting with my client tomorrow, let's go off and have lunch, just the two of us.'

'I feel funny about leaving Gran when I've only just found her again, Michael,' Justine responded, although she longed for them to be alone, just as he did.

'I understand, but unless they've cancelled it, they usually go to lunch with Anita's great-nephew, Ken. He's taken over from his father, and he's their business partner. But you're right, I guess we'd better play this one by ear.'

'Let's do that, decide tomorrow.'

'We might just have to go with them to the lunch,' Michael said, throwing her a knowing look, making a face.

'As long as I'm with you,' she answered, laughing.

'Try and get rid of me,' he answered, and turning her around, he went on, 'Look, there's Iffet coming through the garden. Very chic in a midnight-blue dress.'

A moment later Justine and Iffet were hugging, and then admiring each other's outfits.

Michael excused himself, muttering that he had to get the waiters moving around the garden with trays of drinks.

The two women stood chatting about the documentary, and Justine said, 'By the way, the FedEx envelope from Richard came today, and I can now start working on the advertisement, get things rolling.'

'That's wonderful. Let me know how I can help. Are you bringing Eddie Grange over to Istanbul?'

'I might, Iffet, I'm not sure. I have to get my sequences worked out, plus a storyline developed, but Eddie could be useful, actually. Certainly he could get more stock footage. I'll give him a call on Monday.'

A few minutes later, Michael was back by their side, bringing with him a man called David Grainger, an English novelist, and his friend, Catherine de Bourgeville, a dress designer from Paris.

One of the waiters suddenly appeared, carrying a tray of assorted drinks. Iffet took a glass of sparkling water, David and Catherine white wine; within minutes they were all chatting, finding much in common to talk about.

Michael positioned himself slightly away from the group, watching intently, noticing how at ease Justine was with everyone. She was being gracious and charming.

His phone began to ring, and Michael pulled it out of his pocket, stepped farther away from the group. 'Hello?'

'Good evening, Michael. It's Charlie. Am I phoning at an awkward hour? It must be nine o'clock there.'

'It's okay. My grandmother's giving a little dinner party, and the guests are just beginning to arrive. Are you all right? Is there something wrong? At the bank?'

'Not exactly – however I do need to talk with you. In person. Not on the phone. When exactly are you planning to come to London?'

'To tell you the truth, I was trying to put it off until Thursday. I have to be in Paris on Wednesday morning for a meeting. I intended to stay in Istanbul until Tuesday afternoon, when I was going to fly to Paris.'

'Can you come here for a meeting with me on Monday, Michael?'

'Of course. I'll change things around here. Charlie, listen to me, you don't sound like yourself. What's the matter? *Is* it something to do with the bank?'

'It's more of a personal problem, Michael. I need your advice. You're the only person I can trust to give me the right answers. I also trust *you*. And your discretion and confidentiality. Sorry to call at this hour, but to be honest I've been struggling with the problem all day.'

'Don't worry about the time, you can phone me whenever you wish. Listen, I can call you back later if you like, for a longer chat.'

'No, I can't, I'm afraid. Dinner plans looming. How about tomorrow morning?'

'I do have a meeting with a client at eleven, Istanbul time. So we can speak before ten, which is when I'll go over to meet him. I shouldn't be much longer than an hour. Then I'm reachable on my cell phone.'

'Shall we speak at nine? Your time, of course.'

'Perfect. Goodnight, Charlie, have a nice evening.'

'And you too, Michael. Thanks again. Oh, and I'll have my private plane waiting for you at Istanbul Airport early Monday morning. That way it makes things easier for you. We can meet in the afternoon.'

'That would be a great help, thanks, Charlie.' They both clicked off, and Michael couldn't help wondering what this was all about. Intuitively, and with nothing to go on but his gut instinct, he knew something was terribly wrong. Charlie was going to give him bad news. He suddenly realized he was already bracing himself for it.

Trying to shake off this feeling of apprehension, Michael walked back to the group where Justine and Iffet were standing together, and joined in the conversation. He was clever at disguising his feelings, displayed no emotion whatsoever. He kept the smile anchored on his face, spoke animatedly to them all, being the charming and welcoming host, as he always was when his grandmother entertained.

But he felt as if he had a lump of lead sitting in the middle of his stomach. Worry edged around the back of his mind. He had learned when he was in the Secret Service never to ignore his forebodings. Nor could he now.

After everyone had found their place-marked seats at the two tables on the terrace, Anita, Gabriele and Michael ushered their guests into the dining room where the buffet had been set up. Elaborate flower arrangements, silver bowls of exotic fruit, and white tapering candles in silver candlesticks created a stunning effect on the table, which was covered in a crisp white-linen cloth.

All of the many dishes were elegantly presented. They were the usual Turkish mezes, starters such as *börekas*, dolmas, *lakerda* – salted tuna from the Black Sea – many different fishes cooked in numerous ways, shellfish of every kind and grilled meats. Interspersed between these were large bowls of pasta, rice and vegetables, as well as baskets of local breads.

On a trolley nearby was a whole roast lamb, and it was there that Mehmet stood, waiting to carve, looking very professional in his chef's outfit and his tall white toque on his head. There was a huge smile on his face as he nodded to those guests he knew.

Waiters helped the guests, served them the mezes first, and offered breads and biscuits. Raki was served with the mezes and the fish, and there were white and red wines, fruit juices and water.

Everybody agreed it was the grandest of feasts. The trio continued to play in the background, and the guests chatted happily with each other, laughing and joking. The party was deemed a big success by Michael, who was watching everything carefully, with an eagle eye.

He was sitting between Iffet and Justine, and fully conscious of the latter at all times. He was also attentive to Iffet, whom he had grown to like over the last few hours. He understood why Justine found her so compatible and charming; she was also an intelligent woman with whom he could have a grown-up conversation.

But what pleased him the most was being close to Justine. The idea of going to London and Paris now dismayed him because he didn't want to leave her. Under normal circumstances he would have taken her with him. But that was not possible; she needed to be with her grandmother, and he understood perfectly why this was so.

Looking across the table at Gabriele, he felt an enormous sense of relief. He had never seen her looking better, and she was obviously filled with joy tonight. He also noticed that when she glanced at Justine there was pride as well as love in her eyes. It seemed to him that her heartache was at last assuaged.

Twenty-Four

It was one o'clock in the morning when Michael and Justine were finally alone. The guests had left, the help had finished their work and disappeared, and Anita and Gabriele had gone to bed.

Now they were sitting on the seat overlooking the Bosphorus, relieved to be by themselves at last. They sat in silence, enjoying the peacefulness of the garden after the busy and hectic dinner party. Everyone had enjoyed it, and been delighted to meet Gabriele's granddaughter, and Gabriele had been as proud as she'd ever been. And so had Anita. Both women had glowed all night.

It was Justine who spoke first, when she said, 'Something's wrong, Michael, isn't it?'

'What makes you say that?' he asked swiftly, staring at her, taken aback by her astuteness and perception.

'Because I can *tell*. I knew during dinner that there was a problem.'

'I'm amazed how well you read me,' he murmured, still peering at her in the dusky evening light. 'I thought I was being cool, even nonchalant.'

'You were, to a certain extent. Nevertheless, I saw behind that façade of yours.'

'How? I'd love to know *how*, Justine?'

'There was something about the expression in your eyes. I saw apprehension flickering there, or perhaps it was worry.'

'You're very intuitive and observant, because I'm not that transparent. I've trained myself to keep a neutral face at all times. I learned to do that when I was a Secret Service agent.'

'You do, but I was looking at your *eyes*. Concern was reflected in them. And there's something else, I'm *involved* with you, and *conscious* of you at all times. And I know you without the benefit of time. My grandmother made a comment earlier tonight. She said a woman can know a man for twenty years and never know him at all, and then again, she can meet a man and know who he *really* is instantly.'

There was a pause before she added, 'When I met you, had only spent a few hours with you, I *knew* you, and what you are as a person. And naturally a man can experience exactly the same thing. That's what we're about, isn't it? You and me, Michael?'

'Of course it is. We recognized each other the moment we met. We knew we were meant for each other, and we both immediately understood we had found our soul-mate. I realized you were the woman I wanted to be with . . .' He stopped short, leaned back against the seat, staring out towards the sea, his eyes reflective. *Fate*. She might easily have arrived in Istanbul while he was back in New York. Or anywhere in the world. *Destiny*. It was their destiny to be together, wasn't it?

Justine waited patiently, knowing he would tell her what was troubling him eventually, and she relaxed. The only reason she wanted to know was to help him, if she could.

It was not very long before Michael said slowly, 'I had a call from one of my clients, when we were all having drinks in the garden earlier. He needs to see me urgently in London on Monday, instead of later next week. He wouldn't explain anything on the phone. To be honest, I got the feeling he had bad news to impart. About what I don't know.'

'So now you'll have to change your plans?'

'I will. I was trying to stay until Tuesday afternoon before leaving for Paris, and then going on to London on Thursday, but that just won't work now.'

'I understand,' she murmured, sounding disappointed.

He glanced at her. 'I did tell you I had to be away next week.' She said, 'That's true.'

Michael said, 'And you promised you'd wait for me to come back, if you remember?'

'I do. And I will, Michael. I've no intention of going back to New York at the moment. What about you? How long are you staying in Istanbul?'

'I'll be in Europe for a few weeks. I came over to meet with clients in various countries, and some will be very quick trips. I hope you can join me on a few. Maybe in a week or two you'll feel that you can leave Gabriele, come with me? I want that, I want us to be together as much as possible.'

'I'm sure I'll be able to do that. I think Gran will soon understand I'll always be there for her, whenever she needs me, and for the rest of her life.'

'Oh Justine, I think she knows that already! The whole story has been revealed, she knows the truth, realizes the estrangement had nothing to do with you and Richard. And look at the lengths you went in order to find her.'

'I guess you're right. I'm probably going to be around here anyway, making the documentary. I just need to go back to New York to see Miranda Evans. At CNI, the woman I work with at the network. I hope to make a deal with her. She's always been a big booster of mine – bought my first documentary about African blood diamonds.'

'If I'm not here, I'll be waiting for you in New York. Better still, we'll go back together.'

'You'd do that? Leave when I leave?'

'Of course. I won't let you out of my sight.'

'You're never going to shake *me*, Mr Dalton.'

'Thank God for that!'

They stared at each other for the longest moment. Then Michael made a swift move, drew her closer, kissed her on the forehead. A moment later they were kissing passionately, as they had longed to do since they first met. They were free of all restraint now, understanding each other the way they did.

Justine clung to him, wanting this as much as he did, and she returned his kisses with ardour. They were locked in each other's arms, oblivious to everything except themselves and their feelings for each other.

At last they drew apart, staring at each other, both of them slightly dazed by the impact they had on each other. He knew she was as aroused as he was, and he enfolded her in his arms and held her close. He could hear her heart thudding, as his own was, and he leaned into her and kissed her neck. They sat like this for a short while, knowing what the inevitable outcome was going to be.

He said softly, 'I want to make love to you, and I have since I met you. You feel the same, so don't deny it.'

'I wasn't going to.'

'We can't stay here like this,' he muttered. 'It *will* get out of hand soon and it's not very private here in the garden. It's also getting cooler, there's a wind blowing up.'

'We could go to your room. Or mine?' she suggested.

'I don't know . . . I guess I feel a bit awkward about that.' He sounded hesitant, which was not like him.

Suddenly she realized what was bothering him; wanted to laugh, it was so ludicrous. But she kept a straight face. 'They won't mind, the grans I mean,' she reassured him.

'I know they won't.'

Sitting up, turning to face him, Justine said, 'I think we're being silly, Michael. The grans would have a big laugh if they knew we were sitting out here like this, having a debate about *where* to make love when there are bedrooms in the *yalis*. They're itching for us to get together, for God's sake. Look, I'm thirty-two, going on thirty-three, and you'll soon be thirty-nine. We're grown-ups. So let's go and do what we want to do so very badly, which is make love to each other. Your room, or mine?'

Michael burst out laughing, jumped up and pulled her to her feet. That's what he loved about her, this honesty and directness; it was so fresh and appealing. 'Come on, let's go to yours. That way, if Gabriele comes looking for you, she'll find you where you should be . . . in your bed.'

'With you!' she exclaimed, grabbing his hand, running with him across the garden, both of them laughing, and mostly at themselves.

After slipping through the wisteria and Judas trees, they were in the little area between the two *yalis*. Justine opened Gran's door and went inside, and Michael was right behind her. There was a light on in the hall, and this illuminated the staircase. She went up first; Michael followed. She knew her grandmother was not asleep because, as she passed her room, she saw light shining out from underneath the door. So did he.

They tiptoed down the corridor, and went into Justine's bedroom. As soon as they were inside, Michael closed the door and leaned against it. He pulled Justine into his arms, kissing her deeply, overwhelmed by his feelings.

After a moment, Justine broke their embrace. She stepped over to the closet, took off the tunic and trousers and placed the earrings on the dressing table.

Michael stood watching her, then locked the door, walked towards her, unbuttoning his shirt as he did. They fell into each other's arms in a rush, kissing again. At the same time, Michael struggled out of his shirt as they both scrambled to undress.

A moment later they were stretched out next to each other on the bed. Michael pushed himself up on one elbow, looked down and touched her cheek gently. He kissed her, brought her close to him, held her tightly against his body. He said in a low voice, 'I never thought I could feel like this about someone.'

'How *do* you feel?' she asked quietly.

'*Undone*. Completely undone when I'm with you. And unnerved, and I'm usually completely in control of myself.'

'I feel exactly the same way.' Lifting a hand, she pulled all the pins out of the chignon so that her hair tumbled down over her bare shoulders.

To Michael, she was irresistible, and his hands were soon all over her, and hers were on him. Several times he sighed as she touched him, and when he opened his eyes and gazed at her his heart shifted inside him. He felt a sudden rush of the most intense feeling for her; it overwhelmed him.

Justine stared back at Michael, her expression one of yearning. He saw her desire for him written on her face, and it reflected his. He brought his mouth to hers, began to kiss her once more. Their tongues touched, slid together, and he was moved by the intimacy of this moment.

Unexpectedly, he suddenly released her, got off the bed, strode over to the dressing table, turned off the two lamps. Immediately the light in the room was softer, the moonlight streaming in through the windows filling it with a silver haze.

She watched him walking back to her and began to shake inside. Her excitement was growing; heat rushed through. Even her face felt flushed. It did not seem possible that this was finally happening, that they were together like this in her room. It was all so sudden, so new, and yet absolutely right. She ached for Michael. It was a new experience for her.

'That's better,' he murmured as he lay down next to her,

brought her back into his arms, stroking her face, her breasts, kissing them tenderly. Slowly he began to run his hands over her entire body, fired on by the silkiness of her skin under his hands, and his rampant desire for her.

He looked down at her. Her eyes were closed and he saw the rapture on her face. Her body was very hot now, and it grew hotter under his continuous touching and stroking.

Justine relaxed as Michael continued to explore her body, then she stiffened for a moment when his hand finally touched the core of her, gently at first, then more probing. Unexpectedly, she felt her body arching of its own accord, pushing up towards him; she wanted to be part of him in the most intimate way.

Her ardent response to him inflamed Michael. He slid on top of her, taking her by surprise, and she gasped when he took possession of her. He felt her arms go around his back. 'There,' he whispered against her cheek. 'I'm there at last where I've longed to be. Part of you.'

Within moments they found their own rhythm, were welded to each other, moved as one. Her passion soared with his; her fervour matched his. Now they were moving almost violently, clutching at each other, straining, soaring higher and higher. Ecstasy was sweeping through them both at the same time, but they went on moving, unable to stop, greedily wanting more and more of each other.

Michael finally slowed to a stop, fell against her body, sated; and she put her arms around him, held him close as if never to let him go.

TWENTY-FIVE

They lay together side by side, catching their breath, both of them lost in their own thoughts for a short while. The room was filled with the same silvery haze from the moonlight, and a wind rippled the curtains at the windows. All was peaceful.

Justine felt as if she was floating on air, enjoying a sense of the most lovely euphoria, and all because of this man stretched out on the bed next to her. Unexpectedly, tears came into her eyes, startling her. They slid out from under her lids, trickled down her cheeks, much to her surprise.

Michael turned on his side, reached for her, took her in his arms, and as his face touched hers he felt the dampness.

He pushed himself up. 'What's wrong, darling, why are you crying?' he asked, looking down at her.

'I don't know,' she said through her tears, smiling weakly. 'I suppose because I'm happy. I'm intensely emotional about you, Michael. I've never behaved like this with any other man before, and I'm sort of astonished at myself. I can't remember ever being so passionate or so abandoned. I feel euphoric. Happy. And perhaps that's why I was moved to tears. All to do with happiness and contentment.'

'I feel the same way, Justine. I shared your feelings of longing,' he remarked quietly. 'I fell hard for you, but you're aware of that.'

A small smile flickered around her mouth, and she said in a teasing tone, 'Oh, but *I* believe you were well and truly set up! By those plotting grandmothers of ours.'

'I don't think so, because they didn't know you were going to arrive when you did, floating up out of the Bosphorus like a beautiful mermaid, to quote Gabriele.'

'But Anita had written the letter and mailed it, and obviously she expected me to show up eventually.'

'I think she expected your mother.'

'I bet you Gran didn't, if she knew.'

'Maybe you're right.' He laughed, amused, and went on, 'No, I wasn't set up, sweetheart. But when you almost trampled me underfoot on the jetty and I ran after you, I said to myself, she's for me.'

'Did you really?'

'I did.'

His dark eyes were twinkling mischievously, when he said, 'There was a moment when you stared back at me quite boldly, and then quickly looked away. And you blushed. Dead giveaway.'

She merely smiled, continued to look at him closely, studying the planes of his face, the masculine cut of his jaw, the cleft in his chin, the brows arched above his warm brown eyes, which she now saw were filled with love for her.

How could this man be hers?

A week ago she hadn't even known him. She was filled with astonishment – about Michael, about the unexpectedness of life, this most extraordinary passion he had aroused in her . . . Sheer wonderment filled her with joy.

'What are you thinking about?' he asked, reaching into her thoughts.

'How handsome you are, and how lucky I am, and I still keep asking myself how this gorgeous man in my bed could be mine?'

'Oh, but he is, and then some, and don't you forget it, kid.' He grinned as he said that, then went on in a more serious tone, 'In fact, this man has never been anyone else's before you.'

'But you *were* engaged.' She gave him a puzzled look, frowned.

'That's true, and it was a commitment I took seriously, until I came to understand that the relationship didn't work for me. I knew it would never work. There wasn't even a relationship, if I'm being truthful, just sex. I began to understand that I was withholding part of myself from her. And I've got to tell you, this has become even more apparent in the last couple of days. Since I met you, actually.'

'Why is it different with me?'

'There are no barriers between us, for one thing. I can be myself, be who I am. Also, I trust you, I feel safe with you. I know that's a funny word to use. I think what I mean is that I feel *secure* with you. Because you're loyal, trustworthy; you'll never betray me.'

'And I know you'll be there for me.' Justine reached out, touched his face, 'Anita said to me, "My boy's true blue," and Gabriele said you'd never betray me, and they should know.'

'They're a hoot, those two. I often call them the Gold Dust Twins, and it tickles them to death, makes them laugh.'

'It would, and they're devoted to you. I want to thank you again for looking after Gran these last ten years. I know how much you did for her. I'm grateful you were here sometimes and made her feel less lonely, and that you were so caring, Michael.'

'I always will be. My God, I wouldn't even be here on this planet if it weren't for Aunt Gabri.'

'What do you mean?'

'She saved Anita's life when they were young girls, around fourteen. Every single member of our family loves her for that, as well as for what she is as a human being.'

Justine was gaping at him. She said in a baffled tone, 'How did she save Anita's life? What happened?'

Michael realized his mistake at once. He had made a blunder. Obviously, Justine knew nothing about Gabriele's terrible past, of Anita's fractured early life either.

He noticed the avid curiosity on her face, and he said swiftly, almost dismissively, 'Oh look, Justine, it's Anita's story.' He smiled, adopted a more casual manner, and in a lower voice, murmured, 'I think you should ask Anita yourself. Anyway, she's expecting you to interview her about her life in Istanbul later this week. For the documentary. And she'll tell you all about it then.'

'Perhaps I'd better ask Gran.'

'I wouldn't do that if I were you, darling. Gabriele is shy, doesn't ever want to talk about it, prefers not to rehash it. There's a lot of humility in her, despite all that she is as a woman, and her success in business. She can't stand what she calls boasters and blowhards.'

'How like Gran to be so modest,' Justine replied.

'It is, yes.' He moved closer to her, began to kiss her, and within seconds he was aroused and so was she. They began to make love again, in a quieter and more tender way, and soon they were lost to the world, enraptured with each other.

PART FIVE

The Mystery

The Angel of Death has been abroad throughout the land;
you may almost hear the beating of his wings.

John Bright, House of Commons speech,
23 February 1855

Behold a pale horse; and his name that sat on him was
Death, and Hell followed with him.

Revelation 5: 1

TWENTY-SIX

Gabriele was, by nature, an early riser, and on this bright sunny Monday morning in the middle of May she was up and about at five thirty, had eaten a small breakfast by six, and had done an hour's work in her studio by seven.

Now, as she walked along the wide path in the tulip gardens, which flowed from her property onto Anita's, she felt suddenly uplifted by the sight: hundreds of brilliantly coloured flowers, tall, stately, standing like proud sentinels in the sunlight, the mass of brilliant colour taking her breath away.

She moved slowly, gazing at the different specimens, remembering some of their names, although not all, and at last she was standing in front of her favourite, the snow-white tulip with its petals 'feathered' and 'flamed' in deep burgundy. Unique, utterly unique, she thought. Moving down the path, she came to a large patch of yellow flowers, their petals 'feathered' in brilliant red. The 'broken' tulips, as they were called, were her all-time favourites, although she loved every kind, even the plain, solid-colour tulips. Standing back, continuing to gaze at them, she could not help thinking what a sight they were, something truly beautiful to feast the eyes on.

She sighed under her breath, remembering all the years she and Trent had worked on the gardens. It had been a long, tiring task, but they had enjoyed every moment of their labours; how proud Trent had been when their gardens had won acclaim from everyone who visited them.

As she continued to move around the different paths, taking the pictures she needed to create new designs for her fabric line, she was unaware that Michael was standing at the far end of the lawn, observing her.

His heart melted when he saw Gabriele in these gardens. He had watched her working on them for as long as he could remember, since his childhood, and now a rush of memories flooded him. She was part of his younger days, just as she had been part of Justine's, and that was yet another bond between the two of them. She had influenced both of them in her own way.

Whenever he thought of Gabri, whether he was in New York or London, or anywhere else, he pictured her in these gardens, perhaps because they were such a huge part of her life.

Once, long ago, when he had congratulated her on the beautiful effects she had created with the mass of tulips, she had nodded and said in a low voice, 'I have a compulsion to make beautiful things, perhaps because I've seen far too much ugliness and brutality in my life.'

He had made no comment at the time, but he had never forgotten her words. There had been moments when he had longed to penetrate the mystery that surrounded her; know something, however small, about her past; have her confide the secrets of her other life which were stored inside her. But he had never had the nerve to ask her anything. And whatever Anita knew was buried deep, locked up forever in his grandmother's heart, never to be disclosed.

Michael stepped out onto the pebbled path, and the crunch of his shoes made Gabriele swing her head around.

Her face lit up when she saw him, and she could not help thinking how marvellous he looked this morning. As usual, he was dressed in a pristine white shirt, no tie, dark grey slacks and black blazer. It was his uniform, but he always looked so fresh and boyish in these clothes. They were casual but also businesslike to a certain extent.

Michael had the height and strong masculine build of his grandfather, Maxwell Lowe, but there was a lot of his father, Larry Dalton, in his handsome, chiselled face. And it was to his grandmother Anita that he owed his dark-brown, sparkling eyes, usually full of humour and warmth, as were hers.

A moment later, Michael was hugging Gabriele, saying good morning, and then following the direction of her gaze as she moved her head slightly to stare at the gardens again. 'Just doing my morning check,' she murmured, turning back to him, looking up into his face, smiling.

'They're gorgeous, Gabri!' he exclaimed, admiration echoing in his voice. 'And although I've said it before, I've got to reiterate it again: I've never seen tulips like this anywhere in the world.'

'I agree, they're fantastic. But you must remember, here they are in their natural habitat – they're a Turkish flower, born and bred.' She broke into sudden laughter as she said this, adding, 'I sound as if I'm talking about children, don't I? It's true that they grow happily here on the shores of the Bosphorus, though, and actually *I* believe they flourish so well because they are Asian in origin, have grown in this area for centuries.'

'I love the pure white with the burgundy flames on the petals – they're so unique.'

'My favourite too, and the best I've seen in a long time, this particular lot. Of course, it's the luck of the draw. When you buy a bulb you're not sure what you're going to get.' A sudden smile illuminated her face. 'And to think it's a *virus* that causes the "feathering" and the "flaming" on the petals. For hundreds of years botanists and gardeners tried to discover the secret of the "broken" tulip, experimented in every possible way with bulbs. Yet the truth wasn't discovered until the late 1920s in England.'

'I remember you telling me about the virus when I was about fourteen, and I was really astonished and also fascinated. I'll never forget how stunned I was that the virus was caused by the peach-potato aphid invading the bulbs.' Michael shook his head. 'I was flabbergasted.'

'Yes, you were, especially when I told you they feed by sucking sap from plants and fruit trees, soft-bodied little insects that generally live in fruit orchards. But you didn't come here for a refresher course on botany . . . I suspect you came to say goodbye.'

'I did. I'm flying to London this morning, and before I leave there's something I want to tell you, Aunt Gabri, and also ask you.'

Linking her arm through his, she walked with him down the path. 'You know you can talk to me about anything, Michael.'

He came to a sudden halt, and so did she. Turning to face her, he announced, 'I've fallen for Justine. I feel very strongly about her.'

Gabriele stared back at him. 'I'd guessed as much, Michael.'

'I'm serious about her. And she is about me.'

'You're both in your thirties, you know what you're doing.' An amused look settled on her face.

He smiled then, his dark eyes sparkling. 'So you approve?'

'I do.'

He hugged her to him, and was about to tell her how he had made a blunder last night, but instantly changed his mind, just stood holding her for a moment longer.

Drawing apart finally, they walked together across the lawn to her terrace. Giving her a kiss on her forehead, he offered her his famously cheeky smile. 'See you at the weekend.' He swung around and went towards his grandmother's *yali*.

'Fly safely,' she called after him.

Looking over his shoulder, he blew her a kiss and pushed his way through the wisteria and Judas trees that concealed the little courtyard between the two villas.

Anita was sitting upstairs on the terrace adjoining her bedroom, and she glanced at her grandson as he came outside to join her. 'So there you are, darling,' she said, her love for him illuminating her face. She had been lucky with this grandson of hers. He was what Gabriele called true blue. 'I was waiting for you. Do you have time for a cup of coffee?'

'I sure do, Grandma.' He sat down next to her on the sofa and she poured the coffee, handed it to him.

'There's something I need to tell you. To warn you about, Anita,' Michael said.

Peering at him, she frowned. 'You sound very grave. What's this about, Michael?'

'I made a blunder last night, or rather, in the early hours of this morning, and I'm very sorry. I told Justine her grandmother saved your life.'

'Oh Michael, no! Oh no, you didn't!' Dismay flooded her face and she shook her head. Without meaning to, he had opened Pandora's box.

'I did, I'm afraid. It just slipped out, and it was an error, I knew that the minute I said it. Naturally she was intrigued, curious. I brushed it off immediately, explained I couldn't discuss it, because it was your story, not mine. I told her she should ask you. And I only did that because she announced she would talk to Gabriele about it. I had to stop *that*, Grandma.'

'You certainly did. How did you manage to do so?'

'I told her that Gabri didn't like to discuss it; that she was not the type to sing her own praises. Justine agreed not to ask

237

her, but for sure she's going to ask *you*. She'll bring it up when she does the interview for the documentary. So be prepared.'

'I see.' There was a moment's pause, then Anita asked, 'Have you told Gabri?'

'No, I haven't. That was my intention, but I just didn't have the heart.'

'I understand.' Anita realized that it was an unfortunate mistake on his part, but she couldn't really blame him for a slip of the tongue. However, she was certain that Justine would be extremely probing, asking questions that were difficult to answer. She had been a journalist, was curious by nature; the instinct was, more than likely, still there.

'Will you warn Gabri for me, Grandma? Look, Justine knows nothing about Gabri's past life, I'm certain of that, and neither do I for that matter.' He gave her a hard stare.

Anita sat back on the sofa, looking off into space, her expression one of sadness as she thought about Gabriele, her very dearest friend, whose past was actually as mysterious to her as it was to everyone else. In certain ways, Gabriele was something of an enigma.

Michael waited, drank his coffee and thought about his maternal grandmother. When he was back home in New York, or travelling the world doing his work, she often popped into his head unexpectedly, somewhat in the same way Gabriele did at times.

The image in his mind's eye was of the buoyant, vivacious woman he had had so much fun with over the years growing up in New York and here in Istanbul. Anita, the businesswoman, the famous hostess, full of energy and goodwill; everyone's special favourite, who usually wore every shade of red in preference to any other colours. He had never met anyone who enjoyed life more, gave so much of herself to her friends and family, and whose love was unconditional.

Interrupting these thoughts, Anita finally said to Michael, 'I'll alert Gabri to the situation, but she won't talk about saving my life to Justine. Or confide anything else about her distant past. She never has to me, you know.'

Anita shook her head, and continued, 'She never told me what happened to her during those years we were apart, after I'd come here to live. She *did* save my life in an act of enormous courage, and I have never forgotten that, nor has she, and we are truly bonded. And yet she has never once shared her secrets, and she has hardly mentioned those long-ago years.'

'I find that odd, Grandma, in view of your extraordinary friendship . . . you were kids together.'

'I genuinely believe she can't talk about those *lost years*, as I call them. Once, way back when, she told me she had buried the past so deep she couldn't dredge it up. In my opinion, she doesn't *want* to remember, if I'm honest with you.'

'And she never told you *anything*? Nothing at all?'

'A few little things, but her past is in her own keeping . . . She's never given me any details of those missing years, and I know for a fact that she never confided in Trent.'

Leaning closer to her grandson, Anita went on to explain, 'I'm convinced she's never spoken to anyone other than me. I probably know the most, which is really nothing at all, if the truth be known – a few comments, one small confidence that I promised never to disclose. That's all she's ever given me.'

He was still astonished by this, but he noticed the sorrow in his grandmother's eyes, and he decided to cut this conversation and move on. It served no purpose to continue discussing Gabri's past.

He exclaimed, 'Come on, Anita, let's put all this to one side. Let's be happy that Justine and I met and fell in love . . . it's what *you* wanted, isn't it?' He grinned and put his arm around her. 'Guess what? Justine believes you set me up.'

On hearing this, Anita couldn't help laughing. It wasn't exactly true, but there was no doubt that the moment she had seen

Justine she had known Gabri's lovely granddaughter was the perfect woman for him, the right woman.

Eventually managing to suppress her chuckles, she remarked: 'Justine is a very clever girl. She picked up on the conspiratorial looks I exchanged with Gabri. And you're right, it's wonderful news that you fell head over heels in love. You two are just like your grandfather and me. We met, fell into each other's arms that night, were in the same bed the next night, got engaged a week later, were married a month after that. We were the happiest couple I know, which is often the case with love at first sight. It seems to last forever.'

A few minutes later Michael found Justine in Gabri's small library, which opened off the living room. She looked up as he walked in. 'Are you about to leave?'

'I am. And I've changed my mind; you can come with me if you want, at least as far as the Çiragan Palace. There's a load of traffic on the bridge, according to Kuri. So he called the hotel, booked a car and driver to take me to Atatürk Airport. He'll bring you back after he's dropped me at the hotel. How about that? Feel like a quick boat ride?'

She laughed. 'I'd love it.' Standing up, she walked over to him, and he immediately pulled her into his arms, held her close.

He whispered against her hair, 'I love you, Justine.'

'And I love you too, Michael. I'm going to miss you terribly.'

'I'll call you every day, I promise,' he said.

TWENTY-SEVEN

Anita and Gabriele saw them off at the jetty, waving to them until the boat was in the middle of the Bosphorus. Only then did the two women turn away and walk back into the gardens.

Anita said, 'Let's go and sit on the seat for a few minutes, Gabri. I need to talk to you about something important.'

Gabriele nodded. 'Why not? It's a lovely place to relax on a superb morning like this.'

Once they were settled on the garden seat, Anita said, 'I need to explain a situation that's developed.'

Gabriele turned to look at her, and frowned, bafflement reflected on her face. 'You sound serious, Anita, is there a problem?' She scrutinized her friend alertly.

'I think so.' Anita shook her head, worry clouding her eyes. 'Michael came to see me this morning. He said he made a blunder earlier. He told Justine you saved my life when we were young girls.'

Gabriele was silent; her heart sank. She said slowly, carefully, 'Knowing Michael, it was an honest slip of the tongue.'

'That's right, he meant no harm, Gabri. Apparently, Justine

was so surprised and intrigued he realized she hadn't known this before. He grew alarmed because Justine became overly curious.'

There was a moment of silence, then Gabriele murmured, 'She was always inquisitive, hence her desire to become a journalist.'

Anita explained, 'According to Michael, she began to ask a lot of questions, and he told her that it was my story, that she should speak to me if she wanted to know more. He suggested this because she told him she wanted to talk to you about it. He was trying to divert her.'

'I see.' Gabriele bit her lip, wondering how to handle this unexpected situation, which presented a number of problems.

Recognizing this was troublesome to Gabriele, Anita took hold of her hand and squeezed it. 'I'll say anything you want. What shall I tell her? I *will* have to address it.'

'Yes, you will. We'd better stick to the truth: it's always the best in the long run. She knows we grew up together. So you can just say it happened during the Second World War, and leave it at that.'

Anita was not sure it would work, and she was dreading talking to Justine. The latter was a clever young woman, brilliant in certain ways, and extremely perceptive. Very much like her grandmother. Clearing her throat, Anita asked, 'Shall I say I was in a dangerous situation?'

'No, don't say that if you can avoid it. Just bring the conversation to an end.'

'What if she keeps pressing me?' Anita asked, her concern echoing.

'She might do that, yes. So if she does, tell her the truth. That a short while after I'd helped you, your brother took you to Turkey, because your mother was there with her sister. And that she wanted you both with her.'

Anita nodded, let out a long sigh. 'You know as well as I do that one question will simply lead to another – it inevitably does.'

'If that happens then you have no alternative but to tell her to come and talk to me,' Gabriele said firmly, in a steady voice.

Anita was startled by this remark, and she gaped at Gabriele. Her surprise was apparent in her voice when she exclaimed, 'But you've never spoken about those years with anyone, not even me . . .' Anita shook her head. 'You're not able to do that, Gabri.'

There was no response from Gabriele. She leaned back on the garden seat and closed her eyes, her mind racing. Her body was suddenly as rigid as stone, her face a mask; inside she was floundering, at a loss, not knowing what to do.

Anita, who knew her better than anyone, understood what was going on in her mind. Gabriele was seeking a way to tell her granddaughter something about her past, without creating needless pain for herself. Anita had fretted about her for years, had long accepted that Gabriele's sorrow ran deep, that she had no desire to dredge up memories which would only cause more suffering. Their one little discussion about the lost years, as Anita called them, had been in the late 1940s, after the end of the war when travel had become easier. And ever since then there had not been much else said. Until now.

With a sudden movement, Gabriele sat up and turned to Anita, gazing with intensity at her devoted friend. 'I will try to confide a few things in order to satisfy Justine. But as you're well aware, I am not able to dig very deep.'

'That will be good, Gabri.' Anita's eyes narrowed as she returned her friend's long stare and realized how pale she was. She also noticed the apprehension in Gabriele's blue eyes, decided to change the subject.

Anita remarked, in a casual way, 'I think Justine will want to do the interview with me today, for the documentary. And I shall.' Anita paused, before murmuring softly, 'But the other

243

matter might come up, you know.' There was a note of warning in her voice.

'I am prepared for that now,' Gabriele answered swiftly. 'There's something else we should discuss. We're supposed to go to Bodrum tomorrow, to visit the Malkins, talk about finishing their house by June. We can't put it off, we must go. If necessary, we can take Justine with us.'

'You're right, and we have to get the project out of the way. I have a feeling the Malkins want to move in as soon as possible.' She then thought of Justine. A sense of dismay trickled through her once more, a shadow crossing her face. She wished to God her grandson had been more careful. It was not like him to make such a blunder; on the other hand, he had not understood the ramifications.

Gabriele spent the remainder of the morning sitting at her desk in a corner of her bedroom. It was quiet upstairs, and she had total privacy. Far away from the many and varied activities downstairs, early morning cleaning, flower arranging, and preparations for lunch, she was also removed from the fussing of Ayce and Suna, the two young women who looked after her and the *yali*. They were caring and devoted, but had developed a tendency to mother her, which both amused and touched her. Yet there were times when she needed to be alone, to sort through her myriad thoughts.

Up here in her spacious room overlooking the Bosphorus she could relax and think. She had a clear and analytical mind, and her mental capacities had not been diminished by the passing years.

Now she settled on Justine. She was well aware her granddaughter's inquisitiveness was based on nothing more than a need to know about her younger days because of Justine's love and pride in her. The child she had helped to bring up had always tried to emulate her, and had worked hard at school to please her, and there was a special bond between them.

Tony, Justine's father, had often laughed and said, 'Justine wants to know the backend of everything,' and she knew this was true. There had never been any hidden reason for the girl's constant questions, just that enormous curiosity about everything.

Gabriele sat for a long time staring into space, letting her thoughts drift, remembering things about Trent, her auntie Beryl and uncle Jock, and their times together. Beryl had been a conduit to her past; her mother had been Beryl's sister, and she loved to talk about her beloved Stella. And uncle Jock had been like a father to her.

Her mind went on turning and turning. Then quite unexpectedly the solution to her problem came to her. It made her sit up straighter in the chair with a jolt. She experienced a sudden clarity of vision so acute she knew exactly what she must do. She had the solution. Excitement swept through her.

Pushing herself to her feet, she hurried down the stairs, intent on talking to Anita. Almost running through the small sheltered courtyard to the other *yali*, she felt as if a great weight had been lifted from her shoulders.

TWENTY-EIGHT

Anita was sitting on Gabriele's terrace, studying a floor plan, when Justine returned an hour later. She looked up when she saw her approaching, smiling, displaying her happiness.

'There you are, darling. Michael get off all right, did he?'

'Yes, Anita.' Justine hurried over, and gave her a hug, then sat down in the chair next to her. In a rush of words, she went on, 'Once we arrived at the Çiragan Palace, we went to find the car and driver Kuri had booked, and within minutes Michael was off to the airport. He wouldn't let me go with him.'

'No, he wouldn't. He's never liked goodbyes. I suspect he was very nonchalant when he left, wasn't he?'

'He was. He said, "So long, see ya," and gave me a quick kiss and was gone.'

'That's the way he is, and you'll get used to it.'

'I'm used to it now, I think. I understand him, and I do love him, Anita.'

'It's apparent, and I can see that he feels the same way about you.'

Justine settled back in the chair, looking reflective. After a second or two, she said, 'Michael told me that my grandmother saved your life when you were both young girls. He said you would tell me the whole story.'

After her chat with Gabriele only a short while ago, Anita was now well prepared. 'So he explained to me, before he left. But Gabriele would prefer to tell you about it herself, and she plans to do that tomorrow morning. This afternoon she has a meeting about her Tulipmania fabric line, and I thought you and I could do the interview for your film. You know, chat about my life here, and my thoughts about the city. That would be a good moment, Justine, because tomorrow afternoon your grandmother and I have to go to Bodrum. We're decorating a beach house there for clients. Would you like to come with us?'

'I'd love to see Bodrum, but I can't do it, Anita. I made a tentative date with Iffet to go over the newspaper advertisement with her, so that I can finish my rough draft. You're not upset that I can't go, are you?'

'Of course not, and Gabri won't be either. We know you're staying until Richard comes, so we're relaxed. When *is* he going to arrive, by the way?'

'He's almost finished the hotel installation, and I hope he'll give me a proper date when we speak later today.' Standing up, Justine said, 'I'll just go and get my recorder and notebook. Perhaps we could start now, before lunch?'

'That's a good idea.'

'Where's Gran?'

'She went to her studio to find some fabric samples.' Anita patted the floor plan, and added, 'For this part of the villa in Bodrum.'

Justine nodded. 'See you in a minute,' she said and dashed away.

Anita looked after her retreating figure, thinking how wonderful it was to be young. Anita was old now. Nonetheless, she didn't feel it, and that was all that mattered.

Justine returned within a few minutes, and settled herself in a chair opposite Anita. 'I know you must have been interviewed a zillion times, but I just need to explain that I don't do the regular kind of interview for my documentaries. I'm a little bit . . . well, let's say different, innovative. I like to get impressions from people, how they really feel about things on that level. Is that all right with you, Anita?'

'It's fine. Let's start, shall we?'

'Okay, I'm all set. I want to get some impressions of Istanbul from you. For instance, when you're away, *not* here, and you think of Istanbul, what comes into your mind?'

Anita didn't really have to think about this. Immediately, she said, 'Sounds and smells.'

'I'm assuming you mean the sounds and smells of the city, not your home?'

'That's right. The most striking sounds for me are the hooting of the ferries crossing the Bosphorus, and the squawking of the seagulls in the very early morning . . . they make a lot of noise, those birds.' Anita shook her head, amusement suddenly flickering in her dark eyes. 'And then there are the cats, *caterwauling*. They seem to become very vocal in March, on the prowl, meowing and crying from dawn until dusk. Nonstop. We've also got a lot of barking dogs, and they usually start their racket the instant the calls to prayer begin. I'm talking about the calls of the muezzins from the balconies of the mosques. And here's another thought, a memory that often comes back when I'm out of town. When I walk along Istiklal Street there's the sound of music. That's because there are music shops on that street. I hear all kinds of music – Kurdish and Armenian songs, Turkish pop and folk music . . . I have always enjoyed being on that street.'

'So it's not all cats and dogs kicking up a fuss,' Justine said, smiling at her.

'No, not at all. And as far as smells are concerned, there are so many. My goodness, how can I explain them all? The gardens here at the *yalis*, obviously. The fragrance of the flowers mingled with the fresh salty air suffuses the atmosphere, as you know. Sometimes I smell the fish in my head, and instantly I think of how much I love the sea. And my mouth waters because I immediately associate the sea and fish with the liquorice taste of raki which, as you've learned, we usually drink with fish dishes.'

'What do you feel about the cigarette smoke? I've noticed that Istanbul is a city full of smokers. Does it bother you?'

'A little bit,' Anita replied. 'But there's nothing I can do about that. And there're worse smells. Exhaust from trucks, buses and age-old cars for example. And the garbage when it's a hot day. You really have to follow your nose to get the good smells of the city, Justine. Turkish coffee sending big whiffs of caffeine, the tempting smells of fresh food from bakeries and "home"-style restaurants. If you walk into any good bakery you'll notice hints of almond, pistachios, fresh baklava and bread. Such delicious smells. Then, when I go to the Grand Bazaar, I always head to the shop where the fragrant oils are sold. I get dizzy when I'm there, but it's a nice kind of dizziness, darling. I must take you next week. I will buy you Bulgarian rose oil – nothing like it in the world. And it's to put *on* your body, not in the bath.'

'What do you mean?' Justine asked, frowning, her eyes puzzled. 'Do you mean you rub it on your body?'

'Exactly that.' Anita smiled. 'Just a few dabs here and there, though, not gallons of it, or you'll smell like a Chinese whorehouse.'

Justine burst out laughing. She loved some of the outrageous things Anita came out with, so bluntly, and without really caring what people thought. 'I'll remember to do that, just a drop, Anita. Now, to move in a different direction, when did you come to live in the city?'

'Oh my goodness, I've lived here most of my life, except for the times I spent in England with Maxwell, my first husband as you're aware. And the love of my life. And he was English, as no doubt you know.'

'So how old were you when you came to live in Istanbul?'

'Fourteen, almost fifteen. I came with my brother Mark. My mother was already living here,' Anita responded. 'She was widowed, and came to stay with her sister Leonie, who was also a widow, and who had fallen ill. My mother couldn't really leave her so she brought us here to be with her. Then war broke out, and it was impossible to travel, so we remained in Istanbul after Aunt Leonie died. I went to school and college here.'

'Did you live on this side of the Bosphorus or the European side?'

'Oh, the European side, Justine! I'll take you there next week and show you where I grew up. It's called Beyoglu. It's on a steep hill north of the Golden Horn, and it has been home to the city's foreign residents forever . . . at least for centuries, anyway, and believe me it hasn't changed much. From about the sixteenth century, the great European countries opened embassies in this area, and there are also many historic buildings: mosques, churches, synagogues. Oh, and the very famous Pera Palas Hotel. Now that was a place, and then some, I can tell you.' Anita threw her a knowing look and rolled her eyes.

'What kind of place?' Justine asked. 'Come on, tell me, you've got such a naughty look on your face.'

Anita chuckled, and shook her head. 'I'm not suggesting it was a naughty hotel. It was a superb hotel, and everyone stayed there, from film stars to foreign dignitaries, and even Agatha Christie, the English writer, was a resident at times. It was chic, and during the war the hotel was full of spies, gigolos, crooks, lotharios, diplomats, prostitutes and refugees. The world and his wife were there. In the bar, the lobby, the restaurant.'

Sitting back in her chair, Anita paused for a moment, and then said, 'Istanbul was a city of intrigue during the Second World War. Turkey was a neutral country, and the likes of dispossessed royalty and riff-raff from every country gathered here . . .' She cut herself off, and was thoughtful for a moment before asking, 'Did you ever see that old movie, *Casablanca*?'

'Of course! It's famous, and one of my all-time favourites. Very romantic, and oh boy, Ingrid Bergman was gorgeous,' Justine replied. 'Are you trying to tell me that Istanbul was like Casablanca in those days?'

'Exactly. It was intriguing, dangerous, fascinating.'

'I can just imagine.'

'Mind you, Justine, I wasn't old enough to enjoy all that.'

'All that what?' Gabriele asked, walking onto the terrace, and coming to join them.

'The excitement of going to the Pera Palace, having cocktails there and mingling with all the dangerous people,' Anita answered with a twinkle in her eye. 'My brother sometimes went with his male friends, but I wasn't old enough. And when I *was* the right age, in my early twenties, the war was over and everything changed.'

Gabriele looked amused as she sat down next to Justine. She said to her granddaughter, 'Suna is making one of your favourite things for lunch: goujons of sole.'

'Oh Gran, how wonderful! Pearl tries to make it, and so do I, but neither of us cook it exactly like you do, and it's never right.'

'Very hot fat in the pan,' Gabriele said. 'That's the secret. I'm glad Pearl and Tita are well, and incidentally, I spent part of this morning looking at the photographs of Indian Ridge. I noticed my old gazebo is still standing! Also, the green-slate roof on the gallery is stunning. It links all the buildings together so well. Richard is very talented. I can't wait to see him and meet Daisy.'

TWENTY-NINE

The three women walked across the terrace and into Gabriele's dining room. It was of medium size, with white-painted walls and a blue-and-white tiled floor, and this colour scheme was repeated throughout.

As they seated themselves at the round table, with a starched white linen cloth and blue-and-white china, Justine said, 'When I was wondering how I was going to find you, Gran, I remembered all the blue-and-white tiles you used at your apartment in New York, and I decided I'd go to all the tile makers here to ask if they knew you.'

Anita laughed, and so did Gabriele, and it was Anita who said, 'And most of them know us. But we have our own ceramic company, you know. My great-nephew Ken runs it.'

At this moment Ayce came in carrying a tray of plates which she placed on a sideboard. She took a plate of salad to each of them, returned with a sauceboat of vinaigrette dressing, and put it on the table. With a smile she disappeared.

Gabriele said, 'This is another of your favourites, darling. Endive with orange segments, chopped apple and walnuts.'

'I know it is,' Justine replied. 'You used to say it was your version of the famous Waldorf salad.'

'My goodness, you do remember a lot.' Gabriele sounded surprised.

'I remember *everything*,' she answered.

Justine sat back in the chair, gazing at her grandmother, her face filled with love. 'You used to say I had a photographic memory, and it's true, I do. And there isn't anything I don't remember about my childhood with you, Gran – you made it so special when you came to stay with us.'

Gabriele blinked back sudden tears, lowered her head and pushed her fork into the salad. For a moment she couldn't speak, so moved was she by Justine's words. Again she thought of the long estrangement created by Deborah . . . all the years she had missed out on sharing her grandchildren's lives. It had been so unnecessary, a cruel act on her daughter's part. She pushed away the sad thoughts. Justine was here now, and Richard would come shortly, and that was all that mattered. They were reunited at last.

The three of them concentrated on their food, and once they had finished their first course, Ayce served the fried fish, which came with green peas and French fries. 'Just the way I like them!' Justine looked across at her grandmother. 'And it seems *you* remember everything, too.'

'I do. That's what's kept me going all these years. My memories of you and Richard, and of your father. And Trent, of course.'

It was over coffee that Justine suddenly said, 'It doesn't seem possible that I'm madly in love with Michael. It's Monday today, and I met him only last Friday. That's about seventy-two hours ago. It's all been so fast, it's mind boggling.'

Gabriele did not respond. A thoughtful look crossed her face, and after a moment she said slowly, in the softest of voices, 'Some people might think it fast, but Anita and I know that a *coup de foudre* always *is* fast – a flash of lightning striking. That's exactly what happened to you and Michael.'

Anita nodded her agreement. 'That's right, it is.' She gave Justine a loving smile, and murmured, 'Remember, I told you that it was the same for me. Maxwell and I took one look at each other, and we were goners.'

Justine nodded, liking Anita for being such a good sport, so accessible and outgoing, and truly genuine. Her absolute honesty was refreshing.

Gabriele turned to her granddaughter, reached out and touched her arm lightly. 'Other things can happen much faster, Justine. A much-wanted baby can be born and then die in an instant. A volcano can erupt and bury a city in minutes. So can a tsunami, a tornado, a hurricane. They destroy everything before them, and terrifyingly so, before people even have time to catch their breath.'

Gabriele paused, shaking her head, and after a moment continued, 'A person can have a stroke and die before hitting the floor, get knocked down and killed instantly by a car or catch a stray bullet. All in the passing of *a moment* in time. Disasters happen inexplicably, move fast and strike without rhyme or reason. Never forget that the world is catastrophic. In the blink of an eye a life can change. As yours has this weekend. It will never be the same again. You met the right man in the right place at the right time. You've been one of the lucky ones, Justine. You've been blessed . . .'

Later that afternoon Gabriele went off to her meeting and Anita and Justine returned to the terrace, to talk about Istanbul for the documentary.

'How did you meet your first husband? I'd love to hear about that,' Justine said, turning on her recorder.

'Ah yes, the love of my life. My marvellous Maxwell, and the father of my only child, Cornelia.' Anita seemed to ruminate for a few moments, and then she began to speak.

'As I told you, I came here in 1938. My brother Mark was twenty-two. Although we came because our mother was living here, nursing her sister, there was another reason. Aunt Leonie's husband had just died and left her his company. This had been in his family for fifty years or so, and because of his death it was being run by a cousin of his. But this man was getting on in years, and although he ran it well, he wanted and needed help. The idea was that Mark should enter the business. There was no one else really, and they wanted to keep it in the family. Mark was clever, and he learned fast. He really enjoyed his work. He had studied accountancy, was business-oriented, and so he ran the company for the rest of his life.'

'And this is the ceramic business you referred to at lunch?' Justine asked.

'That's correct. I did most of the designing when I was young. We used these designs, as well as the copies of the Iznik tiles. Because I was so involved with the company, and worked full time, Mark made me his partner, and I worked alongside him for years. Anyway, getting back to Maxwell, I met him through my brother.'

'In Istanbul or in London?'

'Oh not London, no. Maxwell was living here. Mark dealt with an English import-export company called Lowe's of London. It was world famous and, in 1948, the second son of the family that owned the company, Maxwell Lowe, came to live and work in Turkey. He took over the Istanbul branch of Lowe's of London so that his elder brother Sam could return to London, once Maxwell had the hang of things. This switch was made so that their father Ben could retire, and Sam would run the head office.'

'And that's when you met Maxwell,' Justine asserted.

'No, it was actually two years later, in 1950, when Maxwell had been here for two years. Mark asked him to come to dinner. That's how we met.' Anita's eyes suddenly twinkled, and she finished with a bit of a flourish, 'And the rest is history, as they say.'

'So you got married and lived happily ever after. Always here, Anita?'

'Yes. But we did make frequent trips to London. My brother Mark married eventually and had children, and his eldest son Oliver went into our ceramic business, and now it's Mark's grandson that runs it – Ken, my great-nephew. I've mentioned him before.'

'And what happened to Lowe's of London?'

'Maxwell ran it until the day he died, and then *his* nephews took over. It's still here, but run by the new generation of Lowes. I have an interest in it, of course, but I'm a silent partner.'

'Michael told me that his mother went to Harvard, studied law.'

'Yes. She's talented, a clever woman, in fact. But as no doubt Michael explained, she fell in love with Larry Dalton, married him quickly, after her graduation, and has never practised law.'

'Her son takes after her,' Justine murmured, smiling.

'That's true. More's the pity. I can't tell you how worried I was when he was in the Secret Service. I hardly had a proper night's sleep, fretting over him. It's dangerous work, Justine.'

'I understand that. Although the other day he told me it was endlessly boring at times.'

'Maybe. But it was still dangerous.'

The two women went on chatting for another hour, and Justine listened attentively. It was Anita who finally brought the interview to an end.

'I've talked my head off, darling, and I must have a rest now. But we can continue this whenever you wish.'

THIRTY

After Anita had retreated to her own *yali* to rest, Justine went upstairs to her bedroom, fully intending to play back the recording and sort through her notes. But suddenly she felt tired herself; immediately she kicked off her shoes and lay down on the bed.

Earlier, Ayce had closed the opaque curtains to keep out the sun and had turned on the ceiling fan. Her room was softly shaded and cool. Placing the cell phone on the bedside table, she punched the pillows, put down her head and closed her eyes. Within seconds she drifted off, falling asleep almost instantly. It was a deep sleep and dreamless.

When she awakened, Justine glanced at the clock and saw that she had slept for over an hour. There was no doubt in her mind that she had needed it. She and Michael had kept very late hours, and the weekend had passed in a haze of intense lovemaking and quick naps, plus other activities. Exhausted, that's what I was, and probably still am, she thought, and reached for the phone when it began to ring.

'Hello,' she said.

'It's me,' her brother answered. 'Am I calling at a bad time?'

'No, a good time. I just woke up from a nap. I've been inter-
viewing Anita for the documentary, then we had lunch, did
another interview, and finally we both needed to take a rest. Is
everything all right, Rich?'

'I'm good, and the installation is almost finished. It's gone
without a hitch so far, although I'm almost afraid to say that
– I don't want to tempt providence.'

'This is great news. Do you know when you'll come to
Istanbul? We're all anxious to see you,' Justine now said, wanting
to pin him down.

'Another week and then I should be able to take off. I'll soon
be there, don't worry.'

'With Daisy, I hope.'

'Of course.' There was a pause. Richard cleared his throat,
said carefully, 'Do you mind if Joanne comes with us, and brings
Simon?'

Her brother had caught her by surprise, and for a moment
she was startled and didn't respond.

'It is all right, isn't it?' he asked anxiously when she was silent.

'Of course it is. Gran will be thrilled, and so am I.' There
was a slight hesitation before she said, 'You must have had a
nice weekend with her, enjoyed it.'

'Yes, I did, and she did, actually. We spent most of our time
at Indian Ridge with the kids, and being with her made me feel
relaxed. I've not felt so good since . . . well, before Pamela got
sick. Joanne was really fantastic. She made me laugh a lot, and
was a great companion. And—'

'She always has been,' Justine cut in, laughing quietly. 'You'd
just forgotten.'

'That's true, I guess.'

'It is, yes, but I hope you're more than just friends,' she
murmured, wanting to draw him out.

There was silence for a moment before he replied, 'Yes, we
are. She's warm, loving and sexy. For me it was like coming out

of a deep sleep . . . I felt I was alive for the first time since Pamela died.'

'I'm glad, Rich, and it pleases me, knowing you're happy. And especially with someone like Joanne, you know her so well. She understands you.'

'I guess I might have been a bit dumb in the past, not getting it . . . that she had romantic feelings for me,' Richard muttered.

'Never mind, you know now.'

'Listen, Juju, I've something to tell you. I heard from our mother.'

Justine sat bolt upright on the bed and exclaimed, 'When? What did she want?' She was instantly alerted to trouble.

'I got an e-mail from her,' Richard answered. 'Which I just found this morning. She was asking if I know a certain architect in Los Angeles. He's apparently designing a huge house in Tokyo for a Japanese tycoon. She's being considered as the interior designer. She wanted the dope on him, that's all.'

'Did she ask about Daisy? Or me? Or you? Did she wonder how we all were?'

'No mention of any of us. It was so businesslike, I must admit I was a bit ticked off.'

'Keep it that way, and don't reply.'

'She'll only bombard me with e-mails if I don't get back to her. I can't take that. I don't want her to call me. She's so pushy and overbearing.'

'I know. So you'd better reply. And just be as cold and businesslike as her. By the way, is she still in Mainland China or has she gone to Hong Kong?'

'I've no idea, and I've no intention of being friendly. I don't feel friendly towards her. She's impossible,' Richard exclaimed.

'We'll have our day in court.'

'That's right. I suppose you haven't asked Gran what other documents our mother found when she broke into the writing case?'

'I didn't. Nor do I want to question her, Rich. Michael told me something, though. He mentioned that Gran saved Anita's life, and Gran's going to tell me all about it tomorrow before she and Anita go to Bodrum.' Her voice took on a more amused tone as she added, 'They're currently decorating a house for a client in Bodrum, if you can believe that.'

'I certainly can – that's the Gran I remember, always working. How did she save Anita's life?' Richard asked, as curious as his sister.

'Michael didn't say, but I'll tell you when I know myself. It's part of the past, I'm sure of that, all part of the mystery surrounding Gabriele.'

'I agree with you, there's a lot we don't know from her early years. Are you going to call Joanne?'

'I thought I would, and I'll send my usual e-mails to her and Daisy. Let me know when you plan to arrive; the sooner you come the better.'

'I wish we were coming tomorrow,' Richard said. 'I'm suddenly getting really excited about the trip.'

'So am I, and Gran certainly is already. So, have a good day, I'll talk to you later.'

'Whenever you want, my phone's on permanently. Big kiss, Juju.'

After they hung up, Justine stretched out on the bed, thinking about the conversation. She was genuinely happy that Richard and Joanne had managed to take the huge leap into bed.

Her thoughts went to her mother, but only fleetingly. She had no time for her any more, and she only wanted to see her in order to confront her about the terrible lie she had told them years before. Once that had been accomplished she would be free of her, and could walk away. Permanently.

Justine got off the bed and went to the desk, taking her cell phone with her. She dialled Joanne in New York, and within a second Jo was saying, 'Hello?'

'You did it!' Justine exclaimed. 'You finally got my brother into bed.'

'He told you?' Joanne asked, sounding light hearted, laughter echoing in her voice.

'He didn't come out and say the words exactly – you know how reticent he can be at times. But he more or less told me. And I couldn't be happier, Jo, because you're so *right* together. And it's lovely that you and Simon are coming to Istanbul.'

'When Richard asked me if I'd like to go with him and Daisy, and bring Simon, I was really surprised, but naturally I jumped at the chance. And I don't think this is going to be a passing thing with him. I'm certain it's going to last.'

THIRTY-ONE

Later that afternoon, Justine went out to the gardens to wait for Gabriele to come back from her meeting on the other side of the Bosphorus. She sat down on the garden seat, her mind focused on the documentary. She had formulated many ideas last week, whilst searching for her grandmother, and after studying her notes a short while ago she knew she was on the right track. Even though her life had changed drastically in the last few days, she was still hoping to make the film, and Michael agreed that she should.

The crunching of footsteps on the pebbled path brought her head around, and she smiled and waved as Anita came towards her, wearing a colourful cotton caftan and large dark glasses, as chic as always.

'Can I join you?' Anita asked.

'Yes, come on, sit down here,' Justine answered and, leaping to her feet, she gave Anita a big hug.

Once they were seated, Anita said, 'You know, I was thinking about the two interviews we did earlier, and I realized we had only touched the surface of my thoughts and feelings about Istanbul.'

'But they were very interesting, and you certainly captured Istanbul for me, as far as the sounds and smells are concerned. I really conjured up a few of the areas I've already been to, listening to you, and got a true flavour of the city, I promise you.'

Anita looked pleased, then she said, 'But you can't very well film *smells*, now can you?'

Laughing, Justine shook her head. 'You can capture sounds, though, and you'll be talking about the smells as we go around the city together when I'm actually filming. We'll visit the markets, the fish stalls, the food shops, the Grand Bazaar, and we'll paint a living picture of smells, in a certain sense.'

'I understand.' Anita turned slightly and looked intently at Justine. 'Istanbul is *the* place of my memories – that's something else I understood when I was taking a rest. I grew up here. I started my design career here. And, of course, this is where I spent those wonderfully happy years with Maxwell, where together we brought up our daughter, Cornelia, Michael's mother. Naturally, I have some very happy memories of London, the times we stayed for short periods, because Maxwell got homesick occasionally. But my most treasured memories are rooted here.'

Glancing around the garden, Anita murmured softly, 'And especially in this old *yali*, which Maxwell loved so much, as do I.'

'And Gran loves *her yali*, Anita, and she's happy and grateful to be living so close to you. I'm sure she has a fund of memories of Istanbul as well.'

'She does. Gabriele was happy here with Trent. On the other hand, she was happy in England, and naturally at Indian Ridge. Gabri always loved that place in Connecticut, and being there with you and Richard.' Staring hard at Justine, Anita then asked, 'And when *is* he coming? Do we know yet?'

'As a matter of fact, we do. I just spoke to him, and he'll be finished with the hotel installation a week from today, and he plans to leave at once.' Justine refrained from mentioning that Joanne and Simon were also coming along. She wanted Gabriele to be the first to have that news.

When her cell phone began to trill, Justine pulled it out of her pocket, put it to her ear and said, 'Hello?'

'Hi Justine,' Michael responded. She glanced at Anita, silently mouthed, 'It's Michael.'

Anita mouthed back, 'Give him my love,' and rising she walked down the garden path, understanding all about love, and the need lovers had to constantly speak to each other.

'Are you there, Justine?' Michael asked, his voice rising.

'Yes, I'm here, and hello, hello! Your grandmother says to give you her love. We were sitting here on the garden seat, chatting. Now she's gone, being respectful of our privacy. How are you? Is everything okay there? With your client?'

'I'm fine, and everything's under control. As you know, I can't really discuss my business, so just let me say I think I have some solutions for him. And so he's feeling better. What's been happening there?'

She laughed. 'You've only been gone since this morning! So there's nothing new, Michael, at least not here. What *is* good news is that Richard is coming in about a week, and bringing not only Daisy, but my best friend Joanne and her son Simon. And guess what? They've finally got their act together and are involved.'

'That's great, and I can't wait to meet them, and especially Richard.'

He lowered his voice. 'I miss you. I wish you were here. I thought of bringing you with me, but I didn't want to take you away from Gabri. Still, I can't help wishing I had.'

'I'd love to be there, and I felt the same way as you, especially about Gran.'

'Oh come on, fly to London instead! Be with me here. *Please.*'

'Don't tempt me, Michael. Listen, you know I want to, but

my grandmother said she'd talk to me tomorrow about saving Anita's life . . . I think I'd better stay here. I need to know about her past.'

'I guess you're right, but I sure as hell miss you, babe.'

'I miss you too.'

Gabriele's face broke into smiles when she saw Justine hurrying towards her, and she called out, 'What a sight for sore eyes *you* are.'

A moment later Justine was enfolding her grandmother in her arms, holding her tightly. 'I love you so much. I'm still pinching myself that I found you. A stroke of luck.'

'I know what you mean.' Linking her arm through Justine's, Gabriele continued, 'I'd love a cup of tea, wouldn't you?'

'Yes, I would. I'll go and make it, and then you can tell me how your meeting went.'

'Ayce will attend to it, Justine; I'm afraid she gets a bit miffy if anyone starts fiddling around in her kitchen, and Suna's the same.'

'Michael sends his love, and he says he's on schedule.'

'So you've spoken to him, have you?'

'Yes, he called about half an hour before you got back.'

Justine smiled at her grandmother, and squeezed her arm. 'You two are very different, and yet I understand why you get on so well: you're both so loving and compassionate, and in tune.'

'Why thank you, lovey, what a nice thing to say.'

Justine followed her grandmother into the front hall and asked, 'Shall I go and look for Ayce or Suna? Ask for tea?'

'That would be nice, and you might also ask her if she has some Cadbury's chocolate fingers, please Justine.'

'Be right back, Gran.'

Gabriele stood in the doorway of the living room, watching her go, loving her so much, gratified and relieved that this young woman had been so persistent and determined to find her. Gabriele went along with the idea that it was a fluke, a lucky accident, that Justine had done so, but inside she believed it was part of a greater plan. There were those who would disagree, who thought everything that happened in life was random, just chance, and nothing more than that.

Seating herself on the sofa, Gabriele leaned back, glad to be in this beautiful old room, surrounded by many of the things she loved. The windows faced the sea, and now, as the light was changing, the sun moved slowly towards the far horizon. The room took on a hazy golden glow, just as Anita's did at this hour.

Closing her eyes, she relaxed, and opened her mind to a certain memory, as she often did at this particular hour of the day, and she heard it clearly, the music, the violin, echoing in her head.

Feeling the tears gathering behind her eyelids, she sat up with a jerk, blinked, and flicked her fingertips across her eyes. No need for tears, she told herself, and smiled brightly at her grand-daughter as she came back, so coltish and lithe.

'English breakfast tea with lemon, chocolate fingers and ginger biscuits,' Justine announced, sitting down opposite Gabriele. 'So, Gran, tell me what happened at the meeting? Are they going to buy lots of your latest fabric?'

Gabriele nodded, her blue eyes lighting up. 'The whole line, Justine. The new company is taking every design, and in various fabrics – cotton, linen and pure silk. And what's more, they'll distribute them across America. They seem to be crazy about me – or rather, about the fabrics.'

Her grandmother sounded so surprised, Justine stared at her in puzzlement for a moment. 'Why wouldn't they? The tulip patterns are sensational. Congratulations, Gran, you deserve your success.' Then, leaning forward, she announced, 'I've got a surprise for you. I spoke to Richard. He'll be winging his way to us in a week – next Tuesday, to be exact.'

'Oh how marvellous! I can't wait to see him, and little Daisy. Who would ever have thought that I would live long enough to see a great-grandchild of mine?'

'It's going to be very special for you, I know. And listen, Joanne is coming with him and bringing her boy, Simon, who's Daisy's age.'

'It'll be old home week – all of us together again like we used to be at Indian Ridge. I was always fond of Jo.' Gabriele's face was radiant as she spoke.

'I've another bit of news,' Justine said. 'The two of them, I mean Richard and Jo, have hooked up with each other at last. She's been in love with him since we were kids growing up together, and very frankly I never thought it would happen. But it has.'

'*Que sera sera*,' Gabriele murmured, using her favourite saying. 'What will be will be.' She glanced at the door as it opened. Ayce came in pushing the tea trolley, and Gabriele welcomed her warmly.

THIRTY-TWO

Once they had finished tea, which had been a bit more elaborate than Gabriele had anticipated, she sat studying Justine for a moment or two.

Her granddaughter suddenly became aware of this fixed scrutiny, and said, 'Gran, you're staring at me. Do I have a dirty mark on my face?'

'No, darling, you don't. I was just admiring you, thinking how beautiful you look.'

Justine smiled, her face lighting up. 'And you do too, so smart in your black suit and white shirt. Just like a high-powered executive.'

Gabriele shook her head. 'Just an artist, that's all.' There was a pause, and then she said, 'I want to talk to you about something, Justine, but before I do, I must ask you a question. When is Iffet coming to see you tomorrow?'

'In the afternoon. But a time hasn't been set yet.'

'I think you should cancel the meeting.'

'Why?' Justine asked, sitting up straighter. She couldn't understand what this was about. 'Is there something wrong?'

'No, no, not as far as Iffet's concerned.' Gabriele paused, took a deep breath, continued, 'I promised to tell you about saving Anita's life, and I will do that tomorrow, as arranged. But that is all I can actually tell you about my early life, my past—'

'Oh no!' Justine exclaimed, cutting across Gabriele. 'I want to know everything.' Dismay flooded her.

'Let me explain,' Gabriele responded. 'When I was a girl, a teenager approaching young womanhood, I had a difficult life. It was not a happy existence. As I grew older, and my circumstances started to change, I began to bury the past, pushing it deep down inside me. In fact, I buried it so deep I cannot dredge it up. Ever. I obliterated it from my heart and mind, and I have never been able to speak about it. However, I think you have a right to know about my early life, what I was, who I am.'

'Thank you for that, Gran, and I'm so glad you will talk to me, that you've chosen me to hear your story.'

'Oh, but I'm not going to *tell* you anything, Justine.'

'But you said you wanted me to know.'

'I do, and you shall. I have never discussed those years with anyone. No one on this earth knows my story, and—'

'Not Anita?' Justine interrupted.

'Not even her. She knows about my childhood; after all, we grew up together, and I saved her life when we were teenagers. A short while later we became separated by circumstances. We didn't meet again for a few years, and she had no knowledge of my life during that time – nor I of hers. I did confide one thing when we finally met again, and she knew about those people who'd been kind to me, but that's all.'

'You weren't able to tell Uncle Trent either?' Justine ventured.

'No.' Gabriele leaned back against the pillows on the sofa, staring into the distance for a moment. A sadness settled over her.

Finally, she spoke. 'Ten years ago, when your mother and I quarrelled, I came back to Istanbul once she had returned to the States. As you now know, she created the estrangement

between us, told me to stay away from her and her children –
you and Richard. She kicked me out of the family in effect. As
you can imagine, I was stunned. Broken-hearted. I came to
Istanbul because I knew I was safe here. I had my *yali*, and I
knew I was loved and respected by my friends. I had Anita, and
Michael was loving and caring when he was here.'

'I'm happy he was, Gran, that comforts me.'

'He's a good man . . . To continue. Slowly, over the last ten
years, I began to pull up bits and pieces of my past, fragments
of my life, and I wrote them down. Certain parts were buried
far too deep; I could not dredge them to the surface of my mind.
And so they remain unwritten. But there are enough of those
fragments for you to form a picture of my early years. It took
me a long time to write this . . . well, I was going to call it a
memoir, but it's not that. Rather, it's scenes, bits and pieces,
fragments of a life. Do you understand, darling?'

'Yes, I do. It's like a notebook? Is that what you mean?'

'That's what it is, I suppose. I shall give it to you before we
leave for Bodrum tomorrow.'

'Is that why you want me to cancel my meeting with Iffet?
So I can read it?'

'Yes.' Gabriele hesitated for a split second before adding in a
low, concerned voice, 'I think you might find some things . . .
difficult. Knowing you the way I do, you'll want to be alone.
And you'll want to digest everything.'

'I understand,' Justine said, and she did. 'I'll call Iffet later.'

'Don't read it all at once,' Gabriele murmured. 'Take it slowly.
I put the name of the place and the year of each fragment, each
memory. So you'll know where I was and when.'

'If I need to speak to you, can I? Can I call you in Bodrum?'

'Yes, on my mobile.'

'Are you going to allow Richard to read it?'

'Yes, of course. *He must*. He has to know about my early
life.'

'Can I tell him about the notebook?'

'I think I'd prefer him to read it for himself. Better he doesn't know about it beforehand. I want him to understand it properly, to digest it. So don't say anything to him, please, Justine.'

'I won't. What about Michael?'

Gabriele thought about this for a moment or two.

'You can talk to Michael if you feel you must. A few things he does know from Anita.'

'He said he didn't know anything,' Justine replied, frowning.

'That's absolutely true. He has no information about my early life, except in relation to his grandmother. You'll understand why he knows certain things as soon as you've read the first few pages.'

'Is this notebook going to upset me, Gran?' Justine asked slowly, suddenly feeling nervous inside, and anxious.

Gabriele did not answer.

Justine gave her a penetrating stare, and her heart clenched. For a fleeting moment she saw the pain in Gabriele's eyes, and knew the answer to her question.

THIRTY-THREE

The following afternoon, once Gabriele was ready to leave for Bodrum, she went to the safe at the back of the walk-in closet in her bedroom, and took out the large black notebook.

She had kept it locked up for years, and only removed it when she had wanted to add to it. Now for the first time it was going to be read. By her granddaughter. For a moment Gabri hesitated at the safe, suddenly tempted to put the book back inside. No, she thought. I want Justine to know the truth about my life. Decisively, she closed the safe and locked it.

A few moments later she picked up her handbag and went downstairs to find her granddaughter. Justine was not inside the *yali*, and when Gabriele went out into the gardens, she caught a glimpse of her walking down towards the garden seat in front of the Bosphorus.

Gabriele smiled to herself. The seat had become a favourite spot. It was there that Justine and Michael had admitted their overwhelming attraction for each other, and, of course, it was now symbolic to them both.

A couple of seconds later, Gabriele was joining her on the

garden seat, explaining, 'Well, darling, I'm about to go to the airport with Anita, and I just want to give you this.' As she spoke she handed Justine a small Fortnum & Mason shopping bag. 'In here is my book of notes, those fragments I told you about yesterday after tea.'

Taking the shopping bag from her, Justine nodded. 'Thank you, I can't wait to read it, Gran. I'll start this afternoon. And by the way, Iffet didn't mind about changing our date. In fact, it was good for her. She has clients in town and she usually looks after them when they're here.'

'I'm happy it worked out. Now you have plenty of time to read, to digest everything.' Reaching out, Gabriele took Justine's hand in hers. 'I intended to leave the book to you and Richard in my will. You see, to be honest, I never thought I would see either of you again in my lifetime. Not in my wildest dreams. But you found me. And I'm still alive and kicking, so I decided you should have it now. Richard can read it when he arrives next week.'

'I'll keep it safe, Gran, and I do understand it's for my eyes only . . . until Rich gets here.'

'And remember, it was written over the last ten years, and to the best of my memory.'

Later, after Gabriele and Anita had left, Justine took the Fortnum's shopping bag to her bedroom, sat down in a chair and placed the black leather-bound book on the small coffee table.

She sat staring at it for the longest time, wanting to pick it up, to open it, and yet, in a strange way, she was afraid to do so. She was not sure what she was going to find among those leaves.

After taking a deep breath, she finally reached for it, stared at the first page. The title was there.

Fragments of a Life, it said, and underneath was the name of the author. *Gabriele*, and that was all, no last name. Justine turned the page, and read the words at the top. On the left was the dateline *BERLIN*, and on the other side it said *16 NOVEMBER 1938*.

Justine frowned as she stared at the name of the city. Berlin had jumped out at her. What was her grandmother doing in Berlin in 1938? She was genuinely puzzled.

Dropping her eyes, she scanned the page, was reassured that this was her grandmother's handwriting. She knew it well. It had always been distinctive, flowing, elegant, and easy to read.

BERLIN   16 NOVEMBER 1938

I am always happy to come home when I've been away. When I reached the street where we lived I became excited, joyful in my heart. It was growing dark. There was a cold wind. This made me hurry faster. All of a sudden I started to run when our building came into sight. I couldn't wait to see my parents and my little sister Erika. Once I was inside the vestibule, I smoothed my hair and straightened my scarf before climbing the stairs with my suitcase.

Something seemed different. Then I realized that the building was unnaturally quiet. I had lived here most of my life and it had never been so *still*. There was usually the odd noise. When I reached the second floor I noticed something even stranger. The door of our flat was ajar. It was always closed, locked from the inside. Who had left it open like this?

I didn't go in. I stood staring at the door, frowning, listening. Silence. Darkness inside. Finally I pushed the door open, stepped into the foyer. I could see dim light at the end of the corridor, and as I looked to my right there was another pale glow from my father's study. I stood there for a split second, fear invading me. I turned on the foyer light at last, called out, Mutti! Papa! I am home!

No voices of welcome. No happy laughter. No parents. No little sister hugging me. I put down my suitcase. My mouth was dry. I swallowed, steeled myself to walk forward. When I reached my father's study I pushed open the door cautiously with my foot. The desk lamp was on. My father's violin lay on his music table. It was not in its case. This was peculiar. Worrying. It was a Stradivarius. Papa always put it away. Next to it was a sheet of music. I went to look. Mozart.

I walked down the main corridor to the kitchen, peeped around the door, went inside. There were pans on the stove. A chopping board on the counter. Vegetables scattered on the big kitchen table. It was obvious my mother had left hurriedly. That was the only explanation. She would never leave her kitchen in disarray.

Where were my family?

I dare not accept the thought that sprang into my head. I just stood there. Frightened, rooted to the spot. And then I heard it, a noise, like a door squeaking. As I swung around I came face to face with Mrs Weber who lived across the hall.

She hurried to me, grabbed me, held me close to her ample body. I heard a choke, a sob. When I looked up into her face I saw how deathly white she was. The same colour as her apron.

Gabri, you must leave. Now, at once, she told me. Come with me, I have something for you. I asked her where my parents and sister were. She did not answer. She just kept shaking her head. Taking hold of my arm she hurried me out of the kitchen, down the corridor. In the foyer she picked up my suitcase and rushed me out of our flat and across the landing into her home.

Mrs Weber locked her door, led me into the kitchen. The window was open. I could hear the traffic in the street. She turned on the radio. So no one could hear us. I knew that. I was watching her alertly.

Where are they? I asked. I was trembling inside. They've been taken, she whispered, and stopped. I waited, my eyes riveted on hers. By the Gestapo, she said.

The Gestapo. No! No! I shrieked. Not Mutti and Papa. Not little Erika. No, I cried. I was frozen to the spot, filled with terror, tears pricking the back of my eyes, my throat choked.

Mrs Weber rushed to me, saying I must be quiet. *Gabri, please be quiet.* She held me close to her and then took my hand, almost dragged me into her bedroom. She closed and locked the door, pulled out a suitcase from under the bed, explained my mother had given it to her. Asked her to keep it for me some weeks before. She reminded me I had the key on a ribbon around my neck. I took it off, opened the case.

My clothes had been neatly packed. My passport lay on top, along with an envelope. I opened it. There was money inside. And a photograph of the four of us. I picked up the picture, staring at my family. Tears slid down my cheeks. Would I ever see them again? I did not know the answer.

I turned to Mrs Weber, insisted I must get my father's violin. She became vehement, said I couldn't go back for it. They will soon come looking for you, she whispered. They have lists. *Family lists.* You must leave the flat the way they left it. They will return, they will notice.

I started to weep. She wiped my eyes with her handkerchief, brought me into her arms again, holding me close, stroking my hair. Do you know what to do? she asked me. Yes, I answered, my mother told me. She nodded, said, Now we must combine the two cases, put everything in your mother's case. I did as she asked.

Mrs Weber hugged me, led me through her foyer. May God go with you, Gabriele, she said as she opened her front door. I thanked her, looked across at our flat, and went down the stairs slowly. I was blinded by tears.

God? What God? I wondered.

There was no God. I was on my own. I was fourteen.

When I went out into the street it was very dark. I turned left, then right, and left again. I walked straight down the fourth street until I arrived at the building where Anita Fischer lived with her older brother Markus. I had to tell them, warn them. I went into their vestibule, climbed the stairs to the first floor, rang their bell. Waited. I was still shaking inside, brimming with dread. *Had they been taken?*

The door opened. Anita smiled when she saw me. And then her face instantly changed. What is it? What's wrong? she cried, pulling me inside, slamming the door, locking it. They've been taken, my family, I whispered. A sob broke free from my throat. I covered my mouth with my hand, gulped back the tears.

The Gestapo? she asked. I could only nod.

Markus was suddenly standing there. *The Gestapo?* he repeated in a hushed voice. Still I could only nod.

They're out hunting Jews, he asserted, his voice grim, his face turning as white as Mrs Weber's had been. The Nazi thugs came out in the open on Kristallnacht, he muttered, looking from me to Anita. They showed their hand. They want to kill us all. They won't be satisfied until they've killed every Jew in Germany.

I gaped at him. So did Anita. That's not possible, I gasped. Wait and see, he replied.

We went into the living room. Anita left us to make hot tea. Markus and I sat down. He was twenty-two, and clever. Do you want to stay here with us? I shook my head. I have to go to my mother's friend, that's what she told me to do, I muttered, still swallowing my tears. The Russian woman? Markus asked. Yes, I replied. Can I phone her? He nodded.

Markus took me to the small den, indicated the phone, then left me alone. I dialled the number I had memorized on my mother's instructions. It rang and rang. *Ja?*, a woman's voice asked. *Guten Abend, Prinzessin*, I said in German. And then added in English, It's Gabriele Landau speaking. There was a moment of silence. The princess asked in English, Are things not right? No they are not, I responded. She told me to come to her at once. I said I would.

I went back to the living room. Anita, as white as chalk and shaky, had made tea. We sat and drank it in silence. Anita said, Markus got his travel visa today. But I didn't get mine. I stared at her. Can't you go too? I asked. It was Markus who answered. We'll find a way, he said. We must both go to Istanbul together. If we cannot, I shall stay here to protect Anita.

Later, after we had finished our tea, I asked Markus if he would take me to the home of Princess Irina Troubetzkoy who lived near the Tiergarten, the lovely old park my mother so loved. He agreed to drive me there on his motorbike.

Justine put the black leather book on the coffee table, her hands shaking. In fact, she was shaking all over, and her face was wet with the tears still streaming out of her eyes. She could not believe what she had just read, nor did she understand. She had always believed her grandmother was English. But she was not. She was German . . . a German Jew. And therefore *she* was Jewish, and Richard and her mother also. Justine understood she was not who she thought she was, and neither were they. But that did not really matter to her. What was important was the pain and suffering her grandmother had gone through as a young girl. A fourteen-year-old girl, alone in Nazi Germany. A Jewish girl, more at risk than anyone.

A shudder rippled through Justine at this thought. She went into the bathroom, found the tissues and wiped away her tears. Staring at herself in the mirror, she noticed how strained she looked, and her eyes were red-rimmed from crying.

Oh Gran, oh Gran, however did you endure? The tears started again, and Justine returned to the bedroom, lay down on the bed, weeping into the pillow. All she wanted at this moment was to wrap her arms around Gabriele and hold her close, and tell her how much she loved her.

But that was not possible. Nor could she speak to her. Gabriele and Anita were on the plane to Bodrum.

THIRTY-FOUR

Justine remained on the bed, trying to rest. Exhausted from weeping, she felt as though she had no tears left in her. The first pages in her grandmother's black leather book had truly shocked and stunned her. She had been flabbergasted by what she had read, and was filled with innumerable questions that only Gran could answer.

She could not conceive how her grandmother had managed to endure such enormous pain and loss at so young an age. Or how she had survived what must have befallen her later on. Justine was well versed in history, and knew about the Second World War and the Holocaust. She could now only wonder, and agonizingly so, about Gabriele's life during those evil times in Nazi Germany. That she had escaped death was surely something of a miracle.

What had the young Gabriele done? Who had helped her? How had she evaded arrest by the Gestapo? Or hadn't she? Had she been in one of the death camps? And lived. What had happened to Gabriele's parents? *Her* great-grandparents? And what about Erika? Had Gran's little sister survived? How had Gran managed to get to England? When had she gone? What role had Gabriele's beloved auntie Beryl played in her early life? On and on . . . so many questions scurried through her head, were unanswerable at this moment in time. Only after she had spoken to her grandmother would she know the entire story, and she needed to know it all now.

Justine's eyes fell on the black leather book on the coffee table. It was like a magnet, enticed her. After staring at it balefully for a while, biting her lip, she finally went over to the coffee table, picked it up and sat down in the chair. She leafed through the pages she had read before, until she came to where she had left off. Her eyes were glued to the page.

In the end we decided against the motorbike. There was the problem of my suitcase. It was too big. More importantly, Markus was reluctant to leave Anita alone in the flat. I agreed with him. We were living in dangerous times. Who knew that better than I? Jews had a price on their heads. Better that Anita came with us.

Out on the street we quickly found a taxi. I told the driver to go to the Tiergartenstrasse. When we were settled in the back, Markus asked me how my mother knew the Russian woman. She met her with Arabella von Wittingen some years ago, I told him. Arabella is married to Kurt von Wittingen. You've met the prince, I added, he's a sort of roving ambassador, a consultant to Krupp, the armaments king. Oh yes, I remember him now, Markus replied.

I continued to explain: My mother and Arabella went to school in England together. Roedean, near Brighton. She was born Lady Arabella Cunningham. She's the daughter of the Earl of Langley from Yorkshire. They stayed close after leaving Roedean, I finished.

Your mother is English, I keep forgetting that, Markus said. She comes from London, Anita reminded him. I *know*, he replied, peered at me in the dim light of the taxi. You lived in London a lot. Pity you didn't stay there permanently, he murmured sympathetically.

It is a pity, I replied. I wondered why we hadn't. I knew that answer. Frequently my father conducted the Berlin Philharmonic Orchestra. Whenever they wanted him for a series of concerts, he went back. He was a brilliant musician. Some people said he would be appointed permanent conductor one day. Not now, I thought, and shrank down into my coat, fear taking hold. Shivers ran through me. I wondered where he was at this moment. My lovely father. Dirk Landau. Who loved us all so much. Tall, fair of colouring, gentle. A good man. A man who wrongly believed Jews were safe in the Fatherland.

I snapped my eyes shut. Swallowed hard. I tried to hang onto my equilibrium. I must be brave. I must get back to Arabella. At the Schloss in the forest. I had just spent the weekend with them. I would be safe there. And they would help to find my parents. If anyone could do that, it was Prince Rudolph Kurt von Wittingen. A great aristocrat. A well-connected man, my mother always said.

Markus asked, Isn't she a princess? Yes, I answered. Irina's a Romanov. Her mother Princess Natalie was a cousin of the late tsar.

Nodding, Markus said, Nicholas. Assassinated in the Russian Revolution. In 1917. I nodded back. That's when they left Russia, I answered. They roamed around Europe. Refugees. With nothing. They settled in Berlin. Ten years ago. Recently Princess Natalie married. Her husband is a Prussian baron. Now they have a home at last. On the Lützowufer.

Peering at me again, Markus frowned, said, You told the driver to go to the Tiergartenstrasse. I know that. I gave him a hard stare and continued, We'll walk from there. Anita looked at her brother. It's not far, Markus, she said. After this Markus became quiet. We all did. I was pushing down the sobs that constantly rose in my throat. Where were they? Mummy, Papa and Erika? Were they still together? Or had they been separated? That's what they did sometimes, the Gestapo. They separated families. Oh my God, not that, I thought, shivering.

A tear slid down my cheek. Erika was only eight. She would be afraid if she'd been taken from our mother. I felt the trembling starting inside again. Anita reached for my hand. She held it tightly. I thought I was going to choke on the tears in my throat. Anita squeezed my hand. I squeezed back. Whatever would I do if I didn't have Anita and Markus?

We got out of the taxi at the Tiergartenstrasse. Markus paid the driver, carried my suitcase. I led them down that lovely street near the park. We left it at the intersection between the Hofjägeralle and Stülerstrasse, making for the Lützowufer. As I glanced at the Landwehrkanal I thought of another friend of my mother's, who lived in an apartment overlooking the canal. Renata von Tiegal.

Eventually we were on the Lützowufer. I led Anita and Markus to the house where Princess Irina Troubetzkoy lived with her Romanov mother and her stepfather, the Herr Baron.

The house was in total darkness except for one window next to the front door. I knew this was the small office on the ground floor where the baron's secretary worked. Markus lifted the heavy brass knocker, banged it several times. Almost immediately the door was opened. It was Princess Irina herself who stood there. Her burnished red hair was a fiery halo around her head in the light from the foyer. Opening the door wider, she beckoned us inside. Immediately locking the door, she looked us over. Then she pulled me into her arms. It will be all right, she told me in her perfect, slightly accented English. I hope so, I murmured.

Releasing me, she turned to Markus and Anita. I introduced them to her. She smiled at them, said, Let us go into the drawing room at the back. We can talk there. She led us through the shadowy foyer, down the corridor. I knew the drawing room. I had often been there with my mother.

Princess Irina told us to be seated. She went over to a round table where there was a pot of coffee, and cups and saucers on a silver tray. Would you like a hot drink? she asked, turning to look at us, adding that it was a cold night.

We all said yes, and thanked her. She poured, asked who wanted milk and sugar. I carried the cups to Anita and Markus. The four of us sat drinking the coffee near the fire, warming ourselves in front of its blaze. After a short while Irina looked at me, asked, What happened, Gabriele? I told her everything. How I had been staying with the von Wittingens for the weekend, being a companion to the children, Diana and Christian, looking after them. She seemed to know this. I then explained that the prince's chauffeur had brought me back to Berlin earlier today, dropped me off near my home. And that I had found the flat empty. I told her everything Mrs Weber had said to me . . . and that the Gestapo had taken my family.

When I had finished, Princess Irina nodded, her face grim. She looked at me and then at Markus. Slowly she said, Last week something savage and evil was released in this city, the power of the Nazi thugs. They came out in force. Kristallnacht, that's what they're calling it . . . *Crystal Night*. Because of the broken glass, I'm sure. What a pretty name for such a foul and brutal assault. Only they would think of *that*. Windows broken in Jewish homes, in shops, cafés, restaurants and in the synagogues. So many people killed. No, let me correct myself. So many *Jews* killed. It's an outrage. This government is a band of gangsters, murderers. Their savagery is a sign of the times.

The princess paused, looked at Markus and Anita, asked softly, Are you Jewish? They both nodded. She said, You must be careful, be discreet, don't draw attention to yourselves—

The shrill ringing of the cell phone on the bedside table made Justine sit up with a start. She jumped out of the chair, ran to grab the phone, immediately brought it to her ear. 'Hello?'

'It's me,' Joanne said. 'Do you have a minute or two to chat?'

'Yes, I do,' Justine responded, keeping her voice as steady as she could. 'You sound odd, Jo. What's the matter?'

'Bad news, I'm afraid. Daisy has come down with an ear infection.'

'Oh my God!' Justine exclaimed and sat down on the bed.

'The doctor doesn't want her to go to school.'

'So what you're saying is that you won't be able to come next week. That's it, isn't it?'

'It is, Justine. And we're so sorry and disappointed. Richard will be calling you later. He had to fly to Washington earlier today. A meeting about a boutique hotel there. Anyway, those are the facts. *Daisy can't travel for the next couple of weeks.* Richard is worried about Gabriele. He knows how upset your grandmother is going to be.'

'She will be, and so will Anita. It was going to be a big family reunion. But what can you do?'

'Richard wants you to come up with another date . . . when we can come to Turkey,' Joanne said. 'In June.'

'I understand. But I'm not sure what Gran's plans are,' Justine said.

'Okay. Listen, are you all right? You sound as if you have a cold.'

'That's right, I do.' Justine seized on this explanation, not wanting to confide in Joanne at this moment, to tell her about the black leather book and its shattering contents.

The two friends chatted a few moments longer, then said goodbye. As Justine walked back to the chair, the phone she was holding in her hand began to ring again. 'Hello?' she said.

'It's me, Justine,' Gabriele said. 'I just wanted you to know we landed in Bodrum and Anita and I are now at the hotel.'

'Gran, oh, Gran!' Justine cried. Immediately the tears started, and she began to weep. 'Gran, I love you so much. I want you to know that. How on earth could you bear the things that happened to you? I wish you were here; I want to put my arms around you, and hold you close. I want to love and protect you always, Gran.'

'Oh, Justine, don't cry. I knew the fragments, the scenes from my life would upset you, but I also needed you to know the truth, darling.'

'Now that I know some of it, I've so many questions for you, Grandma.'

'I can't answer them now, lovey, I'm about to have a meeting with the clients. Anyway, you'll have all the answers soon, if you keep on reading. I shall call you tomorrow morning to see how you are. And make sure Ayce makes supper for you. Promise me you'll eat.'

'Yes, I will, I promise. I love you, Gran.'

'And I love you too, Justine. Very much.'

THIRTY-FIVE

Justine was about to pick up her grandmother's book when there was a knock on the door. 'Come in,' she called.

Ayce popped her head inside, and announced, 'I have brought tea, Miss Justine.'

'Thank you, Ayce,' Justine replied, beckoning her to come forward.

Ayce did so, placed the tea tray on the coffee table in front of Justine and, with a smile, left the bedroom. After pouring a cup of tea, adding lemon and sweetener, Justine took a few sips, and then picked up the book, anxious to keep reading.

She found the exact place where she had left off quite easily, and scanned the page, her eyes settling on the words:

. . . don't draw attention to yourselves.

They both nodded. We talked for a while longer. Princess Irina spoke about the danger in the streets, especially at night. Rising, going over to a small desk at one end of the room, she sat down in the chair, writing on a pad. When she returned, she handed Markus a piece of paper, asked him to telephone her once they were safely home. This is the number here. I have also put down the number of the von Wittingens' Schloss. I want you to have it, the princess added. I am taking Gabriele there for a few days.

Anita threw me a look of dismay mingled with worry. I said, I will be in touch, I promise. The princess looked at her and said kindly, Perhaps you will be able to come and visit. I shall ask them if you can, Anita. Maybe at the weekend.

This last comment brought a quavery smile to Anita's face. I loved Anita. She was my best friend. We had known each other since childhood. I had helped her cope with her grief when her beloved father died five years ago. Now her mother was in Turkey looking after her sister. A widow who was ill. Anita missed her mother. A lump came into my throat as I automatically thought of Mummy. I wanted to weep. My heart clenched. I could not help wondering if she was all right, what her terrible fate might be. I was glad I was sitting down. I felt weak.

It was Markus who suddenly stood up and, turning to the princess, he gave a small bow. I think we must leave. Thank you, Princess Irina. You have been most kind. Anita also thanked her. I hugged them both. Whispered to Anita that I would see her soon. Together we walked to the front door. Once they had left, the princess turned the key in the lock, bolted the door. She said, We will go to the kitchen, Gabriele. We must both eat. Keep up our strength.

I followed her down the corridor. She explained that the staff were off this evening. That her mother, Princess Natalie, and the Herr Baron were visiting his estate in Baden-Baden. Then she remarked that they might remain there indefinitely. She said her stepfather, an anti-Nazi, anti-Fascist aristocrat was of the old school. That he believed Hitler was going to lead Germany into an unnecessary war with England. Perhaps all of Europe. He thinks Hitler will destroy Germany, she suddenly announced. He says the dictator is a madman, a megalomaniac. I tend to agree with him, Gabri.

I remained silent. But would remember those words. Once in the kitchen she quickly busied herself. A soup was brought out of the cold larder, put on the stove to heat. She asked me to fill the kettle with water. To make tea. I did, carried it to the stove. She returned to the larder, brought out smoked salmon, ham and cheeses from the refrigerator. I felt a pang when I saw the name *Harrods* on the door of it. Mummy loved to go shopping there. My mother, my father, my sister. Where were they now? At this moment? I was filled with fear. Trembling overcame me. I couldn't keep a limb still. I hoped the princess didn't notice. I held onto the edge of the table. Took hold of myself. I must be strong. I must endure. I had to look for them, find them, rescue them. I must save them at all cost. My beloved family. Part of me.

Justine closed the black leather book, leaned back in the chair, tears trickling down her face. Fumbling in her pocket, she found a tissue, wiped her damp cheeks, took several deep breaths. How brave her grandmother had been when she was a young girl. A child really. *Fourteen*. So vulnerable, all alone, fearful . . .

Glancing at the clock on the bedside table, Justine saw to her surprise that it was almost six o'clock. Four in the afternoon in London. Michael had called her early this morning, said he would be in touch again tonight. She wanted – no, *needed* – to speak to him. But she knew better than to disturb him when he was working. She must be patient, must wait.

Placing the book on the coffee table, she picked up the small tea tray and carried it downstairs to the kitchen, where she found Ayce.

Justine said, 'Please don't make any dinner for me tonight. Tell Suna I'm not hungry. I'll have one of those mixed salads you make for lunch, Ayce. The chopped salad.'

Ayce nodded. 'Missy Trent say fruit too.'

Justine smiled. 'Yes, my grandmother would say that. Okay, fruit as well and hot lemon tea, but that's it.'

Ayce looked pleased, nodded. 'What time supper?'

'About eight o'clock, please, Ayce. Not before.'

Justine needed to breathe in the fresh air, to be outside, to stretch, to walk, to think clearly. Once she left the *yali*, she set off towards the tulip gardens, and experienced a sudden sense of enormous joy when she saw the blankets of flowers in all their glorious, brilliant hues . . . reds, pinks, parrot-yellow, purple and orange.

What a spectacular sight they were, growing here at the edge of the sea. And perhaps that was why they *were* there. The flowers were food for the soul; they renewed the spirit. Gabriele's doing. Her gran knew about the damaged soul.

Anyone reading Gabriele's words in her black leather book could not fail to be moved, touched in the same way she herself had been.

But because of her very personal involvement, she had also been chilled to the bone. The words had seared into her brain; she would never forget what she had just read. Not as long as she lived.

She wanted to rush back inside, to start reading again, but she just couldn't face the heartache this would cause her. She knew she must pace herself with the memoir, have moments of respite.

Already Justine was an emotional wreck. That little fourteen-year-old girl was her grandmother, and Gabriele's suffering had been horrendous. And Justine was quite certain there was much worse to come . . .

Now, following the pebbled path, she walked along the edge of the tulip beds, heading for the garden seat that faced the Bosphorus. Their seat now. Hers and Michael's. She shook her head, blinked a little, took lots of deep breaths. How good it was to be out here in this beautiful garden with its tulips and flame-coloured Judas trees, the lilac-blue wisteria . . . and beyond the pink-tinted, golden horizon where the sun was slinking down, disappearing behind the distant rim.

Her grandmother loved beauty . . . it was her antidote to ugliness, brutality, pain, suffering and loss. Justine truly understood now why the gardens at Indian Ridge had always been important to Gabriele. It was she who had made the entire property so spectacular. She had planted many tall trees and flowering bushes, including rhododendrons, hydrangeas, lilacs and the lilac-blue wisteria. Then there was the orchard filled with apple trees, and Gabriele's famous rose garden, which she had tended lovingly and for hours on end.

As a child Justine had been the main helper, the assistant gardener, her gran called her. She had passed tools and the garlic bulbs, which Gabriele said prevented the invasion of nasty little black beetles that ate the roses.

Justine smiled to herself. Remembering so much, and now understanding so much more. Her grandmother was a caring and compassionate woman, as well as so many other things.

As she finally sat down on the seat, Justine wished Michael were here. She needed to unburden herself to him, ask him certain questions. Closing her eyes, Justine relaxed, enjoying the balmy air, the smell of the sea mingling with the fragrance of the flowers. Later, when twilight descended, wrapping the *yali* in its soft blue light, the night-blooming jasmine would spill its heady scent over everything.

After a while, Justine roused herself from her myriad thoughts and stood up. She looked across at Central Istanbul with all its teeming millions and then walked back to the villa slowly.

Upstairs, fragments of her grandmother's life awaited her. She must go back to it again.

THIRTY-SIX

The moment Justine walked into the bedroom she picked up the black-leather book, sat down in the chair, and opened it. For a split second she stared at the title, *Fragments of a Life*, and wondered what was coming next, wanting to know but almost afraid to start reading again.

Finding her place, she stared at the page.

THE MARK BRANDENBURG   17 NOVEMBER 1938
I did not sleep. I cried most of the night. I could not get Mummy out of my mind. Or Papa and Erika. Every part of me ached for them. I longed to be with them. Where were they? How were they? My mind raced. I must find out what happened to them. *Where were they taken?* I must have fallen asleep from exhaustion. The princess woke me at nine o'clock this morning. She was dressed to go out. She told me to get ready, go downstairs for breakfast. Hedy, the cook, was expecting me. She confided she was going to see someone who might help us. The princess bent over me, stroked my hair tenderly, added that we would be going to stay with Arabella von Wittingen. At the Schloss in the Mark Brandenburg.

I did everything she wanted. I was ready, waiting to leave when she returned later. I could tell she did not have good news. She told me that her contact knew nothing, as yet. He would find out, she said, gave me a reassuring smile. We went out into the foyer. She leaned closer, whispered, Don't talk about private matters in front of any staff. Anywhere. I'm sure they're loyal. But better to be silent, she finished. I told her I understood.

It was Hans, the Herr Baron's chauffeur, who sat behind the wheel of the motorcar. He stowed our suitcases. Helped the princess into the back. I scrambled in after her. We sat together in silence. I wondered which way we were going to the Mark after we left the Lützowufer. We were driving towards the Tiergartenstrasse. When we passed the Tiergarten, I thought of my mother. It was laid out like a natural English park, that's why she loved it so much. The car left the Hofjägeralle, went past the Grosser Stern, and the Siegessäule, the winged victory column.

We went down the Unter den Linden. The princess closed her eyes, muttered in a low voice, They have defaced the most beautiful boulevard in Berlin. And grimaced. I knew what she meant. The Nazis had erected rows of soaring columns down its centre and its sides. Each was topped with a Nazi eagle. My mother had called it meaningless, ridiculous paraphernalia. After passing the Pariser Platz, Hans turned right.

I stiffened. We were driving up Wilhelmstrasse. At the end of this street was the Reich Chancellery where Hitler dreamed up his mad schemes with his sinister henchmen. The dreaded Führer was plotting death and destruction behind those walls. I shivered uncontrollably. The princess glanced at me. We are going to the British Embassy, she murmured. Had she read my mind? Opening her handbag, she took out a letter, showed it to me.

It was addressed to Sir Nevile Henderson, the British

Ambassador in Berlin. The car stopped outside the embassy. Hans took the letter. I peered out of the window. My heart lifted. The British flag, the red, white and blue Union Jack, was blowing in the wind. I couldn't help thinking of auntie Beryl. Far away in London. My mother's sister. Was that letter about my mother?

Once we were on our way again, Princess Irina said, Although I have been many times to Kurt's home, I do not know much about the area. Tell me about it, Gabriele, please.

I did so, explaining, The area once belonged to the conquering Teutonic knights. The forests of the Mark Brandenburg were part of their domain, and they stretch into Prussia. It has many lakes, canals and little rivers running through its many villages, and these are quaint, charming. There are three rivers in this area, the Havel, the Spree and the Oder, and several great Schlosses. The two most important belong to Prince Kurt, and Graf Reinhard von Tiegal.

Thank you, Gabri, the princess said. She settled back against the seat and closed her eyes. I did the same. We remained silent until we arrived at the castle where the von Wittingens lived.

Princess Arabella von Wittingen, my mother's best friend, stood waiting for us on the front steps of the Schloss. The moment I saw her, tears came to my eyes. She was tall, slender, blonde, blue-eyed. So similar in appearance to my mother. They were both English women, had the same silky English voices. My mother was not an aristocrat as Arabella was, but she came from a highly respected English Jewish family. Her great-great-grandfather had gone to England from France in the early nineteenth century. His name was Leo Goldsmith. He was a diamond merchant. He created a great business in Hatton Gardens, the diamond district in London. Diamonds had made my mother's family rich.

I wanted to run to Arabella when I got out of the car. I

didn't. I walked sedately, carrying my suitcase. I wanted to be grown-up. The princess followed me with Hans, who was holding her case.

When I got to the top of the steps, Arabella opened her arms. I put down the case. Stepped into them. She held me tightly, said soothing words. Then we all went inside. And Hans drove away. I did not like the chauffeur. I did not trust him. And I was glad we had kept silent on the drive here. Diana and Christian were nowhere in sight, and as I turned to Arabella to ask where her children were, she said, They're with their grandmother. They'll be here tomorrow, Gabriele. It was as if she had read my mind. Like Irina had. Was that easy to do? I must learn to keep a poker face.

Arabella led us into the great room off the hall. There was a huge fire blazing, and on the large coffee table I noticed a teapot, cups and saucers, and a plate of nursery sandwiches, as they were called in England. Princess Irina and I welcomed the hot lemon tea and the roaring fire.

Once we were settled, Arabella said, I spoke to my husband today, and he will endeavour to find out where Stella, Dirk and Erika are. She looked at Irina questioningly. I know you tried also, Irina. I did, the Russian princess said, shaking her head. No luck. But I fear the worst, I'm afraid.

I stiffened on the sofa, stared at her. What do you mean? I asked. My contact, the man I saw this morning, said he's fearful they might have been sent to a camp already, Gabri. I didn't say anything earlier. I wanted you to be here with Arabella when I told you. I wanted you to know we'll keep you safe.

But my family, I began, and burst into tears. Arabella, next to me on the sofa, put her arms around me. This only made me cry more than ever. In my mind and heart she was so closely associated with my mother.

I finally stopped crying, sat up, dried my eyes. I said, Can we get them out of the camp? I don't know, Irina murmured, sounding sorrowful. Arabella said, Let us see what Kurt comes up with. There is something else I would like to discuss with you Gabriele. I nodded. She continued, Your aunt Beryl in London. Have you telephoned her? Does she know what happened yesterday? No. I haven't phoned her. I then recounted everything, explaining what I had found when I returned to the flat. I also told her about Mrs Weber, what she had been able to tell me. I should've phoned, but I didn't think of it, I muttered. I was worried about my family.

The two women exchanged glances, and Irina said, I think I can get you an exit visa, Gabri. Arabella believes we can work it out for you to go to London. It'll take some doing, but we both feel confident we can pull it off.

I shook my head vehemently. I don't want to go! I want to stay here. To find my parents. I can't leave them behind. I won't do that. I must be brave and stay in Berlin, find Mummy and Papa, and little Erika. My voice wobbled as I spoke. I pressed my hand to my mouth. The idea of leaving without my family frightened me.

We're all going to work on it! Arabella exclaimed. We must remain calm and controlled. Handle this step by step. But in the meantime, there's no harm in putting certain things into motion. Don't you agree, Irina? I do, Irina answered, added, I will talk to C. If anyone can help, he can. And he will. He'll get the visa, Arabella. The Russian princess gave me a loving smile. I knew she was kind, caring, and wanted to reassure me. But I wasn't. Not really. Deep down inside myself I knew that once people had been taken by the Gestapo they were never seen again. The Nazis had absolute power. I had heard my father say it many times.

Later that afternoon I put on my overcoat and scarf and went for a walk. The estate was beautiful, even in winter. Great fir trees towered above, almost touching the blue sky, and there was the sound of running water everywhere. The Schloss had lots of little waterways and canals. My mother had a favourite spot here. It was a cluster of rocks on top of a rise. The view of the lake across the valley was spectacular. Mummy had liked to sit there, and read. Or while away an hour doing nothing. Sometimes Arabella made a picnic and brought Diana and Christian. There was always merriment and laughter, much joyousness when they came.

Sitting down in the shadow of the rock formation, I leaned back, closed my eyes. I heard her voice then, saying my name, calling me her darling girl, reciting her favourite poem to me or reading something from a special book.

Would I never hear that voice again? See her smile? Look into her clear blue eyes? Would I never feel her tender touch? Her loving arms around me? Was my mother gone from me forever? And little Erika? My baby sister, only eight years old? And Papa? Would I never hear him play his Stradivarius? Hear his happy laughter, see his joyful face when he was with his little family. My girls, he called the three of us. He loved us all so dearly. And we loved him. We were a happy family.

Although they had not said it directly, I was certain that the two princesses were not too optimistic about finding my parents. It was something I sensed. And I could not shake that feeling.

How do you cope with a loss like that? Justine closed the book and leaned back in the chair. Despair, loneliness, fear, sorrow . . . all those feelings must have swamped her grandmother when she was only fourteen. The thought of it overwhelmed Justine. She could hardly bear to think about it, had to leave the book for a while to recoup, settle her emotions.

Suddenly, she wanted to talk to Michael. She looked at her watch. It was seven thirty. Two hours earlier in London. She hesitated for a moment, wondering if he was in a meeting. And then, taking a deep breath, she dialled his cell and waited.

After a moment his voice was on the line. 'Dalton here,' he said.

'It's me,' Justine answered. 'Is this a bad time?'

'Hi, and no it's not. I just came back to the hotel. It's a good time.'

'There's something I want to tell you,' she said, and the tears came into her eyes.

Thirty-Seven

'So tell me,' Michael said, when Justine remained silent at the other end of the phone.

'I know a little bit more about Gran's past,' she began, and then unexpectedly her voice faltered, and she stopped speaking.

'What is it? What's the matter?' Michael said, sounding anxious. 'Do you have a cold?'

'No, I don't, I've been crying.'

'What is it, Justine? What's wrong?' he asked, his voice rising in concern and alarm.

'Nothing's wrong, Michael. It's just that I've been reading about Gran's early life, and I've been very touched, really moved. And sorrowful, actually. But that's not what I have to tell you.' There was a pause before she said, 'I just found out I'm Jewish.'

There was a silence at Michael's end of the phone.

Justine asked, 'Are you there, or did I lose you?'

'No, I'm here. I'm taken aback. So Gabriele finally told you,' he said.

'Not exactly. What I mean is, she didn't *speak* to me about it. She gave me a leather notebook. She calls it *Fragments of a*

Life, and it's handwritten, filled with bits and pieces about her life, scenes from her past. I'm beginning to realize she has chosen things that are meaningful, changed her life. She's apparently been writing it for the last ten years, ever since my mother quarrelled with her. She was planning to leave it to us in her will, but changed her mind when I found her.'

'Good God! And she never told anybody – well, at least to my knowledge she didn't. I'm glad you know you're Jewish, Justine. The fact that you didn't has been bothering me. A lot. I spoke to Anita before I left for London, and she said that she was positive you had no idea Gabriele was Jewish. Or that she and I were. I told Anita I was going to bring it up with Gabri when I got back, which alarmed her somewhat.'

'I can imagine. But now you don't have to talk to Gran, because I know.'

'It's a relief. And by the way, I was determined you were going to be filled in as soon as possible. I believe you have a right to know about your antecedents and your heritage.'

'I agree with you,' Justine responded.

'And how do you feel about it?' he asked, his curiosity echoing in his voice.

'Obviously I was startled when I discovered that Gran was not only Jewish but German-born with a German father. I had always believed Gran was English. She looks it, sounds it, and is very English in her ways, her manners.'

'Well, she is half English because of Stella, her mother, and I'm sure she absorbed a lot from her, and the aunt in London. I know from Anita that she and her mother were very close, joined at the hip. Then again, they spent a lot of time in England before the war, according to Anita. Later Gabri was married to an Englishman, Peter Hardwicke, your grandfather, and she lived there for a number of years before going to America.'

'Yes, that's true, and I guess that's the only part *you* know, isn't it, Michael?'

'It is. After Gabri saved Anita's life, they were separated, were living in different countries until the end of the war. And that's about the extent of it. Do you know, I'm not even sure how they found each other again. It was in London, though, that I'm aware of, Justine.'

'I'm sure my mother doesn't know one thing about Gran's early life. Otherwise I think she would have been much kinder to her, nicer. Perhaps the estrangement might never have happened.'

'Perhaps. But look, Gabriele has always been very tight-lipped about her life before she went to New York in the late Fifties.'

'I just wish she had told me and Rich when we were children. My father didn't know, I'm convinced of that.'

'How could she tell you, Justine? Gabriele obviously couldn't confide in anyone. If she said she was Jewish, had grown up in Nazi Germany, the questions would have come flying at her thick and fast. It's quite apparent people would have wanted to know about her life, what happened to her as a young woman.'

'I suppose so, and she is very striking, was truly a beauty when she was a much younger woman. Charming, very elegant. People were drawn to her. They *would* have wanted to know more.'

'Gabriele can't dredge up those years. That's the reason she has never talked. And never will. I understand that, Justine. She can't bear to relive what happened to her,' Michael said. 'It's too painful.'

Justine murmured, 'I've been on an emotional roller coaster all day, Michael.'

'I'm sure you have. I hope Gabri will let me read it. What do you think?'

'I did mention that to her, and she said I could tell you about the book. After all, you've been like a grandson to her all of these years, given her love, shown compassion and understanding. You've been extremely close to her. Of course she'll want you to read it.'

'Yes, we've been close and she's given *me* a lot of love in return. I would like to know about those mysterious years in her life. I think that's only natural.'

'Something else came up, Michael. Joanne called earlier today. I'm afraid Daisy has come down with an ear infection—'

'They're not coming!' Michael exclaimed, cutting across her.

'That's right. She can't travel. Not for two weeks.'

After she and Michael had hung up, Justine decided to go down-stairs and have supper. Although she was not very hungry, she knew if she didn't appear soon Ayce would come looking for her.

It was Suna who greeted her when she went into the kitchen. 'Good evening, Miss Justine,' she said. 'Ayce on terrace.'

Justine nodded, murmured her thanks and went outside. She spotted Ayce setting a small table in readiness for her dinner. 'Thank you,' she said as she came to a stop next to the pretty young Turkish woman, smiling at her. 'What a great idea you had. It'll be nice to eat outside.'

Ayce smiled back. 'I bring chopped salad?'

'Yes, please, Ayce, I'd like to eat now.' Justine sat down at the table and picked up the glass of iced tea Ayce had just poured, took a sip. Ayce hurried off.

It was a lovely night, the sky a deep pavonine blue, with stars gradually coming out, and a hint of moon floating above Central Istanbul. Justine found herself relaxing, her mind focused on Michael.

THIRTY-EIGHT

After supper on the terrace, Justine returned to her bedroom. Now that she had spoken to Michael, and had a short respite from the book, she wanted to start reading it again, needing to know more about her grandmother's past.

Within seconds she had settled herself in the chair, picked it up, and turned the pages until she came to the part where she had left off.

When I returned to the Schloss after my walk, Princess Arabella was waiting for me in the great room. Do you feel better now? she asked me. I nodded. I needed to calm myself, I explained. I sat down in the chair opposite her. And waited for her to speak. I could see she looked serious. She said, Let us go to my study, Gabriele. We must make the phone call to your aunt in London. Let us do it now. She must be told. I nodded. Stood up. Followed her out of the room. Her study was across the hall. She went straight to the desk. Beckoned for me to follow. I did. Indicating the chair where I should sit, she picked up the receiver. Handed it to me. I knew my aunt's number by heart. I dialled her in London. Waited.

Eventually it rang through. She answered it. I said, It's me, auntie Beryl. Gabriele. Oh hello, darling, how are you? she asked in her warm but brisk voice. I was suddenly unable to speak. My throat closed. I gulped. Then I managed to say, Mummy has disappeared, auntie Beryl. And Papa and Erika. They were taken by the Gestapo.

Auntie Beryl cried, No! No! Oh no, not my darling Stella, not Dirk and Erika. It's true, I said. Where are you? she cried in alarm. Are you safe? I am with Arabella von Wittingen. Here she is, auntie Beryl. I could hear my aunt weeping, trying to control herself at the other end of the phone. I stood up.

After greeting my aunt, whom she knew, Arabella sat down, sympathized with her, gave her the details that I had passed on earlier. She told my aunt I could stay with them. I would be safe in the country. She also said that Princess Irina Troubetzkoy could get me an exit visa. That they were going to get me to England. Somehow. To her.

My aunt must have told her she would send money, as much as they needed, because Arabella said, 'No, Beryl, we don't need lots of money from you. We don't need any. Thank you. My husband is happy to do this for Gabriele. We will stay in touch. As soon as we have the exit visa for Gabri we will let you know. We'll phone when we have more news of Stella. Then she was listening to my aunt. Soon she beckoned me.

I went to the phone. My aunt said, Take care of yourself, Gabri. I am here waiting for you. And listen to the princess. She has your interests at heart, as if you are her own flesh and blood. I will, I promised. I hung up.

Princess Irina came into the study. She was smiling. I spoke to C. Is he going to help us with Gabri? Arabella asked. Of course, Irina replied, I feel as if a weight has been lifted. Now I am all ready to start working on your project.

305

I looked from one to the other. Arabella said, Come along, Gabriele. We are going to the attics. To rummage. In the trunks. For clothes. My new project. I followed the two princesses as we mounted the stairs.

At one moment I heard Irina say, We're in for a long siege, Belle. I'm afraid C sounds very grave. He thinks the Nazi riots a week ago are only the beginning. He says Hitler has plans to engulf the Western democracies in war. A war like we've never seen. C is dismayed. So are many of the generals. They are angry. They want Hitler out.

Arabella nodded. I'm not surprised. There may well be a revolt. I agree we have to get rid of Hitler. One must always strike at the head of the beast, Arabella added. It's the only way to kill it. The man is diabolical. And totally mad.

There were many large trunks in the attics. Arabella showed me one, directed Irina to another. Take everything out, examine it, and decide if it's worth remaking. The seamstress I have works wonders. I did as she said, examined every piece of clothing. And listened. They spoke freely in front of me. They trusted me.

Princess Irina said, I asked C if he could get Gabri a new passport. But he doesn't know if he can. Maybe false papers. But he prefers to use the legitimate passport. It worries me, though. Why, Arabella asked without lifting her head. It has J for Jew stamped on it. A new Nazi law was passed in October. Oh God, Arabella said in a low voice. What will they think of next? She sounded suddenly despondent.

Irina said, One of my Polish friends told me the other day that Goebbels has a new name for us young international aristocrats from foreign countries. He calls us *international garbage*. Irina laughed. Arabella didn't. She said in an icy voice, And Doctor Goebbels is Nazi filth. She continued to rummage in the trunk.

Suddenly Arabella spoke again. I couldn't believe my eyes

at the British Embassy last week, she said. Somebody there must be crazy. They invited the worst trash, including a few so-called lady guests who looked as if they worked at Madame Kitty's brothel.

This comment made Irina laugh again. But she remained silent. Arabella spoke in a brighter voice as she straightened, and closed the lid of the trunk. She said, Adam von Trott is coming to dinner on Saturday, and Reinhard and Renata von Tiegal. Would you like me to invite C? Irina stood staring at her. I'm not sure. He would enjoy it perhaps, she answered. All of our friends think the way he does. He is not socializing much these days. He has his hands full.

I understand, Arabella said. Kurt has great affection for him. Kurt and C are of the same ilk. By birth, upbringing, tradition and conviction, they are the antithesis of Hitler, all that he stands for.

Irina closed the lid of her trunk. I kept my head in mine. I wanted to listen to them. The Russian princess murmured, Many of the naval officers who work for him think the same way. In fact, there isn't one ministry that doesn't have men who hate the Nazis, condemn what they are doing. All these hateful acts infuriate them. Anyway, I will ask him, Belle.

Arabella told us to sort the clothes into separate piles of dresses, coats, jackets and suits. She told us that Prince Kurt predicted a long siege. Shortages soon. Food and clothes would be scarce. It would be a long and terrible war, she added.

Later I went to my room. I wanted to be alone. I was not in the room I usually had. Instead Arabella had put me in the one that my mother had always considered hers. I liked it. And it seemed to welcome me. I felt my mother's presence everywhere.

Prince Kurt did not arrive until Saturday. He brought the children with him. Christian was twelve. Diana was nine. They were happy to see me. I enjoyed being their companion.

There was only one rule we had to obey. We must speak English at all times. Even when Gretchen, their governess, was present. Princess Arabella insisted on this. It was no hardship. She wanted them to be fluent in her native language. She said I was a good influence because I spoke perfect English.

Later that afternoon, Arabella took me to the library to see the prince. He was kind, spoke gently to me. His news was bad. I sat with Arabella. Listening to him. I was shaking in every limb. He told us, Your parents and Erika were taken to Buchenwald. I made many enquiries. This is the information I have been given. I am so sorry, Gabriele. So very sorry.

I couldn't speak. I couldn't stop shaking. My heart was crushed. I had lost them. I knew that. Whatever would I do without Mummy? And Papa and my little sister? And how would they manage without me? I always made them laugh when they were sad. I gave them all my love. I helped my mother. I looked after Erika. We had been one unit. Now I was one person. Alone.

Arabella witnessed my distress. She took me in her arms and held me close. I wept for a long time. She comforted me. And so did the prince. I asked if my family would be released after the war? He said, Of course they will, Gabri. That day will come. And it will be a day of rejoicing.

Later, when I was back in my room, I held on to that thought. I lay down on the bed, where my mother had slept, and I felt her presence once more. She was there with me. Hovering over me like a guardian angel. I could smell the scent of roses. Her favourite perfume. And if I closed my eyes I could hear her voice. Her lovely silky English voice. I wept for my family until I fell asleep.

That evening friends of the von Wittingens came to dinner. I saw them in the distance. Once I had eaten with the children and Gretchen I went back to my room. I was at ease there. I felt closer to my mother within those four walls. And safer.

Tomorrow Anita was coming to stay. This pleased me. I couldn't wait for Markus to arrive with her. I soon fell asleep. I was exhausted. I must have slept for about an hour, maybe longer. Suddenly I woke up at the sound of voices in my room. I lay still, terrified. Listening. Had the Gestapo come to take me away? Within seconds I realized I was alone. Yet I still heard the voices. I turned on the lamp. My room was empty. The voices were coming from the fireplace. From the room underneath mine, downstairs. The parlour. I got out of bed and went to kneel in the fireplace. I heard Irina say, But even if Hitler is assassinated, there is still the government to deal with. That is true, a man's voice responded. I recognized it. It was Reinhard von Tiegal speaking. He continued, I'm not planning to commit tyrannicide, I'm only speculating about it.

Another man's voice entered the conversation. I knew it was Sigmund Westheim. He said, Any plot to kill Hitler would have to be comprehensive. Power would have to be seized instantly. Chosen men would have to run the government; they would have to be ready to take over the minute he was dead. Take full control.

Kurt said, There are many committed anti-Nazis amongst us. Maybe one of them can formulate a plan to get rid of that madman in the Reich Chancellery. I understand from certain sources that there have been a lot of crazy outbursts lately. He's obviously totally mad. I tremble when I think of the atrocities he'll commit next, if he isn't stopped. I blame Hitler for that unconscionable brutality against the Jews. Kristallnacht was entirely his doing.

Princess Irina said, I understand from Canaris that a vast number of the generals want to stop Hitler. The admiral says that they all fear he will destroy Germany from within.

Prince Kurt spoke out. He said, As head of the Abwehr there's nothing that the admiral doesn't know. After all, he's in charge of German Military Intelligence. He's already doing so much, helping people to get out. Jews, Catholics, dissidents. Those targeted by the Gestapo. He takes terrible risks. Some say it's an open secret he's virulently anti-Nazi. Yet he manages to play the game with Hitler, who admires him. He's walking a tightrope. Yes, he is a good man. We must protect him, be careful what we say, and to whom. There are Nazi spies all over. None of us is truly safe.

I heard the prince cough, then he continued, I propose a toast. To Admiral Wilhelm Canaris. A true hero. *Prost!*

Everyone said *Prost*, joining in the toast. Soon the voices faded away. The parlour became silent. They had gone in to dinner. I pushed my head deeper into the grate, not understanding how their voices had carried up here. But they had. There must be some flaw in the flue or the chimney. I hadn't meant to eavesdrop. I just couldn't help it. And their secrets were safe with me.

I went back to bed, lay awake for a long time, thinking about what I had heard. Their words had cheered me up, given me hope. But they had also frightened me. I didn't want anything to happen to my friends. Especially Irina. Although she was about twenty-seven, she seemed younger sometimes. And she was impulsive and brave. And she had her own standards, she had once told me. She had also explained that the Romanov autocracy had fallen when she was six, her mother twenty-five, which was when they had fled Russia. They had lived in Lithuania, Silesia and Poland before coming to Berlin. Despots and dictators, she would mutter sometimes. Our world ruined because of them and their thirst for power. I knew she would fight the Nazis with all of her strength. I just hoped she wouldn't take too many risks.

Justine put the book down, astonishment written across her face. What she had just read astounded her. Obviously there had been enormous resistance to the Nazis in many quarters. Unexpectedly, she remembered once reading about the German aristocracy working against that hideous and evil Nazi regime. There had been underground movements all over Germany.

Rising, she put the book down and left her bedroom. Running downstairs, she went into the kitchen and got a bottle of water from the refrigerator. After taking a glass, she headed upstairs; she had to read more about her grandmother's experiences.

THIRTY-NINE

As she returned to her bedroom, Justine made the decision to keep reading for as long as possible tonight. She had the urgent need to know more, wanted to bury herself in *Fragments of a Life*. Opening the black leather-bound book, she turned the pages until she came to where she had left off a few minutes before.

THE MARK BRANDENBURG   10 DECEMBER 1938
I was waiting in the small study which opened off the big hall when Gretchen poked her head around the door. I hear a motorcycle, she said, it must be Markus and Anita. Immediately I put down the book I was reading, jumped up off the sofa. Gretchen had gone out into the hall. I followed her. I was excited. Anita was coming to stay for a few days. Markus had brought her out for a visit in late November; I hadn't seen her since then. The two princesses believed it was safer here than in Berlin. I agreed with them. Gretchen was standing on the front steps. I went to join her. She was laughing. I laughed too. For the first time in weeks.

Anita was sitting on the back of Markus's motorcycle.

Bundled up in scarves and a large green tartan beret I had brought back from London for her last year. She was wearing her very best navy-blue coat. Anita had acquired a windburn on her ride from Berlin. Her cheeks were like red apples. She was holding onto her brother tightly.

The motorcycle came to a roaring stop. I went down the steps, followed by Gretchen. I think the young governess liked Markus. A lot. Whenever he brought Anita here, or took her home, Gretchen was hovering. She was a nice young woman. I liked her. I think Markus did too.

Anita, always agile, a bit of a tomboy, jumped off the motorcycle, rushed to hug me. I've missed you, I said. Me too, Gabri, she answered, and grinned at me. As usual when she rode on the back of the bike, there was a rucksack on her back. She slipped it off and stood holding it.

Markus smiled at me and Gretchen. He asked, Where shall I park this? Gretchen said, Round the back near the kitchens. Will you stay to lunch, Markus?

Thank you. I will. Very kind of you, he answered. He roared off around the terrace to the back of the Schloss. Anita greeted Gretchen. Together we all went up the front steps and into the hall. I said to Anita, Prince and Princess von Wittingen have gone to see his mother. The children have gone too. They will return tonight. Princess Irina is here. She will see us later. She has gone riding with a friend. You've met her. Renata von Tiegal. She will have lunch at their Schloss.

I led Anita towards the staircase. Gretchen said she would wait for Markus at the back door, and disappeared down the corridor to the kitchen. Anita was pleased she was in her usual room. It was across the hall from mine. After she had unravelled herself from her coat and the many scarves, taken off the beret, she opened her rucksack. This is for you. She handed me a small package. I opened it, discovered my favourite marzipan fruits. Oh, thank you, Anita, I said. Hugged her.

She took a few other things out of her rucksack and put them away. The last thing she removed was her passport. She put this in the drawer too. I asked, How's your mother? Worried, she answered. She frowned. Shook her head. She said, Mutti is worried about us living here alone. And about her sister, my aunt Leonie. She doesn't get any better. If she dies my mother will come back to Berlin. Oh no, I said, dismayed. She can't do that. It's too dangerous. She's better in Istanbul.

I know. She won't listen to me. Or Markus. Anita sat down on the bed. She said, Berlin is more dangerous than ever. People are disappearing all the time. The man who owns the bakery shop, Herr Schroeder, told me his brother-in-law was taken. The whole family. Anita lowered her voice. The Gestapo are everywhere. A friend of my brother's says some people's phones are tapped.

I simply nodded. I knew things were bad. Princess Irina had been to Berlin several times. She came back with horrendous stories. She, too, had mentioned phone tapping. I looked across at Anita and smiled. It faltered. Her face was suddenly glum. Her sparkly brown eyes were dull. What is it? I asked.

Do you think I can stay here indefinitely? With you? Will Princess von Wittingen let me? But aren't you going to go with Markus to Turkey? I asked, startled. I'm waiting for my visa. It's coming any day, Anita explained. But if it's delayed, I want him to go by himself. I'll join him later.

This talk alarmed me. She couldn't travel alone. All the way across Europe to Istanbul. She hadn't travelled very much. She wasn't a veteran traveller like me.

She won't let me stay, will she? Anita said, tears forming in her eyes. Of course she will, I instantly replied. I'll ask her tomorrow. I got up, went to Anita, put my arms around her. Don't cry, I murmured. I'll make sure everything's all right for you, Anita. I promise.

Hearing this brought a watery smile to her face. I know you will, Gabri. She stood up. We'd better go down to lunch. We found Gretchen and Markus sitting in the study, each drinking a glass of lemonade. Lunch will be ready in ten minutes, Gretchen announced to us. Lotte told me. I nodded. I walked over to the small side table and poured lemonade for Anita and myself.

It was Saturday, which was why Markus was not working. He sat back, comfortable in the armchair, drinking his lemonade. He looked relaxed. Except for his eyes. I instantly noticed the anxiety in them. I asked, How is Albert Wendt? I know he's a good boss, a true friend to you. Markus nodded, sat up straighter. He said, Herr Wendt likes me, so he helps me. That's why I was able to come here today. He gave me the day off. I was taken aback. Oh do you work on Saturdays now? I do. We all do, Markus replied. Munitions are vital. We've got to keep turning them out. We're one of the biggest manufacturers, after Krupp.

Gretchen said, Prince von Wittingen is a roving ambassador for Krupp. Markus said, I know that. We talked about nothing much after this. Markus had clamped up. I don't think he was now comfortable speaking in front of Gretchen, for some reason. He was usually wary. Cautious.

Lotte came and told us lunch was served in the morning room. We followed her. She had put hot dishes on the sideboard; she told us to help ourselves. We went to look in the covered dishes. Lentil soup. A pot roast with vegetables. Apple strudel. Next to the platter of apple cake stood a jug of thick cream. The four of us had bowls of soup, and then served ourselves some of the pot roast. I noticed that the others ate sparingly, as I did. Lotte came back later with a coffee pot, cream and sugar, and left us to ourselves, as she normally did.

Princess Irina returned later in the afternoon. She told me she had no real news from Berlin. The von Tiegals had remained in the country for the last few weeks. Like everyone else, they felt much safer away from the city. And from the prowling Gestapo, the SS, the swaggering ordinary soldiers who were rude and aggressive, were out to make trouble with civilians whenever they could.

That night we had a simple buffet supper in the morning room. Later we played charades. This was one of my mother's favourite games. I kept thinking about her. I couldn't wait to go back to my room, which she had always used. This is where I felt close to her, felt her presence acutely. It comforted me to sit in the chair she had used.

Markus left the following morning. He told Anita he would phone her every night. He always did. To reassure her he hadn't been taken. The three of us watched him roar off on the motor-cycle, looking handsome and very dashing, his scarf flying out behind him. Gretchen sighed, seemed sad to see him go. Don't worry, he'll be back, I murmured, and went inside.

Later that afternoon, Princess Irina came looking for me. She found me in the library with Diana, Christian and Anita. We were playing Snakes and Ladders, the board game the von Wittingen children loved so much. Oh, there you are, Gabriele, she said, moving around the game table in her graceful way. I need you to help me with something. If you don't mind. No, I'll come right away, I said, jumping up.

Linking her arm through mine, in the charming, very personal way she had, we walked out together. Once we were in the hall, she cried in a hushed tone, I've great news! Let's go upstairs, Gabri. I could see she was excited. We sped up the wide staircase together. Once in her room, she said, I've had a message from my friend C. He needs your passport. I have to take it to Berlin. You are getting your visa. You're going to London. To your aunt Beryl. Arabella will be buying your tickets. You will go by train via Paris. Isn't that wonderful news? I shall put you on the train myself.

It is wonderful, I said, smiling, infected by her excitement. I'll get my passport. I hurried out, walked down the corridor. Suddenly I knew what I must do. I wanted to go to London. I was aware I would not see my parents until the end of the war, so why stay in Berlin when I could be with auntie Beryl? But I couldn't leave Anita stranded. She was at risk.

I stopped abruptly in the corridor, turned around and went back to Princess Irina's room. I tapped on the door. She said come in. I did. I can't go, I announced. What do you mean? she asked, frowning at me. I would like to give my exit visa to Anita. Markus already has his. I don't think hers will ever come through. The authorities know that if he leaves alone, he'll be sure to come back. Because of his sister. He won't leave her in Berlin by herself. I think Herr Wendt, his boss, got him the exit visa, but did not request one for Anita.

Maybe that is true, the princess murmured, sitting down heavily at the desk. She stared at me thoughtfully, shaking her head.

I gave her a pleading look. Will you ask C to give my exit visa to her? Please, Princess Irina. I want Anita to go with her brother to Turkey. Their mother needs them. And they are in danger.

What a selfless thing to offer to do, Irina murmured, her fixed scrutiny levelled at me.

Will C do it? I asked. I suppose he will, she said. If I explain. But how do we get her passport? Oh she has it with her, I explained. Markus insisted she carry it with her just in case they ever had to go on the run.

Like we all do, the princess answered, her face grave. This is a very brave thing you are doing, Gabriele. Very brave indeed. But it puts you in danger . . .

So that's what Gran did, Justine said under her breath. Putting down the book, standing up, stretching, she walked over to the window. Gran saved Anita's life by handing her that precious exit visa that the princess had worked so hard to get. What an act of bravery for a fourteen-year-old girl. A vulnerable Jewish girl, whose sister and parents had been taken to the death camps, and who was at risk herself.

Justine leaned her head against the windowpane, and closed her eyes. Tears seeped out from under her lids, slid down her cheeks. How noble, she thought. My grandmother is the most remarkable person I've ever known. I wonder who else would have made that kind of sacrifice?

Could I? She did not know the answer to that. Justine wiped her cheeks with a tissue, and gazed out of the window, still stunned by her grandmother's actions as a girl.

The ringing of her mobile phone brought her across the room to the bedside table. She picked it up, brought it to her ear. 'Hello?'

It was Michael. 'Are you all right?' he asked. 'I suppose you're still reading?'

'I am, yes. I just found out how my grandmother saved your grandmother's life. She gave Anita her exit visa. I suppose you know that.'

'Yes, I do. But I don't know much else about what happened to Gabri after that, after Anita and Markus left Berlin. However, I can tell you this. I've always thought it was the most extraordinary act of courage I've ever heard of in my life.'

FORTY

After filling the kettle and putting it on the stove, Justine sat down on the kitchen stool. As she waited for it to boil she found herself thinking about her grandmother again. How could she not?

Once more her mind was back with Gabriele in Berlin in 1938. What must it have been like to live in those dangerous times, when the most evil regime in the history of the world had been alive and kicking? Terror and fear had been her grandmother's constant companions, of that she was certain, and she had been so very young. *Fourteen.* Justine thought of herself at fourteen, the way she had been at that age, and her mind baulked.

A shiver ran through her and she sat very still. Gabriele had given Anita the chance to escape, to save her life, while she herself had stayed behind. Not knowing what the future held. Most likely certain death. But she had not faltered, had done it out of love for her friend. It was the most unselfish act Justine had ever heard of.

The whistling kettle brought her to her feet. She turned it off, made a mug of English breakfast tea, added lemon and sweetener and returned to her bedroom.

She was using a bookmark now, and easily found the last page she had been reading earlier.

. . . you in danger. Perhaps you must think of this decision for a while. Do not be hasty, Princess Irina finished. I said I *had* thought about it, and excused myself. I went to Anita's bedroom, and told her about my exit visa coming through. I didn't mention C. I knew I must be discreet, very careful not to put him in danger.

Oh, I'm so happy for you! Anita said. Your aunt will be waiting for you with loving arms. She's nice, your aunt Beryl. I like her.

I sat down on the bed next to Anita, and took hold of her hand. I'm not going to use the exit visa. I am going to give it to you, Anita. So you can go with Markus to Turkey. To be with your mother.

Anita was flabbergasted. She turned, gaped at me. Didn't speak for a moment. Finally she said, No, no. I can't do that, Gabri! It's your visa. It would be wrong of me to take it. You must, I insisted. Anita shook her head. Furiously. Her face became set in that way she had. *No.* I won't take it, she said again. I asked her to give me her passport. So that the exit visa could be attached. She would not. And she dug her heels in, as my mother would have called it. She was adamant.

I began to talk to her. Trying to be persuasive. I couldn't make a dent. Eventually I said in a low voice, Listen to me, Anita. I haven't told you this. But I know where my parents and Erika were taken. Buchenwald. My voice broke then and I choked on the words. I took a deep breath. I said unsteadily, I know now that I will not see them until the war ends.

Anita had stiffened. She stared at me. Her face was white, strained, her sparkly brown eyes filled with fear. I realized she was aghast. How do you know? Who told you which camp?

Prince Kurt, I answered. He has access to a lot of important people in the Third Reich. He found out about them for me. I believe him. He is a good man. When the war ends I want to be *here*, Anita. To find my parents. Not far away in London. I might not be able to get back for ages. I must stay here in Germany. *I am going to stay*. Even if you don't use my visa. So why should we waste it? Please use it, Anita. It's foolish not to. After further discussion and tears on both our parts, Anita agreed. Finally. She gave me her passport, so that I could hand it on to Irina, who would take it to Berlin to have the exit visa attached.

I went back to the princess's bedroom, told her everything. She nodded, put Anita's passport in her bag. Then she glanced at me. There was an odd look in her violet-blue eyes, as she said softly, What a wonderful friend you are, my brave little girl. You have the kind of courage I've rarely seen in a grown man.

BERLIN   20 DECEMBER 1938
We stood together on the platform of the Schlesischer Bahnhof. People milled around. It was very busy. There were a lot of Gestapo about, and troops of the Wehrmacht, and people were already boarding the Berlin–Paris train which had just pulled in.

Princess Irina had not wanted me to come to see Anita and Markus off. She was afraid for me. But I had insisted. Anita held onto my hand tightly. Her eyes were full of tears. Markus stood just behind me. His hand was on my shoulder. Once again, he whispered in my ear, Thank you, Gabri, thank you with all my heart.

Princess Irina had come with me, was concerned about my safety. Suddenly she turned around, smiled as Arabella and Kurt von Wittingen joined us. They greeted us cordially. The smile on my face suddenly slipped. I froze. A man was striding toward us. An officer wearing the field-grey uniform of the

Wehrmacht. To my horror he stopped alongside the prince.

Kurt von Wittingen turned, nodded when he saw him. They shook hands. The officer then came and greeted each of us as if he knew us, shaking our hands in a friendly manner. He even kissed Princess Irina on the cheek. She noticed my terrified expression, winked. I then understood this was not an enemy but a friend. The officer said something to Prince Kurt, who stepped over to Markus.

Show me your papers again, my boy, the prince said, sounding as if he were speaking to a relative. Markus took them out of his overcoat pocket, handed them over. The officer also looked at the documents. He said to Markus, Where are your tickets? Markus gave them to him, and said, Return tickets to Paris from Berlin. Coming back to Berlin on January tenth.

The officer inclined his head, handed the tickets back. He lowered his voice when he said, At the border town of Aachen your papers will be checked, your luggage searched. It's normal. There are a lot of Gestapo, SS and troops on this train – that is routine also. Now let me get you both settled in the compartment. The train will be leaving shortly.

I hugged Anita, then Markus. So did the two princesses. Prince Kurt shook their hands, wished them well. They followed the officer onto the train. Anita turned on the top step and blew me a kiss. I blew one back. Then she disappeared from view. I wondered if I would ever see her again.

A moment later she was tapping the compartment window. I waved. Irina and Arabella did the same. The guard was coming down the platform, waving a red flag. The train was hooting, emitting steam. Three SS officers pushed past us, boarded the train. They were followed by more troops, and several women, two with small children.

The officer in the field-grey uniform who had helped Anita and Markus to the compartment reappeared, came to join us.

We all watched the train as it slid out of the station and went rattling on its way to Paris. Then we left the station, went our separate ways.

Irina took me back with her to her stepfather's house on the Lützowufer. We would spend today and tonight there before returning to the Schloss tomorrow. We were to stay in the country until the New Year.

When we got back to the house, Hedy made us hot chocolate and served it with warm doughnuts. We were both hungry. As we settled in front of the fire, Irina said, The officer who came to help them onto the train is with the Abwehr. We thought it would give Anita and Markus a certain legitimacy if they were being looked after by a colonel in German Military Intelligence. I believe it went well, she added. Is he working with C? I asked. She nodded.

The princess was silent for a moment, before confiding, When we were leaving the station, he told me he was given a lot of salutes from troops when he was ushering them into the compartment. It's all about validity. And who you know.

Yes, I agreed. After a moment the princess said, Anita told me they are staying in Paris, then go on to Nice. Yes, I answered. They arrive tomorrow morning at the Gare du Nord. They will spend the night at the station hotel. Not any longer. They want to keep moving. In Nice they will take the freighter to Istanbul, passing through the Dardenelle Straits. Just as she told you.

The princess looked thoughtful. Anita explained that her mother had arranged for them to travel on the freighter. I hope everything works out all right, that nothing goes wrong.

So do I, I murmured.

FORTY-ONE

'It's me, Rich,' Justine said. 'Is this a bad time? I need to talk to you.'

Her brother sounded surprised to hear her voice, and exclaimed, 'It's fine for me, but what about you? It's late in Istanbul.'

'I'm wide awake,' she answered. 'How was Washington?'

'Great. I just got back to New York a while ago on the shuttle. I was going to call you, Juju, but I thought you'd be asleep.'

'I wanted to know how Daisy was.'

'She's doing fine.'

'I'm glad Joanne's around. She's very motherly.'

'What about Gran? Isn't she waiting for me? Anxiously?'

'She is, and she doesn't know about Daisy's ear infection yet since she's still in Bodrum. I shall tell her when she gets back with Anita.' Justine paused, then said, 'I've had an idea. I was thinking it might be great if I brought Gran to New York to see you and Daisy. She'd also love to see Indian Ridge. She still owns it lock, stock and barrel, to put it bluntly.'

'That would be great to bring Gran. Oh God, I hope she doesn't hate the changes I've made at Indian Ridge.'

'How could she? Everything's beautiful. Anyway, she's looked through the photograph album I brought with me. And she was very admiring of your talent, I told you that.'

'I know you did, but a photograph's a bit different from the real thing.'

Now that she had the call to New York out of the way, Justine reached for the leather-bound book and started to read again.

THE MARK BRANDENBURG 4 MAY 1939

It was a beautiful day. The sun was shining and the spring flowers were already in bloom in the garden. There were lilacs coming out and apple blossom in bud. I wanted to go outside. Take a walk. But I had to finish my studies first. I liked the library where I studied every day. It was full of books and beautiful old paintings. The von Wittingen children worked alongside me, were good companions. But this afternoon Diana and Christian had gone to Berlin with their mother. To have their medical check-ups. I missed them when they were away. Christian and Diana were warm, loving and full of high jinks. They kept me laughing even when I was sad. They brought a lot of life to this old castle, helped to create a cheerful ambience.

The two princesses had undertaken my schooling. At the beginning of this year. *My guardian angels.* That was how I thought of them. They loved my mother. So felt responsible for me. They were similar in character. Practical, down-to-earth women who constantly said, 'Let's get on with it.' And did so. Both were aristocrats yet there was not one snobbish bone in their bodies.

Their lives had been very different, though. Arabella, daughter of an English earl, with her own title, had had a loving and stable upbringing in a happy family in Yorkshire. There she had lived in a world that was safe, secure and genteel. She had been protected.

Irina, born a Romanov princess, had lost everything at the age of six when her father was murdered, her uncle Tsar Nicholas II assassinated. She and her mother had gone on the run. Living hand to mouth. Relying on the kindness of others in different European countries. And especially in Poland, where they had made many close friends. Irina often spoke to me about these chums of hers and the days she and her mother had lived in Warsaw. Explained how much they owed their survival to them. Somehow she and her mother had managed to stay alive. Irina was strong, dependable, smart, inventive. Perhaps because of her vagabond life as a refugee. She told me once she was a survivor.

They were like loving aunts. But I never forgot Mummy, with her sky-blue eyes, golden hair, quick mind and loving nature. I thought of her every morning, and of Papa and Erika. And every night when I went to bed. My family were never out of my thoughts. I yearned for them. I believed I would see them again. Once the Third Reich ceased to exist. Irina, Arabella and Kurt said it would collapse one day. In the not too distant future. This belief kept me going. Gave me hope.

After Anita and Markus had left Berlin in December, I returned to the Schloss with Irina. We have remained here. I missed Anita but I was relieved she had escaped. Markus had phoned when they reached their destination. Were with their mother in Istanbul. After speaking with them I breathed a lot easier.

It was several days after this call that Princess Irina told me the building where they had lived was raided by the Gestapo only two days after Anita and Markus had fled Berlin. Many Jewish families living there had been taken away, sent to the camps. This information had come to her from the nice colonel who had been at the station to see them safely off. She told me his name was Colonel Hans Oster, that he worked with C in the Abwehr, German Military Intelligence. Irina's face was grave when she added, Anita and Markus got out in the nick of time, Gabri. God bless C.

I was constantly worried about Irina. I knew she was deeply involved with one of the resistance movements. She went to Berlin a lot. Stayed for days on end. I was full of dread until she came back.

Arabella worried about her. She was unusually tense, anxious when Irina was away. Taking chances, she would mutter to herself. Doing God knows what. Arabella was schooling me in English literature. My mother had always loved books and reading. She had encouraged me. Over these last months I have read many stories by Charles Dickens, Jane Austen, Thomas Hardy, and Shakespeare's plays. Arabella also introduced me to her own favourites, the Brontë sisters, who had lived in Yorkshire in the nineteenth century.

Irina focused on geography. Gretchen invited me to join the children when she taught them mathematics and gave them painting lessons. She was a talented artist. She encouraged me to work at my art. She thought I had a good eye and a great sense of colour. They all encouraged me. They wanted the best for me.

There were times when I wanted to go to Berlin with Irina. She refused to take me. She said it was safer here in the country. At the Schloss. I realized she was right. But I still longed to go to the city I had always loved.

I had just finished working on an essay about Emily Brontë and *Wuthering Heights* when Gretchen came into the library. She asked me to go for a walk. Suggested we take our sketchbooks with us. I agreed. It was such a lovely day for sitting in the sun, drawing.

Princess Irina had instituted a rule when we had returned to the Schloss last December. She insisted on knowing where everyone was when she was in charge. When the von Wittingens were away. I found her in the small study. Asked her if I could go sketching with Gretchen. She said, All right, but please come back in time for tea. I promised we would.

Gretchen and I walked down to the forests. There was a secluded glade near a small lake where we often sketched. We set ourselves up on our folding stools and were soon at work.

The sudden roar of motorcycles invaded the peacefulness, brought our heads up. Startled, we stared at each other. Gretchen exclaimed, I think there are trespassers on the estate. I nodded. Glanced around nervously. So did she. I was instantly on guard. Fully alert. Concerned. Wondering if the motorcycles spelled trouble.

A moment later two soldiers in the field-grey uniforms of the Wehrmacht came rolling down the dirt track on their motorcycles. They saw us, glanced at us, drove on. But a moment later they came roaring back, and braked. Instantly, I stood up. Nervous. Ready to flee. They were both smiling. Looked harmless enough. But instinctively I knew they were not. One of them said, Hello girls, hello there!

Gretchen was still seated. She said, What are you doing here? This is private property. So what? the other soldier retorted, grinning. You are trespassing. Leave this estate at once, she ordered.

I said, Come on, let's go. I began to edge away. Gretchen sat on the stool as if frozen there. Let's go! I hissed. I was filling with dread. Go where? the other soldier said, and got off his motorcycle. He walked over to me. I took a step back. He grabbed me. Not so fast, blondie, he whispered, pulling me closer, staring into my face. I struggled with him. Fought him. Protested. Shouted at him. He held me tighter in his grip. Laughed in my face. He had been drinking. There was the smell of liquor on his breath. I kicked him on the shin. Pounded my fist on his shoulder.

I must have hurt him. He suddenly let go of me. I ran. Gretchen was running too. Unfortunately she tripped. Fell to the ground. I turned back. Helped her to her feet. I felt a hard blow on the back of my neck. I was felled to the ground. The soldier who had called me blondie pulled me by my arms, dragged me closer to the lake. Was he going to drown me?

Run, run, I shouted to Gretchen. She tried to do so. But she was obviously hurt. The last I saw of her she was being thrown down by the younger soldier. She was fighting. Screaming.

I could not move. I was pinned down. He began to slap my face. I managed to claw his cheek. Blood spurted. He yelped. Angry, he hit me harder. Then he punched me in the face with his fist. Like a boxer. He grabbed my blouse, ripped it down the front. Suddenly he slid on top of me. I couldn't push him off. He was far too heavy. I was reeling from the blows. Dazed. Helpless. I screamed. He covered my mouth with his hand. I couldn't breathe. I thought he was going to kill me. He didn't. He raped me instead. Violently so.

Unexpectedly he was suddenly finished with me. I felt a lessening of his weight. I opened my eyes. He was standing, buttoning his trousers, straightening his jacket. He walked away nonchalantly without a backward glance.

I remained afraid. I decided it was wisest to play dead. I lay still. I hurt all over. My face felt raw. It was stinging. I dared not touch it.

He was suddenly shouting for the other soldier. Heinrich! Heinrich! Let's get going! There was no response. Where *was* the other one? What had he done to Gretchen? Oh my God, was she still alive? Or had he killed her?

I heard the sound of a motorcycle revving. I pushed myself

up. The soldier who raped me was smoking a cigarette. Preparing to leave. Then I saw his partner in crime. Crossing the dirt road, buttoning his jacket, grinning. He got onto his motorcycle. They roared off together. Shouting at the top of their lungs: *Sieg Heil! Sieg Heil! Long live the Third Reich! A thousand years! The Third Reich forever!*

I tried to get up. I thought I had been ripped open. I could barely walk. There was blood on my skirt, on my blouse. I stumbled away from the lake. Slowly I made it to the glade. There was no sign of Gretchen. Only two overturned folding stools. Sketchbooks on the ground.

The soldier had walked over from the other side of the dirt track. I limped across. Gretchen must be somewhere there. No sign of her. Then I heard a low moaning. I managed to make it up a short incline. I spotted her lying in a dell below me. I knew I couldn't walk down. I sat on the ground, slithered down into the dell on my bottom. Her face was a bloody mess. Her skirt was around her waist. There was blood on her legs. I touched her hand. She trembled. Afraid. It's me, I whispered. She opened her eyes. Tried to speak. I leaned closer. I can't move you. I'm going for help. She looked scared. I said, They've gone. Just stay still. I'll be back.

I crawled out of the dell, pulling myself up by clutching at grass and roots. Slowly I made it back to the Schloss. I had taken the path that led me to the back of the house. Just as I arrived at the kitchen door, it flew open. It was Lotte, the cook, putting garbage into the dustbin. When she saw me she cried, Oh my God! Gabri! Gabri! What has happened to you? She rushed to me, put an arm around me, helped me into the kitchen. Trudi, the maid, screamed when she saw me. Stop it! Shut up! Lotte shouted at her. Go and fetch Princess Irina, she instructed.

Lotte helped me to a chair. I told her Gretchen was outside. Injured. Badly injured, I thought to add. At this moment

Princess Irina came rushing into the kitchen, looking alarmed, her face stricken. She was horrified when she saw the state I was in. I told her what had happened with the two soldiers. I said we had been raped, Gretchen was still outside. That she would have to be carried back to the Schloss.

Irina was in a fury. But she controlled herself, sent Trudi to find the gardener, Klaus. His hut was in the wood across the back yard. She dispatched Giselle to the caretaker's cottage at the main gate, told her to bring the caretaker, Stefan, at once.

While the maids were gone, Irina took a wet towel and gently wiped my face. She began to ask me more questions, but then Stefan, the caretaker, was suddenly there. A moment later Klaus, the gardener, arrived. I insisted on taking them to Gretchen. The princess came with us. She was carrying one of Kurt's shotguns. I was certain she knew how to use it. Lotte stayed in the kitchen. Boiling water, taking out towels, first-aid kits, herbal medicines of her own concoction.

Klaus, the gardener, was strong. He brought Gretchen back to the Schloss. He carried her in his arms like a baby. He was angry. Stefan, the caretaker, was equally furious about the soldiers. And angry with himself. How had he not heard our screams? I told him we were deep in the forest. Too far away from the gatehouse.

The princess asked him how the soldiers could enter the estate without him knowing. He had no answer. Neither did the gardener. Klaus said we must put a fence around the edges of the estate. A high barbed-wire fence, the princess added. I will tell Prince von Wittingen when he returns from Switzerland.

Klaus carried Gretchen up to her room. Princess Irina helped me get to mine. She tended to my wounds. Lotte and Trudi cared for Gretchen. Once she had helped me, the princess phoned the doctor in the village. He arrived fifteen minutes later. He examined us, treated our wounds with salves, said he would return the next day. He, too, was flabbergasted by this attack, and outraged.

When Arabella returned from Berlin that night she was stupefied. How could this have happened here? This was her home. The family had lived here for centuries. The von Wittingens were prominent landowners, had position. Standing. That this had happened alarmed her.

It's the times we live in, Irina said. We thought we were safe here. But are we? I don't think so. This government is run by criminals, gangsters. Most of the ordinary soldiers are ignorant louts, thugs. We live under the rule of evildoers. At the mercy of dangerous men. Men without principles or humanity.

I thought of her words that night in bed. I usually cried myself to sleep. Thinking about my family, I did so again. But tonight I cried because I'd been raped. I felt violated, humiliated, dirty. My body ached all over. I was sore. My face had been punched. It was cut and bruised. I was worried that the soldier had made me pregnant. What would I do? How could I have a baby at fourteen? How would I bring it up? I had no money. I had nothing. I was alone in the world.

But the following morning I knew I had my two loyal princesses. They were both concerned for me. They talked to me about my rape, tried to counsel me. They were soothing, loving, understanding. They helped me to feel better. They told me they would always be there for me. I believed them. I knew they were true blue. My mother had told me they were.

Justine put the book down and leaned back against the pillows. She was overwhelmed by emotions, filled with sorrow. The knowledge that Gabriele had been raped at such a young age affected her deeply. She could hardly bear to think about it. Had Gran been pregnant? If so, what did she do? Had she had a child? So many questions filled her head, and she wanted to know the answers. But she knew she had to get some sleep. She turned off the light and closed her eyes. Sleep evaded her. She was unable to get those violent images of the rape out of her head.

FORTY-TWO

L ight drifting in through the gauzy curtains awakened Justine early. She had been so exhausted the night before she had forgotten to close the blinds.

Glancing at the bedside clock, she saw that it was only five. When she noticed the leather-bound book on the other side of the bed, she roused herself. She knew she had to keep reading. But first, she needed a cup of coffee.

There was no one else up. She found the kitchen deserted when she went downstairs. Ayce and Suna were nowhere in sight. After preparing the coffee, she made herself a slice of toast; it was a meagre breakfast but it was all she wanted.

Fifteen minutes later she was back in the bedroom, propped up against the pillows, reading *Fragments of a Life*.

BERLIN   1 SEPTEMBER 1939

The first day of September was a bad day for Irina. A day of doom, she called it. Germany was at war. In a sudden lightning strike at dawn, Hitler had attacked Poland. By land and air. The Poles were unprepared for the invasion, according to Irina. She had stayed glued to the BBC broadcast from

London. She listened to the radio all the time. So did many Berliners. Everyone believed it was the best source of genuine news.

The mightiest army ever created in the twentieth century had been hurled at them, Irina had explained to me. She said the Poles were finished. They had not had the armour, the guns or the planes to defend themselves.

She had cried for hours ever since she had heard this news about the mighty and overwhelming invasion. She continued to weep, her head bent close to the radio. The BBC nine o'clock evening news had just started.

We lived alone at the house on the Lützowufer. Except for Hedy, the cook, and the young maid, Angelika. Walther, the butler, had joined the Luftwaffe. Her mother Princess Natalie and the Herr Baron had remained in Baden-Baden.

Hedy and Angelika were both off today. I had attempted to get Irina to eat. But she would not. We had ration stamps. Some foods were scarce. But the local stores opened daily. Even if the shelves were empty. I had been to the bakery. I was too late. All the bread was gone. There was nothing at the dairy. Most of the other stores had only meagre supplies.

I had left Irina listening to the radio. In the kitchen I made tea, added lemon and the last spoonful of sugar, poured the tea into two glasses. She liked hers in a glass.

When I returned to the library, Irina had stopped crying. She was calmer. I offered her the tea. She took a glass. Thanked me. I'm sorry, Gabri, she murmured. I let my grief get the better of me. I believe most of my dearest friends in Warsaw are going to die. If they're not already dead.

Perhaps they've been lucky, I murmured. I wanted to cheer her up. Perhaps, she agreed. But only for a short while, she then said. Hitler will get them in the end. His hatred for the Poles is a well-known fact. He thinks of them as *Untermenschen*.

I gaped at her. He thinks they are subhumans? I gasped. I was staggered by this statement.

She nodded. He invaded Poland because he wants to get rid of the Slavic race. And also because he wants to extend the *Lebensraum* to the east. According to Prince Kurt, Hitler wants their land.

The ringing phone made me jump. I stared at it. The princess picked it up. *Ja, ja,* she said in German, and listened intently. Seconds later, in English, she said, I am here alone with Gabriele. When she had replaced the receiver, she looked at me. That was Prince Kurt. He is back in Berlin. Princess Arabella and the children have stayed in Switzerland. I nodded. He has found a house for them. The princess added, Well, it was in the cards. Perhaps the prince might want to eat. Do we have any food? she asked. A chicken Hedy made this morning, I said. Lettuce. Four potatoes. I won't ask them if they are hungry, the princess said.

I stared at her. *They?* Is someone coming with Prince Kurt? She inclined her head. Two other men. We have to confer. The four of us. Make plans.

When the doorbell rang, Irina went to open it. The prince came into the library, followed by two men in uniform. One was the nice colonel. Hans Oster. I did not know who the other one was. After Prince Kurt had greeted me affectionately, Colonel Oster came and shook my hand. Politely, like I was a grown woman. He then introduced the other man. It was Admiral Wilhelm Canaris of the Abwehr, the head of German Military Intelligence. A powerful man. Known as a saviour and a saint to many. He had obtained the visa for Anita.

The admiral smiled at me in a pleasant way. He had a kind face, soft eyes, and was of medium height. He wears his enormous power with great humility, Princess Irina had once told me. I knew he was a good man. I decided I must leave them alone. I excused myself, left the room. Irina followed me. They will only have a drink, she said. Why don't you eat something, Gabri?

I shook my head. I went upstairs carrying my glass of lemon tea. I sat down in the chair near the radio. It was mine. Arabella had given it to me for my birthday in June. I didn't turn it on. I was thinking about Gretchen. She had been to see us this morning. She came once a month. To keep Irina informed about her health. She was five months pregnant after her encounter with the soldier at the Schloss. I was the one who had been lucky. I had not become pregnant, much to my relief.

Gretchen was a changed person. Apprehensive. Nervous. Diminished, somehow. The experience had frightened her. I felt sorry for her. She did not stay long. Irina gave her an envelope when she left. It was money from Arabella. A kind gesture from a good woman. Arabella felt a sense of responsibility. The assault had happened at her home. Gretchen was lucky in one thing. Her sisters lived in Berlin. In a street just behind the Tiergartenstrasse. They were willing to look after her. She was well taken care of, she had said.

For half an hour I listened to the BBC. I felt closer to aunt Beryl when I did. We spoke occasionally. But sometimes the telephone lines were bad. Full of static. She was still waiting for me to come to London. I glanced at the door as it opened. Irina stood there. Her face was ashen. What is it? I asked. I was frightened. She looked deathly ill.

Princess Irina sat down in the other chair without saying a word. What is it? I asked again. After a moment she said, Oh Gabri, my friends are doomed. As I thought they would be. Hitler plans massive executions. Of the nobility, the aristocracy, the clergy, Catholic priests, political dissidents, Jews and the Polish intelligentsia. They are all going to be exterminated. It will be wholesale slaughter. A bloodbath.

I gasped. But that's not possible, I said. He can't kill a whole country.

She stared at me unflinchingly. Look what he's doing to the Jews in Germany, she said.

I was silent. I thought of my family and trembled inside. I was more afraid than ever for them.

Irina said, The invasion has been brutal. Unspeakable atrocities will now be committed. How do you know this? I asked. Canaris told us. He is sickened by this invasion, by what he has found out, and what he knows will inevitably happen. *My friends will die.* She began to weep.

I went and knelt at her feet, took her hands in mind. They were as cold as ice. I didn't know how to comfort her. I said, Maybe it won't be that bad. It's not possible to murder an entire nation. When she was silent, I asked softly, Is it?

Princess Irina Troubetzkoy lifted her head and stared deeply into my eyes. If you are the Führer – yes, it is possible. Do you know what C said to me? I shook my head. Before he left he said, Read *Mein Kampf* and believe it. Hitler has to be removed, she finished, her voice a whisper. He must be assassinated. If he is not he will destroy Germany.

These words terrified me. They had been here to plot tonight, those three men. With Irina. I was convinced of that. And I was afraid for her. I did not want anything to happen to my lovely Russian princess.

BERLIN   3 SEPTEMBER 1939
On Sunday, two days later, Irina was a much happier person. And so was I. Once again we were glued to the radio in the library. We were listening to the nine o'clock evening news on the BBC, coming from London. At eleven o'clock that morning Britain had declared war on Nazi Germany. Six hours later the French government did the same thing. She had a

338

smile on her face when she said, They will win the war. You'll see, the British will defeat Hitler. She believed more than ever that the Third Reich would tumble. And so did I. This belief gave us hope. And it kept us going through the bad years yet to come.

THE MARK BRANDENBURG 6 MARCH 1940

We went back to the Schloss because Prince Kurt had asked Irina to check on the castle for him. Princess Arabella had returned to Switzerland with Christian and Diana. The prince travelled all the time as the envoy for Krupp. When he was in Germany he lived at his house in Berlin.

Irina told him we would go for a week or two. Not much longer. She wished to oblige Prince Kurt. She also decided we needed a change. There was an air of gloom and despair in Berlin. The streets were crammed full of Gestapo, SS and Wehrmacht soldiers. Thugs were everywhere. The food shortages were getting worse. Many other necessities were gone. The Herr Baron and the Princess Natalie had returned to the house on the Lützowufer. The baron was planning to turn the wine and storage cellars into an air-raid shelter. He believed the British would soon bomb Berlin.

Before we left Berlin, Princess Irina phoned Gretchen. She told her the monthly visit had to be cancelled. On impulse she asked Gretchen if she wanted to visit us. For a day or two. She accepted. We were both surprised. Gretchen told Irina she would come on March the eighth. It was a Friday. And that she would bring the baby. Gretchen had given birth at the end of December. The child was a few weeks premature. It was a boy. She called him Andreas.

Irina and I were alone at the Schloss except for Lotte, the cook. The two maids Trudi and Giselle had both left. They had gone to do war work in Berlin. Klaus, the gardener, and Stefan, the caretaker, were still working here. And their presence made us feel safer. The two men patrolled the estate twice daily. And by now the fence encircled the forests on their outer rim.

Immediately when we arrived Irina reorganized the Schloss. She closed off most rooms downstairs. Covered the furniture with dustsheets. She kept open the library, the small study and the parlour. All the bedrooms were covered with sheets, and closed. Except for her room and mine. This lightened Lotte's work. She had been cleaning since the two maids had left. Irina also hired Marta, the wife of the care-taker. She came daily to help out with the cleaning. I pitched in with the cooking. I wanted Lotte to teach me some of her specialities. We were busy for the first few days. Then Gretchen arrived. The baby was adorable. He had fat pink cheeks, blue eyes and tufts of blond hair. He smiled, gurgled and kicked his legs in the air. Lotte fell in love with him. We all did.

The kitchen was the warmest room in the house. We assem-bled there for most of the day. We had meals there as well.

There was no doubt in my mind that Gretchen loved little Andreas. Despite the circumstances of his conception. Yet she was odd in her behaviour. I said this to Irina. The princess decided Gretchen was distracted, worried. Irina and I called the baby our 'little dumpling'. We picked him up. Walked around with him. Nursed him. Cuddled him. Played with him. Brought fluffy toys for him. A lamb and a teddy bear found in Diana's room. We gave him his bottle. We took him outside in his pushchair. For three days Andreas was the centre of our lives at the Schloss. On the fourth day Gretchen disap-peared. And so did Andreas.

We were used to small meals in Berlin. Lunch was a treat. Lentil soup, bread and some of Lotte's precious bottled fruit. Later, Irina went to work in the study. I stayed in the kitchen. Lotte was going to show me how to bake, make apple strudel.

Gretchen took Andreas upstairs. For his afternoon nap. We never saw them again.

Gretchen did not bring the baby down for his bottle later that afternoon. I went up to her room. She was not there. Neither was the baby. But her suitcase was. And the baby's things. I was puzzled. I looked for her all over the Schloss. I told Irina. Then Lotte and Marta. We began to search for them. Stefan and Klaus covered the estate. The gardens. The forests. The snow had melted. It was still cold outdoors. There was no sign of them. I went back to the Schloss. Checked Gretchen's room again. Her topcoat was gone. And so was the baby's coat, wool cap and shawl. But where were they?

Irina was concerned. She phoned the doctor in the village. He had looked after Gretchen when she was raped. That was my idea. I said, Maybe she took the baby to see the doctor. She had not. Irina telephoned Gretchen's sisters in Berlin. She was not there. Neither had they heard from her. Reluctantly, Irina finally phoned the village police. There was only one officer now. All the others had joined the army. Officer Schmidt came to the Schloss. Listened to our tale. He searched the Schloss. The estate. Klaus and Stefan went with him. By now they were armed with torches. It was growing dark outside. And colder.

Gretchen and the baby vanished. In the blink of an eye. Gone. Just like that. None of us could imagine what had happened. It seemed she had simply walked out. And disappeared. Into oblivion. Her sisters came the next day. They searched every inch of the Schloss. From the attics to the cellars. Went to the doctor in the village. Spoke to the police officer. Went from house to house. Asking if anyone had seen a woman with a baby. Nobody had. So they said.

Irina and I fretted about Gretchen's disappearance. For weeks. For months. For years. It was a mystery. One we never solved. We had many theories. And no way of knowing if any were true. And we mourned them and wept about Andreas.

My God, what a strange story, Justine thought as she closed her grandmother's book. What on earth could have happened to them? She was still frowning as she went into the bathroom to take a shower, consumed by this troubling story.

FORTY-THREE

After her shower, Justine dressed and went for a walk in the garden. Her grandmother did this every morning, and she understood why. There was such beauty out here: the flame-coloured Judas trees, the lilac-blue wisteria and the masses of tulips. The latter were magnificent. Incomparable.

As she stood staring at them, taking in their brilliance, she suddenly realized how much backbreaking work had gone into their planting and care over the years. Gran had told her how hard she and Uncle Trent had worked, especially when they had first started growing the tulips. 'It was a labour of love,' Gabriele had said to her the other day. 'Trent had the same thirst for natural beauty as I did, and this garden became his real passion. And it was satisfying for me to see such beauty come into being. It was an antidote to all the ugliness I'd seen in my life.'

Ugliness, brutality, hardship, deprivation. All those things had dominated her grandmother's life when she was a teenager. No wonder her work as a designer was so important to her, as well as gardening. Gabriele created beautiful fabrics, lovely rooms, exquisite paintings. These were the things that nourished her, counteracted all that darkness and suffering of long ago.

343

Justine sat down on the garden seat and stared at the Bosphorus and Central Istanbul on the other side. It was a beautiful May day. The sky was a crystal-clear blue. The sun was up, bathing everything in its golden light. What a fabulous day.

For a moment Justine wanted to get up and go into Istanbul, stroll through the shops and boutiques. She had the urge to seek out meaningful presents for Gran and Anita and Michael. And Richard, Daisy, Simon and Joanne. She had the need to do something to show them how much she loved them, cared about them. They were her family. Her treasured family. There was nothing better than that.

I'll do it, she said to herself, jumped up and went back into the *yali*, intent on changing and going into the city.

Ayce came hurrying out of the kitchen and smiled when she saw Justine. 'Your grandmother on phone,' she said, beckoning her to follow.

As she did so, Justine realized she had left her cell phone upstairs on the bedside table. Picking up the receiver of the landline on the countertop, she said, 'Hello, Gran darling!'

'Good morning, Justine,' Gabriele said. 'I hope I'm not calling too early.'

'No, of course not. I've been up for a while, walking in the garden. The tulips are gorgeous.'

'They look their best at this hour,' Gabriele murmured.

'Gran, there's something I want to say. I . . . I love you so much, more than I can ever convey. I'm glad you gave me the leather book to read *now*, didn't leave it in your will. Because I am able to tell you how much I admire you, how proud I am to be your granddaughter. To be part of you . . . I think you're heroic . . .' She stopped abruptly. Her voice was shaking; she blinked back the tears.

There was a silence at the other end of the phone, and Justine could hear Gabriele gasping slightly, choking back her tears as well. After a second, her grandmother said, a bit unsteadily, 'I suppose you're still reading, aren't you?'

'Yes, I am, because I do have to stop occasionally to get a bit of rest. I'm going to my room to continue when I hang up. I want to finish it before you return from Bodrum. When will you be back, Gran?'

'I think we'll be able to finish everything by Saturday, fly to Istanbul on Sunday.'

'Gran, there's something I must tell you! I'm afraid Richard can't come now. Daisy has an ear infection.'

'Oh dear, I'm sorry to hear that,' Gabriele responded

They talked for a few more minutes and then hung up. Justine took a mug of coffee out to the terrace and sat drinking it.

A short while later she went back to her room, and picked up her cell phone, about to dial Michael in London. Then she realized it was only eight o'clock in Istanbul. London was two hours earlier. He was probably still asleep.

Sitting down in the chair, she opened her grandmother's black leather notebook and found her place.

BERLIN   10 MAY 1940

The phone had been ringing a lot. Irina had received one call after another. I wondered if something special was happening. At the moment I did my schoolwork in the small office at the front of the house. Where the Herr Baron's secretary usually worked. But she had gone off to Baden-Baden with the baron, Princess Natalie and all of the vintage wine. The wine cellar had become an air-raid shelter. But as yet not too many bombs had fallen.

Once more the phone rang. Riddled with curiosity, I put down my pen, went in search of Princess Irina. I found her in the study where the baron usually did his work. She was hanging up the receiver when I tapped on the door, put my

345

head around it. She stood up. For once there was a smile on her face. Her violet-blue eyes were sparkling.

Something wonderful has happened, she said. I was about to come and find you. What happened? I asked, staring at her. Her whole demeanour was different. I thought, she's happy. The princess said, At eleven o'clock in London this morning, Winston Churchill walked into Number Ten Downing Street as the new prime minister. He has replaced Neville Chamberlain. And all I can say is thank God for that! And hooray! We're in safe hands, Gabriele. Now I know for certain. The Third Reich will be defeated.

How do you know about Churchill? Have you been listening to the BBC, I said. No, she replied. Many phone calls. Prince Kurt told me first. Then C. After him, Hans Oster. Renata von Tiegal. And the Herr Baron phoned from Baden-Baden. He told me Churchill was in power. He reiterated his invitation. We can go and stay with them. I said no. But thank you. He warned me. We're going to be bombed, he said. That's wonderful, I told him. I welcome British bombs.

My aunt Beryl thinks Churchill is brilliant, I confided. She's right. The princess came forward, got hold of my hands, led me around in a dance. I'd never seen her like this. It's high time we had a party. I looked at her in astonishment. She laughed. I'm going to invite Prince Kurt, the von Tiegals, the Westheims. Tonight. For dinner. We'll have champagne. I know the Herr Baron left some behind.

He did. But we've no dinner, I pointed out. An arched auburn brow lifted. No food? I shook my head. Not much. Eggs. Lettuce. We can always get lettuce. *Eggs*, the princess repeated. Frowned. What can we make with eggs? Oh wait a minute. Parisian eggs! she cried. What are they? I asked. Come, she said. Hurried me out to the kitchen.

Hedy looked startled, afraid, as we rushed into her domain. Is something wrong? she asked. No, the princess said, smiling.

Do we still have cans of anchovies? Hedy nodded, baffled. And mayonnaise? The cook nodded again. Then we can have Parisian eggs for dinner. *Ja, Prinzessin*, Hedy said. We are having guests. Hedy nodded, still seemed startled.

We never ate lunch. Food was short. I went back to my schoolwork. The princess said she was going to phone her friends. Later that afternoon she came to the secretary's office. We must look nice tonight, Gabri, she announced. Come with me. Upstairs in her bedroom she took me into the middle of the room. Under the chandelier. Stared at me. Nodded. You have become beautiful, she said. Blue eyes, blonde hair. Very Aryan. You will be safe. Because of your colouring. She touched my cheek lightly. The scars have healed, she murmured. Disappeared. I nodded. I did not want to think about the scars. They reminded me of the rape. And of Gretchen. Lost somewhere out there. Leaving me, Irina went to the cupboard. She took out a blue silk dress. This will suit you, she said. Handed it to me. Am I coming to the dinner? I asked, puzzled. Absolutely, she said. Renata and Ursula Westheim are your mother's friends, as am I. And Arabella. Is the *Prinzessin* here? I asked. Irina shook her head. Zurich. I nodded. I would be intruding, I muttered. No, you wouldn't, she said. They will come at six thirty. I understand, I replied.

In my room I went to the chest. Opened the drawer, took out the photograph of my family. It was now in a frame. Irina had given it to me. I sat down, holding it in my hands. Gazing at them. At *me* with them. I touched my mother's face. And my father's. And Erika's. I'll see you soon, little one, I whispered. Suddenly, something was wrong with the glass. I couldn't see them properly. Then I realized it was my tears falling on the glass. I cleaned it with a towel. Put the frame away. In the drawer was the snapshot Arabella had given me last year.

It was of Anita and me. We were standing in a meadow

behind the Schloss. It was a sunny day. Our summer frocks were blowing in the wind. We were laughing into the camera. Arabella had taken it in the summer of 1938. Two years ago.

I would be sixteen next month. I lay down on the bed. I thought about Winston Churchill. What it meant that he was prime minister. Would he be able to save us? Or were we still doomed? Aunt Beryl said he was the best and the brightest. I trusted auntie Beryl. She was usually right. So we would be saved.

I was ready at six o'clock. I went and tapped on the princess's door. As she had told me to do. Inspection time, she called it. She told me to come in. I did. I gasped when I saw her. She looked marvellous. She wore a purple silk dress and red shoes. There was a string of blue beads around her neck. Her auburn hair was piled high on her head. She was a beauty. She stared at me. Took off the blue beads. Put them around my neck. There, she said. Just the right finishing touch. She glanced at my feet. Shook her head. Brought out a pair of silver sandals. Handed them to me. They're a bit tight, I told her. But worth it, she said. You must always wear blue, Gabri. It's your colour. She found a string of pearls, put them on, took my hand and led me down the stairs. Because tonight is so special, she said, you can have a glass of champagne. To toast Winston Churchill.

I knew Ursula Westheim and Renata von Tiegal. They had gone to school with my mother and Arabella. They were Roedean girls through and through. Ursula reminded me of my mother. She was blonde and blue-eyed like Stella. Renata was dark and exotic. Her clothes were always chic. They had stayed in touch with me for the last two years, always concerned. They never forgot my mother.

I talked to them for a while. Irina was huddled with Sigmund Westheim and Reinhard von Tiegal. I watched them out of the corner of my eye. Plotting again, I thought. Last week I had heard a new name. Claus Von Stauffenberg.

Prince Kurt von Wittingen was the last to arrive. He looked harried. He rushed all over Europe as a senior consultant to Krupp. It seemed to me he could roam around freely. A useful job. He had been alarmed and concerned about Gretchen's disappearance.

He walked over, once he had greeted Irina and the two men. He asked to speak to me privately, after kissing Renata and Ursula on their cheeks. In a quiet corner he seemed to relax. He said, I am still troubled by the situation with Gretchen, Gabri. I can't imagine what happened to her and the baby boy. What do you think?

I was flattered to be asked. Irina and I had discussed it many times. I said: I have three theories, Prince. Tell me, he said, leaning closer. I said, The first is that she had made an arrangement to be picked up by somebody that day at a certain time. But no one heard a car on the estate, he murmured. I nodded. The driver could have been waiting on the main road. Outside the gates. True, he said. The second is that she decided to go back to Berlin for some reason. Went out onto the road, hitched a lift. She's either living safely in Berlin or she is dead. Depending on who she got a lift with. Maybe it was someone who wanted a baby. Who killed her, took the child. Or perhaps she got to Berlin safely and disappeared in the city, wanting to be free of her sisters.

I fell silent. The prince asked, And what is your third theory, Gabriele? That she knew someone in the village. Went to see them. She could be still there. Or maybe somebody in the village wanted her child. And she willingly gave the baby to them. And then disappeared. Or that she met foul play in the village, again because of Andreas.

The prince gazed at me unwaveringly. Not very palatable theories, Gabriele. I just hope she and that child are safe. So do I, Prince von Wittingen, I said.

Hedy and I served the Parisian eggs. They sat on lettuce

leaves, with mayonnaise and anchovies spread on top. Everyone said they were delicious. Irina kept lifting her glass. Toasting Winston Churchill. So did her guests. Everyone enjoyed the evening.

Justine sat back and closed the book. Reading this fragment from her grandmother's past had not been quite so heartbreaking or harrowing. And it had told her such a lot. About Gabriele's preference for blue dresses and scarves. Her fondness for Parisian eggs, and her quick, bright mind. So Gran had had theories about what could have happened to Gretchen. Yet there was no way she could prove any of them to be true. More's the pity, Justine said under her breath.

FORTY-FOUR

Although Justine was longing to continue reading about her grandmother's teenage years in Nazi Germany, everyday life intruded for a short while. Iffet phoned her just to say hello and chat about things in general. Then she spent time sending her regular daily e-mails to Daisy and Joanne. And to Ellen at her office in New York.

It was just after this that Michael phoned her from London. 'Hi, babe,' he said when she answered her cell phone. 'Are you all right?'

'Good morning, and I'm fine. How was your dinner? Did you have a good evening?'

'I did. Everything is now on an even keel. My client is happy . . . well, I wouldn't say *that* exactly, but he's pleased we've managed to make a few compromises. I'll tell you about it when I get back to Istanbul. It's going to hit the papers anyway next week. The financial sections.'

'Oh, was it *that* important?' she asked, surprise echoing in her voice.

'In a way. Because it had to do with an important bank. But as I said, we've reached an agreement. So how's the reading

351

going? I hope it's not upsetting you too much?' he said, sounding concerned.

'Some of it's a bit harrowing at times,' she replied. 'But there are also some happy parts. I'm fascinated.'

'I miss you, babe, and I still wish I'd brought you with me. But we'll make up for it,' he finished.

Justine said, 'You bet we will! When are you going to Paris?'

'In a few hours. I want to get everything done so that I can be in Istanbul on Friday night.'

'That's great . . . Michael?'

'Yes? What is it?'

'I want you to read Gran's book as soon as you get here.'

'Do you think I should?' he asked. 'You said Gabri told you to tell me about it, and that's all.'

'I'll take the responsibility. I want you to read it,' Justine responded.

'Okay. You're the boss.'

Within half an hour, Justine retreated to the bedroom to continue reading.

BERLIN   12 SEPTEMBER 1941

Princess Irina was happy because we had been invited to visit Graf and Gräfin von Tiegal, to give them their correct titles. At their Schloss near Brandenburg. It was not far from Potsdam. The Westheims are staying, she said. It will be nice to see them all. I had also been invited. Reinhard von Tiegal had arranged for a friend of his to drive us out. Another friend would bring us back to Berlin after the lunch. We dressed in the smartest clothes we had. Makeovers from Arabella's wardrobe. Irina wore a fir-green wool suit. I picked a midnight-blue dress with a matching jacket. I thought we looked better than we had in years. Certainly less shabby. I was now seventeen. Tall like my mother. Irina thought I was too thin. I was. So was she. It was from lack of food. The shortages were growing worse.

The drive out was uneventful. I sat in silence. Irina spoke intermittently to the owner of the car. His name was Dieter Müller. He was a friend of Prince Kurt's. He seemed well informed about everything. And in her clever way, Irina pumped him.

We received a great welcome when we arrived at Graf von Tiegal's Schloss. It wasn't too far from the von Wittingens' home. I had a sudden rush of nostalgia. Much to our surprise the prince was at the lunch. He had just returned from Zurich. He said Arabella, Christian and Diana all sent their love. Arabella was working for the International Red Cross, he told me. Christian and Diana were at school. Apparently they missed Berlin and all their friends.

Ursula Westheim sat with me in the drawing room. We chatted about my mother, their school days. I knew that in January 1939 she had taken her son Maximilian and her ward, Theodora 'Teddy' Stein, to Paris. From there Teddy had escorted Maxim to London. They now lived with Teddy's aunt. Ursula had returned to Berlin. To look after Sigmund. They had hoped to get his mother and sisters out. Sadly old Mrs Westheim had died of heart failure in 1940. His two sisters had been killed in an air raid this spring.

We were being bombed by the Royal Air Force. Sporadically. We knew worse was to come. None of us cared. We welcomed it. The RAF would be our saviours. They had beaten the Luftwaffe in 1940 in the Battle of Britain. Churchill called it Their Finest Hour. Irina and I cheered when the Allies won.

Renata came and joined us. And I was allowed a glass of champagne when the toast to Winston Churchill was given. That was another ritual these days. Dieter Müller, Sigmund and Irina were talking near the window. Prince Kurt was in deep conversation with Reinhard. It was usually like this. I was now certain they were all in the same resistance group. It scared me. But I knew I couldn't influence her. She was stubborn. And a fighter.

Eventually we went in for lunch. I smiled to myself when I saw that the first course was Parisian eggs. After that we had rabbit and vegetable stew. Followed by a lettuce salad. Renata had made an apple pie. I knew all of this produce had been grown and caught on the estate.

Over lunch there was discreet conversation about the angry generals who were virulently anti-Nazi and plotting to overthrow the Führer. I heard that name again: Claus Von Stauffenberg. I wondered who he was.

It was Prince Kurt who drove us back to Berlin. Dieter Müller was going to Potsdam. Irina sat up front with the prince. I sat in the back, closing my ears to their chatter. I did not want to know about the schemes they were hatching. I was growing more nervous by the day.

It was three weeks later that Irina and I went out to the von Tiegals' Schloss again. We were taken there by Dieter Müller. He was as concerned as Irina about them.

Irina had telephoned to thank them for lunch, but since then we had not heard a word. And their phone just rang and rang. No one answered. We had not been able to go to their Schloss before. Princess Irina had been ill with bronchitis. She was still not well. But she insisted on going with Dieter. There was no one at the Schloss when we arrived. Only an old housekeeper. She told us the Count and Countess von Tiegal had gone to Berlin. A few days before. With the Westheims.

_ Immediately we returned to Berlin. We did not find them. Nor the Westheims. The four of them had vanished into thin air. They were never seen again.

Dieter Müller was certain that they had been taken by the

Gestapo. Sent to the camps. The von Tiegals are not Jewish, Irina pointed out. But they harboured Jews, Dieter reminded her. They gave them a safe haven. And that was the truth.

Irina and I were devastated. We had no option but to believe Dieter. It was the only theory that made any sense. I wept often when I thought of Mummy, Ursula and Renata. The three Roedean girls in concentration camps. Were they together? How could I know? I was relieved Arabella was safe in Zurich. I wished this war would end.

BERLIN   29 JANUARY 1942
We welcomed the drone of the RAF planes as they flew over Berlin every night. Dropping bombs. The city had become a pile of rubble in some areas. Irina and I were afraid. But at the same time we were jubilant. We sat huddled together in our air-raid shelter. The Herr Baron had built it in the cellar of the house on the Lützowufer. We were thankful he had had the foresight. We were relatively comfortable. We had blankets and pillows. The baron had installed a small toilet and a shower. Irina's stepfather had even put in a phone. These days it didn't always work. But sometimes it did. When the air raids were over we came out of the cellar and lived in the house again. But one night we were unable to do that. The lovely old house took a hit. The whole of the Lützowufer did. Fortunately there was an outside door to the cellar. Eventually we were able to get it open. As Irina and I scrambled out, climbed over rubble and came up into the street we saw an indescribable landscape. There was not a building standing. All had been flattened. We are lucky, Irina said as we stood there looking around in astonishment. We are still alive, Gabri. And we haven't been injured.

We have no conception of what living through a war is like, Justine thought as she closed her grandmother's book. No idea at all. America has never been invaded. I can't imagine how Gran survived. What guts it must have taken to do so.

She went downstairs to make herself lemon tea, and she would drink it in the garden. Her gran's beautiful garden, which was a magnificent tribute to her miraculous survival. Her personal triumph, in a sense.

FORTY-FIVE

Later that same day Justine settled herself in the chair in her bedroom. She was already aware that she did not have much more of her grandmother's leather-bound book to read. She wanted to finish it by tonight if she could. Opening it, she began to read eagerly. Yet at the back of her mind there was a kernel of apprehension about what she might soon discover. These pages had been full of shocks and surprises.

BERLIN   31 MARCH 1945
We lived in a hole in the ground, my lovely Russian princess and I. The hole was in a crater. To reach our hole we had to step into the crater. We then needed to manoeuvre ourselves down a half-shattered flight of steps with edges like jagged teeth. The steps stopped at another smaller hole. We had covered it with pieces of wood. These we'd nailed together. Just beyond was a heavy oak door banded with iron. It was strong. It could be securely locked. Before the house had been bombed, the steps had led directly from the Herr Baron's kitchen to the wine cellar. The other end of the cellar had been used as a vault. It had housed valuable silver, antiques

and priceless porcelain. Long since shipped to Baden-Baden. With most of the wine.

This then was our home. My lovely princess said we were like the troglodytes of Tunisia who inhabited caves. And weren't we the luckiest women in Berlin? I laughed. She enjoyed making such comments. Telling jokes to cheer me up.

We had been 'troglodytes' for three years. Ever since the house on the Lützowufer had been hit by an RAF bomb and destroyed. The whole street had been badly damaged. But we had lived. Miraculously.

Irina and I believed the Allies would soon liberate us. The war would be over in a few weeks. Hitler's ridiculous war that had killed millions. Shattered cities. Ruined countries. Taken its toll on people. Created chaos in the world. And what for?

Hitler said the Third Reich would last a thousand years, Irina remarked to me the other day. He was wrong, wasn't he? It will be finished in a few weeks. In fact, it's finished now. We have the last laugh, Gabri. I agreed with her.

When the Herr Baron had created the air-raid shelter in 1940 he had furnished it with simple things. A large sofa, armchairs, several chests. The big cupboards in the old silver vault were used to house our possessions. Such as they were. The sofa was my bed at night. Princess Irina slept on a narrow cot in the old vault adjoining the wine cellar.

Our years in the cellar have not been easy. The space was cramped, uncomfortable and at times airless. But the brick walls and concrete floor have kept it dry. Free of damp. Irina and I are scrupulously neat. We give each other as much privacy as possible. We are compatible. We laugh a lot. She has a great sense of humour. So do I. This has helped us. It got us through the rough patches.

We were luckier than most. These days many Berliners carried their belongings in paper bags. People lived in hideous conditions. Wherever they could. In amongst the piles of rubbish. In the underground stations. Under public buildings. In alleyways barricaded by garbage bins. Some like us had the cellars of their ruined homes to camp in. We knew a local man who lived in a packing case. Another in a hole in the ground topped by a sheet of metal.

The air raids were now continuous. Nonstop. Ever since the Americans had entered the war. Their bombers flew over the city every morning. At exactly nine o'clock. Then at noon. The RAF came speeding in at night to bomb us. There had been nearly three hundred Allied raids up to now. The city was battered. Filled with high mountains of rubble. Bomb craters. Shattered buildings. Iron girders hanging like bits of floating ribbon from their crumbling walls. There was dust everywhere. In the air. On our clothes. On our skin. On everyone.

The casualties had been enormous. Thousands of people had been killed. Or seriously injured. Hospitals were filled to overflowing. There was nowhere to bury the dead. Bodies were rotting under debris for days on end. Fires constantly broke out. Pipes kept bursting. Spewing fountains of water. At any time a gas line might blow. And another fire would ignite and explode. Lighting up the sky. It was dangerous out there.

Yet somehow this city managed to function amongst the ruins. So did the Berliners. The police were on duty every day. The mail was delivered – if the house, building or office block remained standing. Food shops opened daily. But produce was scarce. The underground trains still ran. Telephone and tele-graph services were operating. Unbelievably, my father's orchestra, the Berlin Philharmonic, continued to play. People attended the concerts. They went to the theatre. To the cinema. To the few good bars and restaurants that were open. They read the daily newspapers. They met their friends for coffee.

Lately fear had become a most palpable thing. Fear of the Russian Army. We were surrounded. By British, American and Russian troops. Berlin was about to fall. Irina and I prayed the Allied armies would reach us first. So did every Berliner. Some women had even planned their suicides should the Russians enter the city ahead of the Allies.

It was the first day of spring today. We decided to venture out. We must attempt to find food. Prince Kurt and Dieter Müller were coming to visit. We left the cellar at ten o'clock. We had been waiting for the Americans to bomb us at nine. But there was no raid. Perhaps it would be at noon. We would deal with that if it happened. Dodge the bombs. Get home.

Irina locked the door with the big iron key. Cautiously she climbed the shattered steps. I followed, moving just as carefully.

It was a lovely day. Sunny. Blue skies. But a chill in the air. Fortunately there was no wind. The level of dust was low. We were in luck. For once there were a few fresh loaves at the bakery. We found four eggs, milk and a piece of cheese at the dairy. Plus a small slab of precious butter. We had enough food stamps to cover these purchases. And some left over for a bottle of fruit. We were happy when we left the dairy.

We walked toward the Tiergartenstrasse. Irina seemed suddenly sad. This street was filled with memories for her. The Westheims had lived here. She had spent much time with them. In their beautiful house. So had my parents. The house was gone. Blown to smithereens. That had all been another time. Another safer world.

We crossed to the Tiergarten. I found my heart clenching as I thought of my mother. She had loved this park. Once it had been filled with trees. They had all been cut down. By the Berliners. They had needed firewood in winter. It had been bombed many times. The tree stumps were like strange charred objects in a blighted land.

The flower vendors were out on the street corners. The sight of them hawking their spring blooms created a curious air of normality. When I spotted the vendors I was carried back to my childhood. My mother had always bought little bouquets from them. To cheer Irina I went and bought her a bunch of flowers. This gesture made her smile again.

We hurried home to our little abode, as Irina called it. Once there I announced I would make an omelette for supper. If Prince Kurt and Dieter Müller were hungry. She smiled at me in her loving way. Thank you for the flowers, Gabri, will you put them in water, please? I did so. We had no vase. Only an old jam jar. But they looked nice enough.

I turned around. To put the flowers on the little table. Irina was looking at me thoughtfully. Just imagine, Gabriele, you will be twenty-one in June. Whatever has happened to the time?

We've been busy keeping ourselves alive, I exclaimed. We both laughed. We were feeling better. We were always refreshed when we had been out of the hole. In the city. Knowing other people were still around.

Kurt arrived first. Bringing with him a huge paper bag. In it were two bottles of Rhine wine. And a small bottle of cognac. The princess was surprised. And grateful. These little treats helped us get through the troubled days and nights. The prince told us he had been in Essen. At the Krupp factories. Then travelling for months on end. When Dieter Müller arrived he also came bearing gifts. Four sausages in a paper bag and a jar of mustard. We can have a veritable banquet, Irina said, after thanking him.

We all had a glass of wine. Exchanged what little news we had. Irina and I cooked the sausages. On our little stove. We served them with fresh bread and butter. And the mustard. We each had a plate on our knee. Picnic style. The sausages, the fresh bread and butter were a real treat. Next Irina served the lettuce salad and cheese. After that we declined the bottled fruit. None of us could eat big meals any more. We had grown used to meagre portions.

Prince Kurt insisted we each have a small glass of cognac after we had eaten. As a digestive, he said, pouring the brandy. Once we had our glasses he sat down on the sofa. Looked pointedly at the princess. And at me. He said, The Russians will be in Berlin in three weeks. The middle of April. You must prepare. Dieter will bring you more food next week. I want you both to remain inside this cellar. Once they've infiltrated the city. Do not go out. Promise me. Irina. And you too, Gabriele.

We did. She went on, I know everyone expects a sexual assault. This is now a city of women. Except for small boys and old men. All the other men are dead or in the forces. The Russians will rape and loot. But mostly rape. I understand that very well.

Just so long as you do, Prince Kurt answered. Dieter will bring you a gun when he comes with the food. And ammunition. To protect yourselves. If that is necessary. We will do that, she said. Then added, I'm a good shot.

I have some other bad news, Kurt announced. I have just discovered something truly appalling. He paused, gave Irina a long stare. *Berlin has no defences.* I know it's unbelievable. But it's the God's truth. There are not even any plans to defend Berlin. No fortifications. They were all in Hitler's imagination. Berlin is not the fortress he claimed it to be. No provision has been made to protect the civilian population. Or evacuate them. Women, children and the old are in the gravest danger.

That can't be true, she began and stopped. She saw the grim look on his face. He said, Attempts will be made by the local government to provide some sort of defence. But there are hardly any troops here. And the police force is diminishing as they're called up for the army.

We'll have to defend ourselves, or flee, the princess said. There's nowhere for you to go, *Prinzessin*, Dieter said. The Russians will soon be in the Mark Brandenburg. If they're not already there. They are rapidly moving inland from the River Oder. Irina asked, Is there any chance of the Allied forces getting to Berlin first? She looked from Kurt to Dieter. Her eyes were worried now. Both men shook their heads. The British, the Americans and the French *will* arrive, Dieter said. But they'll probably enter the city a few days after the Russians.

Refugees fleeing here from the country towns are telling horrifying stories, Prince Kurt told us. About the Russian soldiers. They're voraciously raping as they move forward. We will be careful, Irina promised. But I noticed she was extremely pale. With a sharp laugh, she said, If they find a White Russian like me, a Romanov, they'll murder me after raping me. You can be sure of that.

FORTY-SIX

Knocking on the door brought Justine's head up. She called, 'Come in,' and smiled when she saw Ayce. 'I know you've come to ask me about lunch, but I don't want anything right now,' she said. 'I'll come downstairs and make a sandwich for myself later. Thanks for being so thoughtful.'

Ayce smiled, inclined her head and closed the door of the bedroom.

Justine dropped her eyes and looked at the black leather-bound book on her lap. She turned the page and began to read.

BERLIN   10 APRIL 1945

I kept a tight control on my emotions. And so did the princess. It was the only way we knew how to be. Prince Kurt had told us not to leave the cellar. But this was difficult. We had to go out sometimes. Early every morning we stood in the crater. For air. We would climb the steps. Look around. Then we went down into the crater again. Back inside the cellar. We did the same at night. Some days we even went to the bakery. And the dairy. We did this together. We never lingered. We ran most of the time.

364

It was chaos in the streets. Berliners rushing around. Seeking food. Or news. Dodging refugees from the outer towns dragging their belongings. Circling mountains of rubble. Avoiding craters. Fear hung in the air. We were as frightened as everyone. We knew we were facing Armageddon. The Russians were on the banks of the Oder. Hitting out at the small towns standing in their way. Their huge armies growing larger daily. The Allied armies were closing in. The British, the American and the French. Berlin was their target. We were at the door of death.

It was a cool Tuesday morning. Irina and I ventured out. She locked the door. We climbed the jagged steps. Hurried as fast as we could. We ignored the blighted landscape. Focused on our business. To find food. Dodge the bombs. If a raid came. Get back to our little abode. Safely. To hide.

Only stale bread at the bakery. We bought it. The dairy had milk and cheese. We gave our stamps. Paid. Left. Ran back home. The Americans had not bombed today. So far. We wondered why.

Irina made coffee. We did not eat. We were saving the food for supper. We were expecting Dieter. He had called yesterday. Miraculously our phone worked. His call was brief. He was coming with food. And news. Around six o'clock. I sipped the coffee. I was thinking hard. I must talk to Irina. Ask some questions. I glanced at her. Gauging her mood. She had not been well. She had a weak chest. She caught colds easily. Her face was pale. Drawn. But her eyes were bright. She suddenly smiled. What is it? she asked. An auburn eyebrow lifted. Can we talk about C? I asked. She frowned. Then nodded. Yes, she said, What do you want to know?

You told me he was in prison. Is he still there? Is he still alive? To my knowledge, she said. I don't understand. Why was he arrested last year? I asked. Because he helped people to escape?

She shook her head. Let me explain. Count Claus Von Stauffenberg, a colonel in the Wehrmacht, was a Roman Catholic. Anti-Nazi. Anti-Hitler. He went to Hitler's headquarters. At Rastenburg. In East Prussia. It was last July. He had a time bomb in his briefcase. He placed it next to Hitler. Stayed for most of the meeting. Then left. Flew back to Berlin. He believed Hitler had died in the bomb explosion. A few hours later, everyone knew the assassination attempt had failed. Hitler was still alive. Claus Von Stauffenberg was arrested. That same night. Executed that same night. Without a trial. By a firing squad. Canaris and dozens of other generals, and Colonel Oster, were arrested. Several days later. Sent to Fürstenberg Prison. Accused of being part of the assassination plot. Many were executed. But C is still alive. So is Colonel Hans Oster. The British know all about Canaris. They will save him. I'm praying he has a charmed life. That he lives until they get here.

Thank you for telling me, I said. I'm relieved. I only got this information recently, she answered. After a moment Irina gave me a penetrating look. Where is your passport? In my bag, I said. Can I see it? I nodded. Went to get my handbag. I handed her the passport. She opened it, looked at it. Very carefully. Began to tear it up. Who needs a passport stamped with a J for Jew on it? she said. Please bring me a pan, and the matches. I am going to burn it. I stared at her. Flabbergasted. She laughed. Nobody has papers these days. We've all lost everything. In the bombings. We have nothing. And thus was my passport burned. The ashes flushed down the toilet. By the princess. She looked pleased with herself after she had done this.

We were always hungry by lunchtime. But we did not eat. We had to conserve what bit of food we had. In the afternoons we usually listened to the radio. For the news. For music. Then we slept. When we were asleep we did not feel the hunger pains. For me this afternoon was a bit different. I sat for a long time staring at the photograph of Mummy, Papa, Erika and me. I held the belief in my heart that they were alive. That I would see them soon. The Allies would free them. I was certain of that.

I picked up the snapshot of myself and Anita. Taken by Arabella in the meadow at the Schloss. In 1938. When I thought of Anita I smiled. She was safe. In Istanbul. I would see her again. One day. Unless I got killed in the bombings. Or by the Russians. I thought of Arabella von Wittingen. Luckily she was safe in Switzerland. With her children. But Ursula Westheim and Renata von Tiegal had not fared well. Tragically they had both died in Ravensbrück. In 1943. Maria Langen, a friend of Irina's, had told us this. Maria was imprisoned in Ravensbrück herself. From 1943 to 1944. Unexpectedly she had been released. The three women had been there together. Friends. She came to see Irina. To give her the sorrowful news. We asked Maria if she had known my mother and sister. She had shaken her head. No, she had not, she said. But she had heard they were there. They had been moved from Buchenwald. Later I wept. Irina said, It is a very big camp. They are probably still alive. Hold onto that thought, Gabri. I did. And so did Irina.

We always tried to get dressed up. For Dieter and Kurt. It gave us something to do. Made us feel better. We scrubbed our faces. We brushed our hair. Changed into our shabby but treasured remakes of Arabella's clothes. Waited for Dieter. We did not know why Prince Kurt was not coming. Travelling, Irina said. He would not miss seeing us. He cares about us.

Once the knocking started, Irina and I went to the door. She knocked back. Dieter said against the keyhole: *The blue gentians are in bloom*. It was the password of their resistance movement.

Irina turned the key. As usual Dieter had brought a paper

367

bag of food. Half a salami. A packet of tea. A container of cooked herring. And a bottle of Rhine wine.

Not much, I'm afraid, he said. Irina thanked him profusely. So did I. We were grateful. He opened the wine. The three of us sat down. Irina and I were thrilled to see him. Where is Kurt? she asked. Moving around for Krupp, he answered. Ammunitions are still being made. I haven't heard from him lately. But he'll show up. You should be prepared, he said suddenly. The Russians will start the attack on April the fifteenth. Or the sixteenth. No later. Irina nodded. We trusted his information. He owned one of the most important newspapers in Berlin. Information came to him daily from various sources. He had hundreds of contacts. I know it's hard to stay inside, he went on. But once the Russians hit the city you must not go out. I will come. When I know it's safe. We must hope the telephones keep working. And the radio, he said.

Do you have any special instructions? Irina asked. Don't open the door. Unless you're sure it's me. Then he added quietly, Understood? We nodded. Irina and I took out the bread and cheese. Opened the container of herring. We had our usual picnic. Plates on our knees. As we ate, Dieter told us Hitler was still in Berlin. In his bunker, he said. Rumour has it he'll commit suicide. Before he'll surrender to the Allies. Or the Russians. He won't be taken alive.

Do you truly believe Berlin is defenceless? Irina asked, staring at Dieter. He nodded. Kurt and I have it from the best source. General Reymann. The city's new commandant. He knows that Berlin's defences are an illusion. Hitler's illusion. He believed Berlin would never be in danger. And now it is. All I can say is God help us. We went on talking for a while. Then Dieter told us he must get home. To prepare his wife for the coming trouble. He promised to phone us if he had any important news. Or instructions for us.

Irina and I were huddled in our little abode. She did not feel well. I was apprehensive. I didn't know what I would do if she got really sick. With bronchitis. Suddenly we both stared at each other. We heard the drone of planes. It's the Americans! she exclaimed. A smile flashed. Her violet eyes sparkled. Hooray!

I laughed. She always welcomed the American bombers. And the RAF. I did too. They were trying to liberate us. Even if they killed some of us in the process. For over three and a half years the planes of the US Eighth Air Force and the RAF had pounded us to smithereens. Today was the same. I had lost count. But I thought it was about the 363rd air raid of the war. It was 9.25 a.m. on Saturday morning. We heard huge thuds. The crashing of buildings that had been still standing. The exploding bombs. But the noise seemed far away. Not near us at all. Three hours later the planes were flying off. Leaving the airspace above Berlin. The drone of their engines was receding.

A moment later there was a noise the like of which I had never heard before. It was a weird screaming sound. Not the whistle of a bomb. Nor the thudding of anti-aircraft guns. Something entirely different. So high-pitched it was ear-splitting.

The radio was on. I heard the announcer's voice. *We are under attack! Berlin is under attack! The Russians are entering the city!* The voice stopped abruptly. Music began to play.

I looked at Irina. Alarmed. She rose. Came and sat next to me on the sofa. I put my arm around her. She was trembling. What time is it, Gabri? she asked. I looked across at the clock on the chest. Eleven thirty. She stared at me. She said, Berlin has just become the front line. The Bolsheviks are here in the city and they're going to kill us.

We knew from the horrendous noise outside that shells

were exploding everywhere. On the Lützowufer, above our cellar where we were huddled. Along the Tiergartenstrasse. On the Ku'damm. Even on the Unter den Linden. The city was under siege. The Russians were pulverizing it. We knew we must not go out. Not for days. We were at their mercy. Even when the shelling suddenly stopped we paid no attention. It would soon start again. It did. Out there was rape and death. And if the soldiers didn't get us, we would be killed by flying shrapnel and bombs.

By the late afternoon we were hungry. I made some salami sandwiches and hot tea. We still had a little sugar left. And a precious lemon. We enjoyed our food and the lemon tea. It was a treat. At one moment there was a thud against the oak door. We were startled. Stared at the door. Apprehensively. Was it a bomb? Artillery fire? A soldier standing outside? We waited. Terrified. Nothing happened. I stood up. Don't go out! Irina cried. I'm not, I said. I just need to stretch.

And so it went. Day after day. Night after night. We heard the guns, the bombs, the artillery, the explosions. The crumbling of the remaining buildings. But no one attempted to get into our cellar. No bombs hit us. We slept. Intermittently. Ate carefully to conserve our food. We had no idea how long the siege would last. We did exercises. Read. Slept. Slept some more. Read. Listened to the radio. The news was horrifying. Thousands killed. Thousands more injured. Hospitals stretched to capacity. Berliners crowding the streets. Nowhere to go. Nowhere to shelter. All of the underground shelters filled to overflowing. The dead and the dying abandoned. No ambulances available. Bodies rotting. The streets are too crowded, nothing can move, Irina said.

By the end of April the last battle was almost over. Berlin was burning and the Third Reich was dying a terrible death.

We waited. The phone didn't ring. But we knew what was going on from the radio. People had started to loot. So had the Russian soldiers. The rapes had started. Terrified women were committing suicide. The police were non-existent. They had been recruited for the depleted army. Or the Home Guard. And they had been defeated. Overrun by the Russians. Out in the street were tanks, artillery, machine guns. Guns of every kind. And the Russians were toting them. If we opened the door we would face chaos, danger and death.

We attempted to keep track of the days. But we were exhausted from worry, lack of fresh air and food. Then one afternoon we were both dozing when we heard a loud banging on the oak door. I struggled up off the sofa. Irina was already heading towards the door. I followed her. She knocked back. We both heard Dieter Müller's most welcome voice. *The blue gentians are in bloom*, he said.

The princess opened the door. He smiled at us. He said, Come on. Come out, get some fresh air. We did so. Blinking in the first daylight we'd seen in weeks. It's over, he announced. The last battle is over. And so is the war. We both fell on him. Together we hugged him joyously. What's today's date? I asked. May eighth, he replied. And yesterday, at Reims in France, General Alfred Jodl, the representative of the German High Command, and Grand Admiral Karl Doenitz, the designated head of the German State, signed an act of unconditional surrender to the Allied Expeditionary Force and the Soviet Union. *It's truly over.*

Dieter came and kissed each of us on the cheek. He couldn't stop smiling. I climbed the jagged steps. Irina followed me. Dieter came out of the crater last. I looked up at the sky. It was a very bright blue. The sun was shining. The air was balmy. It felt good on my face. It's a beautiful day, Irina said. I nodded. And then she added, But it's so quiet. This was true. There wasn't a sound. It was so eerie it was startling. I looked around me. I was in shock. I could not believe what I was seeing. A vast unending landscape of flattened buildings.

Piles of rubble, upended girders, bricks and lumps of twisted steel. Deep craters everywhere. Mud holes brimming with water. Everything was covered in black soot and ash. Central Berlin looked like a blighted dystopian landscape on some far-distant planet. And it was unlike anything I'd ever seen in my life. The vista was totally flat. It was a wasteland.

Berlin has been wiped off the face of the earth, Irina said, sounding horror-struck. That's right, Dieter agreed. Marshal Zhukov turned twenty-two thousand guns on a Berlin already in ruins. He wanted to obliterate it. And he did.

FORTY-SEVEN

Although she didn't want to stop reading, Justine knew she needed refreshments. She had a headache. Downstairs in the kitchen she made coffee, took a handful of cookies out of the biscuit barrel on the countertop. She stood there munching on the cookies and drinking the coffee, her thoughts in the past.

Within a few minutes she was back in her bedroom, opening the book, reading the next segment of her grandmother's story.

BERLIN   15 JULY 1945

We've been living in a desperate city, the princess and I. Not a city at all. Demolished. Not functioning. Without proper services. Hospitals bombed or spewing patients into the streets. Disease rampant. Typhoid, diphtheria and tuberculosis causing most deaths. Death is in the air we breathe. Thousands of dead bodies are yet to be buried. Rats run everywhere. People look lost. Dazed. Berliners living amongst piles of rubbish. Camping out anywhere they can. Refugees trailing back. Mostly Berliners who fled during the war. Too many people. Terrible overcrowding. Hotels non-existent. The Adlon, the

Eden and the Kaiserhoff destroyed. A few small hotels open. How lucky we are to have our little abode. Our hole in the ground is a palace.

Suddenly things are changing. To our great joy, the British, the Americans and the French are here. They have taken control of their sectors, which will be known as West Berlin. The Russians are now isolated in their own zone. Known as East Berlin. Far away from us. We are in the West zone. Irina and I breathed with relief when we saw the friendly smiling faces of the Allied soldiers. Our true liberators.

Already things have begun to change. For the better. The Allies have an immense task ahead. The Russians got some services working again. Now the Allies have pushed everything forward. And swiftly. Gas and electricity are back. Telephones are working. Most of the time. The underground, the trams and trains are running. The airport is operating.

Some old taxis are back. Just a few. Petrol is in short supply. The International Red Cross has opened an office. We are truly relieved. Grateful. Life is better.

Irina and I have been sorrowful. We grieved for Admiral Canaris and Colonel Oster. Dieter told us in May that they had been moved, then executed in Flossenburg Prison. Just a few days before the end of the war. How ironic. They might have been saved. We wept for them. Irina was devastated when news came about her friends Adam von Trott zu Solz, Gottfried Bismarck, Fritzi Schulenberg and other men. Members of her resistance group. They died without revealing our names, she whispered. Under torture. They died protecting me and Dieter and Kurt. Such brave men. I endeavoured to comfort her.

One day last week we made a decision. We would go out into the streets. Help clear the bricks. Women in our neighbourhood did this daily. They were called *Trümmerfrauen*. They chipped old cement off the bricks. Put them in wheelbarrows. Took them to a depot. The bricks would be used for the rebuilding of Berlin. Useful work. But tiring. The sound of chip, chip, chipping was a constant irritant. We managed. We laughed. We joked. And then there was a moment when I looked over at Irina one day. We live in a world gone mad, I said to myself. She is a Romanov. A princess. A cousin of the late tsar. Now she is a *Trümmerfrauen*. A rubble woman. Cleaning bricks. In all weather. Wearing old clothes. Living in a hole in the ground. No prospects. Things have to change. I will make them change. I vowed that to myself.

In May I vowed to find my parents. But still I have no news of them. I have been to the International Red Cross. Many Zionist organizations. Jewish refugee groups. And the Society of Friends. It is run by the Quakers. Their names are not on any lists. I will go back next week. I will not rest until I know their fate.

This morning Irina and I are getting dressed up. We are going to lunch. At Dieter Müller's home. He and his wife Louise were lucky. Their house in Charlottenburg was only slightly damaged. Thankfully it's in West Berlin. He is starting up his newspaper again. He has an international name. He and his father were well known before the war. And known as anti-Fascists. He is well liked by the Allies. Especially by General Harold Barlett-Smith. One of the heads of the British Occupation Forces. The lunch today is for the general.

I finished dressing. Went to see Irina. For my inspection. She smiled when she saw me. Gabri, you look lovely. I thanked her. I had on an old Arabella remake. A blue slubbed silk dress. And Irina's blue beads. I'd asked to borrow them again. My old black shoes look awful, I said. She laughed. Nobody will be looking at your feet. They'll be gazing into your blue eyes. Entranced by your gorgeous face. I felt myself blushing. Irina was wearing a pink linen dress. Another Arabella cast-off. It was striking with her auburn hair and violet eyes. She was thirty-three now. And very beautiful. She put on her pearls. How do I look? Like a princess, I said. We both laughed.

A moment later Dieter was knocking on the door. Irina let him in. He was startled when he saw us dressed up. For a moment he was speechless. You're both beautiful, he said. He sounded surprised. Irina murmured, And *clean*. We followed him out. Irina locked the door. Put the key in her red bag. Dieter said, The general was kind. He made his car available to me. With a driver. Irina and I looked at each other. We were thrilled. We got into a car with a British flag on the hood.

We were the only guests. Other than the general and an aide. Louise was charming. She knew Irina well. I had met her once. It was nice to be in Charlottenburg. Away from the rubble. The garden was lovely. One day I would have a beautiful garden of my own. When the general arrived I was struck by his geniality. His friendliness. He seemed impressed that Princess Irina Troubetzkoy was a Romanov. He spoke about Russia with her for a few minutes. Then turned to me. He smiled. Asked me why I was in Berlin? Being that I was an English girl. I explained that my mother was English. My father German. That we had lived in both countries. He questioned me about my parents. I simply said they were missing. That they might have been killed. I added I felt they were alive. Hoped they were.

The general, whom everyone called Bart, asked if I had family in England. I nodded. My mother's younger sister. My aunt Beryl, I said. Then thought to add, And her husband, Alastair McGregor. The general gave me an odd look. Is he by any chance known as Jock?

I was startled. Yes, he is, I answered. Do they live in Mayfair? he asked. Again I nodded. Just off Charles Street.

The general beamed. And is he in the steel business? Yes, General, he is, I replied.

What a small world it is, the general said. He stared at me. You certainly resemble Beryl. You share her blonde good looks. Your aunt and uncle are my good friends, Gabriele. Do they know you are safe and well? Yes. I've spoken to them on the phone. They want me to come to London. To live with them, I told him. I have no papers. I glanced at Irina, who was watching me closely. They were burned when Irina's stepfather's house was bombed, I explained, and smiled at her. She winked.

Were you born in Germany? Or in England? the general asked me. He had a thoughtful look on his face. In London. My birth certificate is, was, British. But I had a German passport. I was considered to be a German by the Germans. Under their law.

We'll see about that, he exclaimed. I consider you to be British. And you should be with your family in London. I'm going to fix it.

I nodded. Then I glanced at Irina. She had become my family. I saw that she was smiling. Nodding.

Did I want to go to England? It would mean leaving Irina. I loved her. She had looked after me. Protected me. Been like a sister to me. We had been through so much together. And how could I leave until I found my family? I then realized that everyone was staring at me.

I said, Thank you, General, thank you very much. I'm going to call your uncle Jock tonight, he announced. He'll need to get a copy of your birth certificate from Somerset House. No big deal. Once he sends it to me I'll do my bit. Don't give it another thought. You're going home. The general had just been a general. He had now taken charge of me.

After we'd finished our glasses of wine we went into lunch. I fell into step with Irina. I took her arm. I don't want to leave you, I whispered. You must, Gabri. You must let the general help you. Nobody ever gets a chance like this. It's a fortunate thing that happened today. I'll worry about you, I murmured. I held her arm tighter. The Herr Baron is coming back to Berlin, she told me. With my mother. I won't be alone. And listen, London's not that far away. She smiled. The war's over. We can go wherever we want, Gabri.

FORTY-EIGHT

S he was almost at the end of her grandmother's memories of her youth. She wanted to know everything there was to know, and yet Justine did not want *Fragments of a Life* to end. She had savoured every word, every line. She had lived through it with her grandmother. And she wanted to know more . . . the rest of Gabriele's life up to when she herself had been born. It was a fascinating story. She opened the book and began to read.

BERLIN   22 JULY 1945

Irina and I are convinced there is something wrong with Arabella von Wittingen. She is back in Berlin. And she has been behaving strangely. Even Dieter is worried. He is coming to see us shortly. Arabella returned to Berlin a week ago. She had not been able to travel from Switzerland. Until now. She went to stay with her mother-in-law in Charlottenburg. The old princess is renting a house from a friend. The von Wittingen mansion in Central Berlin was heavily bombed. It is now a pile of rubble.

Dieter took us to see her. At first she was fine. Happy we

were there. Then she started rambling. About Prince Kurt. He has not been seen since May. When Berlin fell. Then two or three days later. After the last battle. He seemingly disappeared. We have not seen him for a very long time. Nor heard from him.

Wolfgang Shroeder has seen him. Wolfgang, a well-known photographer, is a friend of Dieter. He also knows Kurt. Wolfgang recently told Dieter he had seen Prince Kurt in May. They had exchanged greetings, chatted. Several days later Wolfgang caught sight of him. Talking to some Russian officers. In what is now East Berlin. The Russian sector.

Because of his profession, Wolfgang was always roaming around Berlin. Taking photographs. But he never once spotted Kurt after that. Dieter immediately checked the hospitals again. Could not find any trace of Prince Kurt. There had been intermittent fighting at the end of the war. When Wolfgang had seen him last. Dieter, Irina and I believed Kurt had been killed. In one of the last-ditch battles. His body was never found. It was this that was upsetting Arabella. She had convinced herself he was alive. She insisted he had been taken prisoner by the Russian officers Wolfgang had seen him with.

But why? Irina and I had asked her last week. She had no answer for us. Only this irrational belief that her husband still lives. No body. No death, I said to Irina.

I jumped up at the sound of knocking. Ran to the door. Opened it. Greeted Dieter. Hugged him. Led him into our little abode. A moment later Irina joined us. She embraced him. She said, I have a solution. We must persuade Arabella to return to Zurich. She has the little house there. What better place? The children will be safe. They'll continue their education. She won't go, I said. Dieter agreed. We must be clever about it, Irina said. Point out the disadvantages of Berlin. The advantages of Switzerland. We must promise her that if we hear anything about Kurt we will inform her. Immediately.

Dieter was thoughtful. He said, yes. We must appeal to her love for her children. Diana and Christian cannot live here. There's nothing for them. Only a heap of rubble.

I wasn't persuaded. But I agreed to help them. I pointed out that she would go to the Schloss. Not possible, Dieter exclaimed. The Mark is now in the Russian zone. It's dangerous. I'll tell her. Irina got up, went to make coffee. Dieter said in a low voice, I think Arabella is deranged. I went to see her again the other day. She was incoherent. Her eyes looked glazed. I am worried. He went on. They have a house in Munich. The old princess does. I nodded. Perhaps she'll go there, I suggested. How will she get from here to Munich? Dieter asked, shook his head. Germany is full of refugees on the move. Zurich is simpler. He was right. I told him so.

Irina brought us coffee and Dieter instantly changed the subject. He said, I have a lovely offer. For the two of you. He smiled. Irina asked, What do you mean? General Barlett-Smith, our friendly Bart, would like you both to work for him. At a conference. He's holding it next week. A meeting with Russians and Germans. We were both taken aback. I said, Doing what? Dieter answered, Listening, assessing, making notes. Later giving him your opinions. Does he want us to be interpreters? Irina asked. She was puzzled.

Dieter said, Not exactly. He's going to have professional interpreters. Who speak German and Russian. And obviously English. What he needs are some honest answers. You have both lived here. Before the war. During the war. Now. In its aftermath. Bart says he trusts you to convey something to him. What the Russians and Germans are *really* saying. What they *really* mean. Translations by the professionals won't be the last word for him.

He's very smart, Irina said. So much can be lost in translation. What is the conference about? Do you know? I do, Dieter answered. It's about the rebuilding of Berlin. He laughed unexpectedly. You can still be *Trümmerfrauen*. But in a different way. We both laughed with him. We knew he disapproved of us chipping at the bricks.

A short while later we left our hole in the ground. Walked with Dieter to the Tiergartenstrasse. Took the train to Charlottenburg. Arabella was coming to lunch at Dieter's house. When we were almost there, Dieter said, What shall I tell Bart? I glanced at Irina. She nodded, said, It will be interesting. I agreed with her. I must do it, I announced. He is arranging for my British passport. He's been so nice. He has, Dieter said. You owe him a favour. There was a miraculous change in Arabella. She was her old self. Greeted us lovingly when she arrived. Laughed when she saw us wearing her old summer clothes. From the 1930s. We chatted. Drank a glass of wine. Louise drew Dieter to one side. I did not hear what they said. But he was smiling. When he joined us. The lunch was a success. Louise had managed to procure two chickens. From the black market in the Tiergarten. Food was still short. Everyone resorted to the Tiergarten. It was very active. Food and other items were always on sale. For the right price.

When we were having coffee, Irina asked Arabella about her plans. She said she wasn't sure what to do. Whether to stay in Berlin or not. She seemed to be looking to us for advice. Gently, in a loving way, we told her she must return to Zurich. This was the best plan. For her children. Unexpectedly she agreed. She told us she had been to the Tiergartenstrasse and the Lützowufer. Had been horrified to find their house gone. And by the damage. The wasteland that Berlin had become. It appalled her. No one can exist here, she said. Irina and I agreed with her. Reminded her about our hole in the ground. How uncomfortable it was.

Later that afternoon she hugged us both. Then wept. She whispered sadly, I know Kurt is dead. He must have been killed. In the last-ditch fighting. I am sorry about last week.

My behaviour. I was demented. Clutching at straws. We comforted her. Told her how much we cared about her.

Dieter walked us to the train station in Charlottenburg. Waited with us. When the Berlin train came chugging in, he said, So I'll tell the general you'll work for him? Yes, I said. And please ask him when we start. I believe the conference begins on Wednesday, Dieter said. Which Wednesday? Irina asked. This Wednesday, he replied. We were both flabbergasted. We nodded our agreement. He added, You will be paid.

And so began our little adventure. That is what Irina called it. We had to rush to get our clothes in order. We splurged. Bought shampoo. At the black market in the Tiergarten. And a lipstick each. On Wednesday morning we set off for Charlottenburg. And the conference. The aide to General Barlett-Smith, Captain Walter Frost, greeted us. He had been at Dieter's luncheon. He took us to see the general. Bart was warm, welcoming. Then he explained why he needed us. What he wanted us to do. Once Bart had briefed us, Captain Frost came back. He brought us passes, identification badges, notebooks and pencils. He took us to the conference room. On the way he showed us where all the facilities were. Explained that we could eat at the canteen. He took us into the conference room. Showed us to our given seats. And disappeared. He's dropped us in the deep end, I said. Irina laughed.

We worked hard. We listened carefully. Made detailed notes. Our assessments. I was concentrating on the German officers. Irina on the Russians. At night we wrote a report for Bart. Gave it to Captain Frost the next morning. Every other day we met with the general. To discuss our reports. We met Peter Hardwicke the first day we started. The canteen was full when he arrived. There were only two seats left. At our table. He asked if he could join us. I said, please do. Irina simply nodded, smiled at him.

383

He was nice looking, polite. Possessed a quiet charm. We both liked him at once. He was a captain in the army. He was in the Administration Department of the British Military Police. We realized how impressed he was when we said we worked for the general. That first day he made us laugh. Kept us entertained. He asked lots of questions about Berlin. We answered. A few days later he asked to join us for lunch again. He also invited us out on the town. That was the way he put it. We had to educate him about the town. We explained there wasn't one.

One night, when we were planning our clothes for the next day, Irina suddenly turned to me. Her face was serious. Peter likes you a lot, she said. I like him, I murmured. I know you do. But he has really fallen for you, Gabriele. I began to laugh. Don't be silly, I answered. And laughed again.

BERLIN   5 SEPTEMBER 1945
I shall be leaving Berlin in a few days. My passport and all my papers are now in my hands. In some ways I feel sad to leave. Mostly because of Irina. She has looked after me for the last seven years. We've hardly been apart. We braved the storm of war together. I loved her. There was no one I admired more. But I know I must go. I need to be with aunt Beryl and uncle Jock. And before I leave I must return one more time to the International Red Cross. Visit all the other agencies. I must look at the lists again. The long lists of names of those who died in the concentration camps.

When I arrived at the temporary building for the International Red Cross I hurried inside. I found the woman I had dealt with before. She nodded. Her eyes were kind. I did not know her name. She handed me the new lists. These came in yesterday, she said in a neutral voice. She was an American. I thanked her. Took them from her. Hurried towards a corner. To be alone. I looked at the Ravensbrück list first.

My eyes scanned the page marked with a capital L. My heart clenched. I saw it at once. Her name. *Landau: Stella Elizabeth*. And underneath *Landau: Erika Beryl*. Mummy, Erika, my heart cried. My mother was dead. My littler sister was dead. No, no, no. I heard a terrible scream in my head. The tears fell out of my eyes. Splashed onto the paper. My hands were shaking. My legs felt weak. I was trembling all over. I found the Buchenwald list. Looked for my father's name. It was there. Just as I had known it would be. *Landau, Dirk*. There it was in black and white. My legs wouldn't hold me. I slid down onto the floor. Clutching the lists, tears spilling down my cheeks. Splattering the paper. I would never see them again. I would never hear their voices . . . never, never, never . . . that word reverberated in my head. Papa, Papa, I will always love you. Mummy, Erika, I will never forget . . . never . . . never . . . never . . .

I felt a hand on my arm. I opened my eyes. Looked up. The woman who had helped me was kneeling down next to me. On the floor. Her eyes were full of sadness and compassion. Her face kind. Can I get you anything? she asked. I shook my head. In my mind I silently shrieked. Yes! Yes! Yes! Get me my mother. Get me my sister. Get me my father.

The woman stood up. Came back a moment later. Gave me a clean handkerchief. To wipe my tears. I inclined my head. I could not speak. Silently I handed her the lists of the names of those who had been *murdered in the death camps*.

LONDON   8 SEPTEMBER 1945
I have come back to this welcoming house. Full of love and warmth. I am here in aunt Beryl's arms. I am here with my mother's younger sister. The closest I can ever be to my mother again. Lovely aunt Beryl. She is calm, kind, loving. Uncle Jock is a quiet man. Compassion and understanding are written on his face. They take me up to my room. Allow me to be

alone . . . to think, to rest, to grieve. And slowly the memories are coming back . . . I hear Papa's violin. His music echoes in my head. Mozart. Rachmaninoff. Liszt. Schubert. I hear my mother's lilting voice, her fine soprano. They are here with me now. *I can see their faces.* Erika with her golden curls and shining green eyes. My handsome, elegant father standing by her side . . . and Mummy next to him. Her pale blonde hair framing her face . . . a golden halo, full of light.

Now I know they will never leave me. There is no such thing as death in my lexicon. As long as I'm alive they will live on in me. And they will be with me all the days of my life. And even after that.

Justine sat back in the chair. She still held the book in her hands. Her face was damp. More tears had fallen at the end. A deep sigh escaped her. She was glad her gran had written this memoir . . . fragments of her life, the life she had lived long ago. And had had the courage to do so. She understood how painful it must have been for Gabri to dig deep into the past, into her memories. Into her soul.

As she was about to close the book she saw a small slip of paper attached to the endpaper at the back. It was stuck down with a piece of tape. There was something written on it, in her grandmother's handwriting. She peered at it, read: *Dear Justine. In the safe at the end of my walk-in closet you will find a black leather envelope briefcase. I think you will be interested in the contents. Here's the number for the safe: 17-95-9911. Gran.*

Justine put the book down, took the slip of paper and went to her grandmother's bedroom. Within minutes she had opened the safe, found the briefcase, and brought it back to her own room.

Opening it, she pulled out an envelope. Pale blue paper. Green ink. Faded slightly. *Birth Certificates* had been written on it. She looked inside. There was a copy of her grandmother's birth certificate. And of two others as well. One was her great-aunt Beryl's, the other one her great-grandmother's: Stella Goldsmith, it read.

She sat holding them for a moment. Then put them down. In the briefcase there was a black notebook. Justine looked inside. She quickly read some of the pages. And immediately understood. This had belonged to great-aunt Beryl, and it listed all of the money she had given to Jewish charities over the years. Hundreds of thousands.

Placing this with the birth certificates, she pulled out a packet of clear plastic folders, wondering what they were. A label had Beryl Goldsmith McGregor on it. As she shuffled them she realized they contained a collection of newspaper clippings. One slipped out of her hand, fell to the floor. She bent down to pick it up. And glanced at the headline as she did:

GENOCIDE.

Justine's eyes widened, and horror swept over her as she stared at the headline, then dropped her eyes to the photographs. 'Oh my God!' she cried out loud. She was stunned by the graphic pictures of the most unspeakable evil, depravity and inhumanity. Naked people, living skeletons, emaciated, hairless and hollow-eyed. Piled on top of each other. Thousands. And thousands. She could not bear to look. Turning her head, she noticed the date on top of the front page of the *Daily Express*. Suddenly her eyes blurred with tears and all she could actually read was May, 1945.

FORTY-NINE

'Why did you come back early, Gran?' Justine asked, looking at Gabriele intently. 'I hope you were able to get all that work finished. That there's no problem with your clients.'

'We did, and the clients are happy. And I came back because I was worried about you. Every time we spoke on the phone you were in tears. I began to think I'd done the wrong thing, writing those fragments, the bits and pieces of my life. And I certainly wished I hadn't given the book to you.'

Justine leaned forward, focused her blue eyes on another pair of blue eyes that were the identical colour. She smiled. 'I'm glad you did. I couldn't put it down. I hurt for you, suffered along with you, and I cried for you. I triumphed with you. I also longed to put my arms around you, to tell you how much I've always loved you.' She stood up, went to sit next to her grand-mother on the wicker sofa under the pale blue wisteria tree on the terrace of the *yali*. 'Reading your notebook has made me realize what a terrible world you lived in then, and that we still do now. It's made me appreciate everything I have and what I've achieved. And I know how lucky I am. It also told me who and what I am. Because of you, Gran, how you brought me up, and—'

'Your father had a lot to do with that,' Gabriele cut in. 'Tony was a good man. He helped to give you and Richard all the right values.'

'So did you. You're the most extraordinary woman I've ever known. I am so happy I belong to you, Gabriele Landau Hardwicke Saunders. And should I add Trent?' Justine gave her grandmother a pointed look.

Gabriele shook her head. 'Trent is a pseudonym, just a name to hide behind. A "stage" name, if you like.'

'I'm also pleased that I have your genes, your blonde hair and blue eyes. Thank you for that.' Justine smiled at her, loving her so much.

'Very Aryan looking, aren't we?' Gabriele shook her head. 'Irina was always drilling that into me.'

Justine said, 'What a wonderful friend she was to you.'

'She certainly was . . .' Gabriele's voice trailed off; she studied her granddaughter for a moment. 'I know you were surprised when you found out you were Jewish. Does it bother you, darling?'

Justine's blonde brows drew together in a frown and she threw Gabriele a puzzled stare. 'Of course it doesn't bother me! Why would it? I'm your granddaughter and that's all that matters.'

Gabriele was silent for a moment, thinking how blessed she was to have this amazing young woman in her life. There wasn't a bad bone in Justine's body. Nor a prejudiced one. She was an honest, straightforward, loving young woman with intelligence, perception and humanity. Who could ask for more?

'You're staring at me, Granny.'

'Please don't call me Granny, Justine. It makes me sound so old. I much prefer Gran. And I was staring at you because I was marvelling that you are part of me.'

'And very much like you, Gran. I need to ask you a couple of questions . . . Please don't be apprehensive. I'm not going to ask you to dig into your past. But I would love to know more about your friends from your wartime years. Princess Irina Troubetzkoy, for one. What happened to her? Did she remain in your life?'

Gabriele smiled. It was a smile that illuminated her face, filled it with radiance. 'She did. We had been so close in those terrifying years, that kind of bond always holds.'

'Did she ever get married?'

'No she didn't. But she could have. She had many admirers, many proposals. She was beautiful, glamorous, and men found her most alluring,' Gabriele replied, suddenly seeing the young Irina in her mind's eye, remembering so much.

'So why didn't she marry any of them?'

'I used to wonder that myself, Justine. I didn't find out until the Fifties. One day in Paris she told me that Sigmund Westheim had been her one great love. Not that they were involved. There was no affair. He was married to Ursula. They were just friends. But she was in love with him.'

'I understand. It is one of those awful things that can happen between men and women. It's so sad, unrequited love.'

'She did actually enjoy her life,' Gabriele went on. 'She was very popular socially, always in demand. And she did eventually have Maximilian in her life.'

'Do you mean the Westheims' son?'

'That's right. Irina saved his life, you know, and the life of Theodora Stein, a friend of the family who acted as Maxim's nanny. Irina managed to get three exit visas for the Westheims. In 1939. From Admiral Canaris. Sigi wouldn't go, he wouldn't leave his mother and two sisters behind in Berlin. But Canaris could not always produce the exit visas just like that. In the end, Ursula took Maxim and Teddy out. She sent them to England, to live with Teddy's aunt. Then she returned to Berlin to be with Sigi. A fatal decision, as you know. Maxim grew up in London. Teddy was like a mother to him. He is a brilliant man and he became very successful. You would know him today as Sir Maxim West.'

'The international tycoon! Wow! He's gorgeous as well as clever, Gran.' Justine looked impressed. 'Imagine that!'

'He is and always was good looking. Somewhat like Michael in appearance, wouldn't you say?' Gabriele murmured, smiling at her.

'Yes, that's true. But what do you mean about Irina and Maxim? I'm not following you.'

'After the war, Teddy went back to Berlin to look for Maxim's parents, Ursula and Sigi. She couldn't find them. She did manage to find Irina. It was a fluke. And through the princess she learned what had happened to Sigi and Ursula; to my parents and the von Tiegals. They were a close-knit group, along with the von Wittingens and Dieter Müller and Louise. Anyway, Teddy went back to London, gave Maxim the tragic news. When he grew up and became successful he went to Berlin to see Irina. From that moment on he took care of her financially. The old baron had left her some money when he died, but not much. Maxim invested that for her, and added to it. He treated her like family.'

'What a wonderful thing to do. And did you continue to see Irina?'

'I did. When I lived in London she came to visit me. Sometimes we met in Paris. Or Berlin. But Irina was a bit like Anita. She didn't want to travel. She felt safe in Berlin. Just as Anita is a stay-at-home, and feels safest in Istanbul.'

'I can understand that, Gran. What happened to Arabella? She was the last of the Roedean girls, wasn't she?'

Gabriele's face changed slightly. 'She was, yes. She moved between Zurich and Munich for a while. However, she was never really herself again. And then, in the early Fifties, Dieter stumbled on a strange story. Germans, mostly civilians, who had been arrested by the Russians when Germany surrendered, were finally being released from Lubyanka Prison in Moscow. There was talk amongst them about a German, an aristocrat, who was kept in solitary confinement. They said he had been there since 1945. His age and physical description fitted Kurt.'

'And was it Kurt von Wittingen?' Justine asked, her curiosity aroused more than ever.

'We never found out. The Russians denied there was any prisoner at all. But naturally what it did was give poor Arabella hope. Which was fatal.'

'I can imagine. Did she become confused again?'

'Worse than that, Justine. Deranged. Diana had a difficult time with her.'

'And you never found out anything? Whether it was Kurt or not?' Justine's intense gaze was focused on Gabriele.

'Not exactly. The world did learn about a Swedish diplomat called Raoul Wallenberg—'

'But of course, Gran! I've heard all about him. He rescued people, mostly Jews, got them out of Hungary. He was a bit like Admiral Canaris. He was considered a great hero, wasn't he? Didn't he die in Lubyanka?'

'Supposedly,' Gabriele answered quietly. 'He had been arrested on suspicion of being a spy for the Americans. In 1945. Or so it went. The Russians denied he was ever there. There were so many different stories at the time and, later, no one knew what to believe. However, I believe that Kurt von Wittingen was never taken by the KGB. Or in Lubyanka Prison. I think the prisoner *was* Raoul Wallenberg. Irina and I always felt Kurt had been killed in the last-ditch fighting in Berlin. And that very simply his body was never found.'

Justine nodded, her eyes full of sorrow. 'How terrible for the von Wittingens. Never really knowing the fate of Kurt.'

'Oh, I think Diana and Christian believed the same as us.

Well, they led us to believe this. And Arabella became very ill in the Eighties. She died in 1990.'

'And Diana and Christian?'

'Neither of them married. They're devoted to each other and live at a small Schloss called Wittingenhoff in Bavaria.' Gabriele turned her head, looked at Justine, finished, 'They're very devoted to me. I hear from them all the time. And sometimes I meet with Diana in London, or Berlin. We go back so far, darling – why, we were children together.'

'I know you were, Gran. And do you still go to Berlin? Or does it hold too many bad memories for you?'

'It does in a sense; on the other hand, part of my life was lived there.' Gabriele sat up straighter on the sofa, looked at her granddaughter. 'Can you imagine, I was actually in Berlin on November the ninth, in 1989, when that dreadful wall came down. The following evening I met up with Maxim, Irina, Teddy and Anastasia, Maxim's former wife, whom he eventually remarried. The whole week was like a huge street party, something special to be a part of.' She leaned back against the cushions, looked off into the distance, remained silent.

'Gran, what happened with Gretchen? Did she ever show up?'

'No. But I still think about her and little Andreas. They might be alive. She *had* become odd. I often thought she'd killed the child and herself. I just don't know. *A mystery*. But it haunts me. I told Anita about it years ago and she agrees with me. It was all very strange.'

Justine watched her, thinking how beautiful she was for a woman about to celebrate her eightieth birthday in June. She reached out, took hold of Gabri's hand, squeezed it. 'You're looking so sad, Gran. She died, didn't she? Irina.'

Gabriele nodded, thinking again how perceptive Justine was. 'Yes, she did. But she was *ninety*. Imagine that. She died in her sleep in 2001. Just slipped away peacefully. In Berlin. Which, despite everything, was a city she had always loved. And after all she'd lost and suffered, she did live a grand life, and she was beautiful right to the end. I still think of her. And quite often.'

'However did the two of you manage in that hole?' Justine wondered aloud, trying to imagine that.

Gabriele laughed, 'Our little abode, she always called it. We managed because we had to, Justine. We were scrupulously neat. Kept our few bits and pieces in the wine racks. And in the silver cupboards. We shared the food and water. We were controlled. And we gave each other a lot of privacy. It was *two* cellars, you know. We were often a bit irritable, but we stuck it out. Through a great effort on our parts.'

'I liked the sound of Dieter Müller when I was reading the notebook. Is he still alive?'

'I'm afraid he died in 1996. He was the same age as Irina. He made a big success of his newspaper. It is now run by his two sons.'

Gabriele took out a tissue and blew her nose, patted her eyes. 'All this talk about my old friends is making me far too sad,' she said, and then smiled. 'Dieter felt so responsible for us. He thought if he didn't look after us properly he'd be letting Kurt down. He was a good man.'

'I felt that when I was reading your notebook, Gran. And I'm sorry if I'm making you sad. Just one more question. Okay?'

Gabriele nodded. 'Just one.'

Justine said, 'Peter Hardwicke was my grandfather. How did you meet up again after you left Berlin?'

'I'd given him auntie Beryl's address. He came calling. We started to date. Eventually we got married. We had a daughter, your mother, and things worked for a few years. But everything went wrong. He was nice, but weak. He had a domineering mother, very snobbish. They were bigoted. Difficult. She never liked me, thought I wasn't good enough. We sort of drifted apart . . . I think that's the best way of describing it. My aunt Beryl always thought he wasn't good enough for me. Oh dear.

Families!' She laughed. 'I never thought of divorcing him, you know, because of your mother. Then he died suddenly of congestive heart failure. I was sorrowful, and yet I remember having a sense of liberation.'

'So it wasn't the great marriage Mom has always maintained. The fabulous love match?'

'No, it wasn't, Justine. Now, enough of the past. Let's go in and have tea. I'm sure Anita's chomping at the bit to see you. And no doubt Mehmet's gone to town on the preparations. It's going to be a fancy Ritz tea once again, knowing Anita.'

Justine rose, waited for Gabriele to stand up on her own, not wanting to be chastised for helping her grandmother. She saw Michael out of the corner of her eye, and waved to him, her heart leaping.

A moment later he was hugging Gabriele and then kissing her cheek. Against her ear he said, 'I've missed you, babe.'

She laughed. 'You've only been gone an hour.'

'It seemed like a lifetime.'

FIFTY

Anita was waiting for them in the gold room. As usual she wore a lovely silk caftan and as she hurried towards them she did so in a swirl of blues and greens. 'There you are, my darling!' she exclaimed the moment she saw Justine. 'Gabri's missed you! I've missed you! I can't tell you how easy you are to get used to. You're positively addictive.'

Michael said, 'And that's the truth.' He guided Gabriele toward the sofa whilst his grandmother hugged Justine.

Michael had come back to Istanbul earlier than planned. When he had heard her sorrowful voice, her tears, and understood the full extent of her distress, he had cancelled the rest of his Paris appointments, flown to Istanbul on Wednesday night. He had managed to calm Justine down, console her, give her background on some historical events she needed explained; some information about Nazi Germany. Then, on Thursday and Friday, he had read *Fragments of a Life*, had been enormously moved by it, amazed at how much Gabriele had been able to convey in so few pages. It must have been a hard task for her to plunge back into the past. It had taken courage. But then he'd always known she was courageous. Bravery was written all over her face.

'You're very quiet, Michael,' Gabriele said as they both sat down on the sofa.

'Just a bit tired,' he answered.

She threw him a strange look, frowned, but was silent.

He said, 'So what do you think about the idea of coming to New York with us? And would Anita come too?'

'I think she might. Although she's never been one for travelling. I think that's partly because she fled here when she was a girl, found refuge here. She feels comfortable in Istanbul, safe. She doesn't really want to leave here.'

He nodded, looked across at Justine and Anita, who were chatting to Mehmet, then turned to Gabriele. 'I love her very much, that girl of yours, Gabri.'

Gabriele's eyes were moist as she took hold of his hand and squeezed it. 'I know.' There was a silence, and then Gabri said in a low voice, 'You've read it, haven't you, my little book of bits and pieces?'

'I have, yes. Justine said I must. She was also quite positive you wouldn't be angry. I hope you're not, that you don't mind.'

'Of course I don't. My goodness, you've been like a grandson to me over the years. Especially the wilderness years when I was here all alone, when Justine and Richard were cut off from me. I don't know what I would have done without you, Michael. And you have every right to read it. Because of our closeness, the love I have for you.'

'Which is reciprocated tenfold. Your courage and steadfastness, your strength and discipline amaze me. And I want you to know there were moments when I wept. And it takes a lot to move me to tears.'

She stared at him for a moment, and then she murmured, 'Oh yes, the hard-bitten Secret Service agent, that's you.'

'There are moments when your pithiness does you proud. I might be tough, but hard-bitten? I'm not so sure about that.' He shrugged. 'But perhaps I am in certain circumstances.'

Justine and Anita joined them around the coffee table in front of the fireplace, and Mehmet and Zeynep served tea and nursery sandwiches with a flourish.

Justine sipped her lemon tea, focused her gaze on Anita, said, 'Now that I know a lot about the past from Gran, I'd like to hear something from you, Anita. I have a question.'

'And what's that?' Anita, her head on one side, gazed at Justine, thinking what a lovely young woman she was.

Justine said, 'I'd love to know how you found Gran? After the end of the war, I mean?'

Anita said eagerly, 'I was determined to go and look for her. I decided that first I'd better go back to Berlin. I didn't really relish it. But I needed to find my Gabri, my best friend. So in 1946, I went to Berlin. Naturally I couldn't find her. Or anyone remotely connected to her. Eight years had passed. So I knew she must have gone to London to her aunt and Jock. I returned to Istanbul somewhat disappointed. But I made a trip to London several months later. And *voilà!* I found her.'

'But did you know where to go?' Justine asked, looking from her grandmother to Anita.

'Yes. I have an excellent memory. I remembered that Gabri's aunt Beryl and uncle Jock lived near a street named after an English king. *Charles* Street. Their house was just round the corner. The number had gone out of my head. But that didn't matter because I knew I would easily recognize the house. It was on Chesterfield Hill and the corner of Charles. I rang the doorbell and guess who answered the door?'

'My grandmother.'

'No, no, Justine, your great-aunt Beryl,' Anita said. 'I'd stayed with her once, when I'd visited London with Gabri and her mother. Naturally she recognized me, welcomed me like a long-lost friend. Which I was, in a way. When Gabri came home from the Royal College of Art later that afternoon, she was overjoyed to see me. And we just picked up our friendship where we'd left off all those years ago.'

'Now wasn't that lucky you knew where to go,' Justine said, and winked at Anita.

'Oh yes, I know. I forgot to put the address on the back of the envelope,' Anita murmured, and had the good grace to laugh. 'You'll never let me forget that, will you?'

Justine and Michael walked through the gardens, went to sit on the seat facing the Bosphorus. Their seat. She had become rather quiet towards the end of tea, and had remained silent as they had strolled along the path.

'What's wrong?' Michael asked, stretching an arm along the back of the seat, peering at her.

She did not say anything for a moment, and then finally spoke. 'I'm tormented by the fact that I have trouble reading those old press clippings of great-auntie Beryl's. I always believed I was strong. Tough. I was a journalist, for heaven's sake, Michael. Yet I find them hard to face. And I feel such a sissy.'

Michael put his arm around her shoulders, pulled her closer, held her in his arms protectively.

'Listen to me, Justine. Everyone has trouble reading about the Holocaust, the death camps, the astronomical number of people killed. Imagine this. Battle-hardened troops of the Allied armies, American, British and French, were filled with shock and over-whelming disgust when they discovered those camps in April and May of 1945. They simply couldn't believe what they were seeing – walking skeletons who staggered to meet them, arms outstretched as if to their saviours, held upright only by their will to live, their will to defy the Nazis. The soldiers were aghast, filled with fury. What happened in Nazi Germany was history's most diabolical mass murder. Remember, six million people were killed.'

'I know,' she whispered. 'I've read all the names of the camps. *So many*. Unbelievable, Michael. I couldn't read on. I cried for hours. So what kind of person am I if I can't *read* about the camps, when my great-grandparents had to live there, were *murdered* there?'

'I know, darling, I know. But please don't feel like a sissy, not brave, Justine. Don't chastise yourself. I'm a historian and even I have trouble with those horrendous images and the fearful details. It's mind-boggling. Listen, here's another example for you. General George S. Patton, one of the US Army's most hard-bitten officers, was horror-struck after he had walked through the camp at Ohrdruf, had seen the death houses, his face was wet with tears and he was uncontrollably ill afterward. Eisenhower, the Supreme Commander in Europe during the Second World War, was ashen faced, clenched his teeth as he walked through an entire camp near Gotha. It was Ike who insisted that Washington and London send editors and legislators to view the horrors he had seen. To report on them. Men were filled with such revulsion and shock, they were sick. Disgusted, furious. You're not alone in your reaction.'

She wiped her tears away with her fingertips, and clung to Michael. After a while he was able to calm her. As he held her in his arms, he thought, there is nothing cynical about her. She is pure, open-minded, without hatred, and has an understanding heart.

He said, after a short while, 'Gabri knows you gave the book to me, that I've read it.'

'Was she angry?'

'No, not at all. I was wondering, do you think she'll allow Anita to read it?'

'Perhaps. Yes, I don't see why not. They are so bonded to

each other . . . from childhood. And now they're eighty, or almost.'

'I shall ask Gabri later,' Michael said.

A little later, Justine went to have a rest, but she found she couldn't sleep. A thought had occurred to her when she was sitting in the garden with Michael. And now she swung her legs off the bed, put on her robe, went out into the corridor. She walked down to her grandmother's room, knocked on the door.

'Come in, darling,' Gabriele called.

'How did you know it was me?' Justine asked as she went into the bedroom.

'Well, I doubt that Ayce would be knocking on my door at this hour. I'm sure she's having a rest before preparing dinner.'

'Oh, Gran, you've started packing. It's exciting, isn't it? You're coming to Indian Ridge. Richard will be thrilled.'

Gabriele nodded. 'It is . . . and as you can see I'm very anxious to get there! This case is already half full.' She smiled at Justine.

Sitting down in a chair, Justine said, 'Listen, I've been thinking about something. To be exact. Mom. It occurred to me that if you'd allow me, I'd like to lend her your *Fragments* book. I think her attitude towards you would be very different once she'd read it. I know she's been angry, that she created the estrangement out of discontent and greed. But this memoir would move anyone to tears. It could be a bridge. Do you want to give it a try?'

Gabriele stood holding a dress, gaping at Justine. Her face had turned deathly white. 'I can assure you she won't want to read it.'

'But you don't really know that, Gran. And—'

'Oh, but I *do* know it!' Gabriele exclaimed, her voice rising. 'I told you, when you first arrived in Istanbul, that Deborah broke into my writing case when she was in London ten years ago. I also explained that she had read certain documents, and had then gone into an absolute fury. She was hysterical, out of control.'

'Yes, you did tell me that. You mentioned she saw your old marriage certificate to Trent. But what else did she see? You never said, Gran.'

'She saw the birth certificates belonging to my mother, aunt Beryl and me. She saw aunt Beryl's black notebook listing her donations to Jewish charities. Uncle Jock was a Scotsman, of course. But his mother was Jewish, and his notebook listing his charitable donations was there as well. And there were a few other things which obviously disturbed her in that writing case, including auntie Beryl's carefully preserved clippings about the camps.'

Justine stared at her grandmother, saw that her hands holding the dress were now shaking uncontrollably. And she was ashen faced.

'Gran, Gran, whatever's wrong? What is it?'

'Deborah hates me because I'm *Jewish*. That is why she went into a tailspin a decade ago. When she read the birth certificates, saw Beryl's donations in the book, and the other papers, she was consumed with fury. Your mother is anti-Semitic, Justine. A bigoted, ignorant anti-Semite.'

'Didn't she know you were Jewish?'

'No. I had never told anyone I was. If I had, I would have had to explain about my past. My frightening childhood in Nazi Germany. I couldn't live through that again. *You know this*. I've explained I can't dredge things up. I can't relive the pain. I didn't tell anyone because I don't want to be constantly talking about the past, about myself, my life of long ago. And that's the only reason I keep quiet. Deborah accused me of lying to her, but I never did. I never told Peter because deep down inside myself I knew there was enormous bigotry in him. And his mother was a snob, a social climber, bigoted and anti-Semitic. She was full of racial superiority. And I suppose that's where Deborah gets it from. It was bred in the bone. They brainwashed her.'

'Oh no, Gran, no! This is terrible.' Justine was trembling herself and pale as a ghost.

'It's the truth. And now you know the real reason for the estrangement,' Gabriele said. 'She broke up the family. Denied me access to you and Richard. Took you away from me because I'm Jewish. And there's another thing . . . you knew as a little girl that she hated Uncle Trent. And that was because he was also Jewish. So no, she can't read the book. Because it will only inflame her more. And besides, it's none of her business. I am who I am and to hell with her.'

Justine ran to Gabriele, put her arms around her. 'Gran, don't be upset about her. She's not worth it. And you've got us. Richard and me, and Michael. And we do love you. We're here for you.'

Uncharacteristically, Gabriele began to sob. Justine held her close, trying to calm her, soothing her for a long time. And her fury with her mother mounted. She knew that she would never forgive her for the pain she had caused Gabriele, who had only done her good.

FIFTY-ONE

Michael stood staring at himself in the bathroom mirror, thinking he didn't look bad for thirty-nine. Well almost. His birthday was next month. His face was much less tense these days; he had lost that tautness around the eyes that had been a permanent fixture when he was in the Secret Service. But that was a long time ago.

Nonetheless he was still tough, contained, controlled, disciplined, totally focused, and never displayed emotion in public. He was well aware that his training at the academy in Washington would remain with him for the rest of his life. It was part of him now, second nature.

After straightening the collar of his white sports shirt he turned away from the mirror, went into his bedroom, glancing at his watch as he did so. He sat down in a chair thinking about Justine, and what to do about her. When they had first met, his initial reaction to her had surprised him. And he was glad he had gone to London at the beginning of the week. It had given him a chance to think, to consider the situation, to look at everything objectively.

They were going back to New York early next week. Gabriele

very much wanted to be reunited with Richard, and to meet her great-grandchild Daisy. Anita hadn't liked the idea of being left behind, and so she had made up her mind to go with them.

What would happen to his relationship with Justine when they got there? Would they continue to see each other, living in their own places? Or would they move in together? He had to travel. She had decided to go ahead with the documentary about Istanbul. What would their lives be like?

Suddenly things seemed to be up in the air. He walked over to the window, looked out at the garden, his mind racing. He had never felt so vulnerable before. It was because of her, this girl he had heard about for years, this girl he had fallen for. Fallen hard.

A *coup de foudre*, the French so aptly called it. Lightning striking. But what happened when the lightning stopped? Would it rain? Would the rain wash everything away?

Michael opened a drawer in the chest, took out various items and put them in his trouser pockets, grabbed his phone. There was no way out of this. He would have to talk to her. But first he had a phone call to make.

Once outside, Michael walked down to the jetty, sat down on a step at the edge of the water. He dialled Charlie in Gloucestershire. A moment later his client was saying, 'Hi Michael, what's up?'

'Not much. I just wanted to let you know I'm going back to New York next week. I wondered if I should come to London for a day?'

'No, that's not necessary. Everything's okay. We're all set to make the press announcement on Tuesday. Laura relocates to Manhattan immediately. To run the International Division. Jeremy has been made managing director. And I'm kicking myself upstairs, as you suggested. I don't mind being chairman; I'll still be in charge.' He chuckled.

'I know that. These moves will put a stop to the in-fighting, friction and bitterness between them. The sibling rivalry will just go away. And all the upheaval in the bank will stop.'

'Funny thing how I've never noticed *their rivalry*. If it weren't for you I'd still be in the dark. Who knew my twenty-nine-year-old daughter was so ambitious?'

'Don't forget William Pitt the Younger, not to mention Alexander the Great. They were both holding immense power in their early twenties.'

'I guess I did forget. Thank God you saw my children a lot more clearly than I did. And came up with the solutions.'

'That's what I'm here for. Okay, Charlie, that's it. Talk to you soon.'

'You bet. Have a nice evening.'

Michael clicked off his cell phone and put it in his pocket. He sat on the step for a moment, thinking about Jeremy. A good guy. He would have to be brought into the loop, told that his father and he were unofficial 'watchdogs', keeping their eyes on the bad guys who could create global havoc.

As he ran up the steps he saw Justine heading across the garden, making for the garden seat, and waved, called her name.

She stopped, waved back.

He hurried towards her. As he drew to a standstill he said, 'I was just coming to look for you. I've got to talk to you immediately. It's urgent.'

She stared at him. 'Oh. Oddly enough, I wanted to talk to you too, Michael.'

'What about?'

'No, you go first. Come on. Let's go and sit on our seat for a few minutes.'

Once they were settled she looked at him intently and said, 'You sound so serious. Is something wrong?'

'No, nothing.' He peered at her, noticed the tension in her face, the taut set of her jaw. 'But are you okay?'

'I am, Michael. Gran just told me something that I want to share with you, but it can wait.'

'I've been thinking about our return to New York next week, and what's going to happen to us. What I mean is, do we move in together? Start living together? Or what?'

She bit her lip. 'I don't know. It's only just been decided that all of us should go back to New York. I haven't thought it through.'

'I haven't either.' He turned slightly, his dark eyes focused on her. He studied her intently for a moment, and he knew then, and without a shadow of a doubt, that he loved her with all his heart. 'Marry me, Justine.'

She was momentarily taken aback and did not answer. He said, 'Come on, say yes, marry me. Take a chance with me – let's follow love, Justine. Let's seize life and live it together. It might be a risk, but so what? We've got nothing to lose. And we do love each other, and there's nothing truer than that.'

A smile began to spread across her face, and the tension in her evaporated. 'Of course we love each other! It's a *coup de foudre*, remember. Yes, Michael. Yes. I'll marry you, and the sooner the better.'

She moved closer to him, kissed him, her arms went around him. He kissed her back and they went on kissing, until he finally drew away. He said softly, 'You are the person I should be with, Justine. For the rest of my life. And you should be with me.'

'I know that, Michael. There's nothing more life affirming than our love for each other.'

Michael put his hand in his pocket, pulled out a small dark-blue leather box. 'I've been walking around with this for days.' He opened the box and took out a ring. 'I asked you to marry me; you said yes.' He slipped the ring on the finger of her left hand. 'And now we're engaged.'

Justine gasped as she looked down at the deep-blue sapphire. 'Oh Michael! It's beautiful. Thank you, thank you.'

'I'm happy you like it. There's a story behind it. Last Monday, before I left for London, I went to see Anita. She brought this ring out of her safe, and told me she wanted me to have it for you. She then explained that it was the last gift my grandfather Maxwell gave her before he died. She wouldn't take no for an answer.'

'What a lovely thing for her to do,' Justine murmured, touched by Anita's gesture. Then she jumped up. 'Come on, let's go and find her, and Gran, and tell them we're now engaged.'

As Michael rose up he said, with a frown, 'But didn't you have something you wanted to discuss with me?'

'Oh *that*. It's nothing,' she exclaimed dismissively. She had no intention of letting the wickedness of her mother overshadow her engagement, or spoil the evening ahead. She would tell him later.

Michael grabbed her again and brought her close then, holding hands, they ran across the lawn. They found their grandmothers sitting on the terrace, obviously waiting for them.

Justine hurried to Anita and hugged her, kissed her cheek. 'Thank you, Anita. Thank you for my beautiful ring. I'm so touched you gave it to Michael to give to me.'

'It was meant for you,' Anita said, beaming.

Turning to her grandmother, Justine stretched out her hand. 'Look, Gran, Michael just gave me this. He asked me to marry him and I said yes and we're engaged.' She bent forward and took hold of Gabriele, and held on to her tightly. 'I'm so happy, Gran.'

'And so am I, Justine,' Gabriele answered, her eyes moist. Her joy knew no bounds.

Michael went to his grandmother and kissed her, and then to Gabriele. As he hugged her close, he whispered, 'I'll keep her safe always, Gabri.'

Anita said, 'This calls for pink champagne. Where's Zeynep?'

At this moment, Mehmet arrived with champagne in a bucket of ice, followed by Zeynep with a plate of hors d'oeuvres.

Michael looked from Anita to Gabriele. 'Why do I have a feeling you've both been one jump ahead of us?'

Both of them laughed and made no comment. After Mehmet had poured the champagne, and they had clicked glasses, made toasts, Anita said, 'This is so exciting. We must plan the wedding.'

'No planning necessary,' Michael announced. 'We're going to get married immediately. Well, in the next few weeks. A small wedding, just our families and a few friends. That's what I'd like. What about you Justine? Agreed?'

'Agreed. I think we should have it at Indian Ridge, don't you, Gran? What do you think?'

'Oh my goodness yes, what a fantastic idea! It's the perfect place. And it's the home of the bride, after all.'

'A Jewish wedding,' Anita murmured, glancing around. 'And I shall design the huppah. The four poles will be decorated with white tulips and white roses, and the canopy will be white silk. What do you think, Gabri?'

'It will be beautiful,' she answered, 'And when we get to Indian Ridge we'll look for the perfect spot to put it.'

Michael laughed, and said, 'My mother is going to be so happy I'm marrying a Jewish girl.'

'One who doesn't know too much about Judaism,' Justine murmured. 'But I'm willing to learn.'

'I'll teach you everything,' Michael shot back.

FIFTY-TWO

The little girl walking towards her wore a yellow muslin dress with a slightly billowing skirt, white ankle socks and black patent shoes with bows. She was carrying a yellow rose and looked very dignified as she stepped out with a certain aplomb.

As she came closer, gliding through the shadowy hall, Gabriele saw that she had silky blonde hair and blue eyes, and the prettiest little face she had ever seen.

Suddenly there she was, standing in front of her. Smiling. Doing a little dip of a curtsy. She offered Gabriele the rose, and said, 'This is for you, Gram. I'm Daisy.'

Bending down, taking the rose, Gabriele said, 'Thank you, Daisy.' She kissed her on the cheek. 'It's a beautiful flower and you're a beautiful girl.' The child laughed, twirled around and spotted Justine standing behind Gabriele. She rushed to her, throwing herself against her aunt's body. 'Juju! Juju! You've come back.'

'Of course I have,' Justine said, hugging Daisy to her, thinking how lovely she looked in the new dress.

Daisy asked, 'Did you go to see Mommy? Does she like Heaven?'

They all looked at each other, speechless for a moment. Justine said, 'I went to see Gran in Istanbul.'

'Oh, where's Itsabul?' Daisy asked, and started twirling again, happy as a lark today, moving down the hall.

Gabriele looked down the shadowy space, saw a man standing there, watching them. As he walked forward the breath caught in her throat. It was Dirk Landau. Her father. But obviously it wasn't. It was her grandson Richard, who now at thirty-two was the spitting image of her father. He had the same shaped face, narrow, elegant. The broad forehead, the sculpted nose and a head of wavy hair.

Richard was smiling and increased his pace.

Gabriele moved quickly, and suddenly they were embracing in the hall. Richard was laughing, kissing her cheek, exclaiming, 'Gran, oh Gran, welcome home! I've not been so happy for ages.'

'And neither have I,' Gabriele answered, standing away from him, looking up at him, her eyes roaming over his face. 'You look just like my father, Richard. Now that you've grown up. I can see him in you so easily.'

He nodded. 'Remember, Gran, you've not set eyes on me for ten years. Unfortunately.'

She simply nodded. Turning she said, 'Come and meet my dearest friend, Anita, and her grandson, Michael Dalton. Justine's fiancé.'

The two men stepped forward, looked each other up and down and shook hands. They instantly liked each other. Then Richard walked over to Anita and shook her hand. He said, 'That's rather silly!' He bent forward and kissed her on the cheek, and Anita was instantly smitten.

Justine glanced around and asked, 'Where are Joanne and Simon?'

'They'll be here soon, after everyone's settled in,' Richard said. 'So come on, Gran, let's go and see Tita and Pearl. They're dying to give you hugs and kisses. That was the way they put it.'

'What on earth did you tell them? I mean – about where I suddenly sprang from?' Gabriele asked, frowning.

Richard gave her a knowing look. 'I told them the truth. That there'd been a quarrel. That we'd been led to believe you had died. Then we'd discovered you weren't dead, and Justine went to find you. It's much better than lying. What is it you used to say, Gran? Something like, let's not get our knickers in a twist.'

'That sounds like a Gabri remark,' Anita murmured. 'And where did little Daisy go? I haven't kissed her yet.'

On hearing her name, Daisy came dancing back into the wide part of the hall. She said, 'Here I am.' She was clutching two roses, one red, one white. She went up to Anita, did a little curtsy and handed her the red rose. 'This is for you.'

Anita smiled at her, bent down and kissed her on the cheek. 'Thank you, my darling. I know we're going to be friends.'

Daisy went to Michael, looked up at him, suddenly appeared to be a little shy. She gave him the white rose. He smiled, enchanted by her. 'Thank you very much. It's just right for my buttonhole.' He smoothed his hand across the top of her blonde head. 'I'm Michael,' he murmured gently.

She stared up at him, then smiled and danced away.

Watching all this, Gabriele was overwhelmed. Her heart was full of love for this adorable child. Her great-granddaughter. It's all been worth it just for this moment, she thought. To meet Daisy, to know of her existence, to have a chance to love her while I'm still fit and well. Oh, what a lovely time I'm going to have with her. She's beautiful. A typical Landau. She has our genes, no doubt about that.

Justine had managed to get everyone organized. Richard had taken their grandmother to the kitchen to be reunited with Tita and Pearl. And to meet Pearl's husband Carlos, and his father,

412

Ricardo. Daisy had accompanied them. Michael had gone off with Anita to look at the garden, to find the right spot for the huppah, and get a general idea of 'the lay of the land', as he called it.

With everyone occupied and busy, she ran upstairs, went to check on the rooms. She had given Pearl her instructions from Istanbul on Monday, before they had flown out on Wednesday. They had spent last night at a hotel in Manhattan, which Michael had insisted was the easiest thing to do, because of the luggage. All belonging to the grans. After lunch today they had been driven out here to Connecticut in a limousine. 'Very extravagant of you,' she had whispered to Michael. He had merely grinned, knowing how much the grans were enjoying everything, and especially the streamlined car.

Pushing open the door of the room that had always been her grandmother's, she smiled when she saw how beautiful it looked. Pearl had filled it with flowers. All were Gabriele's favourites. There was a bowl of mixed fruit on a tray. Bottled water. A dish of sweets. All of those little touches Gabriele had instilled in Pearl years ago. Everything sparkled. It was perfect.

Justine had told Pearl to prepare the room across the hall for Anita, and when she looked in she saw that it too was shining clean, all the little mandatory touches in place.

The third room at this end of the house would be used as a dressing room for Michael, a place to hang his clothes, have a bit of privacy. It also gave him his own bathroom. But he would share her bedroom. She smiled to herself. She knew he would insist on that.

Pleased that the rooms on this floor were ready for everyone, Justine went into her own bedroom and closed the door.

She sat down at her desk and quickly made a shopping list for Pearl, then sat back in the chair. Thinking. On Monday night Richard had called her in Istanbul, had told her that their mother was going to be in New York this coming week. 'We must see her, confront her?' he had said. She had agreed, had suggested he make the date. She would fit in with him.

She had a problem. Should she tell Richard about Deborah's rabid anti-Semitism first, and then give him the book? Or let him read Gabriele's *Fragments*, and then inform him of her attitude later?

Late on Saturday night in Istanbul she had confided in Michael, had told him the real reason Deborah had created the estrangement. He had been stupefied for a moment, and then furious. He had suggested that she give Richard the memoir this weekend, and then clue him in afterwards. Now she saw the wisdom in this. That is what she would do.

Moving on, she wrote out a menu for Sunday lunch, which she would give to Pearl and Tita later. Michael's sister Alicia and his parents were coming to spend the day. Naturally they wanted to meet her, and be with Cornelia's mother, Anita. And she was itching to meet them, hoping they would like her. 'Stop worrying,' Michael had said on the plane to New York. 'You're already part of the family, dopey.'

'I'm so happy you like the changes I've made,' Richard said. 'This is your house, your gallery, your estate, Gran. You created it all years ago. But I would have been really upset if you'd hated the offices. I put my heart and soul into them.'

Gabriele glanced at him, exclaimed, 'But I love your glass boxes, Richard. They are just *dazzling*. There's no other word to describe them. And I think the gallery looks magnificent – the way you have opened it up is spectacular. And your rolling walls are a fabulous idea.' As she spoke Gabriele pushed one of the walls, and it rolled across the floor. She walked through the new space, smiling. 'See what I mean. And the sense of spaciousness is lovely and the paintings are so well displayed.'

Richard followed her. 'We have a lot of your paintings hanging on this wall, Gran. In fact, Justine's favourite is right here.'

Gabriele hurried over. She was pleased that her grandchildren had kept her work on view, but thought they weren't good enough to be on display alongside some of the artists hanging here.

After a moment, she said, 'My paintings aren't that bad after all, are they, Rich? Oh, here's the one Justine loves! She was always so taken with it. Look Richard, that's me, just there. And here's Anita, next to me. We're in the meadows of . . . er, er . . . some meadows. I used an old snapshot from 1938 as my inspiration.'

Richard was staring at it. 'I've loved it for as long as I can remember,' he told her. 'I wish you'd painted more, Gran. You have such talent.'

Gabriele nodded. A rush of unexpected memories assailed her as she gazed at the painting of her and Anita: memories of Arabella, Irina and the Schloss in the Mark Brandenburg. Of their little abode, their hole in the ground that had been their safe haven . . . so many memories . . . so many years had flown by. Over sixty years, she thought.

Her eyes were suddenly moist. She hoped Richard hadn't noticed. No time for tears today, she thought. She had come home to her beloved Indian Ridge . . . and she was going to plan a wedding.

Later that afternoon, Justine knocked on Richard's bedroom door, poked her head around it. 'You're not napping, are you?'

'No, I was just sitting here thinking about our mother. I can't wait to tell her off, but I dread seeing her.'

Justine came in, closed the door. 'I know what you mean.' She sat down, held the leather notebook on her lap.

'What's that?' he asked, having just noticed it.

'It's for you, Rich. I want you to start reading it immediately. In fact, it's imperative that you do so.'

'Oh, why?'

'Because you have to know what's in here before we take on Deborah. It's a sort of memoir Gran wrote over the last ten years. Bits and pieces of her life, she calls it. I read it in Istanbul and it's extraordinary.'

'Tell me about it.'

'No, I can't. That's not what Gran wants. She was going to leave it to us in her will, and then decided we should have access to it *now*. And she didn't want me to tell you anything. She insists you read it for yourself.'

'Okay, I'll do that. It doesn't look very long.'

Justine simply nodded, went on, 'Why is our mother in New York?'

'She's doing that big decorating job in Tokyo. I guess she cut short her buying trip in China. She's here to buy art. Important art, she said. Frankly, I'm glad she's in Manhattan. Having to fly out to the Coast to confront her would be a nuisance at this moment, what with your wedding coming up. We don't have the time.'

'It is more convenient that she's here. I can't wait to give her a piece of my mind. Have you made the date with her?' Justine asked.

'I said I'd call her tomorrow. She's staying at The Carlyle.'

'Make it for early in the week, Rich. Because Michael wants to come back out here on Thursday or Friday.' Rising, Justine walked over, handed him the notebook. 'I think you'll have a few surprises,' she said.

FIFTY-THREE

Justine and Richard sat together in the small lounge area of The Carlyle Hotel on Madison Avenue. It was five thirty on Tuesday afternoon. They had an appointment with their mother at six, and they were both nervous about seeing her.

Justine said, 'I know you're still in a fury with her, Rich, and I don't blame you. Anti-Semitism is vile. I think Gran is right. She said it was bred in the bone. Deborah inherited it from her father and grandmother when she was growing up in England.'

He nodded. 'As I told you on Sunday night, it came as such a shock after reading *Fragments*. I was moved by Gran's story, admiring of her and her courage, and loving her more than ever.' He paused, took a sip of water, added, 'Our mother is insane. She's always been a bit of a flake – soft in the head.'

'I don't know about *flake*. Surely wicked is a better word?' Justine replied.

'I can think of quite a few words to apply to her. Greedy for one. Selfish. Self-involved. Manipulative. A liar. A cheat. I could fill a yellow pad about her. By the way, how do you plan to handle this?'

'I don't know, Richard. I thought we should play it by ear. I want to tell her we know what she did, the lies she told about Gran being dead. That we're on Gran's side. That we don't want *her* in our lives. Agreed?'

'Absolutely. And I'll take your lead. As I always have.'

She glanced at her watch. 'I'm glad we didn't tell Gran she's in Manhattan, aren't you?'

Richard said, 'Absolutely. I don't want Gran to be exposed to her in any way. It's the first of June today, she's going to be eighty this month. I don't want her to have any aggravation with Deborah. I want to make this a happy month for Gran. She certainly deserves it, considering the life she's had. And I certainly don't want her to be upset just before your wedding. I'm sure you agree about that.'

'I do, yes. And so does Michael. He's still shocked about Deborah's behaviour, totally dumbfounded that she broke up our family, isolated Gran, her own mother, for God's sake. To say he's livid about her anti-Semitism is an understatement.'

'How much does Anita know?'

'All of it, and she's currently reading *Fragments*. I think she's hurt inside for Gran,' Justine said.

'That's understandable, considering their closeness, the circumstances of their lives.' Richard pushed his sleeve up, looked at his watch. 'It's a few minutes to six. I can't stand this, I'm going to call her, tell her we're coming up.'

'Yes, you'd better do that. We don't want to surprise her. She might have a man in the room.'

Richard threw her a pointed look, said, '*We* certainly knew about her shenanigans, even if Dad didn't.'

'Dad wasn't dumb, Rich, he just turned a blind eye for peace and quiet. And for us. He wanted us to have a stable upbringing. No divorce, no custody fight. No ripping us away from him.'

'I know. Okay, come on, let's go to the lobby, call her suite.' He paid the bill for their water, and they left the lounge area. Richard glanced at his twin, and suddenly laughed.

She stared at him. 'What's wrong? Don't I look all right?'

He chuckled once more, and said, 'You look fantastic. I love the black suit, the white blouse and pearls. Your hair tied back in a chignon. You look as if you mean business.'

'I do mean business. And I'm aiming for the jugular.'

When Deborah Nolan opened the door of her suite, Justine was surprised. Her mother looked exactly the same. She had not changed. She was still beautiful in her own way. How does she do it? Justine wondered as she followed Richard inside.

Deborah said, 'Well this is a nice surprise. I was beginning to think you didn't want to see me any more. It's been several years, kids.'

'You haven't been here,' Justine answered. 'And we never come to the Coast.'

Deborah ignored this comment. 'Would you like a drink? I've got a full bar here. I'm doing a lot of entertaining this week. Art dealers mainly. I've got this huge job in Tokyo. So what would you like, Justine? Richard?'

'Water for me, please,' Richard said.

'The same,' Justine murmured, and sat down in a chair. Her eyes followed Deborah as she moved across to the drinks table, poured the water. She was still trim. She had to be because she was short. Short, dark haired, with grey eyes. As different from the Landaus as she could be. Did that trouble her? Was she jealous of their height, their good looks, their blondeness? Joanne had once said, years ago, that she was. Maybe Jo had been right. She was one of the smart kids on the block.

Deborah brought them their drinks, and went back for her own glass of water. 'Got to stay trim,' she said, eyeing Justine. 'You look great, Justine, and you too, Richard.'

Neither of them answered. After a moment, Deborah said,

'Well, is this a social visit, or what? You both look pretty serious.' She stared at them, a brow lifting quizzically.

'We just wanted to see you, talk about a few things,' Justine answered. 'Incidentally, how was China? Your buying trip?'

'It was great! I covered a lot of ground in a short time, bought loads of blue-and-white porcelain and pottery, antiques. I have a boutique in Beverly Hills. It's called Exotic Places, Faraway Lands. And it's going well. That's why I went to China, to procure stock. I hope to go to India this autumn.'

'I recognize those names,' Justine remarked, staring hard at Deborah. 'Gran used them when she had the showroom with Dad at the D & D Building on Lexington Avenue.'

'Oh yes, I know. The franchises are mine now. I inherited them.'

'Did you really? And talking of faraway places, I've just come back from Istanbul. It's an interesting city.'

'Maybe I should make a trip there. There must be loads to buy. What do you think?'

Justine was silent for a moment. She glanced at her twin, and then at Deborah. 'I went to Istanbul to see Anita Lowe.'

'Who's Anita Lowe?'

'You know her. She was involved with Gran in the ceramic and carpet business.'

'I can't recall her.'

'I went to see her because she was worried about Gran. She wrote a letter. After all, she will be eighty this month and she hasn't been well. She's much better now, thank God.'

'Who are you talking about? Anita Lowe, I assume.'

'No, Gran. Your mother. *Gabriele*.'

'Don't be so ridiculous. She's dead!' Deborah exclaimed.

'No, she's not. As a matter of fact she's alive and well and in Connecticut at this very moment. I brought her back with me from Istanbul. She's installed in her house, the home she loves so much. Indian Ridge. Her house, not yours.'

Deborah was dumbfounded. She sat gaping at Justine and Richard. She was speechless. Her face was a blank. But Justine realized that those luminous grey eyes were full of cunning. She might look stupefied, but there was no doubt in Justine's mind that Deborah was totally alert, already conniving.

Richard said, 'Why did you tell that awful lie? Ten years ago. It was unconscionable. Wicked! You told us Gran was dead, killed in a plane crash. We have grieved for her for years. When we found out that she was alive, that you had caused that estrangement, we realized what a terrible thing you had done. To her. To us. Isolating her from us for years. You ruined the last ten years for her. And caused us immense pain.'

'This is all ridiculous!' Deborah shot back, sitting up straighter. 'I'm not going to listen to all this nonsense. Bullshit, that's what this is!'

Justine was furious but she controlled herself. Opening her bag she took out the letter from Anita, handed it to Deborah. 'This is a copy of the letter from Anita Lowe. I opened it, because you'd always told me to open your mail. I'm glad I did. If I hadn't opened it, we wouldn't have known what a liar you are. Yes, a liar. And a bad woman.'

Deborah had taken the letter, but she wasn't reading it.

Justine said icily, in a threatening tone, 'Read the letter.'

Deborah simply gaped at her.

Justine jumped up, went and stood over her mother. '*I said read the letter. Read it.*' Her voice was so steely, her anger so apparent, that Deborah did as she asked, read the letter, then tore it up.

'The ravings of some senile old woman!' she exclaimed, and threw the pieces of paper on the coffee table.

Richard said angrily, 'You're really incredible. I think you must be off your head. Deranged. Our grandmother is alive, and you know that as well as we do. Yet you keep insisting she isn't. There's got to be something wrong with you. Are you mad?'

'How dare you say that?'

'Oh shut up, and listen!' Justine cried, losing it for a moment. She took hold of herself and continued, 'I went to Istanbul and I found Gran. I spent some healing time with her. And she told me everything. She told me how you broke into her writing case ten years ago, read her private documents. And that in doing so you discovered your mother was Jewish. That this sent you into a tailspin. You were hysterical because you discovered you're Jewish. And that is when you threw her out of the family. And all because you're anti-Semitic.'

'She lied to me!' Deborah shouted, her face turning red.

'No, Gran didn't lie to you. She never lies. But you do. We're well aware of that. She didn't *tell* you she was Jewish. Which is different from lying. And she didn't tell you because she didn't want to relive the pain of the past.'

'*She lied*. I was there, not you. And stop accusing me. How dare you?'

'I dare because I have the right. You broke up my family. Richard's family. You put our grandmother at risk. She was so devastated she became ill. She could have died.'

Deborah kept shaking her head, denying everything.

Richard said, 'You're Jewish too, you know. And so are we. And why does it matter anyway?'

'I am not Jewish,' Deborah screamed. 'I'm not!'

'Yes, you are. And the reason you're denying it is because you're anti-Semitic. Your father Peter Hardwicke and his mother were anti-Semites and bigots. You inherited those horrendous characteristics from them. It's bred in the bone.' Justine had been shouting in Deborah's face, and now she walked away. She was shaking all over. She sat down in the chair, trying to contain her flaring emotions and especially her anger.

Richard exclaimed, 'You're not only a pathological liar, you're a cheat. We know what you did to Dad. We know about all those men. All those trips when we were growing up. You're rotten to the core. I don't want to see you ever again.'

422

'Actually, you're pure evil,' Justine said, and stood up. 'I have nothing more to say to you. I disown you as Richard has. I never want to set eyes on you again.'

Richard stood up. 'I don't know how you can live with yourself. You killed your mother with the lies you told us, your children. You might as well have taken a gun and just shot her. Thankfully, we've brought her back to life.'

In the most normal of voices, Deborah said, 'That's a beautiful sapphire ring, Justine. On your engagement finger. Are you engaged?'

Justine was flabbergasted by her mother's extraordinary behaviour. 'Yes, I am engaged,' she replied in a cold voice, picking up her handbag and walking to the door.

Richard followed her, convinced Deborah was a truly disturbed person.

Deborah rose. 'So you're getting married soon?'

Without turning around, Justine said, 'Yes I am, and he's Jewish. Like me and you and Gran.'

'And me,' Richard added, and walked out with Justine, banging the door of the suite behind him.

In the elevator going down to the lobby, Justine clutched her brother's arm. 'You don't know how hard it was for me to keep my hands off her. I wanted to punch her in the face, and keep on punching her. I've never experienced anything like that in my life. I'm the least violent person, as you know.'

'I wanted to hit her myself. She enraged me. There's something wrong with her, you know.'

'Yes, I believe there is.'

When they stepped out into the lobby, Richard said, 'Where are you going now?'

'Into the bar. Michael's waiting for me. Come on, Rich, he wants to buy us a drink. And I for one need it.'

'So do I. And thank God that ordeal is over.'

Michael stood up and waved when he saw them. They walked

over and sat down at the table with him. 'How did it go?' he asked.

Justine shook her head. 'I thought I was going to beat her over the head. She infuriated me. And I'm sort of thrown by that reaction.'

Michael put his hand on her arm, smiled at her. 'It's all right to feel that. We all have similar reactions in given situations that are trying. The important thing is, you didn't do it. What do you want to drink? And you, Rich?'

Justine said, 'A vodka on the rocks with a piece of lime.'

'I'll have the same,' Richard said. And went on, 'I had the same angry feelings, Michael. And I honestly think Deborah is . . . sick in the head. She kept denying everything. She even denied she was Jewish.'

'Of course she did.' He beckoned to a waiter, ordered their drinks. They sat together for a while, discussing the encounter with Deborah.

At one moment Michael looked at Justine, and frowned, 'I know you didn't tell Gabri that you were going to confront your mother. Do you intend to tell her now that it's over?'

Justine was silent. She looked thoughtful.

Richard asked quietly, 'What's the point?' He touched Justine's arm. 'What do you think, Juju? Shall we tell her or keep it to ourselves?'

'Perhaps we shouldn't mention it, Rich. Why tell her anything about this horrendous confrontation? She doesn't need to know.'

'Correct,' Michael said. 'When there is *no need to know*, keep a lid on it.'

A little later they left The Carlyle Hotel. Richard took a cab home. It was a lovely evening and Michael and Justine walked down Madison Avenue. At one moment she said to Michael,

'I needed some fresh air after that horrible experience. And I can't believe I felt so violent.'

'Forget it, darling. Forget Deborah Nolan. Think about how wonderful Gabri is now because you found her, brought her back to New York. I know she loves Istanbul, but she is also attached to Indian Ridge. You've made her happy, and Anita, too. And you've certainly made me happy, Justine.'

For the first time that day she smiled as she looked into his face. 'You're such a beautiful man, a good man, a lovely man. And I'm relieved you're mine, Michael Dalton.'

'Just keep on thinking that, saying it.' He paused, turned to her. 'Do you think they did set us up? The grans, I mean?'

Justine looked at him, frowning, shaking her head. 'I just don't know, Michael. Perhaps they did.'

'Oh, what does it matter? It worked, didn't it? We fell in love and we're going to be together for the rest of our lives.'

'You bet we are,' she murmured, and took hold of his hand. 'And the best is yet to come.'

EPILOGUE

The Litchfield Hills, Connecticut
July 2004

EPILOGUE

It was July the Fourth and glorious. The perfect day for the perfect wedding with a perfect bride and groom. And Gabriele knew that this family photograph about to be taken was going to be perfect too.

She stood with Justine, a beautiful bride in white satin and lace, and a handsome groom in an elegant morning suit, a white rose in his buttonhole. Next to Michael was his grandmother, Anita, his parents Cornelia and Larry, his sister Alicia. And standing on the other side were Richard, Joanne, Daisy, Simon and Iffet. Who had come all the way from Istanbul to be another bridesmaid.

As she glanced at them all, Gabriele's heart swelled, overflowed with so much love she thought it would burst. She had never imagined a day like this could happen in her life. A day of happiness and contentment. There were no words that could fully express the feelings she was experiencing. To say she was happy was not enough. It was something beyond that.

Long ago she had lost her family. It had been wrenched from her by a vile regime. Ten years ago she had lost another family, this one ripped away by an angry and bigoted woman. She had believed she would never have another family ever again. But now she did. They stood here with her on this lawn at Indian Ridge, surrounded her, and she knew they loved her as much as she loved them.

Suddenly it was over. The photographer was finished with them. At least for the moment. And in a few seconds the reception would be in full swing. Justine said, 'Gran, always wear blue, like Irina said you should. You're beautiful today.'

'And so are you, Justine. Everything is perfect. Even the huppah is perfect, and you both looked so happy standing under it with the rabbi.'

Michael came to her, kissed her. 'Just think, now we really are related. I can call you Gran, can't I?'

She laughed. 'Of course you can.' And then she turned to greet everyone as they came up to her, and Anita did the same, beaming with pleasure.

Justine took Michael's hand in hers, smiling up at him. 'The grans are marvellous. They're holding court like elegant queens.'

'You must tell them that, they'll love it.' Justine and Michael exchanged looks. Together they went over to Gabriele, drew her to one side.

Justine said, 'Gran, we've something to ask you. We thought this might be the best time.'

'What is it?' Gabriele asked, looking from one to the other, wondering if something was wrong.

'We know you love Istanbul and your *yali*, but we hoped you would agree to spend some time at Indian Ridge. Perhaps in the summers,' Michael suggested. 'When it's so hot in Istanbul.'

She was silent for a moment. 'I shall come every summer because this is where my family is. I lost two families in my lifetime. Now that I have my third, I think I have to be . . . with you.'

'Third time lucky, Gran,' Justine said, her eyes suddenly moist. 'Indian Ridge is your sanctuary.'

Gabriele looked from Justine to Michael, and she smiled. It was a lovely smile that filled her face with radiance. She said, 'My family is my sanctuary . . .' And she went on smiling for the rest of the day.

ACKNOWLEDGEMENTS

Several years ago my husband and I met Iffet Özgönül, a professor of archaeology, and became friends. Iffet also runs her own boutique travel business, Peten Travels, and it was she who looked after us so well on our first trip to Istanbul. She has been doing so ever since, on our many visits to the fascinating city where she lives. I must thank Iffet for allowing me to make her a character in this book, and for her tremendous help with research on Istanbul. Our e-mails were constantly flying back and forth the entire time I was writing it, and her enthusiasm was remarkable.

To bring back to life an historical event of long ago, every author has to resort to books by other writers. I am lucky in that the mentor of my writing career as an author was the late war correspondent and historian, Cornelius Ryan. To recreate details of the end of the Second World War in Europe, I re-read Connie's famous book *The Last Battle*. It is as marvellously vivid and moving today as it was when it was first published. Certainly it helped me to truly envision and 'live' the harrowing and dramatic events Connie depicted so eloquently and with such humanity. No wonder it was a bestseller. Once again I found it impossible to put down. He was also the author of *The Longest Day* and *A Bridge Too Far*, and not surprisingly the French Government awarded him the French Legion of Honour.

I wish to thank Lonnie Ostrow of Bradford Enterprises, a whiz on the computer, who managed to get all of my many edits onto the manuscript under great pressure, and with good humour and efficiency.

I owe thanks to Lynne Drew, Publishing Director of HarperCollins, London, for her ideas, suggestions and enthusiasm. Thanks are also due to my editors Susan Opie and Penny Isaac, as well as to the entire team at HarperCollins, London.

My thanks to my editor Jennifer Enderlin for her enthusiasm and suggestions, and to Sally Richardson, President of St Martin's Press, New York, for her enthusiastic support, and the rest of the St Martin's team.

Last but not least, I must thank my husband Robert Bradford for his encouragement and involvement with all my books, but most especially this one. As the first reader his comments and suggestions are invaluable. His love, devotion and support are incomparable, not to mention his infinite patience with a wife always involved in time-consuming books that seem to take over the entire household.

BIBLIOGRAPHY

Bassett, Richard. *Hitler's Spy Chief*. London: Cassell.

Bielenberg, Christabel. *The Past Is Myself*. London: Corgi.

Cannadine, David. *Blood, Toil, Tears and Sweat: The Speeches of Winston Churchill*. New York: Houghton Mifflin.

Clare, George. *Berlin Days 1946–1947*. London: Macmillan.

Everett, Susan. *Lost Berlin*. New York: Gallery Books.

Gilbert, Martin. *Winston S. Churchill, Vol. VI, Finest Hour 1939–1941*. London: Heinemann.

Gilbert, Martin. *Winston S. Churchill, Vol. VII, Road to Victory 1941–1945*. London: Heinemann.

Irving, David. *Göring*. London: Macmillan.

Kaplan, Philip and Richard Collier. *Their Finest Hour: The Battle of Britain Remembered*. New York: Abbeville Press.

Metternich, Tatiana. *Tatiana: Five Passports in a Shifting Europe*. London: Century.

Roberts, Andrew. *The Storm of War*. New York: Harper.

Ryan, Cornelius. *The Last Battle*. New York: Simon & Schuster.

Shirer, William L. *The Rise and Fall of the Third Reich*. Beverly Hills, CA: Ballantine Books.

Simmons, Michael. *Berlin: The Dispossessed City*. London: Hamish Hamilton.

Solmssen, Arthur R. G. *A Princess in Berlin*. Beverly Hills, CA: Ballantine Books.

Taylor, James and Warren Shaw. *Dictionary of the Third Reich*. London: Grafton Books.

Toland, John. *Adolf Hitler*. New York: Doubleday.

Vassiltchikov, Marie. *Berlin Diaries 1940–1945*. New York: Random House, Inc.

Wasserstein, Bernard, *Britain and the Jews of Europe 1939–1945*. Oxford: Oxford University Press.